Versace Sisters

Dear darling Jeff
and gorgeous Simon,
so looking forward
to visiting P-Town with
you.
Love always Lisa
(AKA Cate Kendall)

By the same author

Gucci Mamas

Versace Sisters

Cate Kendall

BANTAM
SYDNEY AUCKLAND TORONTO NEW YORK LONDON

For Wylie Easthope, 3 November 1967–2 December 2008.
An amazing man. LB

For my 'chosen sisters' Tracey Caulfield and Katrina Hardman.
MH

A Bantam book
Published by Random House Australia Pty Ltd
Level 3, 100 Pacific Highway, North Sydney NSW 2060
www.randomhouse.com.au

First published by Bantam in 2009

Copyright © Lisa Blundell and Michelle Hamer 2009

The moral right of the author has been asserted.

All rights reserved. No part of this book may be reproduced or transmitted by any person or entity, including internet search engines or retailers, in any form or by any means, electronic or mechanical, including photocopying (except under the statutory exceptions provisions of the *Australian Copyright Act 1968*), recording, scanning or by any information storage and retrieval system without the prior written permission of Random House Australia.

Addresses for companies within the Random House Group can be found at www.randomhouse.com.au/offices

National Library of Australia
Cataloguing-in-Publication Entry

Kendall, Cate.
Versace sisters.

ISBN 978 1 86325 618 6 (pbk).

A823.4

Cover illustration based on originals by Nick Monu and Pink Tag
Cover design: www.saso.com.au
Internal design by Midland Typesetters, Australia
Typeset in Bembo 11.5/14pt by Midland Typesetters, Australia
Printed and bound by Griffin Press, South Australia

Random House Australia uses papers that are natural, renewable and recyclable products and made from wood grown in sustainable forests. The logging and manufacturing processes are expected to conform to the environmental regulations of the country of origin.

10 9 8 7 6 5 4 3 2 1

Prologue

1980

'BELLA-RENE!'

Her mother's shriek reverberated off the Hills Hoist and assaulted Bella's ears as she sat huddled in her treehouse. She'd been watching the cattle in the top paddock grazing drowsily.

She hastily scrambled down the tree and ran toward the house. What on earth could she want now? Lunch was over and cleared up and it was hours before she had to set the table for dinner.

The grimy screen door slapped shut behind her as she entered the kitchen, gloomy in contrast to the bright day and dank with the lingering odour of grease.

'Yeah, Mum?'

Marlene Walker looked up from the stove at her eldest child.

'Jesus, girl, how many times have I told you not to wear your good dress around the house? You'll be headed for a fall if you keep thinking you're better than the rest of us, you know. Airs and graces, my girl, airs and graces.' Marlene's diatribe was brought to an abrupt halt by a hacking cough.

Wiping the side of her mouth on her flannelette shirt she continued. 'Watch the kids for me, girl, I'm off to the pub to fetch your father home. And put the corned beef on when the saucepan starts to boil, will ya?' she added as she pulled on her favourite acrylic green cardigan and pushed open the back door.

Bella went to check on her little sister but was distracted by the shouts and squeals coming from the boys' room. After ordering Craig, Travis and Keith to take their wrestling out into the paddock she wandered through the few remaining rooms of the weatherboard cottage calling, 'Sera? Serandipity? Where are you?'

She retraced her steps back to the steamy kitchen where the saucepan was now boiling angrily on the old stove.

'There you are, you cheeky –' Bella's voice froze as the world suddenly blurred and slowed. Sera, climbing on a chair to reach her treasured golliwog on the cluttered mantle above the stove, seemed to be moving as though in a dream. Bella could not speed herself up enough to reach her in time.

She saw what was going to happen, saw it over and over in the few seconds it took to become reality, and heard her scream blend with Sera's as the child's chubby foot clipped the handle of the saucepan and sent searing water onto her right leg.

~ 1 ~

2009

'The benefits of the Capture Ultimate Wrinkle Restoring Serum rests in its ability to be micro-absorbed into the pores to polish and rejuvenate the skin. It's certainly one of my favourite products, and in fact we call it the "turbocharger" of the range,' Sera ended her spiel with a genuine smile. 'And for your delicate skin,' she continued, with a nod towards her customer's ruddy complexion, 'I would recommend Diorskin Forever: its creation has been inspired by nano-technology.'

The thirty-something medical receptionist in sensible shoes and supermarket cosmetics was drinking in every word.

'The Forever make-up has an invisible nano-network of micro-airy molecules to maintain classic beauty in even the most difficult environments,' Sera said, breathless with the joy of the cosmetic marvel.

Within fifteen minutes the receptionist had treated herself to the serum, make-up, some blush and a night cream to help reduce any sneaky signs of ageing. She left glowing with the promise of enhanced beauty.

Sera sighed with satisfaction. She loved her job at the David Jones Christian Dior counter because she truly believed in her product and was thrilled to be able to preach the gospel of Dior skincare to the world.

Nevertheless, when her tea break came she decided to spend it popping around to the other beauty counters.

A good slice of her part-time income disappeared this way, but with two children, a husband and mother-in-law to look after, Sera figured splurging on cosmetics and creams was a well-deserved treat.

'Hi Lucille,' she called, surveying the range at the Clinique counter. 'Anything new coming in?'

'Sweetheart, you know I always let you know first,' Lucille smiled. 'How did you go with the Turnaround Concentrate?'

'It was quite good,' Sera frowned, unconsciously sliding her hand over her scarred thigh, 'but I'd still like to see what they come up with next.'

Lucille reached under the counter. 'Well, I don't think you've tried our Continuous Rescue Antioxidant Moisturiser yet, have you?'

Sera was immediately interested and leant gratefully on the counter while Lucille dabbed a few precious drops of silvery liquid into her hand. She could feel the serum tingling gently on her skin. It felt so silky-soft and yet powerful and her skin was shinier and smoother than it had been a few seconds before.

'Oh this is wonderful, Lucille, I can feel it working already.'

'Isn't it glorious, sweetie? I thought I had shown it to you already. It's a collagen enhancer: the powerful molecules in the serum invigorate and rejuvenate damaged cellular pore linings . . .'

Lucille's voice faded as Sera was gripped by a familiar bubble of hope and expectation. Maybe this cream would be the one. Maybe this one would work.

But then again, how many times had she felt this excitement before, only to be left disappointed and out-of-pocket yet again? She knew Bella would scoff at her for reaching for another impossible miracle. She realised with a start that she hadn't seen her sister for weeks, and a familiar mix of sadness and resentment twisted inside her.

The years she and Bella had spent crisscrossing the globe as flight attendants had been heady with excitement and new experiences. Their adult lives had begun exactly as they had plotted back in their cramped childhood bedroom in the house in Mole Creek. Back then, Bella had plastered the walls with pages from fashion magazines taken from recycling bins in better neighbourhoods that promised a glitzier, brighter, more sophisticated world. The sisters tried their best, but could do little to make their tatty hand-me-downs and op-shop bargains look anything like the fashion in the glossy pages. Versace, with its slightly gaudy edge, became their dream label; their secret code for a better life.

And then it had happened: first Bella and then Sera escaped dishwater dull Mole Creek and joined Air Australia, and soon they were shopping for real Versace in Paris, sipping cocktails in Prague, snapping up bargain Burberry in London, bohemian accessories in Italy and La Prairie in Switzerland.

They fiddled their schedules, begged and cajoled colleagues to swap shifts and change routes so the inseparable sisters could fly together or land in the same cities. Their global partying continued even after Bella married her handsome pilot husband, Curtis.

But then Sera met Tony, and happily swapped jetsetting for family life. Somehow she had simply assumed Bella would do the same, but to her surprise her big sister continued her glamorous life alone.

Sera stared at the back of her hand, bringing herself back to reality. She was sure her skin looked younger and fresher.

'What's the biggest size, Lucille?' she asked.

'Why not just take this 5ml trial size and see how you go?' Lucille offered.

Sera brushed the tiny bottle aside. 'That wouldn't be enough for my whole . . . er . . . um . . . face,' she stammered, blushing. 'The serum seems perfect. I'll get a whole bottle.'

'It's your pay cheque.' Lucille shrugged.

'I'll run back over and pay after my shift,' Sera said rushing back to her own counter. 'Oh, by the way, how much is it?'

'One hundred and seventy-five dollars, darling,' Lucille told her. 'Want it on your store card?'

~2~

Bella could barely walk: her back swayed awkwardly and her toes were numb. But she wasn't about to let a savagely tight pencil skirt and toe-aching stiletto pain get in the way of a killer fashion look.

Her catwalk figure drew travel-weary passengers' eyes from their newspapers and airport novels as she cut through the terminal. At five foot eleven, with a pristine blonde chignon and figure-hugging, chocolate-brown uniform, it was her air of confidence that attracted the most admiring glances.

She stifled a yawn. The flight she'd just left had been completely dull, but at least now there was time for a trip to The Grove, her favourite LA shopping destination. Over the past twenty years, Bella had roadtested every shopping district in LA and her careful research had told her that with fifty of the most fashionable boutiques, stores and cafés under its designer roof, The Grove, the latest shopping mecca, was her best bet for finding a great outfit for tonight.

Joining her colleagues on the transit bus, she stowed her bag safely under the seat in front (force of habit) and checked her Rolex for the fourth time since disembarking. It was still there. Check. She rubbed her hands together and examined her manicure. Perfect. She glanced away and then back again. Still perfect. She patted her hair in search of stragglers and, finding just sleekness and order, sighed contentedly.

An hour later she had settled in her room, slipped into Paige jeans, espadrilles and a ruched aqua silk top and headed out into the smog of downtown LA.

The Grove was packed as always, but Bella was adept at cutting through the crowd of gaping tourists and meandering locals. She started at Abercrombie and Fitch, where she was delighted to find grey had been declared this season's new black. She picked up a belt, a pair of straight-leg jeans and a sheer polka-dot top (in grey of course) to wear to brunch tomorrow.

Victoria's Secret was the next on her list – she needed a new coffee-coloured bra and grabbed a black satin number while she was there – followed by a joyful hour in Michael Kors, where she decided on a simple cocktail dress teamed with a tailor-made diamante clutch and matching sandals. As the salesgirl wrapped her purchases Bella sighed. Matching accessories just helped the world make more sense.

In the window of The Gap a crisp white shirt caught Bella's eye. It was exactly the style Sera wore to work at DJs. Bella tilted her head to the side. Yes, she thought, it was perfect. Sera would love it.

She selected five shirts and was almost at the counter before she stopped herself. She was doing it again. She was mothering her little sister. When would she stop worrying about Sera's life, for God's sake? The woman was thirty-six years old and married with two children, but still Bella couldn't stop looking after Sera. It was part of the reason she skipped most of the Stitch 'n' Bitch nights Sera invited her to: the knitting group was fun but it was time her younger sister had her own social group. Bella knew Sera desperately wanted her there, but she was determined to stick to her plan of tough love. Buying Sera's work uniform didn't exactly form part of this plan.

Bella played with the soft fabric of the shirts as she grappled with her decision. She thought back to their childhood, on the other side of the world and light years away from the glamour of the upmarket mall. Not that Bella had really had much of a childhood; instead she'd taken on most of the parenting of her three rowdy younger brothers and little sister.

Their father, a surly man who rarely spoke to his family, fired up a treat down at the pub after a hard day lopping trees and hauling the firewood that was his livelihood. He'd married their mother, Marlene, after she broke the news that she was three months gone with his kid, but that didn't mean he had to spend his life in her miserable company. Marlene wasn't going to let his sour face ruin her days so she sought solace and plenty of good times with the farm hands at the property next door. And there was always the RSL bingo to fill a quiet night.

Bella was a good surrogate mother. She boiled meat and peeled potatoes for the kids' meals, got them all to school, made sure the washing came in off the line and that the boys were home by dark. Looking after her brothers was an exhausting but straightforward chore, rather like zoo-keeping. But Bella worried for Serandipity; the baby of the family.

Her sister was named for the nearby town of Serendipity where Marlene's biggest bingo win had taken place. Unfortunately their mother's spelling skills meant Serandipity was sentenced to a lifetime of explaining and correcting her name.

Bella's own name was originally Bella-Rene and both a nod to Marlene's Aunty Rene and a reminder of her parent's honeymoon, spent cruising the pokie venues of

Victoria's Bellarine Peninsula. At fifteen Bella shortened her own name by deed poll and refused to call her sister anything but Sera. The care their mother took with the spelling of her second daughter's name was indicative of the way their relationship developed: Marlene never really paid much attention to the little girl. Consequently Sera tagged along with Bella from the moment she could toddle and turned to her big sister with the news of her first reader, her first kiss and her first period. Bella was always Sera's first port of call with any developments and that had never really changed.

The store's piped music brought Bella back to reality and she realised she was stroking her Versace handbag as if it was a pet. She'd longed for the glamour of Versace since puberty. If she could just own something from the Italian designer, she'd reasoned, she would be a part of a shinier, happier world. Her first pay allowed her to buy Versace sunglasses and from that moment she was hooked. She saved diligently for a tiny evening bag and when she started flying was able to indulge in Versace salons worldwide. Gone was the awkward, badly dressed country kid, and in her place stood a glowing woman dripping with designer accoutrements.

She put the shirts back down on the shelf and gave them a last pat, then checked her mobile phone for the seventh time since entering the store. No messages. She checked her manicure. Still perfect. She glanced down at her shoes; dust free, thank God. Hang on, was that a mark? No, it was okay. Her breathing calmed; it was just a shadow.

She knew she was overreacting, knew what the checking and re-checking meant. The habit had started on her wedding day when she'd been unable to stop fingering the individual beads on her dress just to make sure none were coming loose. Her compulsive need for perfection, to ensure that everything about her was just right, had escalated from there. Only when she'd checked and double-checked everything could she breathe; only then did she feel secure.

Okay, she thought to herself as she took a deep breath, well done. It was time to play the doting aunty to Sera's little ones.

She cruised through Nordstrom's toy department. All the plastic, commercial rubbish was so boring. Teddy bears? Too babyish. Remote-control toys? They already had plenty. She wanted to get something special, something Sera wouldn't buy them.

At five, Maddy was a girly girl who loved anything shiny or pretty. Bella pursed her lips as she strolled down the boulevard. Ah perfect, she thought, catching sight of a Swarovski shop. She could start a crystal collection for her niece; a sophisticated, valuable collection that would make Madeline feel grown-up.

Next, something for little Harry. Bella laughed at the thought of her fashion-conscious nephew. She knew just the thing. White Calvin Klein jeans. She scooped up a pair with a guilty smile – they were completely impractical for a three-year-old, but she knew he'd love them.

Bella's mobile rang as the shop assistant handed over her stylish CK carry bag.

'Hello, Bella Walker,' she sang into the mouthpiece.

'Oh,' came the deep reply. 'You've changed your name back.'

Bella's heart clenched. It was the intonation that Bella recognised first, the way he stretched out his vowels and his deep, gravelly timbre.

She hadn't heard his voice in weeks and the shock of hearing it – here, anywhere – swept over her entire body. She felt as if she'd been dumped under an enormous wave at Bondi, losing all sense of direction as the air was forced from her lungs and her throat clamped shut with fear.

She stumbled blindly to a bench in the shopping mall's busy thoroughfare, her legs buckling with relief as she dropped to the slippery plastic surface.

'What do you want?' Bella asked, as her initial nausea was quickly replaced with a hot bolt of anger. A cocktail of bitter emotions swirled in her head, tipping her towards another anxiety attack as she fought to squeeze oxygen into her lungs.

Images flashed before her eyes: the young flight attendant in the cockpit moaning as her husband's hand disappeared up her skirt. The coy looks and sly giggles from the other flight attendants that stopped abruptly when Bella walked into a room. Coming home from a trip a day early to find a nubile young blonde naked in her ensuite, happily using Bella's favorite Chanel shower scrub.

How could she have just let him lie to her again and again? She hated herself for swallowing his flimsy explanations; for ignoring the winks, the flirtations, the little secret waves directed at her philandering husband from so many of her colleagues, even as she walked beside him through terminals across the world.

Of course she'd seen them. Of course she'd been aware. Then why in the hell had she denied it for so long? She had tortured herself with this question every day since he'd walked out on her.

Her stomach lurched with unhappiness. How long would it have gone on for? How long would she have lived in her carefully constructed fantasy world, refusing to wake up? God, she was useless and pathetic and hopeless and weak and –

'That's no way to talk to your captain,' Curtis drawled, interrupting her angry thoughts.

'Oh, are you on Flight 421 tomorrow?' she asked, struggling to keep her voice even and detached, but failing miserably.

'Sure am, baby, and I checked the flight-attendant schedule and saw that you are too.'

Flight attendant schedule, she scoffed, more like shopping list. Any fresh meat you haven't tasted yet, darling? There was no way she would put herself through that. She'd ring in sick as soon as she got the creep off the phone.

'Listen, babe,' he continued. 'Can't chat, this isn't a social call, I need you to do something for me.' He spoke with a casual familiarity that made her gasp and she held the phone away from her ear in disbelief. Do something for him? Was he delirious?

Maybe he'd been drinking, Bella thought, ready to tell the snivelling cheat that he was dreaming if he thought there was anything on this earth she would do for him.

'Sure, what's up?' she heard herself respond coolly. Damn my weakness, she thought, stamping her foot.

'I need those divorce papers signed, baby, aysap.'

The divorce papers had been sitting in the bottom of Bella's travel bag for weeks waiting for her signature, but for some reason she hadn't gotten around to it yet. It wasn't as if she didn't want to get divorced. God no. Bring it on!

'Yeah, sure, I'll put them in tonight's mail.' Her breathing had almost returned to normal. See, she thought with relief, I can manage a normal conversation with the filthy, dirty low-life. I'm not going to have a meltdown; I'm doing well.

'Thanks, baby, you're a star. I need them pronto because I'm getting married next month. Oh shit, must fly, ha-ha, pilot joke. My limo's just arrived. Ciao, Bella.'

Although the line was dead, Bella still held the phone to her ear; her face lifeless, her body motionless. She was snap-frozen. Eventually her body's survival mechanism kicked in, forcing her to take a deep, mindless gulp of air.

Her sister, her little sister, she needed her right now, more than ever before. Sera was the only one who could help her through this. She fumbled with the phone. Her fingers seemed numb and disconnected. She gave up. Who was she kidding? She couldn't call Sera. Sera's life was crazy. There was no way she was going to drag the poor thing down further with this crap. The best she could do was to keep her ignorant from this . . . this . . . nightmare. Besides, there was so much background she'd have to fill her in on. The affairs, the betrayal, the hideous night he'd left her. She'd been unable to articulate it to anybody yet. It was too sickening. Nausea surged up from her gut.

Bella's head dropped back and the ceiling seemed to be corrugated and undulating. The floor suddenly tilted and she only caught herself from flipping off the bench by falling heavily onto her hand.

A tangerine-coloured woman passing by took one look at Bella's dilated pupils and the glistening layer of perspiration that coated her cheeks and tutted in a superior manner. 'Junkie,' she muttered and teetered off as fast as her two-inch-high Jimmy Choos would allow.

Bella threw her head between her knees and waited for equilibrium to return. Within a few minutes the blood returned to her head, her breathing slowed and she was able to collect herself.

So he was getting married. Fucking hell. Who to? The same bimbo bunny he'd left her for? Bella felt nausea rise in her throat again, and dipped her head back into her lap for a few more minutes.

But what the hell do I care? she thought. She wanted him out of her life. She wanted this terrible, humiliating episode to be over. Surely this meant she could now be truly free of him and get on with her life? Maybe she'd even consider dating again, though something told her the damage to her heart was going to need time to heal properly.

So what was this reaction about? Maybe it was just the unexpectedness of his announcement, Bella thought. What would her therapist say? A glimmer of an answer shone at the bottom of her mind. The glimmer intensified as it floated up closer to the surface and she realised that she had been avoiding this thought for a long time. Oh God, what was wrong with her! It couldn't be, it just couldn't be . . . Was it possible she still loved him?

~3~

Chantrea Kim exploded from the plane behind the last straggling, jetlagged passengers. A tiny dynamo of energy and frustration, she barrelled past two burly airport security guards, almost bowling them over in her haste.

She'd been stuck on board with that insipid wet rag Caroline for the nine-hour flight from Hong Kong; that woman made the whole trip hard work.

She charged into the first ladies' room she came across, wrestling her pin-tucked uniform blazer off as she pushed through the door. Dumping her bag on the counter, she struggled to pull her shirt over her head without unbuttoning it as she replayed the trip in her mind.

The shrill cry of a grumpy infant blasting like an air-raid siren from the moment its parents took their seats should have given her fair warning that it was set to be a shocker of a trip, she thought, spinning her skirt around to fiddle with the clasp and escape its confines.

Then there was Pudgy Vomit Boy; what a delightful mid-air treat he'd been. The little charmer had sent a spray of projectile spew across three passengers just after take-off. She'd spent her first hour on board cleaning up the remains of his regurgitated Big Mac meal and offering First Class amenities kits to his disgusted victims.

The lecherous advances of the First Officer, who tried to go the grope every time she delivered refreshments to the cockpit had increased her anger further, especially when he'd whispered that she looked 'positively edible' in her uniform. She'd nearly vomited herself.

Then what with Catering short-changing them fifteen meals, one of the economy-class toilet sinks mysteriously blocking up and three passengers with various phobias, it had been a tough flight. She was shitty, tired and over the whole business of pandering to demanding passengers.

Clad in only her black lace bra and g-string, Chantrea flipped back the cover of her wheelie case and began to rifle through it. She pulled on black leggings, a vintage Merivale and Mr John purple glittery top and added a long, purple and apple green crocheted vest. Her burgundy Doc Marten boots completed the outfit.

One more thing to go: she scrabbled in her toilet bag for her favourite accessory, a bright purple hairpiece that she clipped above her nape to create a funky and authentic-looking mullet.

In front of the basin mirror she ruffled her slicked-back androgynous hairdo into spiky points, smeared vibrant purple eye shadow across her almond-shaped lids and high cheekbones to obscure the airline's regulation Clarins Taupe foundation. The bright shade enhanced her south-east Asian complexion perfectly.

She shoved her uniform into her case and flew out of the ladies' room and down the corridor, propelled by the ease and comfort of her Docs. A quick glance at her chunky plastic watch told her there was time to hit her favourite vintage store in Oxford Street before picking Sally up from crèche. A tendril of guilt at this decision gripped her conscience but she quickly brushed it away.

★

Chantrea was always entranced by edgy Darlinghurst with its glitz of hookers and queens, juxtaposed against regular glimpses of celebs – it wasn't unusual to see Cate Blanchett or Daniel Johns mooching along the street among the suburb's beggars, trannies and home boys. Darlinghurst was a wild place with a tinge of Sydney glamour, but like an old slapper's Glomesh purse, its shine was tarnished and torn at the corners.

Chantrea was in her element among the vintage fashions, the daggy cast-offs and dusty interior of the second hand shop, Decades. She quickly unearthed a body-hugging vintage Pucci mini-dress with flared arms, which would be perfect to wear to Stitch 'n' Bitch tonight. It would look awesome with her new espadrilles.

She spent another hour rummaging through the treasures, imagining their past owners and outings, and her diligence paid off with a stunning caftan that had Cher written all over it and a pair of white gloves the shopgirl swore were once worn by Doris Day.

Hugging her purchases to her chest, Chantrea emerged back into the sunlight and headed for a grungy Italian café to drink a double espresso while she watched the passing gay parade.

Her mobile announced a new message with a tinny version of Dead or Alive's 'You Spin Me Round (Like a Record)'. The very camp waiter did an impromptu dance routine to the ringtone as he walked by.

The text message was from her friend Sam. It read: 'What on earth does a hetero father of two bring to a mothers' sewing circle?'

Chantrea smiled. Tonight would be Sam's first foray into the Stitch 'n' Bitch group. When Sera had called earlier in the year to invite Chantrea to join a knitting group, she had laughed openly at her.

'One thing I really can't ever see myself doing – or at least not until I'm eighty – is knitting, thanks,' Chantrea had said.

'But knitting is the new yoga,' Sera had argued. 'It's so cool – everyone's doing it. Anyway, it's really just a good reason to get together and have a couple of chardies . . . and if we do make anything worthwhile we're going to donate it to charity, the "Woollies for Wars" project.'

'Oh good lord, it sounds hideous,' Chantrea had moaned.

'I promise it's very cool and hip,' Sera had insisted. 'It's called Stitch 'n' Bitch.'

The name won Chantrea over. 'Oh, all right, I'll give it a try,' she had agreed reluctantly.

At the first meeting, Chantrea had met Sera's sweet friend Mallory and her neighbour Jacqueline (who was much too uptight for her liking), and had discovered that she had a real flair for knitting chunky, colourful garments in mohair and cashmere.

Tonight she was introducing her own new Stitch 'n' Bitch member, Sam, a single dad from Sally's crèche whom she had chatted with at pick-up and drop-off. He seemed lonely and very sweet, so she had dared him to come and join their group. She was very surprised when he'd agreed.

She chuckled at his troubled text and replied: 'Butterick Sewing Patterns, lace doilies, eyelash curlers and an apron.'

On the timber table that filled the small office of his Bondi Junction terrace, Sam's phone beeped. He apologised to his client, dug the phone out from under the drawings for the Woolloomooloo warehouse conversion and glanced at the message from Chantrea. He grinned.

After he'd walked his client to the front door and vowed to deliver the next update by the following week, Sam checked his watch. He had just enough time to get to the shops before picking up the girls.

Forty minutes later Sam was standing awkwardly in the middle of a barn-like toy shop. Isabelle and Alexandra needed costumes for a fancy dress party that weekend and he had promised to find fabulous outfits for them.

After much bedtime whispering, Alexandra had announced that morning that she wanted to be Mike Wazowski and Isabelle wanted to go as Ariel. Sam had responded with a vague 'Okay' as he listened to Isabelle finish her reader and made school lunches while hastily gulping down his coffee.

But now Sam was in a quandary. In one hand he held a blue velvet Snow White dress, and in the other a blue-and-white-striped B1 costume, and he stared at them both as he wished he had taken the time to ask Isabelle who or what Mike Wazowski and Ariel were. Since his wife had died there had been countless moments where he had been lost without her, and this was just one more to add to the list.

Staff members in the mega toy warehouse were elusive and thin on the ground. Sam turned his head sharply to the right as he caught sight of a blue-uniformed teenager whip by. He turned quickly to the left as his peripheral vision picked up another running across the end of the aisle using a cut-out of Buzz Lightyear as a shield.

He trudged back to the information desk, where he was quickly dissuaded by a long queue of disgruntled customers. Right, this is going to require a proactive approach, he murmured to himself, wandering over to a small boy who was admiring the skateboards.

'Have a go,' Sam said breezily. 'I'm sure they won't mind.'

The child looked up with a grin – it was all the encouragement he needed. He dragged the biggest, meanest-looking board off the shelf and jumped on, shrieking with delight as he flew down the Barbie aisle.

The ploy worked like a charm.

'Hey kid,' a wavering pubescent voice called. 'You can't play with that.'

The voice's acne-faced owner magically materialised and scurried toward them. With a quick scowl at Sam, the small boy ditched the skateboard and fled the scene.

'Damn it,' the gangly teen surveyed the state of the once-pristine Barbie lane.

'Here, let me help you,' said Sam, picking up several Chanel Barbies from the floor.

'Thanks,' the teen mumbled.

'Not at all,' Sam smiled. 'And by the way, I wonder if you could help me?'

The boy's back stiffened as he bent to retrieve a Zen Retreat Barbie. 'Oh, uh . . . well . . . I finish soon . . .' he stammered, looking keenly at his Rip Curl dive watch.

'Costumes,' Sam said firmly. 'I need costumes.'

'Oh, yeah, cool,' the teen replied, relieved to have escaped any greater demand. 'Aisle six. Knock yourself out, dude.'

'No – ummm . . .' Sam looked at the boy's name tag, '. . . Victor.' What optimistic parents, he mused. 'I know *where* the costumes are,' he continued, before the dishevelled creature could escape again. 'I just can't find what I'm looking for. What is "Mike Wazowski"?'

'*Monsters Inc.*?' Victor replied sympathetically, as if sorry for such an out-of-touch old man.

'Ri-i-ight,' said Sam uncertainly.

'He's a round green guy? A ball? With arms and legs? And one eye?'

By now Sam badly wanted to smack each upper inflection out of the teen's mouth.

'Okay,' he said patiently. 'What about Ariel?'

'Mermaid? You know? From *The Little Mermaid*? And *The Little Mermaid II*? Oh, and I think she was also in *The Little Mermaid III*?'

'Do you have these costumes in stock?'

'I dunno, we might. We did. So we could. But we mighta sold 'em, then in that case we wouldn't.'

'Hey, here's a crazy idea, how about you go and take a look for me?'

'Umm, okay then,' Victor replied, his dull gaze on Sam's face for a moment to gauge just how serious this bloke was about him actually walking all the way over to aisle six to check. Picking a pimple on his chin, he decided Sam was pretty intent on it, so he turned and, dragging his feet, meandered to the nearby aisle, with Sam following close behind.

Victor flicked a cursory glance up at the wall of costumes. 'Nah, we haven't got them,' he said.

'What's this one?' Sam asked, holding up a circular green shape with one eye.

'Oh, that's Mike Wazowski?' Victor replied. 'From *Monsters Inc.*?'

Sam held up a red-haired wig and a fish tail with a bikini top attached to the hanger. 'And what about this? Is this Ariel?'

'Nah, that's Ariel. Sorry we couldn't help.' The teenager shuffled away, holding his pants up with one hand. Sam sighed and headed for the checkout.

Jacqueline Bouvier had a to-do list a mile long today. It had been long enough already until those boys of hers had thrown more chores in her direction at breakfast. She smiled indulgently; men, they'd be lost without women to take care of them.

Joshua and Daniel both had exams coming up so Jacqueline didn't mind at all that Daniel asked her to return his DVDs to the video shop, even though it was next door to his school. And Joshua asked her to drop Tyler's Wii games back to his home in Longueville because Tyler was home sick today and wanted them and Joshua was supposed to take them to school yesterday and had forgotten.

And then the silly billy rang up the moment she was back in the door from dropping them off at school (they didn't enjoy catching the bus) – fancy forgetting his sports uniform! Never mind, it was only half an hour out of her way. Well, an hour if you counted the return trip.

Thomas needed his dry cleaning picked up, his fishing rod taken in to the shop (the reel was sticking) and a few bits and bobs picked up at Bunnings. He also needed her to buy him new underpants. She had mentioned this morning that she was very busy and might have to put the underwear job off till another day, but his scowl over the newspaper had convinced her she could make time for that task.

So after Bunnings she'd headed to DJs and bought her husband's customary y-fronts, ignoring the jazzy lycra boxers with their popsicle colours and body-hugging designs. Her Thomas was a traditionalist when it came to his underwear, and she appreciated his consistency.

Finally all her little jobs were done and her time was her own. It was unusual not to be front and centre at home in the late afternoon, but Thomas had a client dinner and the boys were both at after-school sports and so Jacqueline felt justified in indulging in a spot of shopping.

The dessert she took to this evening's do at Sera's house had to be superb. Chantrea was bringing a new member:

a man of all things. Apparently he was a single father and Chantrea had hinted that he was quite the lonely boy.

Jacqueline tapped her foot impatiently as she scanned the shelves of House. She couldn't find just the right serving plate. It couldn't be too feminine, given the male company, yet should be delicate enough to complement her pavlova.

A bag of decorative clothes pegs caught her attention. Each was shaped like a little person, painted in bright colours with such sweet faces. She glanced over at the salesgirl, who was busy showing a customer the glories of baked enamelware. The pegs were too hard to resist.

Now, back to platters. The stainless steel Alessi was very fashionable and would suit a more contemporary space, such as Bella's apartment, but not the sixties retro look that Sera kept insisting was done on purpose but which was clearly just a kitchen in grave need of a renovation. Jacqueline longed to choose the filigreed white metal cake stand, which would look perfect with her dainty meringue but she moved on to a cream, ceramic cake stand devoid of decoration. The texture of her pavlova would work well against it and wouldn't be overshadowed with unnecessary frou-frou. Superb, she thought, gleefully clapping her hands. She paid for the stand, insisted on two layers of bubble wrap, and left the store.

Her phone beeped an incoming message from Sera, confirming Sam's culinary contribution.

'Hope pâté is ok,' she read. Pâté? That wasn't what they'd agreed. She stamped her ballet flat and spun on her heel back to House. She'd have to exchange the cake stand now and get the Alessi after all.

She texted Mallory: 'Don't bring meat product, Sam's bringing pâté.'

*

Mallory Rimmel's phone tinkled with a message just as she was about to step into her favourite jeans shop. She gave Jacqueline's cryptic message a second or two of confused thought before shrugging her shoulders and deleting it.

She skipped inside the dim shop, which was lit only by garish disco lights that flashed in time to the blaring doof-doof music. Skinny-leg jeans wallpapered the shop: acid-washed, rock-washed, dark denim, light denim, white denim, plain denim, distressed and depressed, sand-blasted, rock-blasted, faded, ripped, zipped, tipped and tightened, and every pair of them in stretch fabric.

A retro rainbow of acid-yellow, royal blue and turquoise tops screamed for attention alongside blue-and-yellow-striped tees with ripped necks, luridly coloured leggings and leopard-print miniskirts. Scruffy bins overflowed with a gaudy treasure trove of cheap bangles and baubles.

Mallory was in her element, delighting in each piece and tearing clothes from hangers as she made her way to the change room, conveniently forgetting that fifteen years earlier she'd sent bags of exactly the same outfits to the op shop.

She bought contrasting leggings, leg-warmers and skinny jeans for herself and her fifteen-year-old daughter, Tilly, who was conveniently the same size as her young mum.

As she waited for the sales assistants to finish exclaiming over a friend's new nose piercing, Mallory checked her phone and found a group text from Bella. 'Can't make SNB 2nite, in Santa Monica. Sorry.'

Santa Monica? Mallory thought. Isn't that where Cyndi Lauper lives?

Sera's house had the ultimate Paddington accessory – off-street car parking. As she pulled into the carport behind the house, she once again gave silent thanks for this residential asset.

The wheelbarrow had fallen forwards, forcing her to park halfway out of the shelter in the fine misty rain. The half-bags of mulch that had spilt onto the driveway nagged at her conscience. She'd wanted to fix up the veggie patch for weeks but somehow hadn't got beyond buying mulch and dragging out the rusty wheelbarrow. She sighed and laid her forehead on the steering wheel to prepare for the next challenge – the dinner and bedtime battle.

She could still remember the days not so long ago when she could simply get out of the car, skip up the twenty steps to the back door, walk in, pour a nice glass of wine and sit down to relax. She had taken that freedom for granted and now her body ached to have that sort of simplicity once more – just for a day or two.

An image of Bella reclining in a luxurious bubble bath sprang into her mind and she felt a stab of resentment. There was her sister, in LA, living the high life, not even able to organise her calendar to be back home for Stitch 'n' Bitch once a month. And here Sera was, stuck in mindless domestic servitude.

It was hours since she had finished work. She'd popped in for an unplanned and very naughty pedicure, picked up the kids from crèche, gone two rounds of chaos at the supermarket, picked up her Pill prescription from the chemist, a registered mail delivery from the post office and some wine for tonight. The steering wheel was clammy under her tight grip when she finally sat back and opened her eyes.

'Right!' she said determinedly to her children. 'Let's do it!'

She got the kids out first, unbuckling their harnesses, answering a dozen or so of Madeline's insistent questions and trying to convince Harry not to plunge his fruit stick into his ear. She strapped their overflowing backpacks onto their little bodies, stooped to pick up the crayons and lunchbox that fell from Harry's unzipped Thomas the Tank Engine bag, then bustled them toward the stairs.

'It's raining,' whined Madeline.

'Well, get up the stairs quickly then,' Sera replied matter-of-factly.

Harry was exhausted and stood mutely staring up at his mum, his enormous puppy-dogs eyes pleading for her to carry him. It was pointless to try to convince him to walk when he was so tired, so Sera resigned herself to an extra trip to the car and hoisted him onto her hip. She slung her handbag over her other arm and scooped up a few shopping bags from the boot.

The rain was getting heavier now and the trek up the slippery stairs was difficult with the exhausted weight of the child against her.

'Knock on the door,' she called to Madeline, who had reached the top already. 'Nanna might open it for us.' Maddy reached up, stood on her toes and hammered with her child's fist several times.

Sera staggered up to the top step and lifted her knee to balance Harry's slumped body on it. Standing on one leg, she swapped all her bags into one hand so she could jiggle the uncooperative key in the lock. When she managed to push the door open Madeline instantly darted inside, causing Sera to stumble and lose her grip on the shopping, her handbag and keys, which all fell about her feet.

She deposited her son on the floor and as she bent to retrieve an avocado from under the kitchen table she caught sight of her mother-in-law's slipper-clad feet up on the ottoman, and stuck her head into the lounge room to say hello. A *New Idea* and the TV remote sat atop the pink-and-white angora blanket on Joan's lap. The noisy excitement of the *Family Feud* contestants filled the room.

Joan looked up over her half-specs. 'Oh, it's you. I thought it must have been by the way the knocking was going on and on.'

'Well, why didn't you open the foor for us?' Sera tried hard to keep the impatience from her voice.

Joan's lunch dishes were still on the coffee table. She'd had five cups of tea today, Sera counted.

'What and risk getting wet? It's raining outside.' Joan pressed the remote to drown out Harry's cries. 'Oh, and your mother called.'

Sera groaned. That was the last thing she needed right now. Harry was in full whinge mode. He waved his arms in the air. 'Up, up,' he demanded. The shopping would be getting drenched in the open car boot, but nothing could be done until Harry was calm and sorted.

Sera carried him tired and protesting into the kitchen to distract him with the Wiggles on the small TV/DVD. Harry slipped his thumb into his mouth and settled his head on Sera's shoulder, momentarily transfixed by Dorothy and Captain Feathersword. She quietly opened a drawer, keeping an ear tuned to the living room. Harry clung like a needy koala to her hip. Timing was crucial. One wrong move and the evening would blow up.

She deftly lifted out a baby bottle with her one free hand, filled it with milk and added a very naughty squirt of chocolate syrup, which would be exposing Harry's baby teeth to decay but would buy her a few more minutes of peace. Harry watched what she was doing and, placated by her actions, allowed himself to be deposited on a kitchen chair while Sera made his favourite drink. She screwed the top on slowly and quietly, and handed over the bottle as she nervously looked in the direction of her mother-in-law.

Harry's tired body relaxed and his eyes closed as he eagerly sucked on the sweet milky treat. Sera realised she had been holding her breath for the past few seconds and let out a noiseless sigh.

'I hope you're not giving in to that child,' came Joan's voice. 'He's far too old for a bottle, you know.'

Sera rolled her eyes. She'd been caught.

'He has you around his little finger, my girl. It wasn't like that in my day. You've got to be strict on them . . . hmmph,' Joan's sentence trailed off into oblivion.

Sera didn't have time to argue. She had just a small window of opportunity before Harry noticed she was gone and began to fuss again.

She raced to the back door, leapt over the grocery items which still lay strewn across the floor, ran down the stairs, loaded herself up with bags of shopping, locked the car and staggered back up to the house, where she tripped on the door jamb and once again dropped her shopping across the kitchen, accidentally standing on the bread as she struggled to steady herself.

Joan sat forward in her chair, affronted by the noise. 'Must you explode into the house every time you enter?' she called out. Madeline sat on the floor beside her grandmother, staring vacantly at the television screen. 'Anyway, what's for dinner?' Joan added as an aside and flicked over to see what that lovely Lavinia was wearing tonight.

Harry began to wail, 'Muuum, MUUUM!'

Sera scooped up as much of the dropped shopping as she could manage and made her way awkwardly to Harry, whose wailing had escalated into a full-throated scream. He had managed to pull the teat off his drink, drenching himself and the floor. Sera stepped over the spill and dumped the shopping on the bench.

Harry's wet, chocolatey face was twisted in anger.

The contents of the shopping flicked through her mind – oh no, ice-cream.

Madeline called out that she was hungry.

Joan asked again what was for dinner.

Harry stood on his chair and launched his pudgy, sticky body at her and Sera quickly stepped into the milk puddle to arrest his mid-air fall.

As Harry smeared chocolate topping and milk across her white work uniform she remembered she didn't have a clean one for tomorrow's shift.

She sighed again, and hugged poor little Harry harder. Bugger the uniform, she thought, as she carried the little bundle of chocolate, snot and misery up the stairs to the bathroom. It nearly killed her that she'd had to give up maintaining an organised house. It was frustrating to leave the disaster zone all over her kitchen floor but Harry needed her and that was more important.

'How about we have a bath together, my little man?' she whispered into his ear.

'Mmmmm,' he snuffled, mollified now that he was where he'd wanted to be all day; in his mother's arms. He clung to her neck in case she changed her mind. But, thanks to years of practise, she was still able to undress both of them and draw a bath while holding him.

Sera sat in the bath with her baby and he finally separated from her long enough to enjoy some quiet splashy play. Madeline soon wandered up and joined them.

As Sera was drying them all off afterwards she heard the back door open. 'What the hell . . . ?' she heard Tony say.

She suddenly remembered the state of the house and quietly chastised herself. She felt like such a failure when her husband came home to chaos. God, that was so 1950s housewife of her, she argued to herself. She was a good, caring mother who prioritised her children's needs.

She pulled on a full-length bathrobe and hurried down the stairs.

'Hello darling,' she said, tilting her face up to kiss him. He returned her kiss her distractedly as he took in the catastrophe of melting ice-cream, squashed bread and various groceries spread out across the floor. Joan deigned to peel herself away from the television now that the apple of her eye had returned home.

'Oh you poor love, you look tired and starving – I don't think there's any dinner yet either,' Joan said pointedly.

'I'll be right, Ma,' Tony said, dumping his tool belt in the closet and picking up the shopping while Sera hastily assembled bowls of fruit and crackers and ran back up the stairs with the children's rather feeble dinner.

'Goodnight little guys,' Tony called up to Maddy and Harry as they peeped through the banister. 'See you in the morning.'

As the children munched, Sera read them stories, scratched their backs, tucked them in for sleep, then came back downstairs.

Tony had put away the ice-cream and cleaned up the milky mess on the floor. Sera put her uniform on soak, retrieved the few hidden runaway groceries, and then prepared tinned soup and toasted sandwiches. As she served dinner in front of the television, she glanced at the starburst clock above the manetelpiece. She only had an hour to pull herself and the house together before the Stitch 'n' Bitchers were due to arrive. How was she going to do it?

Joan peered suspiciously at her tuna toastie.

'Bread's a strange shape,' she said.

~ 4 ~

Sera didn't do skirts. Even with long skirts, there was far too much risk of leg exposure for her liking. But what could she do? White linen skirts were a major look this season, and Sera was a woman who hated to miss a trend.

After the chaos of the day and Joan's usual sarcasm it was a relief to finally escape to her room and get dressed for tonight's Stitch 'n' Bitch.

She scrutinised her reflection in the full-length mirror, assessing all angles. Both legs were almost entirely hidden by the ankle-grazing, white linen wrap-skirt, but she still wasn't sure if she had the courage to wear it. Maybe if she stood up all night she could prevent any wardrobe malfunctions?

At least her taupe silk cami and new bejewelled flip-flops from Witchery posed no such fashion concerns. She'd seen the shoes at lunchtime, the shiny stones across the toes glittering prettily, and had been unable to resist such a must-have purchase.

Of course then there had been the problem of squeezing in a pedicure after work and finding the right chocolate nail polish to match the stones. But it had been worth juggling an extra hour of childcare, getting off work early and cancelling her much-overdue smear test one more time, she decided, wiggling her toes happily.

Damn it! She hadn't had time to even think about buying wool or needles for tonight's knitting session. It had been months since she'd finished her last project: a rather tragic-looking scarf which Madeline had refused to wear. She'd made a half-hearted attempt to start a beanie for Harry, in his favorite Roosters colours, but she'd lost her knitting bag somewhere – a cute Olga Berg number she'd picked up in the last Myer sales – and kept hoping it would turn up. That was a great bag.

But really, Stitch 'n' Bitch was just a convenient excuse for wine and a whine, and that was fine by Sera. She just wished Bella was going to be there. They hadn't caught up for ages.

She took a last look in the mirror. Her bare ankles sat vulnerable and exposed beneath the hem of her skirt, unaccustomed to the glare of daylight. She couldn't do it. She ran back to her wardrobe and pulled on a pair of taupe leggings from a drawer overflowing with tights, stockings, footless tights and leggings.

'Hey gorgeous, nice to see you in a skirt. It suits you,' Tony said, coming into the bedroom to change.

'Yeah, yeah,' Sera brushed away the compliment and quickly ducked away as he moved to kiss her. 'You'd better get a move on, your business studies class starts in fifteen minutes.'

'Gettin' there,' he replied, slipping on his Nike laceless street shoes. 'At least Mum's off to her Italian lesson so she won't be underfoot for you and your friends.'

Sera shook her head. 'No, sadly Mavis's car has a flat battery so she won't be able to go.'

'Oh, damn,' Tony halted on his way out of the room, pulling a tight white T-shirt over his broad chest. 'And on the night you're hosting too.'

'Never mind,' Sera replied with a brave smile, 'I'm sure she'll behave when company's here. She's pretty disappointed about missing Italian though.'

'You'd think she'd be fluent by now,' Sera said. 'She's been taking those classes for ages.'

'Yeah, but she never uses it. Anyway, I'm off, gorgeous.' Tony smiled, blowing her a quick kiss as he bounded down the stairs.

Sera checked in on the sleeping children before heading down to the kitchen to prepare some snacks for her visitors.

'I'll have a cuppa thanks, Sera, if you're making,' Joan called.

In the kitchen Sera gritted her teeth and filled the kettle. 'Won't be long,' she sang out with false chirpiness.

Joan shifted to a more comfortable position on her Jason recliner. 'Chance'd be a fine thing,' she muttered under her breath. 'She'll probably get distracted by something shiny.'

Determined not to let her mother-in-law get under her skin, Sera made the tea to Joan's strict requirements. Dunk the teabag three times only, two sugars and very milky, but boiling hot.

As she was sending the teabag to its third dunking Sera tried to think good thoughts about Joan. It was, after all, her mother-in-law's stunning double-storey Victorian terrace they shared in the highly desirable suburb of Paddington. Sera and Tony would never be able to afford such a sterling address if it wasn't for Joan's generosity. But, boy, did it come with a price. Not just the emotional pricetag but the constant renovation the very beautiful but decrepit old building constantly required.

The first renovation Sera had insisted on was to create a day-spa-style bathroom on the second floor. She needed a high-calibre facility for her grooming and beauty routines, and Tony had, as specified, intalled the mirrors only from waist height up so Sera never had to be confronted by the hideous scar that ran from her thigh to her ankle. To keep Joan and her geriatric toiletry mysteries at bay, Sera had also split the ground floor laundry and turned half into a practical, if minute, bathroom for her mother-in-law. As Tony was a builder it was crucial he had a practical space as his home office, so the children shared the second bedroom and the third upstairs bedroom was his office. The original front drawing room opposite the stairs made a perfect retreat for Joan, and the narrow hall led to the living area, which had been the terrace house's original dining room. The kitchen and laundry had been tacked onto the rear of the house in the early sixties.

Sera had much bigger plans for the rest of the house that would see some of the generous backyard sacrificed to become a second living room with an open-plan kitchen, which would allow Joan's TV-lifestyle to continue in one area, while the young family had their own space.

But it would all cost so much. Tony and Sera already had one hell of a mortgage. Although Joan owned the house, Sera and Tony paid for its constant upkeep. Sera had hoped to give up work completely after the kids were born, but with her renovation ambitions, and her taste for labels and expensive cosmetics, she had to work just to keep their heads above water.

But, with fingers crossed, Tony's big job at Potts Point would come off and they'd be able to begin the big reno within a few months. Sera cringed at the thought of six months of using their living room as family slash kitchen slash homework space while the building was under way, but hopefully it would all work out okay.

Shit, she'd dunked the tea bag for too long. And the tea was less than boiling. She sneaked over to the microwave, glancing furtively over her shoulder, and opened it as quietly as possible.

'You're not going to nuke it, are you, Sera?' Joan called out.

'Of course not, Joan,' she replied, swearing like a sailor under her breath as she dumped the tea down the sink. When Joan's perfect cup of tea was finally ready, Sera delivered it to her mother-in-law.

'Shame you're missing your Italian class night, Joan,' Sera said.

'No, not really, my diverticulitis is playing up again so it's for the best. I hope I'm not underfoot for you though, dear,' she said with a sly grin. 'What with your girlfriends' sewing circle. And what's this about a new boy who's joined? He'd be a poof then, would he?'

Sera swallowed her anger. 'No, Joan, he's straight. He's recently widowed and just needs to get out of the house and keep social, that's all.'

'Hmmph.' Joan was decidedly unconvinced. 'Bit odd, a bloke coming to a knitting group though; knitting's women's work.'

'Well, it's not really about the knitting, Joan,' Sera patiently explained yet again. 'It's more a chance to catch up. Like a book club, you know.'

'Book club! Ha! Don't make me laugh.' Joan's eyes never once left the television. 'I wouldn't have thought that Chantrea would choose reading as a favourite hobby and as for that Mallory, I'd be amazed if she could even read!'

Sera walked away before she lost control and slapped the old biddy. Dear Lord, how was tonight going to pan out? Where was she going to sit everyone? She knew there was no chance of Joan retiring early. Even though Sera had made Joan's downstairs bedroom into a quaint, Laura Ashley-style bedsit with its own armchair and television, she still preferred the main living room. 'Not going to be shut away in that prison,' she'd grumbled when Sera first proudly showed her the expensively re-decorated suite.

Sera decided her kitsch kitchen would be a perfect Stitch 'n' Bitch venue for tonight. They could all pretend to be 1970s housewives. Even Sam.

Embracing her theme with vigour, she dug around in the back of the pantry for red and green cocktail onions. Luckily cabanossi was a weakness of Tony's and she sacrificed her vintage cheddar by cutting it into cubes. And with any luck – she rummaged through the drawer Joan proudly titled 'entertaining' – and yes, she hit the jackpot: tasselled toothpicks. She whipped up a little hors d'oeuvres selection and presented it on Joan's finest Bessemer party dish. She was tickled pink with her irony and even donned a frilly apron. All we need now are Splayds, she thought with wry amusement.

'Door,' Joan yelled helpfully when the doorbell rang.

Mallory greeted Sera with her usual squeal of excitement, wrapping her best friend in a rapturous welcoming hug. She was the same ball of energy and enthusiasm that Sera had been drawn to when they met at their tiny Tasmanian primary school more than thirty years earlier.

Their hellos were accompanied by a loud derisive snort from Joan.

'What's she doing here?' Mallory hissed in horror. 'I thought she had Italian lessons.'

'Mavis's car has a flat battery,' Sera whispered back, pulling a face.

'Curse the Corolla!' Mallory scrunched up her little fists in frustration.

'When you two have finished your schoolyard gossip, some manners might be in order,' interrupted Joan.

The young women swapped grimaces, then Mallory re-adjusted her expression to her usual infectious smile. 'Good evening, Joan.' She skipped in and bent over to kiss her. 'Lovely to see you again.'

'Hello, Mallory,' Joan replied proffering her cheek and tearing her eyes away from the free-earrings-with-ring offer on the screen to assess the younger woman's appearance. She peered over her half-specs.

'Plaits, Mallory? Aren't you a bit old for a the schoolgirl look?'

Mallory simply turned up the wattage on her incandescent smile. 'Love your jumper, Joan,' she responded. 'You don't see enough appliqué nowadays, and that's such an interesting gum-tree motif.'

'Hmm, thanks,' Joan said, looking down at her sweater and matching track pants. 'I like teal.'

'As you should. It works so well with your skin colouring,' Mallory assured her as Sera gripped her arm and the two nearly wet themselves with silent laughter. They made it to the kitchen and shut the door behind them before they collapsed in fits.

'You're wicked, you know that,' Sera said, grinning at her life-long friend. 'But I forgive you because you're wearing great shoes.'

Mallory turned her wedged espadrilles from side to side for inspection.

'Thanks, I just hope I don't fall off them: they're very tippy.'

Sera almost regretted her flat bejewelled choice of footwear, but another glance at them reassured her.

The doorbell announced Chantrea and Sam's arrival.

'Ah, it's our knitting boy, is it?' Joan demanded, sizing Sam up like a prize bull as he stepped nervously into the lounge room.

'Joan, this is Sam,' Sera introduced her mother-in-law reluctantly, waiting for a clanger to fall from her lips – and she wasn't disappointed.

'So, got no mates, is that the problem, eh? Is that why you want to sit around with a bunch of married women . . . Or is it something else more interesting, hmmm?' Joan winked meaningfully at Chantrea, who simply smiled and looped her arm through Sam's.

'Yep, Joan, we're lovers and poor old Sam just can't keep away from me; you got it in one,' Chantrea said cheekily.

'Well, there's no need for that sort of talk,' Joan said, returning her focus to the jewellery sale once more.

Sam didn't know where to look and Sera wasn't sure whether to laugh or cry, but Chantrea calmly led the way through to the kitchen and took her place at the table.

'Christ, about time for a wine,' Sera exclaimed, pouring generous glasses for each of them.

'Please,' Sam said gratefully.

'Hit me,' Chantrea added, holding out her glass.

'I'll just have a half,' Mallory said. 'You know how giggly wine makes me.'

Sera reached for Chantrea's glass and noticed with an unhappy jolt that she too was wearing espadrilles. How could that be?

'Yoo-hoo, ladies.' Sera's next-door neighbour Jacqueline popped her pretty powdered nose around the corner of the back door.

'Good evening all,' she said, enjoying her grand entrance. 'And this must be Sam? How delightful to meet you.' She smiled primly in his direction as she proudly placed a magnificent tropical-fruit-encrusted pavlova onto the centre of the table. There were gasps of admiration.

Jacqueline's ears soaked up their compliments for a few seconds, closing her eyes happily to breathe in her triumph before shrugging daintily and lifting her hands in protest.

'Oh, it was nothing really,' she tinkled, swinging the pink cashmere cardigan off her shoulders and hanging it on the back of a kitchen chair.

Jacqueline knew exactly how the evening would pan out. Everyone would bleat about their failings, how difficult their petty lives were and intermittently remark on her pristine life. She knew they were all secretly jealous of her; with her two perfectly behaved teenagers, her loving orthodontist husband and her perfectly maintained home. Her life didn't have the cracks the lives of the others did. Her life was as unblemished as the petals of an English rose.

~5~

Sera should have been relaxed and relieved. They had escaped Joan's scathing tongue with little damage done. Everyone was comfortable, the snacks were cute and kitsch and the team was knitting industriously. But she wasn't relaxed at all. Instead she could feel a familiar fashion-disaster headache forming around the edges of her mind.

How could she have misread the footwear zeitgeist so badly? How was it possible that both Mallory and Chantrea had picked up on the espadrille trend while she – the proudly up-to-the-minute Sera Walker – was so obviously out-of-step with the look of the moment?

Her fashion radar had clocked the espadrille, taken careful note of the new look, but had somehow miscalculated the shoe's fashion trajectory. She knew they were going to be big – almost as big as white linen – but not yet; not tonight, for goodness' sake. Besides, they were in four years ago. How dare they come back into fashion so quickly?

She shook her foot vigorously, now thoroughly disenchanted with her bejewelled flip-flops which suddenly seemed gaudy and silly.

'You look gorgeous tonight, darling,' Chantrea said to her with a smile.

'White linen is going to be so big this season,' Mallory said.

'Love the chocolate toenails,' Jacqueline added.

Sera smiled vaguely at them all, their kind words sailing past her, wasted. She surreptitiously checked out Jacqueline's footwear as she pretended to concentrate on her knitting; even Jacqueline's standard issue ballet flats seemed more appropriate than her own spangled sandals. With a final angry glare at her stupid, shiny flip-flops, she forced herself to tune back in to the conversation and focus on helping Chantrea with her mohair scarf.

'Oh my . . . well . . . those nibbles do look absolutely intriguing, but I think I'll say no,' Jacqueline said with the tiniest of shudders, as Mallory passed around Sera's kitsch hors d'oeuvres.

'So Chantrea, how was work today?' Sera asked.

'Oh, it was a fairly standard Honkers flight, complete with vomiting child and blocked toilet, but back in time to pick up Sally, which is always a plus,' Chantrea said with a faint smile which didn't quite reach her tired eyes.

'I can't imagine how awful it must be to have other people bring up your child,' Jacqueline said.

'Excuse me?' Chantrea demanded, her face flushing with instant anger. 'What do you mean by that?'

Sera and Mallory swapped nervous looks while Sam bowed his head over his wool.

Chantrea was a prickly sort at the best of times, but particularly defensive about the amount of time Sally spent in child care.

'Why nothing, darling,' Jacqueline replied, all wide-eyed innocence. 'I'm just saying –'

'Yeah, well don't, Jacqueline.' Chantrea's spiked hair seemed to bristle with energy. 'It's all right for some whose work week doesn't get more stressful than Thursday bridge morning and a weekly appointment with Mr Sheen but some of us have a bit more on.'

Mallory wanted to laugh, but one look at Chantrea's face told her that this wasn't the time for girlish giggles.

'Oh dear, I'm sorry if you thought I was attacking you. I wasn't, I was just sympathising with your situation,' Jacqueline replied quietly.

'More hors d'oeuvres girls,' Sera thrust the tray of nibbles between the women in an attempt to ease the discomfort.

Chantrea sighed and ran her hands through her hair, her short burst of anger spent. 'Oh, I'm sorry, too, Jacqueline. I know I'm touchy about childcare.'

'So are your girls at school yet, Sam?' Jacqueline asked, happy to focus on a safer topic.

'The older one, Isabelle, is in Prep this year but our –' a look of pain crossed his faced and he corrected himself '– er, *my* little one, Alexandra, is in the kindergarten room at Baby Face Childcare with Chantrea's Sally.'

'How lovely, and does their mother share custody?' Jacqueline asked.

'Jacqueline!' Chantrea said sharply.

'No, that's okay, Chantrea,' Sam reassured her. Turning to Jacqueline he explained, 'Their mother died two years ago so I'm doing the single parent thing.'

'Oh, my dear, I am so sorry.' Jacqueline touched her fingertips to her temple with concern. 'And it's so much harder for a man to do the work–kids thing than a woman.'

'JACQUELINE!' This time, a chorus of voices admonished her.

'Okay, I think it's time for some pav,' Sera announced, carefully checking to ensure her leg was fully covered before she rose from the table. Jacqueline needed distracting, and her giant airy meringue was just the thing for the job.

Thankfully, Jacqueline became distracted with the serving of her dessert. And with the help of more wine, the group relaxed into laughter and idle chatter, the big issues of life put to one side for the moment.

~ 6 ~

The white light stippling across the charcoal carpet told Joan it was still night time. She'd long accepted she would never again enjoy the luxury of a full night of unbroken sleep.

She stood up, slipped on her maroon velvet slippers and shuffled down the hall to tend to her impatient bladder. She was fully awake now, she realised, as she washed her hands and squinted at the blurry reflection in the mirror. It was truly a blessing that your eyes went at the same time as your skin's elasticity, she thought. If you got a clear view of what your face looked like after ten rounds with Father Time you'd give up for sure.

She shuffled down the hall to the kitchen to make herself a cup of tea. In Joan's mind tea was the answer to everything, a cure-all that never failed to remedy any ailment – from conniptions to the shakes, that little black leaf worked magic. It had never occurred to Joan that her complete dependence on the Tonic of the Colonies was most likely the cause of her insomnia.

Waiting for the kettle to boil, her eyes darted around the room, drinking in the memories that were always so much more potent at night. This had always been her favourite room of the house. So stylish at the time it had been decorated. She remembered when the olive-green doors and orange laminex benchtops were the height of fashion. She remembered the moving-in day and how as a young bride she had unpacked her first shopping bags as excitedly as a little girl playing house. Bonox, Vegemite, Bex, Arnott's Iced Vo-Vos, Gravox: all lined up in orderly domestic rows ensuring her success as the dutiful wife she had vowed to be the week before in front of family and friends at St Matthias'. It didn't take too many more trips to Donahue's market before the novelty of grocery shopping wore right off, though.

In her mind Joan saw the hordes of friends and neighbours laughing and drinking in the kitchen and living room, she heard the Beatles on the stereo, saw martinis in stylish glasses. All the girls with their Audrey Hepburn fringes, elaborate black eyeliner and up-to-the-minute fashions.

The photograph that stood on her nightstand had been taken right here in the kitchen on their first anniversary. She was wearing a bottle-green sleeveless dress with a tight bodice that ballooned out at the waist to a knee-length skirt. Barry was slim and blond, but quite severe-looking. He never smiled for the camera, or much in real life for that matter. No one looking at the young couple would guess at the silence that had already grown between them, or how hard Joan had to work just to keep up the appearance of a happily married life.

Even now she kept the photo beside her bed only because it seemed the right thing to do.

In the photo she was serving Barry a drink from the lead-crystal punch bowl that had been handed down from her great-grandmother. It was tradition to give it to the first bride in the family.

Sera had seemed pleased when Joan had handed it on to her on their wedding day but Joan doubted that she appreciated the significance of the piece. She looked at the bowl now, shoved in the corner of the bench, overflowing with the detritus of family life. Everything from Lego and bills to hair elastics and prescriptions blocked the glorious sparkle of the bowl. She hadn't seen the cups in years. They were probably all broken by now.

Joan sighed and looked out the window at the crazy paving patio that had been a feature of the backyard since before Tony was born. A huge sadness crept over her as she remembered the summer it was laid.

Her tea had finished steeping. She dropped the teabag in the sink and wandered back to her room.

~ 7 ~

'Muuum!'

The wail travelled down the hall to shake Sera from slumber. She tried to focus on the glowing red lines of her clock radio. Six am. Fantastic, a sleep-in.

She sat up and rummaged quietly in her bedside table for her make-up bag, and expertly applied a layer of powder, blush and lip gloss and ran a brush through her hair. In eight years of marriage Tony had yet to catch her once without make-up on in the morning, and she wasn't going to let it happen anytime soon.

'Mmmm . . .' Tony stirred and opened one eye. The other side of his face was mashed into the squashed pillows. 'Hello beautiful,' his husky morning voice greeted her. 'Come here and let me look at you,' he pleaded with arms outstretched.

'Don't be silly,' she snorted, slipping out of the bed. 'I've got a least an hour of work to do before I'll even look human, let alone beautiful.'

Downstairs Sera's spotlessly neat kitchen was filled with autumn sunshine, which made the ugly space almost bearable. She always left the kitchen perfect before going to bed at night. At least that was one area she could keep in order.

Bella was just the same, she remembered, though her sister was a major neat freak about all her living areas. Sera was more interested in styling and decorating her home than keeping it immaculate, especially with two small children thwarting her every move, but she knew she'd never let her home fall into the kind of chaos she and Bella had grown up in.

Just remembering the pigsty that had been their home, and how their mother never seemed to notice the mould in the shower or the stains on the carpet, was enough to spur Sera on to extra cleaning efforts in her own home.

Marlene's housekeeping indifference had spilled over into her mothering, Sera thought, trying to remember a time when her mother had shown concern or worry over her. And yet Joan flew into a maternal frenzy if Tony broke as much as a toenail. On the rare occasions they spoke, her own mother would never even ask how she was. Not that Sera cared any more. She shook her head defiantly as she stood and enjoyed the early morning sunshine that poured through her kitchen windows. Marlene was just too caught up in her own dramas to think about her daughters. Which reminded her of Joan's message the other night; she still had to call her mother back. Probably some minor drama she needed someone to listen to.

'Stuff her,' Sera announced to the empty kitchen. It wasn't as if she needed to be mollycoddled anyway. She turned to the tap to fill the kettle and caught sight of a dirty brown used teabag flung thoughtlessly into her stainless steel sink. A tannin stain had spread an ugly and dark shadow across the shiny surface.

'For God's sake,' she spat angrily. Was the woman trying to melt her brain on purpose?

She suddenly remembered the brochure that had arrived in yesterday's mail. She sifted through the rubbish in her crystal bowl, sighing at the mess it contained. The punch bowl meant a lot to her; she was humbled to think that she'd been entrusted with the care of such a family heirloom.

The ceremonial handing over of the bowl on her wedding day was a sign that Joan was on the verge of accepting Sera into the family; a really significant moment. After the wedding she had placed the heirloom in pride of place on the long kitchen bench to show Joan how much she treasured the gift, but try as she might to make it otherwise, every member of the family used the bowl as a dumping ground. Out of desperation she'd filled it with water one day and floated a couple of orchids on the surface. That night Tony, out of habit, tossed his mobile phone and keys into the floating garden.

And when the kids came along she'd had to push the bowl back to a safer spot at the back of the bench. She didn't want to put it away because it was such a pleasure to look at, especially when the sun hit it at a certain angle, throwing tiny refracted rainbows around the kitchen.

Right, she was going to clean it out today, she decided. She'd wash it until it sparkled and maybe use it for fruit instead. She'd get on to it after taking the children to daycare, as soon as she'd taken the lawnmower in for a service, but before she made dinner, and maybe after her DJs' shift . . . She sighed in defeat. Maybe tomorrow.

Sera rifled through the paperwork in the bowl and found the envelope she was after. She felt a twinge of guilt twist as she opened it, looking over her shoulder before slipping out the letter.

Dear concerned family member, the form letter began. *When the people we love reach a certain age and perhaps are no longer able to effectively look after themselves or are perhaps a little too distracting to be minded by family members in their own home, we want to ensure they're cared for in a loving and sympathetic manner.*

Here at Sleepy Hollow Aged Care Facility we genuinely care for our guests, offering a wide range of programs and activities to help keep minds and bodies active. For example, daily lectures include: 'Our Friend Fibre', 'Life Between Meals', and 'No one's Trying to Steal Your Purse'. Our exercise and gaming program is extensive, including such activities as: 'Wheelchair Rambles', 'Constructive Criticism of Others', 'Cane Jousting' and everyone's favourite 'When-I-was-Your-Age Bingo'.

'Whatcha readin'?' Tony came in and headed straight for the Saeco espresso machine.

'Nothing, just some junk mail.' Sera shoved the brochure back into its envelope and slipped it to the bottom of the pile. She'd throw it out. What was she thinking? Joan was hard work, but this was her house, after all.

While her husband fixed himself some toast to eat in the car, she picked up the last envelope in the pile. It contained fabric swatches for the children's room. The current state of the kids' room made her eyes hurt. It was always so ugly. Mismatched furniture, different paint schemes, toys spilling out all over the place. She was thrilled to have discovered a gorgeous Designer's Guild fabric that worked for both genders. By making the whole space uniform she knew it would look beautiful, and the kids would be so happy. How could they not be happy in a beautifully decorated space? It always worked for her. When she surrounded herself with beauty she felt relaxed and at ease.

The swatches spilled out into her hand and she gave a squeal of excitement. The quality was better than she'd expected. The colour combination of acid green with pale orange contrasted perfectly with a darker pumpkin hue. One fabric was in wild 70s floral shapes, which would look wonderful on Maddy's bed and covering a matching tub chair, while the bold geometric-striped version in the same three colours would look just sensational on Harry's bed. Their Roman blind could be in the pumpkin with the green pelmet and the walls could be in the lemon. It would look incredible. Of course it would cost a small fortune, but it would be worth it for ten years of beautiful wake-ups. She knew the kids would like it . . . they just had to; she'd already paid the non-refundable deposit.

Tony dropped a kiss on her cheek and rushed off.

'Hi Mum, bye Mum,' he garbled through Vegemite toast as he rushed past his mother in the corridor.

'Your wife should feed you a proper breakfast, Tony,' Joan called after him. 'It's not good for the digestion, eating on the run, you know.'

'Why should Sera make me breakfast, Mum? I'm perfectly capable, and I'm late. See ya.' The door slammed shut.

'Morning, kids,' said Joan.

'Nanna!'

Sera put the kettle on again. Tea would be needed ASAP. She smiled at the kids' greeting of their grandmother. The children adored Nanna, and no wonder – she spoilt them rotten. Sneaky lollies before bedtime, horrible cheap variety store clothes they loved, and Joan ignored Sera's rules and let them watch her mind-numbing soaps about ugly people in ugly houses.

'Morning, Joan,' she said as she delivered her mother-in-law's morning cuppa.

'Morning, Sera. Good God, did you just walk past the cup with the teabag? It doesn't look very strong.'

'Three dunks, Joan, just the way you like it. I can make it again if you like.'

'No, it's okay, I'll suffer in silence.' Joan gave the hot beverage another cursory glance and put it on the side table. Sera quietly moved a coaster under the cup to protect the teak.

'Look what I've got, kids: presents!' Joan leaned over to the side of the Jason recliner and pulled out two Best and Less bags. Oh great, Sera thought.

The children swung around from their cross-legged position in front of the television, rushing to investigate their gifts.

'I know you're sick of your baby blue and pink doonas in your room,' Joan began.

What? No! Sera thought.

'So I went out and bought you brand new bed linen.'

OH FUCKING HELL, NO! Sera's brain shrieked as a smile froze solid on her face and her eyes started to water.

'YAY! Look, Mum, look! It's Dora the Explorer!' shrieked Maddy. 'I love Dora!'

Sera looked over, expecting to see Joan smirking. But she was just smiling at the children, enjoying their pleasure. Harry was struggling to get his bag open, but finally the contents spilled onto the carpet.

'SPIDERMAN! Spiderman, Spiderman, Spiderman!' he chanted his hero's name in delight. Just when Sera thought it couldn't get any worse, Joan brought out more parcels.

'Now, I know how much your Mum likes everything to match . . .' Was that a sarcastic twinkle Sera could see in the old bat's eye? '. . . so here's the rest of the linen.'

The kids cheered at their sudden boon. Sera felt light-headed. Matching Dora and Spidey fitted and flat sheets and – dear God, no, please don't let it be possible – yes, the icing on the cake: matching valances.

In all her days of being excruciatingly aware of aesthetics, avoiding colour clashes, subtly rearranging cushions in friends' houses and choosing to sit on waiting-room chairs with fabric that complemented her day's outfit, Sera had never seen anything in worse taste. And she was stuck. This stuff was going into her house, into her own children's bedrooms. Her precious children would surely be influenced by this crime against interior design. She tuned back in to the conversation. 'Remember that win at Bingo last week?' Joan was telling her grandchildren. 'Well, I thought who else would I rather spend my winnings on? You can't take it with you, you know.'

That was it. Sera had to intervene. 'Kids, Joan,' she said sweetly. 'I am so sorry but I've already paid a deposit on a gorgeous bedroom suite ensemble in one hundred per cent cotton.'

The children and Joan all looked up at her as if she were speaking a foreign language.

'It's a beautiful colourway, in hues of pumpkin, tangerine and lime.'

'Good lord, sounds like a salad,' Joan said unhelpfully.

'I no like pumpkin,' said Harry, his bottom lip firmly stuck out and the Spiderman doona clasped firmly to his little chest.

Sera wasn't giving up. 'I have the swatches here to show you. It's a very pretty story, to suit both boys and girls.'

'Story? I like a story.' Harry's ears pricked up.

Sera ran into the kitchen to get the colour swatches, then dashed back to explain to her little boy. 'No, darling, not that kind of story. Silly mummy! A "story" is what the interior designer calls the range of different fabrics that are the same kind. See?'

She fanned out the colour swatches for the children's approval.

'I want story. That's not story, that's sewing. I want story,' Harry whined.

In desperation, Sera turned to Maddy. Surely her stylish daughter could be relied upon to make the right decision. 'Maddy? What do you think? Daisies, look.' Sera held out the swatch to her little girl.

Maddy, more diplomatic than the average five-year-old, said, 'I really like your material, Mummy, but I love Dora more than anything in the whole world. More than even fairy bread.'

Sera caved in. She couldn't take away their doonas, she wasn't that bad a mother. Sure, she forbade them from playing outside before guests were due so they didn't wreck their designer outfits, and yes, she had been known to pop the odd fair streak in her little girl's hair – it was just so dark – and okay, she'd considered cosmetic surgery for her little boy's sticky-outy ears, but she wasn't about to destroy their happiness over interior design. Yet.

'Sorry about raining on your linen parade,' Joan apologised as Sera slumped in defeat. 'A case of miscommunication. I guess.'

'Never mind,' said Sera, heading for the kitchen to toss the swatches into the bin. She fished around the bottom of the crystal bowl, took the letter from Sleepy Hollow and rested it on top of the pile.

~ 8 ~

The lift doors parted like theatre curtains on opening night. Bella was the principal actor on centre stage and the LA sunshine streaming through the floor-to-ceiling French windows was her spotlight. She was on. She pasted a smile onto her immaculately made-up face and began the day's performance. As she passed the ornate gilt mirror she snuck a quick peek at herself. Perfect. Her coral shirt was tucked neatly into her taupe pants. Her ponytail was sleek, her skin dewy and her lips glistening with gloss.

She headed towards the checkout desk and joined the long queue. As she waited her gaze rested on an enormous crystal bowl full of water set on a table in the centre of the foyer. Large water lilies floating on its surface reminded Bella of the time Sera had tried to de-clutter her crystal bowl. Hilarious! Not so funny for Tony's new phone, but a great story.

She thought about her little sister in Sydney. The crystal bowl had been a wonderful welcome gift from Joan. Sera was so lucky. Bella didn't have feelings of inclusion anymore. Not that she ever did really. When she'd been married to Curtis she was just playing the housewife role. She'd set the scenes so carefully, down to slippers at the door and casserole in the oven. Like every part of her life, really; it had all been an act. She'd so badly wanted to belong to a clan. Like Sera did. She'd tried to be a family with Curtis. What a fool she'd been.

In her mind the crystal bowl transformed into a cereal-encrusted bowl on the kitchen table back on the farm. 'Staring at it's not going to get it clean,' her mother's voice echoed from a distant time. Marlene was at the kitchen table filling in one of her many competition forms.

Bella sighed and picked up the bowl, running water in it to soak, then moved over to give the frying pan the same treatment.

'I've got to get to school, Mum,' she said.

'Not till you've put those sheets out to dry, my girl, they stunk of mould last week.'

'But Sera has to be on time today, she has an excursion.'

'Does she?' her mum muttered. 'How am I expected to pay for that?'

'I've already paid. It's just to the petting farm up the road. It was only five bucks.'

'Good girl. Pass my bag, will you?'

Bella passed her mother's tatty old leatherette handbag to her. She wished her mother had a bag like Carrie's mother. A different one each day to match her outfit. Always neat and tidy.

She felt a slight warmth at the 'good girl' from her mother. It was nice to be appreciated. She waited for her mother to give her back the five dollars.

'Ah, here it is.' Marlene pulled out a dog-eared Scratchy. 'Thought I'd lost it.' She began scratching madly with her split, stumpy thumbnail. 'Dishes aren't going to do themselves, my girl. Thought you were in a hurry to get to school or somesuch?'

Looking back, Bella could see that Marlene had simply given up on mothering. She was over it by the time she'd found herself pregnant with her fifth child and was happy to hand Sera over to the eldest. Bella knew that in a big family everyone had to pull their weight, but sometimes she worried that Sera would think she was her real mother; not Marlene.

She loved her little sister so much and wanted to be there for her; but she got so tired sometimes and just wanted to read magazines on her bed, instead of bedtime stories to Sera.

But Marlene's gambling problem had kept the family constantly broke; their grocery money squandered on poker machines, Tatts tickets and horses. Bella had been devastated the Christmas morning that Marlene told three-year-old Sera that Santa had 'got lost' and there would be no presents that year. She was determined it would never happen again. So from then on, Bella saved her supermarket pay for stacking shelves to buy Sera and the boys birthday and Christmas presents.

But no matter how many gifts she bought her little sister, it never lessened the guilt she felt over Sera's accident. She tried so hard to make amends for that one fateful minute in time – in every area of her life. She strove to be perfect at everything. To be a good friend; the best employee; an immaculate guest.

As a teenager, Bella's only moments of peace came when she lay looking at her Versace wall. Gianni Versace embodied everything she dreamed of. It was all gold, glitz and glamour.

Even the iconic Medusa face that was the designer's logo seemed to reflect her own: eyes closed in an attempt to shut the chaos out; sad mouth. She'd drawn a large Medusa, coloured it gold and stuck it on the ceiling above her bed so she could take the shininess of Versace into her dreams.

The Versace models were tigresses; they were big and strong; in charge of their lives, their ambitions, their outfits. She wanted to stride across a Venetian palazzo in silk palazzo pants; she wanted to lounge on a daybed. She wanted to know what a daybed was. These were her schoolgirl dreams. And her wall, decorated with big torn-out magazine ads, kept them alive.

When she turned seventeen, Bella had been determined to leave her messy, broken life behind her and hopped a plane to Sydney. She had planned to leave the destruction zone of her teens; her gambling mother, her drunk father, her dishevelled brothers and even her broken little Sera – all that she felt responsible for – and start again. Start from scratch and be the very best, most perfect person she could be. Then she had sat on the plane next to Curtis.

And for a long time she'd fooled everyone. Bella always looked immaculate. She seemed on top all the time. Her friends were amazed at how ordered her life appeared. Perfect Bella. But it was all fake.

She took another glimpse at herself in the mirror across the lobby and inwardly screeched. What she saw was a messy, completely fucked-up unit. She left the queue and rushed to the ladies'. She had serious maintenance to do.

~ 9 ~

'Watch where you're going, you stupid bitch!' the truck driver yelled above the blaring of his horn, gunning his engine to speed past.

Sera swore in shock at the verbal attack, a surge of adrenalin and embarrassment coursing through her as she realised she had pulled in front of the semi-trailer without even looking in her rear view mirror.

'Christ, I've got to concentrate,' she berated herself aloud as dots of perspiration pricked through the mask of her foundation.

'Mummy, was that man a road-rager? He looked like a road-rager, he was mad at you.' Maddy's voice trembled.

'It's all right, darling,' Sera answered, flicking Maddy a glance in the mirror. 'He's just having a bad day.'

The morning was not going well. They had left the house fifteen minutes late due to an unscheduled, but essential handbag rethink. Sera had suddenly remembered her lunch date with Jacqueline in Rose Bay and knew she had to have her oversized Coach handbag or she'd just as likely not get served.

And changing bags was no small task. It wasn't simply a matter of relocating her phone and wallet; there was her make-up bag, document holder, refresher towels, keys, hand mirror, diary, notebook, pens, moisturiser, latest scar cream, mail, childcare centre payment . . . and the list went on. With the kids wanting to tell her stories, asking for food, arguing among themselves and Joan's dour insights and cup-of-tea requests, it was miraculous she got out of the house at all.

And now Oxford's Street's peak-hour traffic seemed to be conspiring against her even more than usual: she'd almost hit a pedestrian and been verballed by a truckie. The perfect morning.

She zipped in front of the traffic to avoid being stuck behind an illegally parked car and got another blast for her efforts.

At last she pulled into the crèche's circular drive and took her place in the line of DVD-playing four wheel drives waiting to dispatch designer offspring. The parents rushed in laden with children and backpacks and scurried out peering anxiously at their Omegas and iPhones.

Sera swung into the first available spot. 'Come on, come on.' She shepherded her charges towards the door while Maddy shrugged on her backpack and managed to drop her entire herd of My Little Pony toys, hat and jumper onto the wet ground one by one.

'Maddy, for heaven's sake,' Sera said, exasperated. 'That's what a bag is for, to carry things in. Harry, stop!' she yelled, pulling the energetic toddler out of the path of an impatient Mercedes, while simultaneously plucking a pink pony from a puddle.

She delivered Harry to the three-year-old room and finally arrived at Maddy's kindergarten room, where she helped her hang up her backpack and stow the ponies in her locker. Planting a kiss on her daughter's head, she was just about to escape when Miss Susan bailed her up. 'Oh, Sera, we never see you. You must be thrilled with Maddy's developmental progress of late.'

'Oh, Miss Susan, yes absolutely, we're both dead chuffed,' Sera assured her. What was the woman beaming about?

'To have learnt how to tie shoelaces so quickly, well, it's quite an achievement.' Oh, bugger, the teacher was on to her. Miss Susan obviously knew jolly well Sera had no idea what she had been referring to. 'She even earned an elephant stamp from the school director, which isn't a daily event, let me tell you.'

Sera remembered how difficult that stamp had been to scrub off the back of Maddy's hand the week before and how Maddy had cried about losing it. Guilt pounded in her temple. She hadn't realised it had been an award. What's wrong with a bloody certificate, she wondered.

Miss Susan continued, as if reading Sera's thoughts. 'We don't give out certificates because we prefer to give our kinder group an opportunity to explain their success to their parents over the evening family meal – it's a chance for them to shine.'

Good Lord, evening family meal? Sera couldn't remember quite when that had last taken place. The in-flight service on the last Jetstar trip to Melbourne probably didn't count.

'The stamp on the hand acts as a reminder for the child to tell his or her parents about their goal achieved.'

Sera's headache intensified. Maddy had been wailing that evening that she had something important to talk about, and Sera distinctly remembered telling her to stop being a baby and promised to listen to the story just as soon as she got Harry off to bed. But then Harry had done a poo on the bathroom floor and she'd never got around to hearing the story. Now she was in trouble. Maddy was standing proudly waiting for the overdue recognition from her mum. But Sera had to save face in front of Miss bloody Susan.

'Yes, of course,' she began, 'Maddy's been tying her own shoes all week and it's just the kind of thing we expect of her. Naturally we're proud.'

Sera's heart sank at her own words. She knew her little girl was staring at her in amazement. Sera always packed their bags, tied their shoes, even pulled on their clothes for them because it was just plain quicker. Sometimes she meant to help them help themselves, but they were always in such a hurry.

After Miss Susan turned away, Sera leant down to give Maddy a hug. She whispered, 'You're amazing, I'm so impressed. Promise to show me tonight?' But Maddy took the slight with her as she turned to her friend to discuss pony games.

Defeated, Sera sadly said goodbye and got as far as the classroom door before Maddy called out 'Wait' and ran into her arms, the offence forgiven. 'Bye, Mummy, I'll tell you all about what My Little Pony does today after kinder if you want.'

Sera smiled and smoothed the baby hair back into her daughter's plaits.

'That'd be great. I love you, Madeline,' she said.

'I love you too, Miss Susan – oh!' Maddy laughed. 'I mean *Mummy*.' She skipped away leaving Sera stinging with sadness.

She trudged back to the car, all urgency to make her 9 am shift momentarily forgotten as her thoughts swirled. Harry's first steps were at this place. Maddy had read her first word here. Sera had missed last year's Christmas concert by accidentally mixing up her roster.

As she waited at the traffic lights, she thought of her own childhood. Her mother had never been at any of her school events and it was Bella who helped her learn to tie her shoes.

~10~

Sera arrived at work rattled from her crazy morning. Luckily there weren't any early customers so she had time for some therapeutic make-up application.

Sera loved that her job required her to wear 'full face' at all times. For a woman who wore lipstick, foundation and blush to do the weeding, getting made up for work was a serious business that required applying as much cosmetic product to her skin as humanly possible. Her eye make-up was a glowing testament to Dior's entire new range of metallics and her lipgloss was so thick her morning cappuccino often slipped off her mouth.

Three hours into her shift, she checked her reflection again to ensure her hair – piled elaborately on her head and supplemented with several hairpieces – was still firmly in place and then retrieved her handbag from behind the counter, glancing at her watch to make sure her break time had officially started. The girls at the Chanel counter got very catty about break times.

She headed for the mall, smoothing her uniform and smiling brightly at the customers. As she rounded the corner behind Girls' Wear she spotted Sam and his daughters obviously in some sort of bother, as the little one was holding herself and jiggling while the older one remonstrated with her dad, who looked stressed and tired.

'Hi, Sam,' Sera said.

Sam and his little girls looked up blankly at the lady with the big blonde hair and the huge eyes.

'Sam, is everything okay?

'Er, I'm sorry, do I know you?'

'Sam, you were at my house last week. It's me, Sera.'

'Ohhh! Sera, of course, sorry. I didn't recognise you. You look, um, well . . . different.'

'Oh, yes, of course, I'm in my work look. Can I give you a hand here?' Sam's little girl was now doing a Riverdance-style jig.

'Alexandra needs to go to the toilet but I can't convince Isabelle to take her in,' he admitted.

Isabelle, mature beyond her years, turned her enormous brown eyes onto Sera. 'Stranger danger,' she said simply.

'How about me, darling?' Sera asked with a big smile, holding out her hand. 'Would you like me to help you?'

To Alexandra's three-year-old eyes Sera looked like a princess, with her cascading blonde curls, rainbow eyelids and bright pink shimmering smile. She agreed immediately and eagerly took Sera's hand.

When they emerged from the toilets Sam offered to buy Sera a coffee in thanks.

'You don't need to do that, Sam,' she told him. 'But I am on my lunch break so I'd love to join you.'

They wandered to the food court and the girls raced to the mall's nearby jungle gym.

'Jacqueline's right, it is harder for guys sometimes,' he lamented. 'The whole parenting thing seems to have been biased toward women – starting from day one with the breastfeeding stuff. Don't get me wrong, I know there's plenty I can do as a father but sometimes I just feel completely overwhelmed and under-equipped. Like piggie-plaits for example – no matter how many different versions I try I have no idea what she means and I just get yelled at.'

Sera laughed. 'Oh don't worry about that, it doesn't matter which gender parent you are: if you have a daughter you'll never get the hairstyle right.'

She dropped her smile and touched his hand. 'So how is it really, Sam? I can't begin to imagine how hard it must be for you.'

'Yes, I won't try to be brave; the last couple of years have been tough,' he sighed. 'It's really hard to explain but no matter how sad *I* feel about her dying or how much *I* miss her or how much *I* need her, the worst bit is that it's nothing compared to how much those little girls need their mum.'

His voice cracked on the last word. 'Oh bugger.' He bit his bottom lip, throwing his head back. 'It's so embarrassing, sorry, I still can't . . .' Sam held a wad of napkins over his eyes. 'I still get so damn mad at her sometimes. I'm really going to have a stern word with her when I see her again,' he said, smiling wryly.

Sera smiled at him.'It's okay, Sam, take your time,' she encouraged.

'What I've found most challenging is establishing the same kind of unbreakable bond the girls had with their mum – it had always mystified me.' He took a bite of his sandwich and continued. 'Like, how she used to say, "What's wrong?" even though they hadn't told her there was a problem. And how she'd know to suggest exactly the right activity. I suggest tickle-chasey and everyone bursts into tears.'

'Well, you're obviously doing something right,' Sera said as Alex came over to drop off her jumper and give her dad a big smooch. 'How did you do it? Cast a magic spell?'

'Don't laugh, I considered it!' Sam chortled. 'No, one night it occurred to me that I can't be a woman, I can't be their mother, but I can be a pretty good dad. I just have to do that the best way I can. For instance, Grace had a green thumb, but very formal taste. Our courtyard was sculptured and meticulously maintained. It was her passion.'

He finished his sandwich and kicked back, his hands folded behind his head as he got more involved in telling his story.

'I'm not proud of it, but soon after she died I went a bit crazy. After the initial shock all I could feel was intense anger.'

'Really?' Sera asked in surprise. 'How unusual.'

'Well, not really,' Sam explained, 'according to my grief counsellor, it's perfectly normal. Anyway, I was in a rage for weeks. I could barely breathe. Luckily the girls were staying with their grandparents in Noosa. It hit me in waves when I least expected it. I wanted to kill, maim, scream, destroy anything that would release this . . . this, unmitigated fury that she could leave me.

'One day, when I had a savage hangover after a night of drinking, I felt horrendous and suddenly the rage took hold. I wanted to take vengeance, to punish her for doing this to her beautiful innocent little girls – and to me. I just went mad. I went out to her precious, pristine garden with an axe. I hacked up bushes, ripped up pavers, chopped down trees. I even smashed the mosaic table setting she'd made herself. I really regret that one. But I couldn't see straight. It went on for hours. I didn't rest until every retaining wall, water feature, box hedge and succulent was annihilated.' He stopped and drained the last of his coffee, looking over with a peaceful smile at his girls as they practised a dance routine.

'Oh my God,' Sera breathed. 'So what did you do next?'

'I fell into a slump of utter exhaustion. I was filthy, my hands were bleeding and my clothes were torn. The sun was setting and everything was glowing a kind of orange colour. And her garden was gone. All of it, and nothing I could ever do would bring it back.'

Sam stopped and looked Sera in the eye. 'I know I sound like a monster, Sera, and I don't really go around telling people this story. You're just so easy to talk to.'

She took his hand in a maternal squeeze. 'Sam,' she said, 'I don't know how I would react or what I would do in your position. I'm not judging you, just listening, okay?'

He nodded silently and continued. 'So, anyway, as I said it was all gone. In the same way that Grace was gone.' He paused for a second. 'And the only option left to me was to accept it.'

Sera nodded. 'What did the girls say when they came home and saw what had happened?' she asked.

'Well, that was the blessing in disguise. Rather than try to be like Grace and create a design masterpiece, I prepared several sections of the back yard so when the girls came home we could create the world's best veggie garden.'

'Oh, how wonderful,' Sera sighed in relief.

'Yeah, it's really great,' Sam said, his enthusiasm reflected in his smile. 'The girls just love it. One section is for our root veg, one section is herbs, one is for all our leafy veggies – the girls are even eating spinach now, can you believe it? And one section is just full of any random flower seed that tickles the girls' fancy at the nursery. It's like a rainbow in there: poppies, lilies, sunflowers. There's no rhyme or reason, and it's the girls' favourite part, of course.'

'How brilliant. You must show me sometime.' Sera said.

'Yeah, it's been just great and I've learnt the most valuable lesson from it.'

'What?' Sera asked, leaning forward with interest.

'Well, by just pottering, with no telly, or other distractions of life – you know, ballet, homework, swimming – just by working side-by-side, that's when all the little conversation streams start to flow. That's when Isabelle tells me about the girl at school who said she was fat, or how she feels about being the only girl at school whose mum died.'

'Sam, you're really something else, you know.'

'Nah, just a dad doing his job.'

'Can we go home now, Daddy? My tummy hurts.' Isabelle suddenly appeared at his side.

Sam leaned over to Sera and whispered with a conspiratorial wink, 'Tummy hurting means she's bored.'

'Ah, you even speak the code,' Sera replied in admiration.

'Sure, Issy, let's go. Say bye to Sera.'

'Bye, Sera,' said Isabelle as she pulled on her cardigan.

'You're pretty,' Alex whispered.

'You're pretty too,' Sera whispered back and tapped her on the nose.

'See you at next month's Stitch 'n' Bitch, Sam.' She waved at the family as they departed.

'Yeah, see you then. Oh, and Sera,' he called as he hitched two Barbie backpacks over one shoulder and a purple poncho over the other, 'if you teach me how to purl I'll bring you a tussie-mussie of herbs.'

~ 11 ~

The weeks had flown by, and much to Jacqueline's joy tonight it was her turn to host Stitch 'n' Bitch.

'Ooh, how delicious, I really must have those for tonight's "Sweets for the Sweet" theme,' Jacqueline whispered as she stroked the pastel 1950s-esque ceramic dessert tumblers in Bed, Bath and Table. In scrumptious tones of baby blue and pink, mint and lemon, they were just the thing to serve her trademark parfait in tonight.

She sighed happily and hummed to herself as she continued her plotting and planning. The organisation of the event had filled her mind for days and provided a lovely break from her usual routine of meal preparation, household maintenance and school duties.

She had already analysed and discarded a range of recipe options, carefully scrutinised her platters for chips or blemishes and polished all her cutlery. The other Stitch 'n' Bitch members might scoff at her, and she knew they did, but that didn't stop them gobbling all her delicious offerings with gusto, did it?

Jacqueline Bouvier's scones were the pride of the Mothers' Committee cake stall, her teacake declared by the principal as 'sterling', her home-made ice-cream had legendary status in the street and no one had ever had meringue melt in their mouth quite like hers. She had a culinary reputation to maintain, so the others could scoff all they wanted.

Of course she was extremely well-qualified for the job of hostess; far more qualified than any of the others, who just simply tossed any old thing on the table with little care or thought, for Jacqueline was a proud graduate of Institut Villa Pierrefeu, Switzerland's finest finishing school.

She'd excelled in *Mobilier* and could spot a fake Louis XIV at fifty paces; Etiquette and Deportment were a shoo-in thanks to her natural grace and posture; *Ménage* had been hard work, but she knew she'd need the invaluable skills of toilet cleaning and razor-sharp hospital corners in her planned future career as a wife.

It was thanks to the school that she'd met her husband, Thomas. He'd been in Switzerland completing his orthodontic training at a highly respected medical institution and was invited to one of the many soirées the college hosted for the young ladies to practise their burgeoning skills.

As the only other Australian in the room, she'd been instantly attracted to him and the two had relished the opportunity to natter quietly away in English (out of principal Madame Neri's earshot of course – there would be hell to pay if Jacqueline were caught speaking 'colonial').

The two kept in contact by mail after Thomas returned home and when Jacqueline graduated (with an A in everything except floral art) she flew into Australia and into his arms. He'd delighted in his Swiss Finished fiancée and never missed an opportunity to show off her prowess to colleagues during their many dinner parties.

She took another look at the parfait dishes, decided they were just too sweet to leave behind and took them to the counter to pay. She quickly decorated the table in her mind. Everything would be in pastel and floral. Perhaps Sera wouldn't mind whipping up some cupcakes. And maybe Bella had time to make a praline mille-feuille – such a pretty dessert. She selected napkins in a range of soft colours to complement her new dishes.

Making polite small talk with the salesgirl while her purchase was wrapped, Jacqueline was suddenly distracted by a pretty display on the counter. Delicate, slender parfait spoons in silky resin, each one in a slightly different hue, were arranged attractively before her. A gentle white swirl through the pinks, greens and lemons made the spoons appear to be concocted of icing. She picked up the sample batch, tied together with a silk ribbon. A familiar gurgle of excitement started to bubble inside her. She looked up at the shopgirl. Her back was turned as she wrapped the tumblers in tissue. Jacqueline simply had to have the spoons.

Sera was at home feeling guilty. She'd only worked a half day but had left the children at crèche for the full day because there was an important personal task she needed to do.

But first, Sera thought, food for tonight's Stitch 'n' Bitch. She pulled out a packet of frozen party pies from the freezer. Jacqueline would shoot her, she thought, as she looked down at the icy sheen covering the box. But with only an hour before Joan got back, and picking up the kids and starting dinner, it was the best she could do. She briefly toyed with the idea of whipping up a cake, but experience told her that desserts were not her strong suit.

Decision made, she tossed the box on the draining board to thaw and went upstairs to the bathroom with the parcel she'd just collected from the post office.

She sighed as she entered her haven. It was so rare to have it to herself. There was no space or budget stretched for an ensuite after building Joan's bathroom downstairs, but at least the family bathroom was large and luxurious. She'd even got her stand-alone egg-shaped bath, thanks to Tony's trade connections.

The latte-coloured bath sheets and huge cream rectangular floor tiles were set off by tiny sandstone mosaics on the walls. Tony and Sera had spent a happy rainy afternoon, with newborn Maddy in her capsule, scouring the dusty treasure trove of Italian tiling importers Wyse and Son, next door to Parterre in Woollahra, to find thirty individually painted ochre-on-sandstone tiles for the feature wall. The mirrors were all waist high as per Sera's strict orders, and tinted ever so slightly, just enough to give one's complexion a flattering muted appearance.

She ripped open the package in her hand and tipped out the little box. Gently she opened it and removed the instructions. The little round glass tub certainly looked as if it could contain the promised land. She was so hopeful. The website had guaranteed drastic reduction in the appearance of scarring. She was dubious at first – she'd tried so many – but the more testimonials she read, the more she believed that this was the one; this was going to be the magic ointment she'd searched for all her life. Of course she had thought that last month when she'd bought that cream at work, but one had to remain optimistic.

She opened the lid . . . nothing. She'd been expecting a glow of radiance or the Hallelujah chorus at least. She smiled at her ridiculousness, and tried not to notice that the seventy-five millilitres of cream looked much like the cream in every other tub and jar in her cupboard.

A regular apothecary shop lurked behind her bathroom vanity door. She had spent thousands of dollars searching for the elusive cure, all in vain. Until now, maybe? Even though this one looked the same, it was different, she argued to herself. This one was made from sea kelp and whale blubber – and everyone knew what great skin whales had. Except for the barnacles, of course. She did feel quite guilty about purchasing such an illicit product online (what would Mallory the animal lover say?), but if it minimised the scar it was worth it.

She read the instructions three times, mouthing them silently to herself; determined to get the application process just right. And then, dipping her finger reverently into the cream, she smeared it gently from her thigh to her ankle in a smooth downwards motion. She set the timer on her bathroom radio for five minutes.

The scar began to tingle from her outer thigh to halfway down her calf. Its puckered edges were becoming hot and painful. The tingly feeling intensified. It started to burn. She gripped the side of the sink and clenched her teeth. This was great, anything that hurt this much was sure to be working. She looked at the clock, willing the five minutes to be over so she could rinse it off.

Only thirty more seconds to go. Tears of pain were rolling down her face. She jammed a flannel in her mouth in case Joan or Tony came home and heard her yelps. Five, four – she turned on the shower – three, two, one. She plunged her leg into the cool relief of the water with a gasp of relief. Oh, thank goodness. She looked at the welt that ran down the length of her leg. Instead of being puckered and purple it was now swollen and a bright angry red. Hmmm, she thought, not yet prepared to admit defeat. Maybe it would take a few hours to settle down.

She sat on the edge of the bath, staring at the red scar. Tears pricked in the back of her eyes. She wasn't stupid. She knew the image she presented to the world. She knew she must come off as a complete dollybird. The eye-lashes, the fake nails, the hairpieces; but it was all a distraction device, a way of drawing the eye upward and away from the hideous scar.

Tony tried to tell her he didn't see it, but how could he miss it? It ran down her entire leg. It wrinkled and puckered. It didn't tan but blotched, and even fake tan only minimised it slightly.

She remembered the day the accident happened. She wasn't allowed to climb. She knew the golliwog had been taken away from her as a punishment for being naughty but she'd climbed up anyway.

It hadn't hurt much at first. When she clipped the handle of the saucepan she'd fallen to the ground with the boiling water and her bum was what really hurt straightaway. But then the white pain of boiling flesh took over. She'd screamed. Bella had rushed over and poured iced water from the fridge onto the leg, but that had only made it worse. She remembered pushing Bella away, screeching at her to stop.

The ambulance had been a blur. Bella couldn't come because Mum and Dad were still out and she'd had to stay with the boys. But later that night they'd all come in to see her in hospital and she remembered clinging to Bella, not letting her go. Her mum didn't bother coming in again after that. Only Bella came.

She'd returned home after four weeks. The scar didn't really bother her much during her childhood, and when she became a teenager and the neighbourhood boys avoided her because of her burned leg she was relieved. As the local wallflower she never had to deal with facing her deformity through others' eyes.

But then she turned fourteen and everything changed. Bella had been gone for over a year and she got sick of being teased for being the only virgin in her school year. When the new boy, Jeremy Waterton, fancied her it had seemed like the perfect opportunity.

It had been an embarrassing fumble in the back shed on the farm. He'd tried to pull her jeans off, while she kept them up as high as she could. He didn't understand why. Didn't she want to do it? Cos they didn't have to if she had changed her mind, he reassured her. No, she definitely wanted to do it. But with her jeans on. They found a position that worked. He was thrilled with the arrangement and they met in the shed several times over the next few weeks. She was floating. She really felt loved by Jeremy, she felt romanced and excited by her foray into the world of sex.

Until it all came tumbling down around her. 'You're a dirty pig, Sera,' her brother Keith spat at her one afternoon in the kitchen after school.

'Why, what do you mean?' she said and looked up from her homework.

'It's written all over the boys' toilet walls – "Sera Walker does it doggy style".'

The shame. A dark burn crept up her legs and itched her scar until her entire body was ablaze.

'Just quit it will ya, Sera, you're embarrassing!' Keith said as he grabbed an apple and left the room.

She *was* embarrassing, he was right. The memory of that day reminded her now of how worthless her scar made her feel. She rarely let any guy get close to her after that. It was only when she met Tony and he had made her feel so special, so beautiful – for a while at least – that she had managed to let her guard down.

She looked down at her ugly leg. God, she hated it! Hated her stupidity for being sucked in by another stupid cream. She needed more than cream to fix how broken she was.

After drying herself off, she pulled on a pair of jeans and boots. Jacqueline would be home in ten minutes. She had time to blow-dry her hair, re-apply her make-up, then nick next door to see if her neighbour needed anything done for tonight.

'Jacqueline?' Sera called out as she tapped on the glass kitchen door. 'Hello? Anyone home?'

Jacqueline entered the kitchen from the hall and walked over to unlock the back door. 'Hi, Sera,' Jacqueline said, 'I've just walked in. How are you?'

'Fine thanks,' Sera lied, ignoring the almighty burning on her right leg. 'Been shopping?' she asked, looking at the bags in Jacqueline's arms.

'Yes, getting ready for tonight,' Jacqueline replied seriously. 'After much deliberation, I've decided on parfait.'

Sera tried to rustle up an appropriately enthusiastic response. 'Parfait? Why . . . yum!'

'Yes, it was a tricky decision. I toyed with peach Melba, then flirted with lemon meringue pie, but of course I did meringue last time at your house so that was out of the question straight away. I even considered Bombe Alaska, can you imagine!'

Sera looked at her neighbour in wonder. Was there seriously nothing else in the woman's head? 'No,' she replied. 'I can honestly say I can't imagine.'

'Well, the revelation came to me thanks to these delightful parfait tumblers I got at Bed, Bath and Table today. Are they not the sweetest things?'

'So beautiful!' Sera agreed 'They're gorgeous!'

'I know, and look – matching napkins,' Jacqueline said, reaching back into the carry bag.

'What a pretty colour combo,' Sera sighed, laying it all out on the kitchen table in front of her.

'And you won't believe this.' This time Jacqueline reached into the pocket of her camel trench coat.

'MATCHING PARFAIT SPOONS!' she cried, thrusting the bounty towards Sera as if it was burning her.

Okay, that's a bit too excited, Sera thought, noticing the high flush in Jacqueline's cheeks as she proffered the spoons. 'Yeah, they're great, too,' Sera responded warily, taking them from her neighbour's hand. She put them down gently next to the rest of the shopping and started backing away. 'Now, is there anything else you need from me?'

Jacqueline, back in the safe territory of catering, asked Sera if she could possibly whip up some cupcakes.

Sweetheart, Sera thought to herself, you must be high if you think I'm 'whipping up' fairy cakes between now and seven pm. Out loud she simply suggested, 'What about party pies? Lots of people like savoury.'

'Party pies?' Jacqueline said with distaste.

'Home-made, of course,' Sera quickly fibbed.

'Oh, home-made. Well, all right then. I guess it'll be okay.'

'Great, well, see you later on then.' Sera made a quick escape.

When she'd left, Jacqueline turned back to her shopping, her eyes resting for one happy second on the parfait spoons until the joy was replaced by a surge of bile in the back of her throat.

~12~

'Onions caramelising, children not punching on, mother-in-law with cuppa, reflection in kitchen mirror not quite swamp monster,' Sera murmured to herself as she checked her end-of-the-day list.

'Darling,' she said as Tony walked in from work, 'how was your day?'

'Hello, beautiful lady,' he said, grabbing her around the waist and leaning her back for a big smooch. She laughed uneasily and wriggled out of his grasp.

'Hi yourself,' she replied brightly to cover up the brush-off. 'Can I pour you a wine?' she asked sweetly.

'Yes please,' he replied, popping into the living room for a quick wrestle with the kids and a hello to his mother.

'Sera?' Tony said as when came back into the kitchen.

'Yes, darling?' she replied brightly, but in her head she was screeching *Fuckety fuck fuck bloody bloody buggery bugger*, because she'd been married long enough to know that when your husband started a conversation with your christian name it meant trouble.

'Can we talk?' he asked.

'Sure, honey,' she said with a smile. What the bloody hell have I done now? she thought. Whatever he says, whatever he wants, just agree with him. Don't cause a scene in front of Joan and the kids, swallow your pride, just nod and tell him he's right and he'll stop and go away, she told herself.

Tony checked that the doors to the living room and corridor were both closed.

'Darling, I'm just really worried about you, about us, about everything at the moment,' he began.

I wonder if I'll be able to make Stitch 'n' Bitch in time, Sera thought, surreptitiously glancing at the microwave clock.

'You know I love you, don't you? You know I think you're the most wonderful woman in the world? I think you're clever, a great mum . . .'

She couldn't let her face betray her anxiousness at being late. Bother, she thought, smiling and nodding in agreement at the words as they came out of her husband's mouth.

'And you're so beautiful, just the way you are, without the make-up, the heels, the elaborate outfits –'

'Huh!' The exclamation exploded involuntarily from her lips.

'Sera, you are. I don't know why you have it in your head that you need to spend so much time and money on your appearance. It's starting to impact on our family.'

Okay, she was cross now, no point in just playing along. Her hands went to her hips. 'Everybody pays attention to their appearance in our social group. Especially now that we're on the wrong side of thirty-five! Don't be so selfish. I'm not the spunky little twenty-something anymore you know, Tony. It takes hours to get my hair to look halfway decent, hours of work each week to get my complexion to look unblemished.'

'But, Sera, this is my point: nobody is as concerned as you are. You're becoming obsessed!'

'Oh, rubbish.'

'Really, what time did you pick up the kids from child-care last Tuesday?'

'Six o'clock,' she said, guiltily averting her gaze.

'Again? It's happening so often. Why so late when you finish work at three?'

'What is this, the Spanish Inquisition? What I do with my time is my business. How dare you?!'

'Look, Sera, I don't want to be a tyrant here, tracking your every move, but I don't think it's fair that our kids have to stay in childcare until after dark just so you can have a pedicure.'

'IT WAS AN EMERGENCY!' she shrieked at him. She caught a glimpse of herself in the opaque glass of the sliding door shut behind him. That banshee with hands on hips, leaning forward, lips snarling, gums bared was no beauty queen.

'Please don't scream at me, Sera,' Tony replied quietly. 'We can talk more about this when you're calmer.' With that he left to chase the kids upstairs to start their bath and bed routine.

The only sound that trickled into the kitchen was the whoop of audience participation from the game show until Joan's sharp sentence cut across the cheers. 'Airs and graces, my girl.'

'But it was an emergency,' Sera whispered. Then she shook her head. Right, I'm off, she thought, untying her apron and grabbing the party pies. She called out to her mother-in-law, 'I'll be at Jacqueline's, Joan. Let Tony know, please?'

'Hmmmm, that'd be right,' came the response.

Sera shut the kitchen door on Joan and her opinions and marched down the back steps. 'Airs and graces' – the expression catapulted her straight back to her childhood. She sat with a thump on the garden bench. She wanted to talk to Bella, to have her console her and reassure her that she was a good person. But Bella was on the other side of the world; still living the life of freedom that Sera had given up. She sniffed away tears.

She just wanted to be pretty, was that too much to ask? She had always been in awe of her big sister's beauty; of her long, straight blonde hair, her magnificent figure: boy hips teamed with woman breasts. But most of all, Sera envied Bella's legs, her long, long, perfect unmarked legs. Legs in the shower being shaved, legs in a bikini sun-baking, legs jumping off the jetty into the dam. Legs in mini-shorts pumping madly down to the pub to fetch their parents home for dinner, jumping rope, running races, climbing up to the tree house, stretching out from a shortened school uniform.

Sera tried so hard to compete. She used to scour *Dolly* magazine, beg her mother for new clothes, fiddle for hours experimenting with hairstyles and make-up; anything to be in the same league as Bella.

Her mother was no help at all. She thought her daughter's titivating was a joke and never missed an opportunity to tease her in front of her brothers if she caught her 'mucking around with lipstick'.

Sera had lived in her sister's long-legged shadow her entire youth, even following her over to the mainland and into the flight industry; anything to get away from the dour, dopey expressions of her family as they sat around eating their tinned Spam with their slack jaws wide open.

Tony had been her first love. They had met on a flight. She liked the way he joked with her. He liked her beautiful face. She liked his beautiful face.

He told her she was gorgeous and for the first little while she believed him. By the time she decided that he'd been making it up just to be polite, they were already married with a baby on the way. And boy, that was an ugly time of life; she shuddered, remembering her swollen ankles and elephantine stomach. She didn't realise that her skin had glowed, her eyes had sparkled and her hair had grown thick and glossy. She didn't hear it when Tony had told her over and over.

So Sera dedicated herself to getting beauty into her life whenever she could. She was always searching for the next nail polish, gardenia bush or curtain fabric. All she wanted was enough lovely things to obliterate the memory of the shabby farmhouse with its overgrown front lawn, the tin roof so rusted it could no longer hold onto its gutter and the ugly kitchen with its dirty smells. And her scar.

Sera looked at her backyard in the late summer darkness. A heady scent from the last flush of the rose-bushes wafted over and she smiled as she looked at their full droopy heads. She thought of her beautiful children tucked up in bed, and felt a rush of guilt that she hadn't kissed them goodnight.

She looked up at the rich silk drapes over her bedroom windows. Her world was beautiful. A tiny smile came to her lips as she stood to go next door. There was beauty everywhere. She leant down to pick up the box of pies that had fallen next to the fish pond. She caught a glance of her reflection in the still water.

Well, nearly everywhere.

~13~

Chantrea's car screeched into the Babyface Childcare carpark. Today of all days, her flight had been delayed. Parent–teacher interviews freaked her out at the best of times: she always felt as if she was the student and the teacher was assessing *her* performance. She glanced in the mirror and ran her fingers over the temporary tattoo on her bicep. What had she been thinking? This was not a good week for experimenting.

Sally's room leader was conservative at her most way-out. Plaid was her idea of crazy. An eager young graduate, Nancy Thistlethwaite had rushed into the childcare system with a knapsack full of good intentions. It had been her dream to take the clay of the infant mind and mould it into intricate and sophisticated sculptures.

She had quickly discovered the crèche system was more about red-tape than cultural enrichment; that there were more soiled underpants than child prodigies and the thrill of intellectual conversation with like-minded souls in actual fact turned out to be bitter twenty-year-olds backstabbing each other in the tea-room, but Nancy remained steadfast in the face of tedium and was still determined to make a difference.

Chantrea rushed to the school's front door, passing a couple of mothers on their way back to the carpark. Chantrea vaguely knew them both – certainly enough to know that they prided themselves on being loosely linked to Sydney's social royalty. In their minds, the closer one's connection to the Murdoch family the higher up the blue-blood ladder one was.

The woman with the platinum bob, Suzette Martin, spoke with a nasal upper-class twang and was aristocratically beautiful – as refined as white sugar. Suzette's cousin had actually sat next to young Sarah Murdoch last year at a luncheon. Her companion, Virginia Cross, looked like a duller version of Princess Anne, with her dowdy fashions and dishwater-brown hair. These women's Bellevue Hill homes sprawled across one of the city's most exclusive slopes, with pristine gardens and to-die-for views.

As Chantrea rushed toward them they stopped chatting and appraised her with critical stares.

'Evening, ladies. Gorgeous night, isn't it?' Chantrea chirped, smiling widely at them.

'Err, what? Oh yes . . . lovely . . . quite,' Suzette stammered, clutching at the pearls around her neck.

'Yes . . . rather,' was the best Virginia could manage. Accustomed to freezing others into embarrassed silence, both women had expected Chantrea to lower her eyes and walk past in silence.

Chantrea grinned happily to herself as she watched the women's reactions. She had learned years ago that attack was the best form of defence, and the sweeter and more well-mannered the attack the better.

She glanced through the classroom door to see Nancy deep in conversation with another mum, so she slipped back outside to enjoy the warm evening. Sitting on the playground bench, Chantrea quickly realised she could hear Suzette and Virginia chatting in the car park, their voices carrying on the still evening air.

'Of course I'd much rather not have to use childcare at all, but three short days a week isn't much,' Suzette was saying.

'But of course, darling, it's so good for their development and socialisation. My young Edward only comes two days.'

'It's just a scandal that some mothers use this facility almost as a boarding house for their children,' Suzette said. 'Do you know there's a little five-year-old who's always the first in and last to leave every day of the week?'

'That's just appalling. Why do these people even bother to have children anyway?'

'Disgusting, isn't it?' sniffed Suzette. 'It's that little Cambodian girl in the kindergarten room; her mother is that wild-looking creature we just passed,' her voice dropped at this point and Chantrea couldn't hear what was said, but their peals of laughter made it clear it wasn't complimentary.

She sat grim-faced and shocked. How dare they? Sally wasn't here *that* often.

'Oh, it's typical though.' Suzette had returned to her normal speaking voice. 'You know what those Asians are like.'

'It's terrible how they come to this country just for the free government hand-outs,' Virgina sniffed.

Chantrea's head was spinning. She sat motionless, trying to process the ugly racism that made her feel separate – different and inferior – with just a few casual words and it didn't feel good. Not good at all.

Just then the kindergarten door opened and it was her turn. Chantrea felt scrambled and lightheaded, which made it hard to concentrate on the interview, but she heard enough to know that all was well with her daughter. As she nodded numbly, her mind raced. Did she leave Sally here too much? Were the women right? Was Sally suffering?

As she got up to leave, Nancy made a comment that brought her hurtling back to the present. 'Of course there is one thing that interests me,' she said.

'What?' Chantrea asked wearily.

'It's probably nothing,' the young woman said. 'It's just that she's become fascinated with her culture.'

'Culture? What do you mean? Like ballet? Art galleries?' Chantrea asked, very confused.

'No, *her* culture – the fact she's Cambodian,' Nancy explained.

'She's Australian!' Chantrea said defiantly.

'I know she was born here, I mean her heritage. She's become very interested in her background and has actually been sharing some fascinating insights into her people,' Nancy explained.

'Her people! What in the hell . . . ?' Chantrea was now speechless. What was this woman on about? She glanced up at the 'Who I Am,' wall behind Nancy and it suddenly struck her. The rows of children who attended crèche in this predominantly Anglo-Saxon area all stared back at her, many with the Nordic blue or green eyes. They had white-blond hair and English surnames.

And there was little Sally. Chantrea had always looked at her beautiful brown-eyed daughter with the golden skin and the dark brown hair and seen her for what she was: a gorgeous baby girl. But now she could see what others saw. She had a Cambodian daughter.

Chantrea had thought by giving her an Aussie dad and an Aussie name her little Sally O'Leary would be able to fit in. She didn't want her precious little angel to have to go through all the shit she went through. She didn't want Sally to have to contend with the racial taunts; the teasing; the loneliness. And now it seemed Sally was actually boasting about being different. As a child Chantrea would have given anything not to have been born in South-East Asia; not to have been one of the 'chinks' at her western suburbs primary school.

'It's been wonderful, actually,' Nancy kept raving. 'The other children are fascinated. She's been telling us about Angkor Wat, teaching us some Cambodian words and even bringing in Cambodian food for us to try.'

'WHAT?!' Chantrea exploded. What in the hell was going on? Even as she asked herself the question she knew there was only one answer to this mystery.

Her mother.

~14~

'Oh, you're early.' Jacqueline did not sound impressed.

The light from the hallway bathed Chantrea in a warm glow as Jacqueline opened the door, but the welcoming atmosphere was spoilt by Jacqueline's frosty greeting. Earliness was akin to tardiness in Jacqueline's book of etiquette.

'Yeah, sorry . . . it's just . . . I finished up early at school.' Still feeling sensitive, Chantrea uncharacteristically started stammering her apologies until she glanced at her watch and realised she was only five minutes early. 'Oh, for God's sake, Jacqueline, it's twenty-five past.'

'Hmmm,' demurred Jacqueline, 'well, you might as well come in. Sera's early too.'

She led Chantrea into the 'good' room where Sera was already seated. 'Make yourself at home and I shall fix us all Fluffy Ducks,' she smiled, heading for the kitchen.

'I am never going to forgive you for including her in this group,' Chantrea hissed to Sera after she'd hugged her hello. 'She's a fucking nightmare.'

'I know, I know, I'm sorry,' replied Sera, rolling her eyes. 'She was so nice to me when we moved in, though.'

'Didn't you see at the time how superior she could be?' Chantrea whispered.

'Well, she did bang on a bit about her precious boys, but that's just a proud mum, isn't it? You're right though, she is getting worse.'

'Ya think?' said Chantrea, leaning forward to select a dainty hors d'oeuvre from the floral tray. 'Bleargh!' She spat it into a pastel-coloured napkin. 'What the hell?'

Sera fell laughing onto the over-stuffed chintz cushions. 'I was going to warn you, but then I decided, bugger it, it would be way more fun to watch your reaction! She made asparagus spears out of icing. Tonight's theme is apparently "Sweets for the Sweet".'

'Bitch,' Chantrea grumbled, shoving the evidence into her handbag.

'So how are you, anyway?' asked Sera, when her laughter subsided. 'I haven't seen you all week. Everything still crazy busy?'

To her great surprise, tears sprang into the eyes of her tough friend.

'Oh no, what's wrong?' Sera leaned forward with concern.

'Bloody bitches at bloody crèche. Bloody cows,' Chantrea sniffed. She quickly related the evening's events.

Sera knew Chantrea kept her past to herself, in fact she only found out where she'd been born after an in-flight mix-up once, when a Chinese passenger was having difficulty communicating and the purser asked Chantrea to help out. Sera had never seen such an explosion.

'How the fuck dare you!' Chantrea had hissed at the white-faced purser, 'Just because I look Asian you think I can suddenly speak the hundreds of languages and dialects scattered around the entire region? You'll be asking me to translate for the Pakistani passengers next. What about you? Why don't you go and translate for those Croatian passengers? You've got bulbous round eyes and so have they. You must be cousins!'

The purser had tried to calm her down. 'Look, Chantrea, I just thought I'd ask. I don't know, do I? I thought you'd speak Mandarin because you come from China.'

'I'm from Cambodia, you ignorant bitch,' Chantrea spat, storming into the galley. The purser had reported her and Chantrea had been suspended for several weeks.

Now Sera was outraged at what she was hearing. 'That's disgusting, how dare they!' she fumed. 'We need to go to the police; they can't go around saying things like that!'

'That's a bit much, Sera,' Chantrea said. 'Anyway, I couldn't give a shit. They can rot in their Escada for all I care. What I am so angry about is my bloody mother.'

Sera had often heard Chantrea complain about her mother, the hard-working and feisty Dara Kim. To make ends meet, Sera and Dara lived together, both working long hours and co-parenting Sally. Although Chantrea hated that her mum raised Sally half the time – often completely ignoring her parenting rules – she desperately needed her help.

But Sera had never seen Chantrea so angry with her mother as she was tonight.

'I can't believe it, I just can't believe it.' Chantrea was practically shaking as she clasped her hands and leaned forward staring at the ground. 'I thought it was over, I thought I'd shaken it. I had made the break, I'd put that . . . all that . . . horror behind me . . . behind us.'

'Chantrea, I'm sorry, I just don't understand. What's to be ashamed of? Why aren't you pleased that Sally is proud of her heritage?'

'Proud?' Chantrea looked up at Sera, her eyes glowing with bitterness. 'What can Sally be proud of, Sera? That her mother's a refugee? A stinking boat person?'

Sera hadn't realised her friend had arrived in Australia as a refugee. She stared at Chantrea wide-eyed. They sat looking at each other, with only the gentle tick of a crystal clock on the mantelpiece punctuating the long silence.

Suddenly Jacqueline's voice floated down the corridor. 'I'll be there in a shake of a lamb's tail – the Fluffy Ducks are nearly ready.'

'Hellooo!' Mallory trilled from the front door a moment later. She always let herself in and yodelled through the house, which Jacqueline found incredibly annoying. But, overloaded as she was with a tray-full of ornate cocktail glasses, a jug of yellow foaming liquid and an array of little paper umbrellas, it was quite handy that Mallory was able to let herself in.

'Mallory, darling, do come in,' Jacqueline twittered triumphantly – still managing to maintain her control as a hostess, just seconds before Mallory's little foot actually crossed the threshold.

'Mwah, mwah.' Jacqueline air-kissed the latest arrival from a distance, over the tray of goodies, then indicated with her head. 'They're all in there, darling, I'm just serving cocktails.'

'Hiya all!' Mallory bobbed her pretty head from side to side in greeting. With her golden plaits and smocked mini-dress she looked remarkably like an extra from *The Sound of Music*. And as always, Mallory was blissfully oblivious to the room's thick air of tension and quickly dispelled it with her sunny presence. She had the happy knack of being able to radiate warmth, happiness and good intentions wherever she went.

Mallory and her husband Vince had had their surprise daughter while Mallory was still in her teens and the child's birth seemed to have stopped the clock for them both. They listened to Triple J, had Facebook pages, decorated their home with pinball machines and hip-hop posters, and Tilly, their fifteen-year-old daughter, was more like a flatmate than a child.

Mallory rather enjoyed the number of people who mistook Tilly for her kid sister. 'Omigod, it's like sooo funny,' she'd say with a giggle.

Mallory had always wanted lots of children, and for years had tried for more babies until she found out that Vince had different ideas and had taken himself off for a sneaky vasectomy. It was a terrible loss for Mallory but she eventually forgave Vince and came to accept that Tilly would be her only child.

'Oooh, I'm starving,' she announced as her hand shot out to grab a canapé.

Sera and Chantrea swapped small smiles, anticipating her reaction.

'They're sugar,' explained Jacqueline. 'It's a "Sweets for the Sweet" evening. Except for Sera's pies,' she added.

'Ooh, what fun,' squealed Mallory as she popped the sugary 'vegetable' into her mouth. 'Yum! It's delicious, aren't you clever!'

Jacqueline smiled serenely at Mallory's praise. 'Thank you,' she said simply, but inside she felt warm and soothed. Getting up at four am had been worth it after all.

'Now,' said Mallory, moving on quickly, 'what's happening? What did I miss?'

'Oh, nothing really,' Sera said. 'We've only just arrived.' She accepted an elaborate cocktail from Jacqueline. 'Delicious, thank you.'

'Good lord, we're all going to get diabetes after so much sugar,' said Chantrea, putting her drink back on the table. 'I don't have much of a sweet tooth, I'm afraid. Are those pies nearly ready? I'm starving.'

Jacqueline glowered at Chantrea. 'I'll just see how they're going,' she said.

'God, imagine the calories!' Sera moaned when Jacqueline was safely out of earshot. 'I've gained two and a half kilos from that drink alone,' she complained, while sucking in and patting her tummy.

'Tell me about it,' whinged Chantrea. 'I've had to go up to a size ten in my uniform. I've NEVER been a size ten.'

'You know,' giggled Mallory, shovelling another sugar asparagus into her mouth, 'no matter how much I eat I just can't put on weight.'

When the doorbell sounded, Sera went to open it. 'Hey there, Sam,' she said to the leafy figure she found on the doorstep. 'Why are you camouflaged as a bush?'

'Tussie-mussies for everyone,' he exclaimed as he entered the house, handing out small bouquets of herbs to the girls. 'There's sage, chives, coriander and continental parsley. Oh, and mint of course. There's bucketloads of mint. I had no idea that mint absolutely takes over. I can't get rid of the bugger now. And I don't know what to do with the stuff, apart from the odd leaf in yoghurt with Greek food, does anyone know?'

'I do,' came the enthusiastic response from Jacqueline from down the hall. 'Let me get you my peppermint ice-cream recipe.'

'Of course, I knew you'd have something Jacqueline. How are you?' Sam turned to follow her voice and present her with a bouquet of herbs.

'You don't think he's gay, do you?' said Mallory, looking at her herbs in doubt.

'No!' the other two women said immediately and in unison.

'Have you seen the shoes?' added Sera. 'So grubby, and he wears the same Converse Allstars every week.'

'And last week he was definitely a bit on the nose,' said Chantrea.

'Absolutely,' agreed Sera. 'Not too stinky or anything, but definitely BO. Like he'd been working in the garden and not showered before he came out. What gay man would do that?'

'I guess,' demurred Mallory, 'and I suppose the fact he's asking me about my friend Phoebe the bikini model . . .'

'What?!' said Sera eagerly. 'Give us the goss!'

'Oh, I just saw him down at the beach with his girls and I was there with Tilly and Phoebe. I introduced them and that night he called me and asked about her.'

'Wooo,' the girls teased as Sam returned to the room.

'What's all this, then? What are you talking about?' he asked suspiciously as he helped himself to a Fluffy Duck. He reached forward to the platter of asparagus canapés but caught Chantrea's eye as she shook her head slightly, so he sat back without the food.

'We're talking *about* you, not *to* you,' said Mallory.

'What?' he said. 'You can't do that to me, what are you saying?'

'I spoke to Phoebe,' said Mallory, grinning like an imp.

'Oh yes,' Sam replied, sitting back and faking nonchalance.

'She's keen to go out with you.'

'Really?' he squeaked and sat forward. 'I mean . . . *really*?' and he lowered his voice to a manly baritone.

'Yep, she thought you were cute.'

'Holy macaroni, I won't know what to do, what to say!' he said, looking around at the group with a scared expression.

'Well you can start by *not* saying "Holy macaroni",' Chantrea said dryly, pouncing on the party pies as soon as Jacqueline entered the room.

'It'll be fine, just be yourself,' said Sera, patting his knee and feeling like an old married woman.

'We're just sorting Sam out with a date,' Mallory explained to Jacqueline. 'He wants me to come and style him beforehand.'

'No I don't!' Sam protested.

'Yes, you do,' Mallory said, patting him on the knee too and ignoring his protests.

'But . . . ?' he blustered, looking to Sera for support.

'You do,' Sera agreed.

'Now, where to take her?' Mallory pondered.

'Hang on, this is my date,' protested Sam.

'Not now that you're with a group of women,' Sera smirked. 'But seriously,' said Chantrea, 'where will you take her?'

'I know, what about The Lounge?' Mallory suggested excitedly. 'It's the most happening club at the moment.'

'What about the Park Hyatt?' Jacqueline suggested. 'So refined.'

'Oh, you're such a grown-up, Jacqueline,' said Mallory. 'Honestly, that's far too stuffy.'

'Fine,' Jacqueline declared, then changed the subject abruptly. 'What about a brunch?'

'For Sam's date?' Sera asked, confused.

'No, but wouldn't it be delightful if all of you brought your families here for a brunch? We could have it Sunday week. I'll cater; you just need to bring yourselves and your families.'

No one spoke for a moment, as they considered the logistics of children, parents and in-laws.

Jacqueline took their silence to mean approval. 'It's all settled, then,' she said, delighted to have another social event to plan. 'With this dreadful weather I think I'll do a chartreuse and white theme.'

The group members finally reached into their bags to retrieve their knitting projects.

After an hour or so of diligent handiwork, slightly slowed by the effects of the Fluffy Ducks, they packed up their craft items and farewelled their hostess.

Sera walked down the front steps with Chantrea. 'Do you want to pop in for some salt to balance tonight's sugar-fest?' Sera joked lightly, knowing her friend still needed to talk.

'Are you sure it's not too late?' Chantrea asked.

'Of course not,' Sera replied.

When they entered the house, Sera saw to her great relief that mother-in-law had gone to bed.

They raided the kitchen for some blue cheese and crackers, accompanied with a nice dry chardonnay, then installed themselves at the kitchen table.

'So,' said Sera. 'Spill it.'

~15~

Chantrea stared into the flickering candle on Sera's kitchen table. Sera watched as as a mask of blank indifference slid over her friend's features and finally she began to speak as though in a trance, her voice a monotone.

'In April 1975, I was five years old. We lived in Phnom Penh,' Chantrea began. 'I was just little, so I was oblivious to the civil war. I knew the grown-ups were worried; I could hear my parents talking until late at night. Sometimes I heard bombs in the surrounding suburbs and gunfire was commonplace but I didn't take much notice. I was more interested in my dolls and my best friend, Phinny Ung, who lived in the apartment next door.

'Then the government surrendered to the Khmer Rouge. My parents were worried because my father had been an official in the old government's military department, so we knew our family could be targeted by the new regime. My mother was a famous musician: she played the Khmer flute. The Khmer Rouge was against traditional Cambodian culture and many well-known artists and musicians were being taken into custody. Many were never seen again.

'One night Phinny Ung and her family were taken away by soldiers. Her father was a minister of the old government. We woke up to the screams. I can still hear them sometimes. My parents said we had to leave the city and go to my aunt's house in the country. We packed everything we could into our car and left before dawn. I can remember feeling excited, it was like we were going on a holiday – I had no idea.

'But everyone in Phnom Penh was trying to do the same thing. The new government had decreed that every person in the city must return to the village of their birth. The noise of the traffic and the chaos on the streets was deafening. I just sat in the back seat clutching my doll. The car inched forward only a few metres every hour. Mother forced me to lie down and not look out the window because people were being beaten up by soldiers and left for dead. It took us twenty-four hours to drive the short distance to the outskirts of the city, but then the car ran out of petrol and there was nowhere to get more.

'We walked for hours. My feet bled and I remember falling asleep standing up several times. My father carried a bag with water, rice, a cooking pot and other essentials, but he still managed to carry me a few times. He was a very strict man but he never once yelled at me or got angry when I fell down. My mother was pregnant and white with exhaustion by the time we stopped to rest.

'She used her bag to make me a bed under a tree and as I fell asleep I remember seeing my parents making a small fire to burn all their documents. We started out the next day before dawn, joining hundreds of thousands of others. It was like a great sea of people; of pain and death. I will never forget the smell that filled my nose and mouth.' Chantrea stopped to wipe away the tears that streamed down her face and Sera clutched her hand.

'It was the smell of rotting corpses; the people who weren't strong enough to continue, or who had been killed by soldiers. It was over 40 degrees every day and the smell got worse as each day went past. I fainted a few times and my father had to pick me up and keep me moving. I think by then I had stopped feeling anything; the horror and the pain of it all just floated over me.

'One day I watched as a soldier ripped a woman's tiny baby from her arms and threw it against a tree. It was as if it wasn't real; it just couldn't be real. Then he dragged her into a hut as she screamed for help. We just kept walking. What else could we do? I can only talk about this now because I did years of therapy in my twenties. I had to; the nightmares were ruining my life. I'd wake up screaming and desperate for water.'

'Water?' Sera asked.

'It was maybe the most horrific part,' Chantrea replied. 'The thirst. Our water ran out after the first few days. We survived on stagnant water in puddles, but it was never enough. As we passed village after village that was burnt to the ground and deserted, I knew my parents had given up hope of finding my aunt.

'We were with a group of about eighty-five people all heading in the same direction, all hoping for something or someone to save us. One evening at twilight, about five days after we'd left the city, some of the men left the dirt road we were travelling on to go and look for water.

'We were so hot, waiting there as the sun went down, being eaten alive by mosquitoes. Suddenly there was a huge explosion. Mother threw herself over me and I started to cry from shock. The men had triggered a land mine, which killed several of them. The three who returned with a can of dirty water had to look into the faces of the women who had just lost their husbands. One woman threw herself into the dirt and lay there for hours, tears running out of her eyes, but making no sound at all.

'And that night the soldiers came.' Chantrea shivered. 'We were all asleep in the field when we were woken by teenagers with AK-47s. They pulled us up and made us walk; I don't know where. They wouldn't let us stop all the next day and into the night. Some people dropped onto the side of the road with dehydration or sheer exhaustion.'

Her voice deepened and slowed.

'When anyone fell the soldiers would laugh and spit at them, and then . . . then they rammed the butts of their rifles into their skulls and left them to die.'

Her voice cracked. 'My mother fell and the soldier was there so fast. I screamed and tried to protect her. He . . . he hit her . . . hard with the rifle butt . . . hit her stomach. She doubled over in pain. I was so scared. My father leapt to her side and helped her to stand. I kept screaming, screaming . . . I didn't want her to die. Then they made us stop to make a camp, and forced all the boys and men to go with them. I didn't know that when my father kissed my mother and me it would be the last time I would ever see him.

'Thirty husbands, fathers and sons left with the soldiers while we, the women, children and old people, waited by the side of the road. That night my mother lost the baby.

'Later the soldiers returned without the men, but covered in blood. They hauled us all back onto our feet and pushed us along the road. My mother could barely walk, but she whispered to me that she recognised the area we where travelling through – it was where she'd spent many happy years as a child.

'We marched until midnight, when we reached a destroyed Buddhist temple. The soldiers gave us a few spoonfuls of rice to eat and we collapsed onto the hard stone floor. During the night mother woke me. She had played in the deserted temple as a little girl and knew there was a hidden room behind the altar. The soldiers were outside smoking and laughing. We sidled slowly to the altar and squeezed in between the desecrated stone Buddha and the hard wall. What had seemed to be an alcove was actually a very thin opening that led into a cold, windowless room. We sat there, squashed, holding our breath until dawn. After the soldiers herded the group away, we snuck out, crouching to avoid being seen.

'For the next two weeks we crept along the roads and snuck into villages to steal food, until eventually mother managed to slip us past the border guards into Thailand. We travelled for long, hot painful days again until we reached Bangkok and mother found a Red Cross centre.

'Then my mother showed me a secret she'd been carrying the entire time. She'd sewn a small package into the hem of her dress. "These emeralds and diamonds are from the necklace your grandmother gave me," Mother said. "They are our ticket to the promised land, Australia."

'It was the first time she had even hinted that we might have a future. Even though there were only the two of us left, for the first time in almost two months I saw a trace of hope in her eyes. She exchanged the stones for ten thousand baht, which was a pathetic amount, but enough to save our lives. She had heard of a ship's captain who would take us to a wonderful city called Darwin, where we could get food, a house and jobs.

'There was a boat waiting for us at the jetty within days. But it was just a fishing boat, not fit for passengers. Instead of a hold full of squid, the hold was full of refugees like us. It was a living hell and I don't know how we survived it,' Chantrea's voice wavered again. 'The captain kept us locked and cramped in the hold and handed out tiny serves of rice and fish. We had cans for toilets that we had to empty out of the portholes. Most of us had severe gastro and seasickness. And the promised passports were just another lie.

'One night the captain unlocked the door to let us out, telling us we had reached Darwin. In the darkness all we could see were monstrous waves. I can remember looking out in terror at the swell, the black shoreline and then at my mother. I didn't have to say a word. She nodded at me. We had to swim from there.

'A few people couldn't swim and held back in fear but the captain and crew just tossed them in like scrap fish guts.'

Sera gasped and tears filled her eyes, but Chantrea continued without pause.

'The water was surprisingly warm and by complete fluke a wave picked Mother and me up and pushed us towards the shore. For a few seconds I felt euphoric – suddenly it seemed like this new country was reaching out to embrace us and welcome us.

'Of course, knowing what I'm sure you do about how welcome refugees were back then – and still are for that matter –' she added bitterly, 'you'll know that my joy was short-lived. Soldiers were waiting for us on the beach. I expected them to start shooting at us; but they loaded us into trucks and drove us to a refugee hostel for the night. The next day they took us to a place that looked to me like a jail – the detention centre.

'But at least we were safe and alive and we spent the next few months recovering somewhat. My mother lobbied furiously for us to be granted residency visas, which took nine months, but eventually we were on the bus to Sydney to start a new life.

'We had seen Sydney a lot on the television in the detention centre and Mother and I knew it was the city for us. She said its vibrancy and beautiful people reminded her of Phnom Penh, before the war began.

'Thanks to *Sesame Street* and *Playschool* I had picked up English pretty quickly in the detention centre, so my mother thought I would fit into the local school system easily. But honestly, Westville Primary was more like torture.

'The group that ruled the school made the Ku Klux Klan look like the Martin Luther King fan club. They were out to get anybody who wasn't Anglo. My friend Kimmy, who'd just arrived from Vietnam, was found hanging from a tree by her foot one day. The cops weren't even called. The teachers couldn't or wouldn't do anything.

'My friends and I did everything we could to avoid them, but they wouldn't leave us alone. Once, Bill, who was the biggest one, with thick red hair and a AC/DC tattoo he'd done himself, hissed into my ear what he and the other boys were planning to do to me in his bedroom that afternoon. I went ice-cold with shock – all I could think about was the woman and the soldier I'd seen on the road out of Phnom Penh.

'So I played up in class from then on to make sure I always got kept in after school, so I could be safe. I couldn't tell mother. She was so proud to have a little Aussie schoolgirl daughter and she was working such long hours at a grocery store just to feed and clothe us.'

'Oh darling,' Sera murmured.

'So I decided to become a fighter,' Chantrea said grimly, squeezing her hands into fists. 'I learned street fighting and pretty soon the taunts stopped and for the first time I started to feel safe and in control. After I finished school, I worked odd jobs here and there for five years and then finally decided a uni degree was my chance to get ahead. That was where I met Danny – Danny O'Leary. He was studying medicine and had all the girls on the campus swooning at his feet.'

Sera sat up with interest; she had never heard Chantrea speak about Sally's father before.

'I think it destroyed his fragile ego that I wasn't immediately taken by his blue eyes and charm.' She sighed. 'Sera, it's already been a long night, are you sure you're up for the whole messy saga of my life?'

'Absolutely,' Sera nodded. 'You can't stop now.'

'Okay, well, Danny . . . the more he tried to catch me, the more I ignored him. I think it just became a contest to him . . . I dunno . . . anyway life at home with mother was mental. I wanted to be free of any reminders of our life in Cambodia, of our "heritage", but she kept insisting I should speak Cambodian, be proud of coming from such a beautiful country.

'I tried to tell her that Australians hate Asians; that she should stop announcing where we were from to the world, but she said I was the one who should be ashamed.

'So I started going out with Danny, and figured marrying him would be my ticket out of my culture. Not very feminist of me, but there you go,' she grimaced.

'I got pregnant within about five minutes of our very drab little registry office wedding, and after working so hard to catch me, Danny lost interest and formed a pretty close relationship with dope. He was stoned more than he was straight and it was downhill from there. He failed his exams and then just quit uni altogether. He wouldn't get a job to support us, so I had to give up study just after Sally was born. It all still makes me so freakin' angry,' she said quietly.

'I can understand that,' Sera said sympathetically.

'So I worked in a travel agency during the day while Danny was supposed to be caring for Sally – but even that was too much effort for the lazy arsehole.' She began to shake with anger, and wiped away more tears. 'One day during my lunch-break I went home to check on them. Danny was passed out on the couch and there was bong water spilt all over the floor. Poor little Sally was lying in her cot, purple with screaming.

'So I packed up and left, went back to live with Mother in Westville. Of course she was over the moon to have Sally in her clutches; thrilled that my marriage to an unsuitable skip was over and that I was back where she could nag and hassle me all bloody day long. I never heard from Danny again. Bastard.

'But look, it's been okay living with mother, at least she helps me out with Sally. I could never have become a flight attendant without her support, and I need a good job so I can save for Sally's education and buy a bigger house one day. It's only when she starts shoving all the Cambodian crap down Sally's throat that I really get angry. I can't believe that she's been doing it behind my back all this time.' Her voice was choked with emotion.

'Being Cambodian has only ever brought me pain and suffering and I always vowed that Sally wouldn't have to go through anything like that,' she said.

Sera wanted to say that Australia was a different place now, a place of racial tolerance and inclusion; but from her sheltered perspective how would she know? Was the country any fairer or more tolerant than it had ever been? Maybe Chantrea was right to try to prevent Sally identifying with a part of her culture that could set her apart from her peers.

'So that's it, Sera, that's my story and for obvious reasons I'd appreciate you keeping it to yourself,' Chantrea said, looking at her watch. 'It's one am. I better go.'

Sera hugged her friend. 'I'm here whenever you need me,' she said.

'Thanks, darling, it means a lot to me.'

Sera watched from the door as her friend was swallowed up by the night.

~16~

The winter air may have been chilly, but the sun was a shining reminder of summer in Sydney.

'You never get sick of it, do you?' Sera sighed as Mallory's BMW X5 transported the two women across the Sydney Harbour Bridge.

'It's just magnificent,' Mallory agreed, glancing over to the white sailboats dotted across the harbour like stars on a navy blue sky. 'So, anyway, Vince is just doing so well since they made him General Manager. He's gets a wicked bonus every month and we get to go out in the company motor cruiser whenever we want!'

Sera smiled tightly. She'd never been a big fan of Vince. She found him quite challenging to be around. He was . . . now what was the word again? She thought idly as she gazed over the sprawl of North Sydney as they came off the bridge. That's right, a wanker.

Mallory had met Vince when she was waitressing at an exclusive Hobart boutique hotel just after she had left school and they'd been together since. Although Sera and Mallory had been inseparable since first grade, Sera found it hard to swallow Mallory's whirlwind romance and subsequent shotgun wedding to the Melbourne salesman who was ten years her senior. She just couldn't believe that Mallory, with her gorgeous, selfless personality, was actually happy with Vince – a bloke who thought nothing of cutting his toenails while entertaining guests.

Sera blamed herself a bit. She felt as if she'd deserted Mallory; fleeing to the mainland to follow Bella into a flight attendant career the minute she'd finished school. Maybe that was partly why Mallory settled so quickly for the boorish Vince.

Vince was flashy, a bit thick and a bloody show-off. He made Sera's skin crawl with his reflective Dolce e Gabana sunnies perched atop his spiky haircut, his pink Paul Smith T-shirts and Diesel jeans – and he was such a skinny little short-arse too.

'And last night he bought me the most beautiful bunch of long-stemmed roses, what a romantic!' Mallory was still talking.

'What's the occasion?' asked Sera suspiciously.

'No occasion, he just said he loves me,' Mallory sighed, shoving her enormous Gucci sunglasses further up the bridge of her freckled nose.

'Hmmm.' Sera firmly clamped her teeth shut to avoid making a sarcastic comment. It was sweet of Mallory to insist they have a girls' day out.

'You work so hard,' she'd whined, 'it's about time you and I got out and had some fun.'

Sera had had to admit it was tempting. She had not had a day to herself, aimlessly shopping, lunching and trying on make-up, for weeks. After a morning spent at Mecca Cosmetica, they were now headed for their next stop: a well-earned lunch break at the luxury boat dealership where Vince worked. Sera had tried to convince Mallory to have lunch on their side of the harbour but Mallory had insisted she had a surprise for her.

'So, what's this surprise you've got in store for me,

anyway?' Sera asked her as they drove through elegant and leafy Neutral Bay.

'Well, it's not a surprise so much as more of a bit of a lark,' Mallory said, smiling. 'There's a new salesman at the dealership. He's absolutely gorgeous.'

'So?' Sera said. 'We're married, remember?'

'No, no, you don't get it. You know how toffy the school is my Tilly goes to?'

'You need to show your personal balance sheet to get in the door.'

'Yeah,' Mallory agreed, not even slightly offended. 'Well, the schoolyard gossip is that the wealthy wives of Sydney are buying their husbands' boats from Royal First Leisure Cruisers thanks to this new guy. The rumour is that he's seducing the Mothers' Committee one by one.'

'What?!' Sera was delighted at such a scandal.

'I know; it's hilarious. You've got to see it to believe it, though. If we stay at the café having lunch long enough you're bound to see what I mean.'

The towering white hulls of enormous boats greeted the two women as they walked into the dealership.

Mallory scanned the room for her husband. A brittle laugh drew the girls' attention to where Vince was leaning over the reception desk, his pinstriped bottom in full view. The giggle had come from the bleached blonde, mini-skirted receptionist who was looking at Vince with huge doe eyes.

'Oh, good, there he is,' Mallory said. 'Hi, honey!'

Vince gave a startled jump. 'What are you doing here?' he demanded.

'We're having lunch at your café. Thought we'd surprise you,' Mallory said gaily, reaching out to embrace her husband. He caught her arms and pulled them away. 'Not in front of the team, darling,' he muttered.

'Sorry,' Mallory said immediately and put her arms down.

Sera happened to flick her eyes to the receptionist, and was shocked to see the look of pure poison she was sending Mallory.

'Hi,' Mallory said sweetly, unaware of the clear hatred she had provoked. 'We haven't met. You must be Sharee.' She stuck out her hand in greeting to the new girl.

'Yes, hello,' Sharee replied and offered a limp tattooed hand in response. Her poisonous look may have dropped, but it didn't make her ferret-like appearance any more attractive. Boy, does she need a make-over, Sera thought, taking in the brittle white hair littered with split ends and the excessive eye make-up.

'Welcome aboard, as they say in the nautical world,' Mallory said chirpily. 'We're just having lunch if you'd like to join us.'

'No, I'm working,' Sharee said sulkily and turned away from Mallory to shuffle a pile of papers.

'Okay then, maybe next time,' Mallory said and she and Sera walked over to the café. 'Odd girl,' she commented as they sat down. 'As long as the boss is happy with her, I guess,' she giggled.

Oh dear, Sera thought, poor Mallory.

After ordering lattes, sparkling mineral water and semi-dried tomato, rocket, and prosciutto focaccias, they sat back to watch the passing parade.

It was like being on a different planet – Planet Over-Indulgence. Arriving in luxury-taxed cars, each more prestigious than the last, the potential customers all glowed with Port Douglas tans under their casual polo shirts and sports jackets. In contrast the all-male sales team in their Hugo Boss suits looked as if they had come straight from Wall Street.

The female after-sales team looked sultry in their tight suits with generous cleavages and highlighted hair piled up on top of their Bratz-sized heads. After customers splurged on a floating caravan the girls went to work, selling them the essential, can't-live-without accessories: depth sounder, glass tinting, weather-guarding, anchor.

Mallory and Sera soaked up the atmosphere and theatre of the dealership, gobsmacked by the displays of wealth and folly.

Suddenly Mallory grabbed her friend. 'I don't believe it!' she said, indicating the Stingray on the other side of the showroom. 'That's Suzette Martin – her kids go to Eton Grammar. She's married to Marvin Martin, the mobile phone guy.'

'*No way*! She's the bitch who backstabbed Chantrea at crèche the other night,' replied Sera.

With their table hidden behind a palm tree, the ladies watched the woman descend the ladder at the back of the boat. An outrageously good-looking black man followed her.

'Yep, that's him,' Mallory confirmed in a whisper.

'He looks like serious trouble,' said Sera.

'Oooh yeah,' agreed her friend. 'I'm so glad Vince doesn't have to do anything like that to make his sales targets.'

~17~

Thomas lifted his head in irritation at the crash of china. The last broken household item, smashed six months before, had been a brand new fruit bowl. His careful nightly examination of the online bank statements had told him it had cost one hundred and forty-nine dollars and ninety-five cents from Parterre. Such carelessness.

He looked in the mirror and smoothed down his goatee. He was pleased with its recent salt-and-pepper sprinkling. He felt it made him look distinguished. He pulled down his white cuffs so they peeped out precisely an inch from his navy reefer jacket.

It was a nuisance that Jacqueline had chosen to interrupt his precious Sunday to entertain her knitting group, but he was secretly looking forward to displaying his enviable lifestyle. He'd washed the Mercedes, personally supervised the dusting of his new pair of Ming dynasty horses and approved Jacqueline's well-thought-out menu. She might be a klutz, but she certainly had admirable traits in the kitchen.

He already knew Tony and Sera from next door, of course. Sera was a sweet girl; clearly not from the right circles, but quite charming.

He slipped on his leather loafers and went downstairs to check on progress in the kitchen. As he passed the boys, bent over the chess set, he ruffled Joshua's hair to congratulate him on his ingenious move of his bishop.

The formal dining room was resplendent in the promised shades of chartreuse and white. The water glasses were lime and the stark white of the napkins and china leapt from the pale green tablecloth.

In the kitchen his wife was aproned and bustling as she cracked eggs into a large mixing bowl with one hand and flicked the pages of a recipe book with another.

'The dining room is a delight, my dear,' he said, pecking her on the cheek.

She flushed at his kind words. 'Oh, it was nothing,' she said, but before she could relax into the compliment, he followed with, 'What was the crash I heard?'

'Oh that – I'm so sorry, darling, it was the mate to this mixing bowl, I'm afraid it hit the deck before I could stop it.'

A raised eyebrow was his only response as he turned on the tap to wash his hands.

'Well, I've done all I can here, I guess,' he said, mentally assessing his checklist. He'd taken the cover off the barbecue, pleased to see it gleaming, he'd showered, the car was clean and his study was presentable and worthy of an eminent physician. 'I think I'll run a chamois over the Merc,' he said.

'Good idea, darling,' Jacqueline replied and flicked a nervous glance at the clock. 'I'm nearly done, I've just got three more dishes to create and a hollandaise sauce and I need to give the patio a quick sweep.' If that was a hint, it fell on deaf ears.

Thomas assessed his pride and joy as he sauntered down the front steps. The Mercedes Benz S-Class Saloon was a successful man's car. He'd lusted after it for years and had finally taken the plunge last financial year. He took the chamois out of the glove box and picked off errant leaves from the car bonnet.

He didn't know much about Vince Rimmel, Mallory's husband. They had met only once, very briefly, when he'd toyed with the idea of becoming a boat owner. Thomas realised Vince was a very wealthy man, but his flashy accessories and obvious manner reminded him of a celebrity sportsman. And his wife Mallory was a twit. Not the type someone of Jacqueline's calibre should be associating with.

He did enjoy the haughty air of that flight attendant Bella, Sera's sister. She embodied the type of refined superiority he admired in people and he was sorry to hear she wouldn't be coming today.

He hadn't met this new fellow, Sam Harvey, yet. An architect – reasonable profession – still, he sounded a right twat joining a women's knitting group.

Chantrea was an interesting type, quite the siren. Although he'd initially baulked at her wild ways and forthright speaking manner, he found he quite enjoyed their conversational sparring and discovered she had a sharp intellect.

He looked up at a sound from next door and saw Tony leaning out to pull his office window closed. He put his arm up in greeting.

'G'day mate,' Tony called out cheerily. 'See you shortly.'

Tony pulled the window in and turned back to his MYOB accounts. He'd managed to invoice every outstanding client this morning. So what if the windows were a disgrace? He could clean them this afternoon.

He was quite looking forward to brunch. His dash downstairs to help Sera was punctuated by scooping up the detritus left in the wake of the kids: a Dora doll, a Spiderman gun, a hair-ribbon tied between two banisters, a drink bottle . . . what was the bulge in the Barbie bag? His tape measure. Of course. He popped everything in the toy storage drawers in the living room and put his tape measure up out of reach.

Thomas was all right, dry as toast and a shocking snob, but get a beer into him and he loosened up. The girls were a right laugh, though it was a shame Bella couldn't be there. When he'd first started dating Sera he couldn't understand why his new girlfriend was so devoted to her sister, but he soon discovered that Bella was his wife's backstop and best friend. When Tony and Sera had first married, she couldn't choose a curtain fabric without ringing Bella for advice. She was a lot better now, but they still spoke often.

Sera was bending over at the dishwasher. 'There's a sight for sore eyes. What an arse!' he laughed, pinching her behind. 'Tony!' she squealed and wriggled away.

'Do you need any help? I've done all my homework!' he said and selected an apple that was annihilated in three quick crunches.

'What job do you want? Finish the dishwasher or dress the kids? Your pick.'

'Dishwasher, definitely!' he said, taking over from her.

'Chicken,' she laughed as she ran upstairs.

'Not those jeans, I HATE those jeans!' Tony heard Harry's shrill voice drifting down the stairwell. Tony shook his head. He knew the jeans in question. They were so precious to Harry that Sera had bought an identical second pair. But obviously the second pair was not identical because Harry could discern some subtle difference between the impostors and his favourites.

The phone rang. Tony picked it up: 'Tony Wilson,' he said.

'We bringing booze, or what?'

Vince Rimmel. He had a most disconcerting habit of presuming everyone knew who he was. 'G'day Vince, how's it going?' Tony had to force a pleasant tone.

'You know how it is, mate, fleeced the lambs again this week, you know what I mean, eh? Eh?'

Tony didn't but just agreed with him and moved on to address Vince's initial question. 'Don't know about the grog question, mate, hang on a tick.' He yelled up the stairs, 'Sera, Vince wants to know about grog.'

'We're taking a bottle of champoo!' came the reply.

'Champers, mate, probably appropriate for a brunch,' he said back into the mouthpiece.

'Right, I'll bring French,' said Vince. 'Chicks love that shit.'

Vince hung up without saying good-bye. He hitched up his black jeans and cursed the tailor who hadn't cut the hems short enough. His white Puma street shoes had lift, though, so that should stop the cuffs from dragging on the ground. He checked the top of his head, yep the Dolces were firmly in place.

He didn't want to go to this stupid bloody brunch. Mallory's friends were all boring wankers. That Thomas bloke, especially, was a fuckwit, and Tony acted like his shit didn't stink. Those air hostess sisters was stuck-up princesses, but their Asian friend was all right. And it was always a good opportunity for networking.

He went to check on Mallory's progress. Tilly wasn't back from her sleepover yet, so with any luck he could get one away before they left. He felt a headache coming on and there was nothing like a quick root to cure all ills. He was in luck. Mallory was still in her panties. She looked fantastic for mid-thirties. He admired her tight body as she shuffled through her underwear drawer. 'How about it, Mal? Time for a quickie?'

'Oh Vince,' she giggled, 'you're insatiable!'

'I am at that, love. How many last night, three? Four?'

'Um, I think two – ah, here it is,' and she pulled out the pink and turquoise bra that matched her knickers.

'It was at least three,' he muttered.

She pulled a hot pink sheath dress over her skinny form and slipped on a pair of aqua open-toed pumps.

'Hello!' came a young voice as the front door slammed shut.

'Tilly!' called Mallory, and when her daughter appeared at the bedroom door they embraced. 'How was it?'

'Sooo good, there was a Justin Timberlake special on MTV.'

'Omigod, he's so hot!' Mallory said.

'I know!' her daughter replied.

'You were meant to be here an hour ago, Til,' growled Vince, taking his frustration out on his daughter.

'Yeah, whatever,' she replied and, rolling her eyes, slung her overnight bag in the corner and went to the kitchen for a Diet Coke.

'You ready, hon? We're going,' Mallory said as she followed Tilly into the kitchen.

'Do I have to come? Those two boys are, like, so boring. All they want to do is talk about Dungeons and Dragons and shit.'

'Pulease?' Mallory put on her puppy eyes.

'Oh all right, only if I can bring my DS.'

'Deal,' her mother said.

After handshakes and air kisses all round on arrival, the families retired to the patio for pre-brunch mimosas. The younger children were plonked in front of a DVD while the older children steadfastly ignored each other and the men supervised Thomas's barbecuing.

'Is that S-Class out the front yours?' Vince demanded.

'Yes, she is, as matter of fact. She's a magnificent beast,' Thomas replied coolly.

'Heard they've got problems with the ABS. Aren't there recalls on them?' Vince asked.

'No, no problem at all. Would you like a drive?'

'Nah, thanks mate, I'd be worried I might be seen behind the wheel of an old man's car!' Vince brayed.

It was so generous of Jacqueline to insist on inviting the grandmothers, Sera thought, as she watched them chatting together. Joan seemed relaxed, while Dara Kim happily showed photos of Sally in dozens of poses.

Chantrea and Sam were talking about the horrors of single life, a conversation Sera didn't think she could add much to, so she glanced around for the hostess. Of course, she was slaving away in the kitchen. Mallory was with her, drying dishes.

She went inside to help. 'It smells marvellous in here,' she told Jacqueline. 'What can I do?'

'Oh, you're a darling. Here, just zest this lemon for me while I pop this tea out to Joan.'

Out on the patio, Sera's mobile trilled from the table. Tony glanced at the caller ID. 'Whoops, better take this in quick smart: it's Bella.' He hurried it inside to his wife.

'Darling!' Sera squealed into the phone when Tony handed it to her. 'Guess where we are? We're having the most delightful time at Jacqueline's! I'm so glad you called. I wanted to ask you . . .'

Tony returned to the terrace and sat opposite Sam and Chantrea. 'Glad we didn't miss *that* call, let me tell you!'

'They're very close, are they?' Sam said.

'Thick as thieves, mate. Bella's really been Sera's rock, you know, her whole life. I thought I was going out with both of them for a while there in the beginning. When Bella's husband was away, Sera would insist Bella join us on every date.'

'God, what a nightmare, having big sister chaperone you,' Sam said.

'Yeah, it was a bit weird in the beginning. Every time I asked Sera a question she'd look at Bella when she answered, like she needed her approval,' Tony explained. 'But they had a pretty rough upbringing, you know. Bella practically raised Sera. Their parents were never there, the house was always filthy and life was pretty chaotic.'

'That explains a lot about Bella the clean-freak,' Chantrea said, 'and why she goes to so much effort to make sure everything is just so.'

'I think she's got Obsessive Compulsive Disorder,' Tony admitted. 'I thought she was just a snob when I first met her, but it's more that she's uptight and hard on herself, not everyone around her.'

'Are they still so dependent on each other?' Sam asked.

'It's different now. Bella's been really distant lately; she doesn't come to Sydney often these days. She says it's because of her roster, but I reckon she's trying to give Sera some space to be her own person. Also, I don't think Bella's marriage is going too well. You know Curtis, Chantrea. What do you think?'

Chantrea's looked down uneasily. 'Um, I don't really know what's up with him. I don't like to say anything, but he hasn't got a shining reputation, if you know what I mean,' she said.

'That's awful,' said Tony. 'Poor Bella, she deserves better. She's great, Sam,' he tried to explain. 'She remembers birthdays, she sends gifts for no reason, she calls just when Sera needs her and she's very sweet with the kids. Oh, and did I mention she's outrageously gorgeous with legs that go on forever?'

'Settle down, tiger!' Chantrea said, smiling. 'It's true though, she is.'

'Then I hope things work out for her,' said Sam gallantly. 'She sounds like she could use a break.'

~18~

'Oh damn!' Sera leaned forward and checked her reflection in the mirror. She wiped away an errant streak of chocolate icing that ran from her eye across her cheekbone.

Bella was finally going to be in town today and Sera was determined that everything would be perfect. The children would be little angels, the picnic would be worthy of a Donna Hay shoot and she would look every bit as groomed and gorgeous as her perfect older sister.

Because Joan's erratic schedule couldn't guarantee they would have any privacy, Sera had made the zany suggestion of a winter picnic in the Botanic Gardens.

'A picnic?' Bella had said on the phone from the other side of the world. 'Why?'

'Because it'll be fun and besides the kids will love it,' Sera had responded.

'Oh, the kids, yes . . . of course,' Bella said with the air of someone who had the freedom to float across the globe on a whim. Of course she loved Sera, her brothers and her many nieces and nephews, but rather than hovering and become an irritating know-it-all childless aunt, she'd cut herself free, indulging in brief visits and generous gifts instead.

The lifestyle she'd chosen afforded her a degree of self-protection, too. If she was always on the move, she'd never have to put down roots or make a nest; she'd never risk making another huge mistake. The world's best hotels were home enough for her.

The day of the picnic began with Sydney's customary pale blue sky, which later darkened to a richer blue. The clouds went to Melbourne, the wind to Adelaide and the rain spent the day in its favourite place, Hobart.

Sera had been in a styling frenzy all morning. Everything had to be just right. It had taken her an hour to prepare the children's outfits alone.

For herself, she'd finally settled on black leggings and the bright yellow dress she'd bought last week. She spent ages blow-drying her hair, curling it, then straightening it again. She applied her full work-day make-up, and finished with a liberal dusting of bronzer for that natural glow. With her enormous black Miu Miu bag slung over her arm, she almost felt good enough.

Downstairs, she finished icing the chocolate cupcakes and packed put her lime-zest aioli into an old coffee container. The chook had roasted nicely, she saw to her satisfaction as she wrapped it in foil, and the coleslaw she'd picked up from Essential Ingredients looked tempting.

The children were whizzing around the house, beside themselves with excitement about seeing Aunty Bella. She always brought the best presents.

Bella was already sitting on a park bench under a tree when they arrived. She looked stunning in her tan canvas pants and white Abercrombie and Fitch polo top with a pink and white rugby jumper slung around her shoulders. Her hair was pulled back into a long blonde ponytail, straightened with such precision that she must have had it done at a drycleaners. Even her white Dunlop Volleys looked elegant. As Sera drew closer she watched her sister methodically check her watch and mobile three times each, and her hair twice. She's so perfect, Sera thought to herself. Why can't she just relax?

'Darling,' Bella stood and gave her sister a warm hug. 'So good to see you. You look wonderful.'

'Thanks, Bella,' replied Sera. She wanted to return the compliment, but telling Bella she looked good was like telling Stephen Hawking he's clever.

'Hello, Bella,' the children shyly chorused.

'Hello, Madeline, hello, Harry. I have presents for you.'

The kids squealed in excitement and ripped into the parcels. The excitement quickly turned into confusion, and Harry looked up enquiringly from the white jeans to his aunt. Then his little face broke into a sunny smile of approval. 'Yay, jeans! They're cool ones. I put on now?' He struggled out of his perfectly matching Gap navy-and-white striped trousers and pulled the white Calvins on.

'White jeans for a three-year-old boy, Bella?' Sera asked, as Harry wandered over to the picnic basket in search of a snack. Bella's occasional blind spot about child-rearing never failed to give Sera a smug glow of satisfaction.

'What?' Bella asked. 'He likes them.' She didn't care that they had a lifespan of two minutes. Her nephew loved them.

'Uh-oh,' came a little voice. A ripped packet of Twisties was spilling all over Harry and his snow-white jeans. He rubbed the orange crumbs into his thighs and ran off to climb a tree.

'Thanks so much, Aunty Bella,' said Madeline. 'It's wonderful.' Her Swarovski crystal swan glittered in the sunlight.

'Oh my God, you'll break it,' Sera said immediately.

'No, I won't,' came the obstinate reply.

'Let me mind it,' Sera said.

'No!' Maddy insisted.

Sera shook her head and looked at Bella. 'Crystal, Bella?'

'What?' Bella repeated, smiling at her niece's obvious enjoyment.

'They're wonderful presents, thanks for thinking of them,' Sera said, not wanting to sound ungrateful. She was a tad disappointed, however, that there was no expensive overseas gift for her. 'So how's jet-setting all over the globe? Still fun?'

'Lifestyles of the rich and famous, that's me all right,' Bella replied sarcastically. 'You've been there, you know it's not what it's cracked up to be.'

'I only did it for a year. The Hobart–Melbourne leg was not what I would call exotic. I love your world: lingerie in Milan, hairstylist in LA, perfumery in New York.'

'It's not really your one-stop shop, is it? Sometimes I would just like to go to Bondi Westfield like you and get it all at once.'

'Yeah! Good one, swap all that for Westfield.' Sera was painfully aware that evil green fingers were snaking around her throat. She changed her tone. 'I guess you're right. Having kids might put the brakes on your career but we have so much fun together. I'm really enjoying them at the moment. They really complete me.'

Sera knew she was being bitchy, she knew it was completely unfair to throw Bella's childlessness into her face, but she desperately wanted to have something – anything – that her perfect sister didn't.

Her smug smile faded as a squeal shattered the calm of the gardens. 'Muuum,' Harry shrieked. 'Maddy's hurting me, she pushed me over,'

'He started it,' came Maddy's swift defence. 'He wrecked my crystal swan's fairy garden.'

'Did not!'

'He flicked a dead bird into it.'

'She's a liar!'

'Mum, did you hear that?'

Sera smiled at Bella. 'You get used to it,' she said, in what she hoped was a serene manner. 'I've just learned to ignore it.' Another piercing cry sent the ducks flapping away from their peaceful float. 'Actually, they're never like this. I don't know what's gotten into them,' Sera said, while her left eyebrow began to twitch. 'Just ignore it.'

'Oh, I'm ignoring it,' Bella said and plucked a grape from a Tupperware container.

'Have you spoken to Mum lately?' Sera asked. The lapsed communication with her Tassie family left Sera with a sense of guilty relief. She was glad she hadn't had to deal with her mother's whiny neediness lately but still felt bad for not being in contact.

'Yes, she rang last week when I was in Rome,' Bella said with a groan.

She didn't ring me, Sera thought, then instantly chastised herself for being so foolish. Silence from her mother was what she wanted.

'Oh, yes, what did she want?' she asked.

'She wanted me to go online and top up her TAB account because she was on a "sure thing" in Dapto.'

'You can't be serious,' Sera exclaimed. 'I hope you didn't do it!'

'What could I do? I tried turning her down but she ran the whole "You never come and visit" guilt trip on me and fifty bucks seemed like a cheap way to get off the phone.'

'I'm glad she didn't call me, I would have ended up in a fight with her.'

'That's probably why she didn't call you,' Bella said.

'Yeah, and also I never returned her call from a month ago. How's Dad, has he found work yet?'

'No, apparently his back's gone out again. He didn't sound too perturbed about it.'

Suddenly their conversation was interrupted by an an ear-splitting scream from Maddy.

'RIGHT! That's it!' Sera leapt up and screeched in her best fishwife voice, 'I can't believe you two! Wait till I tell your father.' She marched behind the picnic and off across the grass. 'I've had it up to here with this behaviour! The one time I ask you both to behave –' Her voice reached a strangled squawk as she rounded the tree and found the two children in a garden bed, mid-wrestle.

'I don't care who started it; you're both old enough to know better. Harry, look at those new jeans! Ruined!' She looked at the two mucky children in exasperation and pointed a finger. 'This is your last warning. I swear to God I am going to kill you both with my bare hands if you don't stop wrestling each other.'

Sera returned to Bella, shaking her head in disappointment at her own behaviour. Her happy-family veneer had slipped and shown the ugly chipboard beneath.

'Kids will be kids, don't worry about it,' Bella said, trying to reassure her sister. 'White King will get the dirt stains out of the jeans.'

Sera munched on a sandwich and stared out sulkily into the distance. A couple walked past hand in hand, giggling inanely at each other's every word. She wore a mini-skirt. He thought she was beautiful.

'God, I hate it sometimes,' Sera said.

'Hate what?' Bella asked.

'Everything.'

'Oh, don't be like that, Sera, you've got a wonderful life.'

'If it's so wonderful, why do I feel so miserable?'

'Well, tell me about it,' Bella offered.

'Bloody Joan's driving me up the wall,' Sera began.

'Yes, I could see the writing on the wall there,' admitted Bella. 'It was always risky moving in with the monster-in-law, especially one so fiercely devoted to her precious only child. What's she done now?'

'Oh, it'll sound pathetic but it's the doona covers . . .' And Sera launched into the sad and sorry tale of textiles and fabric swatches; poly-blend and Best and Less. 'I just wish I could be you sometimes, Bella,' Sera blurted out when she was finished. 'Just floating around the world from city to city, cocktail bars and rockstar parties, duty-free, carefree, fat-free – you've just got it made and here I am, trapped. Trapped in the drudgery of which freaking dishwashing liquid to buy. Drop kids off, pick kids up, go to work, come home from work, supermarket, farmers' market . . . it's so bloody boring I could scream but I have to do it because I'm trapped.' She stopped for a breath. Her self-pity threatened to overwhelm her.

When Bella didn't leap to her aid with a hug like she usually did, Sera looked up. Bella was glowering at her.

'How dare you?!' she said.

Sera's eyes widened: this wasn't the tea and sympathy she had been expecting.

'How bloody dare you?! You wouldn't have a clue about my life, not a single clue.'

'Well, I sort of do, don't I?' Sera said in a little voice. 'I mean you do travel to lovely places quite a bit.'

'My God, Sera, you have got it all. You have a wonderful husband, a house most people would kill for, a great job in an industry you've always claimed to love and you've got two healthy, amazing children. How can you sit there and complain?'

'Well, it's not all beer and skittles,' Sera said, her bottom lip trembling, 'not like your job.'

'Sera, my job is bloody hard work. You try dealing with spoilt brats day in and day out, putting them to bed, feeding them, helping them get over their every tantrum. And I'm talking about grown-ups. I'll tell you right now, your two kids have got nothing on fourteen first-class passengers – all of whom make sure I know I'm well beneath them.'

'Well, yes, I guess that's a bit annoying –'

'Thanks to a decade-and-a-half of international travel my periods are completely shot and I have constant jet lag. No matter how hard I try I cannot keep the fluids up to stop the dehydration and have to constantly take fibre to stop my body from bloating till it explodes like a dead seal in the sun.'

'Oh,' said Sera. 'I hadn't thought of that.'

'I don't have a true home or family thanks to having equal time in almost every time zone in the world; the closest relationships I have are with the crew I happen to be working with and even that changes every flight.'

'What about Curtis, surely you see him a lot?'

'Curtis left me three months ago, Sera.'

'Bella! Why didn't you tell me?' Sera was shocked.

'Because, quite frankly, every time I call you have so many concerns of your own I don't like to bother you.'

'Oh darling Bella, I'm so sorry, I am so very sorry.' Sera reached out to put her hand on Bella's shoulder but it was immediately shrugged off. She should have known – it was fairly obvious, the slime-ball had even hit on her once. Perhaps she should have told Bella after all. 'What happened?'

'Oh, he had an affair. Well, he had several, if truth be told. I was just too stupid to see them.'

'Bloody hell, Bella! You poor thing.' Sera stared at her

sister in disbelief. The poor woman, and all this time she'd been bottling it up inside. 'You're not stupid, you're just loyal. You just wanted to believe in true love.'

'I was stupid. I married too young. I really jumped from the frying pan into the fire, didn't I?'

Sera reached out for her sister's hand as thoughts of their home life came flooding into her mind like a cloud descending on the sunny day. She remembered the yelling; the boys wrestling and punching, their parents fighting, her mother whingeing and moaning, never happy with anything. She remembered the overpowering smell of cigarette smoke. It was all so depressing; the shredded curtains, broken furniture . . . and the noise, so much noise all the time. Noise. She snapped back to the present. Noise. Where's the noise? She stood.

Bella looked up from her own reverie. 'What's wrong?'

'No noise,' Sera said in a tight voice. She ran back to the lawn where she'd last seen the children. Maddy was scratching out a picture of her swan in the dirt with a stick. She looked up at her mother.

'Mummy, I love my swan sooo much, look – '

Sera interrupted her daughter. 'Maddy, where's Harry?'

'Dunno,' she said.

'HARRY!' Sera yelled. 'HAAARRY!' She ran forward two steps. She looked to her left: Macquarie Street was a dangerous road, should she run there first? She looked behind her: the lake. He couldn't have gone around past them, could he? She'd have heard the splash . . . wouldn't she? Or would she? She looked to her right: half a kilometre away she knew a sheer twenty-foot-drop was fenced off, but since when did a fence stop her little climbing monkey? A feeling of panic began to engulf her.

~19~

Chantrea was early – a whole day early. Sally would be so thrilled, she thought, as she jumped out of her VW and rushed into Babyface Childcare, bubbling with the anticipation of sharing a stolen day with her little girl.

After the parent–teacher interview, she had lain awake in bed thinking of how much she wanted to give Sally to ensure she had a childhood different from her own. But Chantrea missed her so much when she was at work and she knew Sally would prefer to play at home some days. She wanted things to change, but she wasn't sure how to start.

Her mother kept telling her she was crazy for sending Sally to Babyface instead of a community kindergarten; for saving all her money for the fees for a private school when Sally turned six. But Chantrea was steadfast. She *had* to send Sally to a private school and hold on to their stylish Bondi Junction address – even if it was only a cramped unit. Chantrea was sure her address helped get Sally invited to the best kids' parties.

Although other mothers were generally polite, Chantrea often felt like she was the token Asian at coffee mornings. But she didn't care. Sally was making friends, she was accepted and nobody knew her history. Her world was in order; except for the nagging feeling that she and Sally were missing out on something deeper and more important: time together.

She had decided to start with some small changes. She'd start with taking today off and surprising Sally by picking her up at Babyface to spend the afternoon with her. And she might even speak to the roster manager about cutting back on some of her shifts; she was a killer budgeter, she'd just have to pull the reins in tighter.

Now she was putting her plan into action, she felt like a naughty schoolgirl wagging classes. She smiled happily at the crèche director and strode confidently into the kinder room with a huge grin.

Nancy gave her a confused look. 'Did Sally forget something yesterday, Chantrea?' she asked.

'What?' Chantrea shook her head. 'No, I've come to pick her . . .' her words trailed away as she realised her daughter was not among the group sitting cross-legged on the carpet. 'Where is she?' she asked, her heart beating hard and colour draining from her face as a hundred terrifying scenarios flashed through her mind.

Nancy was quickly at her side, patting her hand. 'Oh, no, Chantrea, everything's fine, don't panic. She's just having one of her home days. I'm so sorry, I assumed you knew.'

'A home day?' Chantrea tried not to shout.

'Well, yes, that's what your mother calls them.'

'But Mother works. Who's looking after Sally?' Chantrea demanded.

'I'm sorry, Chantrea, I don't know. Oh dear, I hope we've done the right thing,' Nancy said.

Chantrea was back home within ten minutes. Her mind was boiling over. Surely Sally wasn't sick: her mother would have called if she was. And she couldn't be home alone, could she? With Chantrea's crazy mother, anything was possible.

She pulled her car to a screeching halt in front of the

block of three units. The heels of her boots clicked angrily along the path as she rushed past the first two tiny homes until she reached her own even smaller place at the rear.

Squeals of laughter and strains of music filled the air, and part of her relaxed as she knew that at least Sally was safe. She peered in the skinny glass window that flanked the front door and was astounded to see her mother and her daughter leaping around the room like a couple of deranged primates. Her immediate relief was quickly replaced with a new flare of anger.

She burst through the front door. Sally, perched atop the couch about to leap into the air, froze at the sight of her mother. Her grandmother, squatting on all fours, did the same.

'What the hell is going on?' Chantrea demanded, catching sight of the dining room table, which was covered in monkey face-masks, paintings and sketches done in a suspiciously Cambodian style. 'What's going on here?' she repeated, her voice dangerously icy.

'No mind you,' her mother was shrill with the indignation of being caught. 'Just some fun for a little girl.' And she rushed towards the table to start clearing the craft away. 'We're having fun, aren't we, Sally?'

'Yeah!' Sally sprang back to life. 'So much fun, look we made Hanuman the Monkey God pictures and now we're doing the Hanuman monkey dance.' She demonstrated some elaborate dance steps, complete with well-practised hand movements.

Chantrea noticed a slender tube in her daughter's hand. 'What's that, Sally? Is that the god-awful noise I heard when I came in?'

'Yeah, Mum, it's Granny Yay's Khmer flute. I'm getting really good.' To illustrate, she raised it to her lips. Brittle, haunting notes came from the instrument.

Chantrea's hands flew to her ears. 'Stop it, stop it at once, that's a terrible noise. Give that to me!'

'But Mum!' Sally stared at her mother with an injured look.

'How do you say this to such a talented child?' Dara Kim scolded. For a little woman she could be quite fearsome when antagonised. 'This is a wonderful gift she has, wonderful talent.' Raising herself to every bit of her four-foot-ten-inch frame, she said proudly, 'She takes after her grandmother.'

'Yes, she does – by going behind my back and doing things expressly forbidden in this house,' Chantrea spat. 'Sally, go to your room.'

'Mum!' Sally protested.

'Now, Sally. Go to your room.'

'Not fair, you stink!' The five-year-old sulked off, stamping her little feet down the hall until the slamming of the door brought silence over the house.

'You can't do this, Mother,' Chantrea began. 'You can't make her into a Cambodian girl.'

Dara Kim was livid. The knuckles on her clenched fists went white. 'And you can't deny two thousand years of culture from my country. Who are you? The Khmer Rouge?'

Chantrea had had enough, she'd been fighting to escape her Cambodian background most of her life, but everywhere she turned, someone, something would remind her that she was different, an outsider. And now this: the ultimate betrayal. Her little Sally was turning into someone from that godforsaken country of torture and suffering. It was too much to bear.

'Mother, that's it! I will not tolerate it for one more moment. If you can't drop this stupid Cambodian stunt and embrace our new life, I will leave.' The look on Dara's face spurred her on. 'I will. I'll take Sally and we'll move to another city and you won't be able to find us.'

'You would not dare take my little Sally away,' Dara whispered. Chantrea could tell that the older woman knew she'd lost.

'Don't tempt me, Mother.'

She headed for the door and was just about to slam it angrily behind her when her mother hissed: 'Pol Pot's regime killed one point seven million of our people. Ninety percent of our artists and musicians are dead and gone. Who is going to pass on our culture to our young if I don't?'

Chantrea shut the door quietly and returned to her car.

~20~

Chantrea sat on the edge of Tingara Reserve, staring out through her tears at Rose Bay.

She swiped at her eyes with the back of her hand. How dare her mother do this?

Just look at this magnificent place they called home. Why couldn't she just move on? Chantrea wondered, kicking at tufts of grass at her feet.

She took some deep breaths to quell her sobbing and as her tears subsided she sat back to take in the landscape around her. It was such a special place. Some boats drifted peacefully along the water, while others bobbed merrily at their moorings; the glorious sandy beaches stretched wide and inviting beside the glittering harbour; rugged cliff faces rose above the golden sands and beyond all this was the beauty of the bushland.

Pictures from her Cambodian childhood flashed into her mind – at first the horror and the loss – but then some smaller, happier memories; tiny fractured images of her father and her great-aunt's village; her mother's gentle laugh and a sense of home and family and warmth. Her eyes filled with tears again. She thought about her mother and all she had been through and lost. To her mother, Cambodia still held some joyful and significant memories, but she wished Dara Kim would let them move forward into the bright, happy future that beckoned. She knew her mother loved Australia, and was often the first one to suggest weekend family nature walks or museum visits. But what she couldn't know – couldn't see – was how persecuted Sally would become if she took on her Asian culture.

Chantrea decided to wander along the spectacular Harbour Walk. The breeze wasn't cool enough to make her regret her bare arms and the sun warmed her back, soothing her into a calmer state of mind.

The Rose Bay café and promise of a double espresso beckoned her over and she stood waiting to be seated.

'Table for two?' the waitress enquired, glancing at someone behind Chantrea.

Confused, Chantrea turned to see Jacqueline standing a foot away chatting on the mobile. 'Yes darling,' she was saying. 'I'll pick that up for you after I drop off the boys at soccer.'

A slight shadow of disappointment slid over Jacqueline's face as she registered Chantrea, but she replaced it with a bright smile almost instantly. And although Chantrea would have preferred to fly economy than have coffee with Jacqueline, she nodded to the waitress and steeled herself to endure the faux enthusiastic greeting that women from Rose Bay to Sandy Bay and back to Bay Street employ daily.

'Darling! So wonderful to see you!' exclaimed Jacqueline with all the excitement of a socialite who's just discovered fat-free crème brulée.

'Jacqueline, what a lovely surprise,' Chantrea replied, leaning in for the double-cheek European kiss.

They weren't the best of friends. They had completely opposite views on mothering and childcare, with Chantrea believing women needed to maintain a life outside home and children, and Jacqueline feeling that an effective mother was at home, on call, all day. And while Chantrea suspected Jacqueline of deep-seated racism, Jacqueline simply had deep-seated bag-ism and hated Chantrea's biker-chick taste in handbags.

But here they were, enemies trapped in the cage of social nicety. They sat down at a table, ordered coffee and pretended to be delighted to have run into each other. Jacqueline twittered about her shopping morning, her silly boys and their forgetful ways, and her darling husband who was so busy he'd forgotten their anniversary, not that she minded, of course.

Chantrea smiled weakly, while inwardly shrieking, 'Please, God, just kill me now.'

'So what brings you to Rose Bay, Chantrea?' Jacqueline asked, putting on her best listening face. 'You're usually such a busy little thing, flying all over the place. It's rare to see you out and about, having some time off.'

Chantrea brushed the question away. 'Oh, I just had a day off, so I thought I'd take a walk, it's gorgeous down here.'

Jacqueline, who had a talent for saying the wrong thing at the worst time, added, 'But why aren't you with your little girl? Such a rare opportunity.'

'My mother has her today. They're busy doing, well, stuff together and I just get in the way.'

'But how can you get in the way? It's such a little family, you should be together,' Jacqueline insisted.

'Look, Jacqueline, it's complicated. They're doing stuff that I'm just not into, okay?' Chantrea leaned forward and grabbed her glass of water, slopping some over the side in anger.

'What's got you so upset?' Jacqueline was suddenly genuinely concerned.

'It's nothing, it's stupid really. It's just that my mother

eaching Sally about her Cambodian culture. I ike it at all.'

'Ahhh,' Jacqueline said knowingly. 'Mothers, grandmothers and daughters, always a tricky business. So what is she doing? Letting her eat Asian sweets or letting her stay up all night watching TV? I was very miffed with my mother in the early days when she'd spoil the boys rotten.'

'No, it's not that. It's . . . well, it's really difficult to explain,' Chantrea began, but in her eagerness to set Jacqueline straight she had launched into her fears of Sally not growing up as a complete Australian, her concern that she might get bullied because of her heritage, and her shock that her mother had gone behind her back.

Jacqueline listened carefully and sympathetically. Chantrea finally finished her story and sat flushed with embarrassment at having spilled everything to Jacqueline, of all people.

'You'd be amazed, Chantrea, but I completely understand where Dara Kim is coming from,' Jacqueline said.

Chantrea found it hard to avoid sarcasm. 'Yes, you're right, I am amazed, Jacqueline. How could you understand? You are worlds apart from my mother.'

'She's a mum, I'm a mum, and she's just trying to do the right thing by you; she loves you.'

Chantrea was hot with rage. 'If she wanted to do the right thing by me, she'd do what I want her to do and stop this nonsense.'

'No, that would be indulging you,' Jacqueline said gently. 'She obviously feels strongly that your heritage is crucial to your family. Like every mum, she wants to do what's good for you, not necessarily what you want her to do.'

'Well, I guess that makes sense,' Chantrea said slowly,

her anger cooling. 'But why can't she see how important it is for me to leave all that behind?'

'You're rebelling. You don't see it yet, but when she's gone, you will wish that you'd asked her more about her family and your country's past. You're very lucky to be from such a beautiful country, Chantrea, I've been to Angkor Wat with my International Art Appreciation Group. The artwork and history of that place is quite remarkable. What do we have here for history? A few boatloads of criminals? If an Australian wants to delve further than a few generations we *all* have to go back to our motherland, be it Poland, Germany, Vietnam or England.'

Chantrea was stunned to find that Jacqueline was starting to make a lot of sense. Jacqueline laughed, 'Of course, the Cambodian music is a bit harsh; there's no rhyme or reason to it.'

'Hang on a minute.' Chantrea flared up. 'My mother was a famous musician before we left Phnom Penh. She played the Khmer flute and it has a very beautiful sound. Sally's quite talented at it too.'

'Oh, well, each to his own.' Jacqueline said. 'If your girl has got any musical appreciation whatsoever she should hear my boys play violin. You should consider it for Sally, a beautiful sound and an incredibly versatile instrument. And always such fun at a party.'

~21~

Sera took a deep breath, trying not to panic. 'Bella, you run down to Macquarie Street,' she ordered. 'Maddy, stay at the picnic and watch the lake. I'm going to the public toilets.'

Sera raced to the public toilets. She burst into the men's, startling a businessman who was just zipping up. 'Harry, are you in here?' she called. She ran to the ladies' but found no sign of him.

Outside the toilets she whirled around, looking in every direction. A mounted policeman was in the distance. She called out and ran down to the horse and officer.

'My little boy,' she blurted out breathlessly, 'he's only three. Have you seen him?'

'Hair colour?' The police officer cut directly to the facts.

'Dark brown,' she replied. This felt sickeningly surreal.

'Last seen wearing?'

'Red shirt and blue and white striped pants, no, white jeans . . . oh God,' she said, crumbling with fear for her little boy.

The policeman radioed in the information and told Sera to stay put as he headed off at a trot.

Sera raced back to the picnic to see if there was any news, but she could tell from Bella and Maddy's faces that Harry hadn't been found.

'Maddy darling, think!' she begged her daughter. 'When did you last see Harry?'

'Well, we were drawing pictures,' Maddy started.

'Yes, go on,' Sera prompted desperately.

'And then he saw a duck and told me to look at it, and I said I couldn't cos I was too busy.'

'Then what?'

'That's it,' Maddy shrugged her shoulders.

'I bet he's followed the duck. Maddy, stay with Bella.' Sera rushed off towards the lake, panic thrumming in her ears. She scanned the calm water. No ducks. Sera willed herself to sense Harry's location; to tap into some maternal psychic connection. Nothing.

The last thing she'd said to her son was that she was going to kill him. Her hand flew to her mouth to stop herself from vomiting. What if he was . . . she stopped helplessly on the pathway and looked around, wildly. He'd now been missing over twenty minutes. That was just too long. Bella and Maddy were questioning passers-by.

Where were the ducks? She looked down the hill. The mounted police officer had been joined by another and they were in conversation, gesturing back at Sera. Where was that gardener from earlier? If anyone knew where the bloody ducks were, it would be him.

Suddenly she caught sight of the gardener, digging up a dahlia bed.

'The ducks, where are the ducks?!' she screeched, bolting towards him. She forced herself to draw a breath. 'My three year old is missing. He was last seen following the ducks.'

'I just saw a family of ducks,' he said. He spoke slowly and clearly in a voice he obviously reserved for the slightly touched or maternally panicked. 'They're under the Moreton Bay Fig, over there, ' he said, pointing.

'Thank you,' she cried, hope flooding her mind as she fled down the massive lawn towards the fig tree.

She could see the waddling ducks, but no Harry. She ran closer, her leggings riding up but she barely cared.

'Harry?!' The cry came out as a muffled sob. She tried again. 'Harry!' She stopped running and listened. The ducks stopped moving and looked. He had to be here. There was nowhere else to look after this.

Then she saw a little foot protruding from behind the tree's enormous root. It was followed by a shoulder and then by a face that broke into a smile. 'Mum, look, ducks.'

Sera's knees failed. She dropped. Her face fell into her hands. When she looked up her little guy was toddling towards her with a pinecone in his outstretched hand and a worried look on his face. 'Don't cry, Mummy, you're a beautiful mummy.' She embraced him and burst into body-racking sobs.

As she waited with Maddy near the picnic, Bella wasn't panicked. She knew kids; on the farm the boys would roam for hours without anybody worrying them. She was sure Harry would be found soon. But as the minutes ticked past, she began to grow a little more concerned. Honestly, who'd have children? They were such hard work. Sera was more snappy and tense than ever, the adults never got to complete a sentence and now this ridiculous mad panic. Thank goodness she'd never had any, she thought smugly.

Finally Sera reappeared with Harry in her arms, the relief on her face obvious. Unexpectedly, Bella felt tears in her eyes. This was a picture of motherhood that she had never known. All the years she had spent corralling, chasing, yelling, feeding and cleaning her siblings hadn't been motherhood at all. That had simply been work, thankless work with little reward or emotion. She could see that this was different, and she was shocked.

Maddy started to wail. 'What is it, darling?' asked Bella. 'Harry's fine, see?'

'No, look,' the little girl sobbed. In her hand lay the precious Swarovski swan with one very broken neck.

~22~

Sam was looking for a man; any man. Since he'd been widowed, school pick-up had become a scary plunge into a tangled jungle of female desire and unwanted attention.

If he could just spot another dad in the playground he'd be fine; but on his own he was easy prey for many of the school's single women.

He scanned the milling parents as he headed toward the school: not a Y chromosome in sight. He sighed, his thoughts drifting to his date tonight with the bikini model. What the hell had he been thinking? He wasn't the sort of bloke who dated models, for chrissakes. Come to think of it, he wasn't the sort of bloke who dated at all.

What was he supposed to talk about with this woman? Did women like her want to be complimented, or was that cheesy? He still hadn't decided where to take her; he didn't want to come across as too contrived. But, on the other hand, without a plan it might look like he didn't care. What did they like to do? What did they like to eat? What do women want? He laughed at himself. If he knew that, he'd be a millionaire.

He wandered through the school gates, all thoughts of the impending date leaving his mind. He needed to keep his wits about him here. Last week he'd received three meaningful smiles and one phone number before he got to the school door.

He called them the Seekers. The divorced women desperately looking for a partner; someone to ease the burdens of child-rearing; to help with the mortgage and fulfill what appeared to Sam to be quite insatiable needs – if the way they casually pressed their bodies against him in the crush of the playground was anything to go by. He couldn't remember women being quite so forward back when he was single all those years ago – and it scared the hell out of him.

There was one particularly determined mother, Muriel, who had been stalking him since the day after he had buried his wife. She had the stealth (and the dress sense) of a leopard, the personality (and laugh) of a kestrel and all the subtlety of a rubbish-foraging raccoon. She made him terribly nervous. In their first playground conversation she had jumped from asking how old his kids were to why he wasn't wearing a wedding ring with a startling lack of segue.

He excused his way past the sea of gigantic handbags attached to teeny, tanned women to position himself away from the crush of the group, but with a view of the school door. He hadn't seen Muriel yet so he allowed himself a tentative sigh of relief.

'Hiya handsome.' Curved talons snaked around his left bicep. God, he'd be crap as a gazelle.

'Muriel,' he exclaimed and took a step back from her cleavage before he tumbled into the chasm.

'So how's it going, Sammy, sweetie, you poor man?' Muriel purred, affecting what she hoped was an endearing, yet sympathetic, pout.

'No, no, all good, we're great, fine, no problem.' Sam knew he was stammering but was overcome with a primal need for flight. He looked nervously around the playground for an escape path, but he could only see another group standing nearby sizing him up as if deciding which vegetables would go nicely with Coq au Sam.

'It's so difficult, isn't it,' she sighed dramatically. 'The meat market is so tough, believe me, I know.'

I bet you do, Sam thought. He saw another dad, Dave, coming in the gate. He used all his willpower to reach Dave's mind and get him over, but as a professional athlete, Dave had very little in the mind department, and was probably using it all up just for walking. Usually Sam found Dave's constant sporting commentary to be very draining, but he'd happily endure the Wallabies' latest game blow-by-blow if only Dave would come and save him.

'I think it would be lovely to just find someone to be friends with, you know.' Muriel looked up at him, batted her falsies and grinned. 'Friends with perks. You know what I mean, no strings.'

'Yeah, sounds like a plan,' he muttered, not really listening as he madly flicked his eyes over to Dave who finally registered, put a great plank of an arm in the air in greeting and started pushing through the forest of handbags.

'Really?' Muriel squeaked, alerting Sam to further danger. What had he said?

'Er, yeah, for you I mean, whatever you need, I'm sure it's a good plan, for you that is, I mean . . . DAVE, MATE! *Great* to see you.' He put his hand out for a handshake that was well worth every metacarpal-crushing moment.

'Sam, Sam, old buddy boy!' Dave punched Sam on the deltoid – a blow that he was pleased not to be knocked sideways by. 'How are those piss-weak All Blacks, dude? We got 'em big time, didn't we?'

'Yeah, Dave, that was something else all right.'

Muriel dropped back into the female jungle with a disappointed sigh.

The bell finally rang and Isabelle came running out into Sam's arms. 'Come on, sweetie,' he said, 'let's get out of here and pick up your sister.'

~23~

Bella's luxurious flat boasted sweeping harbour views that compensated for its fourth-floor position in a very ordinary Darling Point 1980s high-rise. Rushcutters Bay Park, the Cruising Yacht Club, Sydney's impressive skyline, the Opera House, the Harbour Bridge and the boat-filled waters of Point Piper and Double Bay were laid out below her tiny balcony.

Bella's main criterion in searching for her first piece of Sydney real estate was finding a magnificent view, and her persistence had paid off. She had quickly set about indulging her love for Versace in designing the flat's interior. Although she and Sera had spent their teens and twenties idolising the gilt and glamour of Versace fashions, which seemed the antithesis of everything their drab childhoods had been, they soon matured into the lure of new designers.

Brands such as Ralph Lauren, DKNY and Lisa Ho became their labels of choice in their late twenties; and while in her late thirties Sera still enjoyed a gaudy touch in some of her fashion, Bella had toned her own look down to sophisticated Armani as she moved toward her fourth decade.

Except at home. Bella opened her front door and smiled as she surveyed the two-bedroom flat that was her Versace castle.

The living room walls were awash in navy flock embossed with gold fleur de lys. A royal blue studded couch stood centre stage scattered with gold Medusa-head tassled cusions. Persian rugs in jewelled tones led towards her bedroom. The queen-size bed was engulfed in the burgundy and hot pink of a faux mink throw, brocade canopy and velvet headboard.

Bella took off her pumps and after carefully brushing them, stored them in the first of her ten cupboards; the court shoe section.

She slid out her hairpins, placing them one by one in her hairpin holder, then threw her head upside down and scratched her head, wildly tousling her usually constrained locks. But before she could indulge in the freedom of unkempt hair she quickly swept it into a casual ponytail and checked it four times for lumps. Then she folded her clothes into their allocated storage spaces and dragged on track pants and her favourite worn flannelette shirt.

Suddenly she was filled with an overwhelming urge to check that the front door was locked. She had checked it when she'd come home (twice) and knew logically that it was locked. She took a deep breath, counted to ten, and the urge passed. She quietly congratulated herself on her strength.

She opened her MacBook Air and stared out at the city lights while her emails downloaded. She would usually have called Sera by now, perhaps arranged for a coffee in the morning. But she just didn't feel like it. She felt terrible about losing her temper with her little sister in the Botanic Gardens; it wasn't like her to snap like that.

After all, it wasn't Sera's fault that Bella had grown weary of always being the listener. Sera was just doing what she had always done; dumping all her problems on her sister and expecting her to fix things for her.

But Bella had just had enough. She was worn out. The failure of her marriage had been a painful shock that had seriously battered her self-esteem. The sense of loss was overwhelming – not just of Curtis – but of the ideal of a happy marriage that she'd strived so hard to achieve. So hard, in fact, that she'd been able to deny the truth of their relationship for years.

She had few real friends. Curtis had discouraged her inviting guests around, so she had isolated herself and concentrated on him for the past few years. Now she was alone.

She'd worked long hours since the end of the marriage, simply to distract herself and to avoid the sheer loneliness of sitting in the quiet flat. Even thinking about making the effort to reconnect with her old friends made her feel exhausted; and she didn't think she could face the humiliation of explaining her situation.

She turned to her laptop and scanned her emails. She saw there was one from Sera.

'Dear Bella, I'm a stupid, selfish cow. How can you ever forgive me? You've always been there for me and I didn't even notice you were suffering. Please call me when you're in Sydney so we can have a proper catch-up sans kids. Love Sera.'

Bella smiled and picked up the phone.

'Two hundred and four, two hundred and five . . .'

'Darling, how are you?' Sera was effusive as she swept into the Four in Hand bar.

Bella was pleased to see her sister, but anxious that she hadn't managed to finish counting the whole row of white tiles at her feet before she'd arrived. She shook the agitation from her head and stepped down from her stool at the bar to give Sera a hug.

'You look wonderful,' Sera enthused, determined to heal the rift between them.

'So do you,' Bella replied less convincingly as she took in Sera's orange face and garish eye make-up.

'That was a rotten catch-up on the weekend, I'm so sorry,' Sera started once she they had settled back at the bar and ordered Tanqueray and Tonics.

'Don't be silly. I'm the one who should be sorry, I should know when to shut up,' Bella said.

'Well, let's not dwell on it, it's behind us now. The important thing at the moment is you. What's happened with Curtis?'

Bella's mouth felt as if were full of cotton wool. She couldn't verbalise it, she just couldn't admit she'd failed. She checked her white T-shirt, it was immaculate, she looked at her nails; her watch; her shoes.

Sera grabbed Bella's hands to stop their compulsive fiddling. 'Stop it, darling, you're so twitchy. It's just me, you can trust me, I won't judge, I'm just here to listen.'

Sera's soothing words worked. Bella told her everything; the betrayals; the two-timing; the constant criticism that coloured her marriage. The sense that no matter how hard she tried she couldn't get Curtis' approval; could never be enough for him. Sera shook her head in shock and sadness. Her poor Bella.

Bella had believed his criticism; had swallowed his rejection and tried to fight harder to be better at everything just so that he might love her again. 'I really thought that if I could just be less of a failure; if I could be a better, happier, more beautiful woman, he'd want me again. Now I guess I can see that he was just projecting his own shortcomings on to me; that he needed me to be the cause of his discontent because it meant he didn't have to take any responsibility for his own issues.

'It's taken time and therapy, Sera, but I am starting to come out of the shadows of that relationship bit by bit, and do you know what?' Bella faced her sister with determined eyes. 'I will never, ever let anyone treat me that way again. I will never depend on someone so fully for my own self-esteem again.' Tears ran down her face and she whipped them away savagely.

Sera's heart ached to see her sister in such pain. 'I'm so sorry I wasn't there for you, Bella,' she whispered.

'I wasn't there for myself,' Bella sighed. 'I stayed with him for twenty years – and for what? Now here I am – single, no babies, no friends left, and a back-breaking career to keep up.

'And now he's getting married.' Her tears turned to sobs and Sera put her arm around her sister's shoulders as grief stormed through her.

'You don't still have feelings for him do you?' Sera asked with trepidation.

'I don't know, at first I thought I did, but I worked it through in therapy. It's more just the overwhelming enormity of the wasted years I can't shake.'

'Oh, thank God for that,' Sera said, relieved. 'In a way it's good that he's getting married, it's the ultimate closure for you, now you can move on.'

The waiter returned with more drinks and the sisters continued to talk long into the night. By the time Bella returned to her apartment she was exhausted but relieved. The evening had been cathartic; Sera had been a wonderful support. It was just what she'd needed.

~24~

Sam's neighbour Jenny looked after his girls every now and then, and the three were happily reading *The Little Mermaid* by the time he was ready to go at eight o'clock that evening. He'd half expected them to beg him to stay home, and was a bit disappointed at not having a reason to cancel.

He got into his Saab and negotiated his way through the back streets until he got to the main drag of Paddington. He couldn't believe how nervous he was. What was a daggy thirty-seven-year-old father-of-two doing thinking he could cut it with a bikini model? Who did he think he was, Hugh Hefner?

He got to the Darlo Bar early to give himself time to sit quietly – well, as quietly as possible on a boisterous Friday night – and drink a Stella to take the edge off his nerves.

The Darlo was a remarkably soothing space to be, despite the noise. His architect's eye enjoyed the retro-kitsch mix of 50s and 60s styles. It was exactly like being in someone's home with its low-maintenance, low-glamour style. The crowd was a collection of hip dudes in skinny-leg jeans playing pool; inner-city types with metallic accessories; a pair of Armani-suited businessmen with loosened ties trying their luck with some leggy blondes; and a Goth waitress chatting with a group of old booze hounds who'd been drinking here for decades.

Then his date, Phoebe, sauntered in. The women in the bar looked up: the attractive ones in envy, the unattractive ones in awe. One of the guys playing pool nudged his mate and pointed with his chin. His buddy was already drooling.

The bar staff stared openly. Two trannies perched daintily on bar stools gave her the once over. 'She's fucking hot. I'd do her,' said one in a deep voice.

'You bitch!' the other shrieked, slapping her friend on her bulging bicep.

Sam had no idea how he would be able to muster the strength to stand and greet this goddess. He was thankful for every inch of his six-foot-three frame as he took in her Amazonian height enhanced by stiletto boots. Her tiny chocolate-and-lime crocheted dress sat daintily over her tanned skin.

'Phoebe, lovely to see you,' Sam said, smiling nervously, and he pecked her on the cheek.

'Omigod!' she squawked. 'I didn't realise how much you look like Mick Jagger!'

'Oh, really?' Sam said.

'Yeah, so much. But not now he's old, not like you're old or something, but you know, like from when he was younger, you know, like your age.'

The magic died. The patrons went back to their business. The trannies bickered over their Mai Tais, the pool player potted the white off the black, the other punters returned to their chatter and Sam found himself talking to a sort-of-pretty girl.

'Can I get you a drink, Phoebe?' he asked.

'Omigod, yeah, what am I, a camel?'

'Ahh, no . . . I don't think you're a camel . . . um . . . what would you like?'

'What a charmer!' she said, through peals of laughter. 'Beer for me thanks, hon.'

Sam headed for the bar. Did she just call him 'hon'? He hated that or any form of endearment from people he didn't know well. Grace had hated it too. He smiled as he thought of her. Oh jeez, what kind of a pathetic loser was he? Here he was on his first date with a beautiful woman, reminiscing about his dead wife. Tragic. But Christ he missed her. He'd have given everything he had to go home now and hold her just for one more night.

He got the drinks and returned to his date.

'. . . So anyway, I said to the photographer, no fucking way am I shaving it all off, leave me a bit of muff for God's sake. I mean what's a Brazilian without fucking Brazil, I ask you? Well, it was on! I'm not working with him again EVER!'

Sam was quite thrown by this. Had she been talking to him the whole time he was over at the bar? Or was she just a mid-conversation starter?

'Really?' he asked as politely as he could.

'Yeah, totally!'

She sat back and waited. It was obviously his turn.

'So what's it like being a model?' He could have slapped himself. What a lame question, he sounded like a dick-head.

'Omigod!?' She squealed as if he'd just asked her the meaning of life. 'It's like sooo amazing. Honestly, I am so glad you asked.' And she went on. And on. And on. He thought at one point she was going to stop. But it was just an intake of breath. Then she went on again.

Eventually she had to stop because she wanted a refill of her beer. When he returned she said. 'Listen to me going on, why doncha? Tell me about you. You've got, like, kids or something?'

Sam smiled proudly at the mention of his favourite subject. 'Yes, I do. I have two girls, their names are –'

She interrupted, 'I love kids, it's so hard to believe, but I was a kid once you know.'

'Well, yes,' Sam said, 'we all were.'

'Omigod,' she gasped, 'that's, like, so insightful, you're like a philosopher or something. I'm so old, you know, don't you think? Do I look old? How old do I look?'

'Oh, gosh, I wouldn't like to say,' Sam muttered.

'Go on,' she leaned forward and gave him a playful shove. 'Say how old you think I am. I won't get cross, promise.'

'Okay, I dunno, twenty-seven?'

'What!? How can you say that to me, you big meanie?' She crossed her arms and slumped back into the couch.

'Well, tell me, how old are you?'

'I'm twenty-seven, but that's not the point.'

'Okaaay then,' he said slowly and excused himself to go to the men's room.

They ordered pizzas and finished their beers. Luckily the music got louder and Sam didn't have to listen anymore, he just nodded a lot and tried to look vaguely awake.

Finally it was time to walk her out to find a taxi. She'd started having vodka shots with every beer and was now considerably unsteady on her very pointy heels.

'Absolutely, taxi to my house,' she slurred. 'You are so hot, wanna come?'

'No, I'd better get back to the girls.'

'Oh, that's right, the old guy with the kids,' she muttered, falling into the cab. 'You're lovely,' she called as the cab pulled away from the kerb. 'Call me.'

'Good-night,' he called.

'You are lovely,' came a deep voice and Sam turned to

see one of the trannies leaning against the wall smoking a cigarette and giving him a slow, long-lashed wink.

When he got home, Sam leaned heavily against his front door. That was utterly exhausting. What was wrong with him? He had a beautiful woman practically throwing herself at him and he just couldn't get into her at all. It had been two years since Grace died, but maybe he just wasn't ready. Maybe Grace was his one true love and he shouldn't try to replicate that. Maybe he was meant to be alone.

He walked into the kitchen for a glass of juice, catching his reflection in the window. He hadn't changed that much since his mid-twenties. He was still wiry, still had his thick black hair – probably dressed a bit old-fashioned nowadays. But he was the same guy. He thought back to his single days, before Grace. He'd been attractive to women, but dating seemed easier in those days.

His mobile beeped. He checked the in-box to see a new text. It was from Phoebe.

I <3d 2nite
4u A3
@teotd ur2gtbt
TMB
P

What in the hell did that mean?

He saw the 2nite obviously referred to that evening, but the rest might as well have been Latin. He painstakingly sent back a message, hoping for the best.

Thank you for a lovely evening.
Sam.

The return message came almost the nano-second after he hit send.

AYSOS

He'd have to get Mallory to decipher that, he decided, turning off his phone with a sigh.

He lay in bed and stared at the ceiling. He remembered what it was he loved about finding a partner. It was chemistry. He was addicted to chemistry. It might have taken months of celibacy but when he would find the woman whose lips made him ignite, whose walk made him weak and whose voice made him sigh, then he knew it was going to be a remarkable relationship. Those special occasions hadn't happened often but when they did it was like having a catherine wheel in your guts. It had happened with Grace. It certainly hadn't happened with Phoebe.

When Sam awoke the next morning, gritty-eyed and furry-tongued, the memory of last night splintered into his mind. Oh, jeez, that bloody woman! As his consciousness crawled further into the new day he became aware of a small foot pushed against the side of his head. He tried to stretch his legs but a weight was pinning him down. He looked down and saw his two girls starfished across the doona.

Sleep-tousled hair awry, their bodies leaden, there was little point trying to move them and it was almost time to get up anyway. He grabbed Ol' Blue, his favourite weather-worn pale-blue hoodie, dragged it on and, gently closing the bedroom door, headed into the kitchen. As he put the kettle on he noticed a tear in the cuff seam. Damn, he loved this jumper. He tugged at the hole, wondering how to fix it.

He had bought it with Grace on a camping trip to the Hawkesbury River just after they'd met. He remembered it clearly; the startling blue skies, and Grace's excitement at her first camping trip. He'd teased that she was a princess who had never had to rough it, but he'd been so keen to impress her that he'd spent a fortune in Aussie Disposals buying every camping gadget he could find.

He'd remembered everything except his own bag, and by the time night fell on the first day he was shivering in his boardies and T-shirt. Grace had warmed him through the night, and as he lay in her sleeping arms, listening to a tawny frog-mouth seducing the nearby frogs, he thanked the sweep of stars above for sending him this amazing woman.

The next morning, with Sam looking ridiculous in Grace's small pink tracksuit top, they'd driven into town and giggled at the meagre wares at the General Store. He'd settled for the blue hoodie that proudly boasted the name of the town.

As the kettle boiled, he looked down and read the words on his jumper again. Pitt Town. Pitt Town; how he ached to go back.

~25~

Joan knew there was no one home next door, but just to be sure she tapped on the back door before entering using the emergency key Sera kept for Jacqueline. Joan stared at the immaculate kitchen, which looked as if it had been prepared for a *Vogue Living* shoot.

She glanced into the museum-like living room and tutted. Personally she'd prefer to live with Sera's relaxed housekeeping than in this cold, perfect world. Each objet d'art was painstakingly positioned and even the cast-iron fire tools were spotless – Joan could have rubbed them on the peach silk couch and not made a mark. Magazines were fanned at precise angles on the antique coffee table.

Joan's gaze lingered on the drawer of the antique lady's writing desk, noticing the highly polished inlaid mother-of-pearl handle.

For goodness' sake, thought Jacqueline as she steered her classic Mercedes Benz towards home. How would she cater for twenty sweaty soccer players tomorrow night? Daniel shouldn't have invited the whole team back at such short notice.

Oh well, she thought, brightening, she could make it a Hawaiian theme and ask Thomas to do a barbecue. That should cheer up this dreary wintery week. She'd make a smorgasbord of pineapple-based side-dishes. As she pulled into the garage she wondered if the boys would like to wear floral leis to set it all off.

Joan wandered back to the kitchen and studied the timber drawers with their crystal knobs. She slid one open.

The drawer was full to overflowing. The poor woman, Joan sighed. She sorted through novelty clothes pegs, long-handled parfait spoons and dozens of other items, until she found what she was looking for.

At the sound of the Jacqueline's car, Joan slid her Charles and Diana teaspoon into her cardigan pocket, slipped out the back door and hurried down the path.

Jacqueline lugged her shopping bags out of the boot. The last shivers of excitement from her shopping trip ran through her as she pushed the key into the front door lock. Inside, she dumped her shopping onto the kitchen table and looked around at her sparkling kitchen with pleasure. Then she noticed that her drawer, her special drawer, was open. Her stomach lurched.

~26~

Although winter's rains were lashing down, the renovations had begun. With a determined charge, the bobcat knocked down another wall and Harry screamed in delight. 'Whoah, Mum,' he yelled, 'you shoulda seed that one!' He jumped up and down on the kitchen chair as he watched the backyard devastation.

Sera bustled in with school bags hanging from the crook of her elbow, a hairbrush in one hand and a kinder notice in the other. She smiled at Harry. 'Exciting isn't it?'

'Yeah, Mum, look, they're wrecking it, they're smashing it!' Harry had watched the machine's progress with glee since it had lumbered noisily into the backyard at eight that morning.

Sera couldn't believe her hard-fought battle for the kitchen renovation had finally been won. She'd soothed Tony's concerns about increasing the mortgage, and dealt with Joan's unexpected and vehement opposition to the destruction of the daggy little patio.

The woman had only given in because she could never say no to Tony, but Sera had thought she'd heard her crying in her room this morning and worried that her mother-in-law might be showing signs of Alzheimer's.

But finally, the project was under way. Tony was in the backyard briefing the driver before he had to rush off to his new Potts Point job and Sera was planning to spend part of the day researching tiles and benchtops.

At the end of the week the builders would start. The first step was pulling off the entire back wall, then gutting the kitchen before building started. It would all take about six months.

Sera knew Tony was worried about the cost of the project, but she was sure it would all be fine. They'd get everything at trade prices because of his job and to save on labour, the two of them would work on the house during the weekends. She loved this idea; envisaging herself in a pair of worker's overalls, her hair up in an Aunt-Jemima-style kerchief and an endearing smudge of plaster dust on her nose.

She didn't need a flashy expensive house, just some space to spread out.

Of course they would need new furniture – they couldn't watch TV on the floor, could they? And obviously a new TV, a lovely big plasma screen. The kids would be thrilled.

She'd tried to tell all this to Tony: that she could do it on a budget and that Laminex would be fine. He'd patiently explained to her that given its location the property couldn't be under-capitalised. It was Paddington. Future buyers would expect a certain standard. They couldn't just slap up a pre-fab extension. It needed to blend with the house, it had to have a matching high ceiling, the exterior had to be seamless, the windows needed to be of a high quality.

Sera was frustrated by this logic. She was trying to save money while he was insisting they spend up big. They had eventually agreed on a budget and she was determined to stick to it, so they could both get what they wanted.

She looked at the microwave clock. Cripes, time to get in the car. She popped in on Joan on her way out, and found her sitting on her bed, staring miserably out of the window. What an old stick in the mud, Sera thought. It was such an exciting day. Joan should be happy they were improving the house.

'You right there, Joan?' shc asked.

Joan turned her red and swollen eyes toward her.

'Do you care?' She sniffed sadly.

'Of course I care, Joan. What's wrong?'

Joan sighed. 'This is my family home – the home I came to as a bride – and I can't bear the thought of it being hacked into like this.'

'Oh, Joan,' Sera said, 'I'm so sorry you feel that way. But it's for the best. There are five of us who live here now, and we want it to be comfortable.'

'There's a lot of history here, Sera, a lot you don't know about.'

'What history, why don't you tell me?' Sera enquired gently.

Joan looked long and hard at her and Sera felt like she was being assessed, as if Joan was deciding if she could be trusted.

'You don't understand and you never will,' Joan finally said and turned back to the window.

Sera gave up, gratefully closing the door on Joan and her misery.

~27~

The spacious change room in the rear of D'Accord was as well appointed as Oprah's walk-in wardrobe. The wall of mirrors reflected the silk-upholstered wingback armchairs and the cedar coffee table offered a refreshment of chilled herbal tea and dried fig morsels.

The evening gown Bella was trying on was proving to be quite problematic. She didn't know how she'd ended up in the midst of a flurry of chiffon, considering she'd popped in to buy a simple shift dress. It was the power of the Rodeo Drive sales staff. These women were pedicured killer bees, furiously attacking any potential customer as soon as they walked in the store. They could sniff out a person's financial worth with a subtle inspection of bag, sunglasses and shoes. And the drones immediately presented anyone wearing this season's Valentino, as Bella stupidly was, to the Queen Bee – the Store Manager, or in LA terms, the Vice President of Procurement Motivation. This incredibly persuasive woman had Bella ensconced in the carpeted cavernous space before she could say 'liposuction'.

The bodice of the empire waistline dress seemed to stop at her underarms and the seam cut right across the middle of her breasts. The dress's shoestring straps indicated that it was definitely a no-bra frock but the flimsy cups of the gown offered no support at all. As Bella was carefully picking up her right boob for the third time to convince it to stay in the top of the dress, the Queen Bee stuck her head through the heavy taffeta curtains.

'Need any help?' she smiled brightly.

'Umm, well, the dress seems to be an odd shape,' Bella said. 'The bodice is too high for my bust.'

'Oh, let me see. I just saw it on a girl with a much bigger bust than you and it fitted perfectly. It might need adjusting.' In a modesty-free manner usually reserved for one's mammogram technician, the woman grabbed Bella's breast and shoved it in place. It dropped down heavily a full ten centimetres again.

'Oh, my dear, it's not the dress that's an odd shape. It's your breasts. Who on earth did them?' The saleswoman looked sympathetically at Bella in the mirror.

'Did them? No one *did* them, they're originals.' Never having breast-fed, Bella considered her B-cups reasonably pert considering forty years of gravity.

'Really? Oh, dear. Original breasts.' The woman made a show of pursing her lips. 'I'm so sorry, madam, but I don't think we have anything in this store that will fit you.'

Bella looked at her in amazement. 'Nothing? Nothing at all in your entire shop will fit a woman without breast augmentation?'

'Well, we cater for the majority, you see. I might be able to help you with one line in pants, though.'

'Pants? Is that all?' Bella started tearing the dress off and pulling on her street clothes.

'Yes, unless . . . have you had buttock implants?'

'No!' Bella said.

'Hmmm, well we do have one style that we reserve for our *au naturel* customers.'

'Don't worry about it,' Bella said. 'Thank you anyway.'

The woman retreated, allowing Bella privacy to finish getting dressed. Bella zipped up her boots and sat back in the armchair. She took a sip of the tea. She could guarantee it was fat, caffeine, lactose and sugar free.

How did she end up living in such a bizarre and crazy world? A place where she actually walked voluntarily into shops that catered only to plastic people. A world where she indulged the spoilt and pampered as they winged their way to places of further pampering and spoiling.

She hadn't planned on this strange life of floating in a global bubble. She remembered back to when she started flying. How she thought she was helping her marriage, being productive, earning an independent income.

Now she was so thoroughly entrenched in independence she had cut herself off from everyone. She didn't even have a houseplant that depended on her.

And then had come the thrill of her Sera joining her at the airline. She got to show her the ropes. Naively, she told Sera at the time that it was all about world travel, expanding her horizons, learning about other cultures. Turned out it was just about shoe shops and hotel amenities. Where did that all go wrong?

It had been a great day when Sera had arrived in Sydney. Of course she'd brought all her usual drama with her and unpacked that before her toiletries bag, but that's what Bella was there for.

'What do you mean you didn't tell them?' Bella remembered standing in the kitchen of her and Curtis's small apartment with her hands on her hips. Seventeen-year-old Sera had been there for three days.

'Dunno, just didn't. They won't notice.' Sera had been sprawled on the couch watching music videos.

'Sera, you're their daughter; they'll be worried sick about you. And sit up straight when I'm talking to you.'

Bella walked over and pushed the off button on the remote control. 'If you're going to cavort off to another city two states away, you have to start taking responsibility for your actions. Get on the phone and ring Mum now.'

'Do I have to?' Sera whined.

'Yes! They'll have the police scouring Hobart for you.'

Sera picked up the phone and rang her parents' number. She let it ring twice then tossed the phone down. 'No answer.'

'Give it here,' Bella said crossly and pressed re-dial.

'Hi, Mum,' she said. 'It's me. Sera's here with me . . . oh, did you? How did you know . . . oh, right. Yes, I see . . . yes, that makes sense. No problem. Speak to you later.'

'See, she wasn't worried, was she?' Sera said. 'So they don't care.'

'Well, no, she wasn't worried, She overheard you on the phone booking the flight so she thought you'd be here. She said that you must have had your reasons for not saying good-bye. They do care, Sera, they're just different, you know. It doesn't mean they don't love you. You must have really hurt them taking off like that.'

'They'll get over it. What's for dinner?'

It hadn't taken long for the two girls to break open a bottle of sauvignon blanc and sit down to a meal that went long into the night. They'd laughed and talked, made plans and reminisced. As Bella cleaned the kitchen at one o'clock in the morning, she looked at her baby sister asleep on the couch and was so happy that she'd come. Her little Sera was finally back under Bella's wing where she belonged.

Bella sipped the last of the tea and stood, swinging her bag over her shoulder. She shouldn't have been so overprotective with Sera. She should have encouraged her to stand on her own two feet more often. But she hadn't, she'd let the guilt take over and had babied her from day dot. When they'd caught up several weeks ago at the Four in Hand, Sera had been wonderful, but her kid sister was reverting to her old ways and a tangible, growing resentment between them was the result. They really needed to have a talk.

As Bella left D'Accord that sunny afternoon she made a promise never to go back.

~28~

'Sally, you're pulling my arm out of its socket!' Chantrea scolded gently. 'I'm coming, I'm coming.'

'But, Mummy, it's my favourite shop in the world. Hurry up.'

The family's outing to Bookley Books in Newtown was Chantrea's way of offering an olive branch to her mother without actually admitting defeat. Dara Kim was just relieved that life was calm in her family again.

As usual King Street was abuzz with energy and eclectic locals. Bohemians philosophised over soy lattes, uni students in Doc Martens combed vintage shops for treasures and young families in tie-dye and dreadlocks shopped for organic groceries. Blonde daytrippers from the North Shore toted stacks of shopping bags and exclaimed, loudly and in well-rounded vowels, how 'unique' and 'interesting' Newtown was.

Chantrea asked Sally and her mum to wait as she checked on the price of a Dior handbag in the window display of Play It Again, Sam. As they waited, a small girl and her grandmother stopped nearby to cross the road.

'Hello, what's your name?' Sally asked the little girl.

'Patsy,' the little girl answered shyly.

'*Ter ke/neang yeay tha me*?' The girl's grandmother asked Patsy in Khmer what Sally had said.

'*Ke/neang yeay tha sour sdey heay sor chhmous nhom*,' Patsy interpreted for her and turned back to explain to Sally. 'My grandmother is on a holiday from Cambodia. She can't talk English.'

Sally beamed at her new friend, 'This is *my* grandmother and she is from Cambodia too.'

The two elderly women smiled at each other and began to chat in Khmer.

'Mum,' Chantrea called from the shop door, 'they only take cash. Do you have thirty dollars on you? I'll have to go to the bank.'

Dara Kim turned to pass Chantrea the money as their new friends went back to crossing the road. Patsy waved goodbye just as a bus slowed to pull in at the stop, but to Sally's horror Patsy's grandmother moved to step off the gutter into the path of the vehicle.

'*Te chhoub ian kroung*!' Sally shouted shrilly, and the woman pulled her foot back sharply as the bus hissed to a stop, just centimetres in front of her ashen face.

Chantrea and Dara Kim had watched in shock, frozen in the doorway of the shop. Patsy's grandmother was pale and shaking as she bent to thank Sally in a volley of Khmer. Sally responded, understanding every word the woman said.

Dara Kim and Chantrea rushed to embrace Sally as Patsy and her grandmother assured them they were fine and made their way towards the pedestrian crossing.

Sally looked worriedly at her mum. 'Sorry, Mummy, I know you don't like Cambodian talking, so I don't do it when you're around.'

Chantrea was too shocked to speak. Her child was not only bilingual, but also quick-thinking enough to prevent a tragedy. She looked down at Sally, and something shifted within her. Suddenly she understood everything her mother had tried to tell her about their history – and their future.

'Darling, I am so proud of you. And you know what? I think I'd like you to help me learn Khmer too.'

~29~

'Damn!' Bella cursed her own clumsiness as 1A's chutney flipped onto the floor.

'Oh my, the perfect Bella makes a mistake,' Asif teased as he walked into the galley. 'What could this mean?' He raised an immaculately arched eyebrow and bumped hips with her on his way past.

'Oh, shut up, Asif.' Bella's comment bounced right off his broad shoulders and he grinned.

She peeked in the tiny oven to check on the chipolatas. Two more minutes. She stood staring at the storage boxes stacked around the galley. *Cups*, the label read. *Cups*. She read it again. *Cups*. Fucking Curtis! *Cups*. Nice simple soothing cups. She knew the cups were neat, tidy and organised inside the boxes. *Cups*. FUCK HIM!

Although it had been ages since he'd called to announce his engagement, she'd only mailed the signed divorce papers before this morning's LA flight. And she was fine. She was sooo over him. Good luck to him and his new wife. She didn't care. She'd let it all go. *Cups*. Neat, tidy cups.

She opened the crate. Yep, there they were, all organised. Nothing out of place. Just like her: together, organised and calm.

The sizzling chipolatas reclaimed her attention and she plated them artistically, wiping away a minuscule speck on the china and creating a tiny smear, which she wiped again, more vigorously. It seemed to have disappeared, but she wiped again, just to be sure.

Poor Sera, she was a great mum. And so busy. She tried to keep up with her job, keep her mother-in-law happy, and now the renovation would mean more stress. She should give her a call. She wiped the corner of the plate again, peering at the pristine china for any hint of a streak.

Maybe she could organise a few days' leave, and whisk Sera and the kids off to for a mini-break at some lovely five-star place in Sydney. A flush of excitement gripped her. She could take the kids to see some city sights, book Sera in for a massage and some pampering; maybe she'd even organise a week of dinners to be delivered while the kitchen was out of order and then she –. Bella abruptly stopped herself. Damn, she thought, I'm doing it again.

'There's nothing there, my OCD one,' said Asif, bringing Bella out of her reverie with a jolt. 'Just serve the bloody thing, will you?'

'Oh, right, yes, of course,' Bella murmured and hung the tea towel, neatly folded, onto the rail, then quickly whipped it away and tossed it into the laundry box. 'Oh dear, where's my head? That tea towel has food on it: I could have single-handedly caused a cross-contamination incident.'

'Oh, Bella,' Asif sighed, now more worried than teasing. 'You've got to let this stuff go a little bit, my darling.'

Bella ignored him and finally got the chipolatas to her passenger. As she passed the young girl in seat 2A, she stopped to see how she was.

'Are you having a nice flight, Ruby?' she asked.

'Yes, thanks. I'm doing a scrapbook of my ballet concert,' the nine-year-old replied. 'See?'

Bella stepped into Ruby's generous first-class space and sat down on the little seat opposite. 'You're a ballerina, how lovely!' she said and smiled at the photos of Ruby in assorted costumes.

'Yes, here I am in the mermaid costume, and there's me in the *Nutcracker*, and look at this one, this is my favourite: I'm a princess.'

'They're lovely,' Bella said, smiling at the photos. 'Wow, you're all so suntanned, was the concert in summer?'

'No, that's the fake tan they make you put on.'

'Surely not,' Bella said in amazement.

'Yes, my mum wasn't at all happy.' Bella followed Ruby's gaze to where her mother dozed in the seat across the aisle. Ruby dropped her voice: 'I was too embarrassed in the beauty salon to take off my bathers so I had strap marks on my shoulders. I got in so much trouble with Miss Petrice, the ballet teacher.'

'I hope it didn't spoil the concert for you,' Bella said.

'No, it's all right. I've stopped now. I'm doing gymnastics instead, which is way more fun. I liked ballet but I didn't like the exams and stuff.'

'Well, I bet you'll make an even better gymnast,' Bella said, returning the scrapbook and standing to leave.

'Thanks,' Ruby said, picking up her glue stick.

Bella smiled at Ruby's bowed head. She rarely found herself bonding with children on flights. She'd cluck over the babies with the rest of the crew, and make sure any young charges were comfortable and happy, but something about this girl really struck her and she had found herself enjoying her company on the long flight.

She had always thought mothering was all about washing and cooking and had never considered the possibility of actually enjoying a child's company. The thought nagged at her mind the next day as she wandered the chic boutiques of Rodeo Drive. Was it just that there was something special about Ruby or was something changing inside her?

For the first time, something inside Bella relaxed and she breathed life into a hope, a desire for a future she'd thought she could never have, and in that moment she knew exactly what she wanted in her life.

~30~

The women walked through to the lounge room. Mallory's house was like an homage to a Big Brother set. Sera loved the teenage feel, which suited Mallory's family perfectly.

Low macro suede modular suites extended into day beds, flanked by plastic moulded Space furniture pedestal tables. A pinball machine hulked in one corner and a large arcade ski game balanced the room in the other corner. *Dolly* magazine, *Grazia* and *Cosmo* were strewn across the coffee table and the walls boasted signed rock concert posters. A platter of nachos was awaiting the start of tonight's Stitch 'n' Bitch.

Sera's attention was drawn to a new artwork hanging over the Jetmaster. The metal square framed a series of varying-sized stainless steel circles, all jostling for position. They'd been delicately placed to give the illusion of bubbles floating to the sky.

'Mallory, I just love your new sculpture,' she said. 'Who's the artist? I haven't seen anything quite like it.'

'Oh, no artist,' Mallory laughed. 'I just whipped it up one rainy afternoon.'

'You're kidding. But how?' Sera had always been very impressed with Mallory's artistic flair, but this was a professional looking piece.

'I just went to the plumbing supplies section at Bunnings, bought some bits and pieces and glued them all together.'

'But it's so precise and delicate. You've really got an eye for form and placement.'

'Oh, thanks, just a bit of fun,' Mallory replied, then glanced towards the front door as its chime announced a new arrival. 'Oooh, goody,' she said. 'Our guests are here.'

Drinks were poured in record time as the group was desperate to hear about Sam's latest efforts on the dating scene. Mallory's thumb was a blur over the keypad of his phone.

'Oh my God, Sam, she wants to have sex with you!' Mallory squealed.

'What?' Sam almost choked on his beer. 'How do you get that?' he demanded, leaning over Mallory's shoulder as she deciphered the text he had received from Phoebe after their one-and-only date.

The Stitch 'n' Bitchers were gathered at Mallory's house for their monthly get-together, but so far all they had managed to achieve was a detailed dissection of Sam's date with the bikini model.

Rubbing his head self-consciously and blushing bright red, Sam looked to Jacqueline and Chantrea for support and got nothing more than wide-eyed nods of encouragement.

'Mallory?' said Chantrea. 'What does it say?'

'Well, the first line here, that's "I loved tonight."' Mallory explained as she pointed at *I <3d 2nite*. 'See, the less-than sign with the three? That's a love heart on the side, then the "d" that follows puts it in the past tense. Then she writes "*4U A3*" which everybody knows means "For you anytime, anywhere, anyplace." Obviously she means sex.'

'Oh, obviously,' Sam said sarcastically, then buried his face in his hand. 'Man, I'm so old, so out of touch.'

Mallory went on with the cryptic code-cracking. 'Then she says *@teotd ur2gtbt*, which is "At the end of the day you are too good to be true". Then *TMB* means –'

'Yeah, "text me back", I'm not that old, I got that one.'

'So you're in, buddy.' Mallory grinned at Sam. 'Are you going to follow it up?'

'I sent back a message saying that I'd had a lovely evening,' he admitted.

The girls exploded with laughter. Even Jacqueline couldn't hold back a rather unladylike chuckle.

'Oh jeez, Sam, the horny bikini model says she wants to bonk your brains out and you reply like you've just been out with Gidget,' Chantrea said.

'I thought I was being gentlemanly and polite!' Sam tried to defend himself.

'So, did she respond?' Sera asked.

'Yes. Though I've no idea what she said. Just scroll down, Mallory.'

Mallory read quickly, then smiled sympathetically at Sam. 'Well, your gentlemanly charm killed the chance of sex. She's put "AYSOS", which means; "are you stupid or something".'

'Oh shit.' Sam couldn't help it, he threw his head back and laughed as the girls joined in, until they were all gasping and wiping tears from their faces.

'Dating is so awful,' Sam groaned. 'You have to laugh or you'd cry. And,' he admitted self-consciously, 'there's more.'

'What?' they all cried.

'You can't hold back now, Sam,' Mallory said, laughing.

'No, okay. Well, I did go on another date last week. It was with a woman I was friends with at uni and I ran into her in Oxford Street with the girls on the weekend. She'd heard about Grace and when she said she was also single I asked her out for a curry.'

'Good work, Sam-the-Man,' Mallory gave him a high-five. 'So?'

'Well, it all went pear-shaped, so I called it a night and went home.'

'What?' Chantrea leapt to her feet in indignation. 'Back up, proper details please.'

'Okay,' Sam relented. 'Well, when she got to the restaurant, I remember thinking she was really overdone. You know, make-up trowelled on, very fussy clothing, and her top was really low and revealing.'

'Hmmm,' Chantrea said, 'it sounds like she was pretty desperate.'

'And then she went on and on about her marriage break-up, her failing architectural career . . . even her eczema!'

'Gross! The rule is no skin disease stories on a first date,' Chantrea said. 'So what was the goodbye like?' she asked.

'Well,' Sam answered, blushing again, 'that was the worst bit, I went to peck her on the cheek but she turned her face and went the tongue pash!'

'Ewwwwww!' the women groaned as one.

'I know, it was dreadful. I think I'll stay home and watch *PlaySchool* re-runs with the girls in future.'

Sera basked in the warmth of her friends' conversation and laughter, and for the first time that day felt relaxed and calm. What with the renovation, and taking on extra shifts at Dior to help pay for it, she hadn't had time to catch up with many of her friends since the last Stitch 'n' Bitch and had really been looking forward to the night. And she was so relieved to be getting on better with Bella again. It had shaken her to the core to be scolded like that at the park.

And it was such a relief to get away from the chaos of her half-renovated house for the evening.

The group talked long into the night and barely a stitch was dropped, let alone purled. Chantrea briefly touched on her difference of opinion with her mother, opening up a barrage of mother and mother-in-law stories. Mallory regaled the group with the latest gossip on the Jamaican salesman at Vince's Luxury Yacht dealership, dropping hints about the latest socialites seen disappearing with him into the cabin of the luxury cruiser. And Jacqueline informed them of a new technique for tomato stain removal.

Eventually it was time to head home. As they exchanged air kisses Jacqueline casually remarked, 'Sam, you know your second date? The old friend?'

'Yes,' Sam said, buttoning his jacket.

'I'm sure if she'd been less needy she would have held on to her man in the first place. It sounds as if she pushed him away.'

The other women gaped at Jacqueline, but Sam simply pecked her on the cheek, smiled and said, 'Good night, Jacqueline.'

~ 31 ~

They were shopping for funeral clothes – well, at least Mavis was – and Joan was happy to go along for the trip and get away from the mess and noise of the renovation.

Mavis wanted a smart burgundy wool blazer for her brother-in-law's wake and Joan was keen to explore Westfield's new orthotic shoe shop, so they parked the car, had a cup of terrible tea in the food court and headed off on their own errands.

After giving the harried young shop assistant a workout racing to the store-room and back again so she could try on several pairs of shoes, Joan selected a navy blue loafer and a cream mesh lace-up and returned to the mall, satisfied with her purchases.

Suddenly she recognised the familiar figure of Jacqueline, entering L'Occitane, just up ahead of her. Joan hid behind a large sign hanging in the shop window, but still had a clear view of her neighbour browsing inside the shop.

A handsome young sales assistant hovered nearby, encouraging Jacqueline to try a new hand cream. Jacqueline gave him a beguiling smile and pointed to a product on the other side of the store. As he turned away, Joan watched as Jacqueline swiftly slid a small bottle of something into her coat pocket.

The assistant returned with the product she'd requested, but Jacqueline simply glanced at it, shook her head and left the store with a triumphant toss of her hair. Joan noticed the flush of color in Jacqueline's cheeks and the bright smile on her face: she was clearly on a high.

Jacqueline's heart was pumping as she fingered the perfume bottle in her pocket. She wanted to laugh out loud at her audacity and daring. The thrill buzzed through her body, heat glowed on her face and the back of her neck. She strode quickly away from the shop, wanting to separate herself from the scene as soon as possible. Within a few paces logic kicked in again and she realised she was heading the wrong way. She needed to go back towards David Jones to pick up the boys' school shirts.

She turned and suddenly her heart banged against her chest. Her breathing shortened. Joan was standing right outside L'Occitane. Had she seen her? Had she been caught? No, surely not. Not like this, not by the interfering old bat from next door. Jacqueline sat heavily on a bench in the centre of the mall's wide thoroughfare, her delight evaporating into anxiety.

Surely Joan wasn't that observant. And as if the old woman would be loitering around spying on her, anyway. No, it was impossible, impossible that anyone would ever find out. They couldn't. She was the perfect one; the Supermum. The One Who Did No Wrong. Shoplifting was such a feral petty crime. So embarrassing.

But what if she had been seen? What could Joan do? Then it hit her. The ultimate punishment! Her hand went to her feverish cheek as the thought seeped in. Not that. Anything but that. She'd rather go to jail. If Joan had seen her, then Jacqueline Bouvier – the perfect, the saintly, the untarnished Jacqueline Bouvier – could become the subject of neighbourhood gossip!

~32~

Mallory had the top down and the music up as she whizzed over the bridge, happily singing along to the Veronicas and revelling in the unseasonably warm, spring evening air.

Her lovely Vince had been so distracted lately. Working back late every night, important phone calls that took him out to the backyard for lengthy conversations – he even worked on Sundays now, the poor love.

And their sex life had suffered recently, Mallory thought with regret. He'd just been too tired or stressed to indulge in their usual level of feisty, regular and adventurous sex. Mallory couldn't understand why other women whinged about having sex with their husbands – even Sera saw sex as a chore. Mallory shook her head incredulously.

But tonight's the night, she thought with an excited grin. Vince was working late at the dealership again and she knew he would be alone. She had a basket full of oysters, chocolate, champagne, and UDLs of Jack Daniels and Coke for Vince. She was planning to seduce him at work.

She pulled her Golf into the parking lot of the pet supplies warehouse next door to the dealership so she could sneak up on him. Under her trench coat she wore red crotchless knickers, a push-up lacy bra and suspender belt.

Mallory sneaked through the back door that led directly into the staff room, placed the basket on the kitchen table and opened the door into the office area. He wasn't at his desk and the office lights were off, so Mallory pushed open the heavy glass showroom door.

From the huge spa, pergola and faux patio in the corner of the massive space came the roar of the Jacuzzi jets. Vince had installed it to create an air of luxury, he'd once told her.

Giggling with excitement, Mallory tiptoed closer to the softly lit spa. She rounded the enormous bow of a boat to be slapped hard in the face by a sight that took several seconds to sink in.

What the fuck? Sex? In the spa? Mallory registered Sharee's bleached, bedraggled mane, and her tattooed anaemic back hunching mid-thrust.

'Oh, yeah baby, you're my little fuck-puppy, aren't you, baby?' came Vince's growl.

Mallory paled; the floor tilted. She grabbed the boat to steady herself. That was Vince's nickname for her. She shuddered, suddenly cold in her lace and satin. It wasn't only her nickname that was being shared. That was her husband, pumping away in the surging water.

At the door of her car, Mallory vomited. She ripped off her bra and suspenders in disgust, her hands shaking violently, and left them where they fell on the cracked bitumen. She pulled a cotton dress from the backseat over her shivering body and slumped into the front seat, only to lean out the window and vomit once more.

She had to get away – she didn't know where to, she just had to fly, as fast as she could, get to safety, away from the danger, away from what she'd seen.

As the car skidded into the street, tears cascaded down Mallory's cheeks, dissolving the glue on her false eyelashes. She tried furiously to brush them away but the left one re-applied itself to her upper cheekbone, blocking her vision.

She stomped on the accelerator as she turned onto the highway and slammed straight into the garbage truck reversing out of a driveway on her left. There was no time to brake. Her little Golf made hardly a dent in the massive truck as it buckled and folded into the metal.

The sickening sound of shattering glass, the shriek of the truck's brakes and the squeal of twisting metal penetrated the rhythm of the hydro love-making.

'What in the hell was that?' Vince said, pulling away from Sheree's probing tongue.

Sheree looked up momentarily in the direction of the noise, and listened.

'Who gives a shit?' she said, and leaned over to pick up the facemask and snorkel.

~33~

Jacqueline was worn out. She'd been extra, extra good this afternoon. She'd volunteered for school tuckshop duty, and washed, polished and vacuumed not just her car, but Thomas's car as well. She'd straightened up the garage, purchased every requirement for the boys' summer school uniform, booked dental appointments for all three of her boys and cooked and served dinner – boeuf bourguignon, their favourite. After dinner, when her husband had retired to his study and the boys were upstairs doing their homework, she'd whipped up a lemon-poppyseed cake and dropped it around to Thomas's father at the nursing home.

It was after ten when she finally dropped the keys on the hall table and entered her kitchen. Her jaw dropped. Sitting opposite, eating a mandarin, was Joan.

'Hello, Jacqueline,' Joan said.

'Joan, what are you doing here?' Jacqueline asked.

'I thought we needed to have a little talk,' the older woman said calmly.

Jacqueline feigned innocence. 'Goodness, Joan, what on earth could be so important we have to discuss it in the middle of the night? Shall we talk another time, perhaps when –'

'Don't bother, Jacqueline,' Joan replied quietly and the other woman wilted in defeat. 'Pop the kettle on, will you, love?' she added.

Jacqueline gratefully slipped into hostess mode, preparing tea and offering Joan a cup with shaking hands.

'Sit down, dear.' Joan nodded at the seat opposite and, anxiously, Jacqueline sat. 'It's tough, isn't it, love?' Joan started.

'What do you mean?' Jacqueline said, suspiciously.

'Life, kids, husband, home – it's all very difficult.'

'I cope, thank you very much,' Jacqueline said defensively, glancing behind her to ensure the kitchen door was closed.

'I know you *cope*, Jacqueline, I think you do an amazing job. You're truly the ultimate home-maker.'

Jacqueline's fragile ego revelled in the compliment and she relaxed a little.

'And how someone can be so busy, yet still be able to whip up the most amazing fruit flan I've ever tasted, is truly a miracle.'

That had her. Jacqueline beamed: she was putty in Joan's hands.

'And look at this place. It's a museum piece, it must be difficult to keep it so immaculate all the time.'

'Well,' Jacqueline confessed, 'it isn't easy. But Thomas insists it's perfect when he gets home each day, so I have no choice really – he works so hard. There's a lot of pressure on an orthodontist, you know.'

'What about you, though? You work extremely hard too, there's a lot of pressure on you as well, you know. You've got a far more important job; you're raising two young men to go out into the world and be productive members of society. All Thomas does is make pretty smiles prettier, and charge like a wounded bull for the privilege.'

Jacqueline laughed and then her face dropped. 'I know, Joan, it is a great deal of pressure. I lie in bed at night worried sick about the boys – do I over-mother them or under-mother them? Do I do the right thing by Thomas and keep the house to his standard? I just need to get it right. When it's all okay, Thomas is happy, then I'm happy and then the family is happy. You see? It all starts with Thomas.'

'You know,' said Joan, 'you remind me of how I used to be with my late husband, Barry. He was such a severe man. So strict. Of course, in my day it was expected that women stayed at home. Those who worked were frowned upon for neglecting their families.'

'Exactly right,' Jacqueline said primly. 'I couldn't agree more.'

'But at what cost, Jacqueline?' Joan asked. 'At what cost to us as women? I did what you do now: I did everything for my family. We sacrifice sleep, our appearance, our friendships, our youth. And all for what? So our children and husbands can go out into the world and achieve? What about us?'

'But Joan, that's what I chose, to help these men be great.'

'Have you ever considered that a great woman can be greater than even a man?' Joan asked.

'Of course she can,' said Jacqueline, folding her arms. 'But not me. I couldn't have a career, I'm not that clever.'

'Oh Jacqueline, you're very hard on yourself, and this kind of pressure can manifest itself in dangerous ways, my dear,' Joan said gently.

'What do you mean, exactly?' Jacqueline's voice was steely.

'I think you know what I mean. I'm not blaming you, I understand. You feel stifled and invisible. It happened to me too, dear. I did things that jeopardised my marriage and threatened my reputation. I hate seeing it happen to you.'

I don't know what you mean,' Jaqueline insisted, refusing to meet Joan's eye.

'Jacqueline,' said Joan, looking pointedly at her neighbour's special drawer on the other side of the kitchen. 'I know it's just a form of escape for you, but it's dangerous, this little habit of yours.'

'Please don't tell anyone, I'm begging you,' Jacqueline implored, grabbing Joan's hands. 'It's such a thrill, at the time, but later I feel so sick and I just hate myself.'

'I know, love, I know. It's a dreadful feeling, guilt, isn't it?'

'But then I do it again, the very next week,' Jacqueline continued. 'And again, and again. And every time I get away with it, I'm so relieved and so overwhelmed with guilt that I vow I'll never do it again. But then I do! I don't understand,' she cried.

'It gives you a feeling of control and nobody's caught you – yet – so it's your little secret. The sense of freedom it gives you must be exhilarating.'

'Yes, that's it! It's the freedom!' Jacqueline looked up at Joan with red-rimmed eyes. 'I just want to break the rules completely, be wild and bad for a few minutes and to have a tiny corner of something just for me.'

'Why don't you consider getting a job?' Joan asked.

Jacqueline stared at the table top, scratching an invisible mark. She eventually looked up.

'Oh, Joan, I couldn't. I just couldn't. I wouldn't be able to, I'd be hopeless.'

Joan tsked. 'That's a shame, love, because I think you can do anything you want to.'

~34~

The room was black. As Bella's eyes adjusted to the darkness she tried to remember which city she was in. Location dislocation was a common side-effect of her job.

Before she actually worked out her geography, she identified a sick, heavy feeling inside. She felt terrible. Why?

Then everything came flooding back. She had taken herself on a mini break to Palazzo Versace in Surfers Paradise in the hope of distracting herself from today's big event: Curtis's wedding.

Memories of her own wedding day rushed in and were as vivid as if her walk down the aisle had been last week. But by the time the tears of self-pity had travelled down the side of her face and pooled in her ears, Bella had pulled herself together.

She sat upright and grabbed a Kleenex. Right, she had an intensive schedule of self-indulgence to throw herself into and no quickie wedding ceremony in the Maldives was going to distract her.

She pushed the bedside button on the electric curtains and they slid open to shine warm Queensland sun on the room's opulent creams and golds. Bella focused on the relaxing surroundings while trying to calm her breathing.

*

At the day-spa Bella wrapped the fluffy bathrobe tighter around herself again, touched her hair, checked her nails, looked down at her pedicure; then did it again, and again. It was only when the other patrons started giving her odd looks that she realised what she was doing. She picked up a waiting room magazine and forced herself to focus on it.

Later, under the beautician's gentle hands, rather than letting her mind dwell on Curtis and his wedding day, she thought back to her morning. She must have checked her reflection at least ten times to make sure there was nothing in her teeth, no stray lashes, no lipstick bleed. Then she thought she'd found a spot on her bag, and that took another fifteen minutes of wiping, re-wiping and buffing before she was satisfied that it had simply been her imagination.

The beauty therapist left her to meditate while her face mask set and Bella felt the familiar tentacles of panic begin to entwine her. Her mind flashed up images of Curtis marrying a younger, prettier girl and she suddenly realised that with thoughts of him came physical reactions. As he came into her mind she had unconsciously sucked her stomach in and checked her nails.

The link was clear; she could see that now. Her obsessive tendencies were triggered by the emotions she felt about Curtis. But she didn't want to count floor tiles and spend her life in front of mirrors aiming for some idealised version of perfection. She was so sick of feeling inadequate. Maybe today was an opportunity to put an end to her compulsions. Just understanding the trigger had been a big step, and now she felt ready for more progress.

Bella held up her left hand and flicked at her index finger's acrylic nail until the plain stubby nail underneath was exposed. She looked at her ruined manicure and distress surged through her, but she took a deep breath and looked again.

This time it didn't look so bad. Maybe she could find out who she was under all the desperate striving for perfection. She laughed to herself nervously.

~35~

Mallory wanted the drugs back. Drugs to cancel out the pain, but mostly to stamp out the ache in her heart. She could cope with the agony of her broken ribs and crushed hip, but the emotional pain was too much to bear. Each time a nurse released more opiate into her system she sank blissfully away from the wrenching sting of betrayal that haunted her conscious moments.

But today they'd taken down the drip, said she would manage without it. Mallory knew they were wrong: she didn't know how she would ever manage again.

It's funny how they talk about heartache, Mallory thought, staring out at the heavy grey rain clouds threatening the CBD. The pain really is in my chest; like a serrated knife plunging straight into my heart. The doctor said that pain was from her broken ribs. But she knew better.

Showering today, for the first time since the accident, had been excruciating. But she'd welcomed the physical agony, spitting out the weak painkillers the nurse had given her. If she couldn't have drugged oblivion, she figured, it might help to lose herself in the searing pain of her battered body.

The woman she'd seen in the full-length bathroom mirror had aged fifteen years. She hadn't recognised the sad, downturned mouth and the hooded eyes. Her hair hung flat against her face in lifeless sheets. Her lips and cheeks, usually rosy with exuberance, were grey. A greenish-yellow bruise on her cheek and under her eye was the only colour in her face. Her collarbone jutted from the top of the white hospital gown that swamped her skeletal frame.

Now, as she lay back in her bed, she watched the clouds release their burden onto the skyscrapers and her eyes followed suit. She'd given up trying to control her tears in the days since the accident. It seemed like all she had done was cry.

When her lovely friends had heard what had preceded the accident, they had ministered to her broken ego as gently as the nurses had tended her broken bones. Sera had held her hand, listened patiently and dried her tears. Sam had offered to beat Vince up and then spent an hour gently brushing and plaiting Mallory's unkempt hair into her familiar plaits, as he did with his own daughters. His gentle touch had made her cry even harder.

When Chantrea heard, she'd ranted and raved and kicked the metal-legged visitors' chair and come up with plots to slash Vince's tyres, graffiti the walls of his dealership and hide dead fish in the boot of his car.

Jacqueline had tsked in disgust and for once had no suggestion for how Mallory could have been a better wife; it seemed even she knew an arsehole when she saw one.

Mallory turned her head at the sound of the door opening and stared numbly at her husband as he entered her private room, his arms filled with long-stemmed roses.

'Hi, how are you doing?' he asked, placing the flowers gently across the foot of her bed.

'Fine,' she said flatly.

'You had us worried. Thank God you came out of the coma.'

'Mmmm,' Mallory said, wishing she was back in that lovely dark place.

'Darling, I am so sorry,' Vince said, with a quiver in his voice. 'You have no idea how sorry I am.' He picked up her hand and squeezed it tightly. She looked at him, desperately wanting to believe him.

'I love you, my little Pookie, you know I love you more than anything.'

'What about Sharee?' Mallory asked. 'Do you love her?'

Vince scoffed. 'Of course not. It was a stupid, stupid mistake. A one-off. I'd had too much to drink. I wasn't thinking straight. I'd been working so hard I wasn't using my head at all. You must believe me, Pookie, you must.'

'Vince, I wish I could, I really do.' Mallory's eyes started to fill again.

Vince rubbed his own eyes with the heel of his palm and sniffed. 'Please, Mallory, you and Tilly mean so much to me. I don't know what I'd do if you left me.'

'I'm sure Sharee would take you in,' Mallory said bitterly.

'There's nothing between us, honestly. It's all over; she's just a filthy little scrag. She hit on me that night and I fell for it. I'm a weak, useless man and I let my dick rule my head for one stupid moment. What can I do to get you back, my beautiful wife?'

'Well,' Mallory said looking at him doubtfully, hoping she was doing the right thing, 'we'll have to have marriage counselling.'

'Absolutely,' he said with a grin, knowing he'd won. 'Anything else?'

'You'll have to sack Sharee,' she said.

'Sacked! Gone! Outta there! I'll do it today.'

'Oh, Vince.' She melted. The nightmare was over; they'd get through this together.

He wrapped his arms around her broken little body as she sobbed into his shoulder. 'It's all right, darling. It's all right, little Pookie, Vincie's here. I'm going to protect you, I'll never let you get hurt ever again.'

'Oh Vince, I love you so much. I thought I'd lost you,' she said between sobs.

'No, don't be silly, you'll never lose me, ever. I'll always be here for you, I promise, my beautiful little girl. I promise I will never ever let you down again.'

~36~

What to wear, what to wear? Another blouse flew off its padded hanger to land in a heap on the floor. Jacqueline's hands shook as she flicked through the array of floral, silk and knits.

She pulled another contender from the wardrobe and held it up against herself. Beige was respectable. Beige was humble yet reassuring. She threw it to the ground and sank down onto her bed.

What was she thinking, going to a job interview, for goodness' sake? She should never have taken Joan's advice. Her time would be better spent visiting poor Mallory in the hospital, or taking casseroles over to young Tilly. Now here she was with this ridiculous plan, already creating chaos and reducing her to a jittery, dishevelled mess. She looked at her reflection. Her baby paunch hung over her stockings, her auburn bob straggled across her face and her eyes were dull with sleeplessness.

Who'd want her in a patisserie? Patisseries were refined, elegant places where mille-feuille pastries were delicately layered into fine lacy towers; where high tea was sipped from fine china. And Laurent Boulangerie Patisserie in Double Bay was all that and so much more. It was French!

Finally she decided to team a knee-length black skirt with a crisp, white blouse, emulating the uniform of the elegant staff at the world-famous patisserie. She pinned her silver cupcake brooch to her shirt for luck.

Jacqueline's knees were shaking as she entered the shop. The customers were three deep as orders for brioche, baguettes and olive sourdough were drowned out by demands for éclairs, croissants and galettes.

André, the manager, had a thick Gallic accent that belied his unlikely ginger hair and freckles. He held out one of the café's wrought-iron chairs for her, glared at her slim CV and then back at her.

'So, 'ow are you? Eh?' he demanded. 'You are enjoying the sunshine?'

'Yes, thank you,' Jacqueline replied nervously. 'It's lovely outside.'

'What about inside? You like zis place? What do you think?'

Jacqueline turned to gaze at the enormous white chandelier, the black-and-white flocked wallpaper, the delicate three-tiered cake stands, the flashes of pink that accented the purely Parisian space. And the pastries, the breads, the gateaux, the mountains of elegantly prepared delicacies that seemed to shimmer in their display cabinets.

'Oh yes,' she breathed, 'it's the most beautiful shop I've ever been in.'

'Good! That is very good! You will work here. You will work at Laurent.'

'But, I . . . I haven't experience . . . I can't use a cash register.' Suddenly she was stricken with self-doubt. This guy was crazy hiring her, but she was forty and had never worked in her life.

'Bouff!' he exploded. 'We have a cashier. Look at you: you are beautiful, you have a passion for pastry, you have ze uniform. And you love my shop. Zis is good, it is a beautiful shop. You even have zis little silver cupcake brooch here, it's nice; I like it. Start Monday. Eleven.'

Jacqueline sat dumbfounded as he stood to click his fingers and roar at an unseen worker out the back. 'Monique, *ici maintenant. Les escargots sont terribles*!'

'I yell at them in French,' he confided to Jacqueline, 'because it sounds so much nicer.'

In a daze Jacqueline said goodbye and stepped out into the bright Sydney sun, blinking at the unexpected turn her life had just taken.

Then one hand flew to her cheek in panic. How on earth was she going to tell Thomas and the boys?

~37~

It had been a week since Bella had called Sera. She was coming to Sydney and she wanted to have some special time with her, alone. After Mallory's accident, Bella realised that life was too short for being cross at your sister. So she had arranged a five-star hotel suite for the weekend so that they could giggle, bond, chat and try and mend the rift that remained between them.

Sera had been relieved when Bella had rung with the offer. They were getting on so much better since their night out in Paddington, but things were still a bit on edge. Anyway, she and Tony were having a rough patch and a night away from the house would be a welcome relief.

Normally Sera would have spent hours planning her outfits and matching accessories for this brief foray into her old world. But this time it was different. She could sense from the brief call that Bella just wanted to see her, the real her. And besides, she was getting a little sick of the constant battle with maintenance. Not that she'd give up her acrylics or anything drastic like that, but she just felt more relaxed about the get-together. It was to be two sisters hanging out, not a fashion parade.

When the kids and Tony were happily eating their Saturday morning pancakes, and Joan had her cup of tea, Sera ran upstairs and donned the first outfit her hand touched: a black shirtdress and black long leggings teamed with pearls – perfect. She threw a beige and red ensemble into her favourite oversized Versace handbag (a gift from Bella) and jumped in the car with barely a backwards glance at her family.

This was going to be fantastic. It would be lovely to get back to their friendly relationship of the past and hopefully put the strain of recent times behind them.

Bella was thrilled at the thought of seeing her sister. It felt like ages since the two had shared time alone and she congratulated herself again at the brilliant idea of having a girly weekend. She had booked them both into the day-spa for a double massage on the Saturday afternoon. Once she would have gone for a facial acid peel but lately she'd realised her ageing face wasn't improving much under such extreme treatment. Maybe if the stress was eased away from her shoulders and back muscles then her face would relax and hopefully result in a more youthful appearance anyway.

She knew Sera needed some physical therapy too, judging by how tightly wound she'd sounded on the phone. She could always change it to Botox if she wanted to.

As always, Bella worried about her little sister. The beauty challenge seemed to be taking its toll on her. No matter how grounded or real a woman is, Bella thought, life in Sydney or Melbourne or LA or New York virtually guaranteed it wouldn't take long for hair or eyelash extensions, breast enhancements or fake tans to assume the status of normality.

But she knew that Sera's desperate struggle for beauty stemmed from somewhere so much deeper than merely living in a glam town. She knew it was the scar – the one thing the sisters couldn't talk about.

Bella had tried to bring it up once, asking Sera if it was

still bothering her. Sera had pretended that Bella had asked a different question and had rambled on down another path entirely.

Sera blamed her, Bella knew. Of course she did, she had every right to. Bella had been the one in charge and she hadn't done her job properly. Their own mother had often been absent and, sure, she had been fairly pathetic, really. But she had done her best, given the poverty, their useless father, the five kids under six. Bella had always known it wasn't her mother's neglect that had forced her into the role of Sera's carer, but her own guilt.

But that was then and this is now, she thought with a surge of positive energy, as she stepped out of the taxi and smiled at the uniformed doorman as he smiled at her long tanned legs.

Now was all about two sisters reconnecting. The first thing she had to do, though, she thought as the upholstered lift whisked her up to their suite, was change out of this mini-skirt. She never wore short skirts around Sera.

Sera pulled into the sweeping drive of the hotel. The doorman grinned at her cleavage as he helped her out of the car. 'Valet, madam?' he enquired.

'Yes, thank you,' she said and pulled the neckline of her top together.

She'd stopped on the way at Signature and bought Bella a little gift to thank her for the mini-holiday. The crisp white parcel with its perky raspberry bow balanced in her hand as she caught the lift up to their floor.

'Darling!' Bella said as she pulled the door of the suite open.

'Darling!' Sera replied and they embraced in a linen-crumpling hug. Two wide cupid bows of lipstick remained on each woman's cheek as neither had bothered with the fake air-kiss of their peers. They laughed and spent the next fifteen seconds thumb-wiping off their marks of genuine affection from the other's cheek. But the warmth of the kisses remained. On the surface it seemed as if any unresolved tension had long passed.

'Come in, sit down,' Bella said and swept her arm around the enormous room, which was decorated in the neutral colour palette of the truly wealthy. The white chandelier was a great cluster of resin antlers. The cushions were plentiful and luxurious in their range of metallics and had been perched daintily on the caramel and cream upholstered couch.

'This . . . is . . . awesome!' Sera gasped and spun around in the centre of the room. 'Honestly, I'm so excited I could jump on the bed,' she squealed.

'Be my guest,' Bella said and opened the double doors that led off each end of the sitting room to show two emperor-sized beds swathed in crisp white linen and faux fur chocolate throws.

'Seriously?' Sera looked to her sister like a child asking permission from her mother.

In answer, Bella kicked off her shoes and leapt onto one of the beds, springing away madly and laughing at Sera's surprised look.

Sera leapt up too and the women held hands and jumped up and down like a couple of kids. Bella reached over and hit the remote and soon MTV in quadraphonic sound was bathing the girls with bubblegum pop that only accelerated the silliness.

Eventually, when a truly stupid song came on, they fell in a heap. Sera's head rested on Bella's stomach.

'Do you remember Bananarama's "Venus"?' Sera asked.

'How could I forget?' Bella replied and smiled. 'How many times did the DJ play it for us during that summer?'

'I had the best summer of my life that year,' Sera said. 'Remember that fake ID you made me?'

'It was either fake your ID so you could come to the pub with me, or I'd have had to stay home and babysit you. How bad was it the night we turned up and Mum was at the bar?'

'Yeah, that was bad,' Sera said quietly.

'But she didn't even notice you, you got away with it!'

'Yeah, that was the bad bit.' Sera got up. The fun and games were over. Time to change the subject. 'So how was the flight today?'

'Oh, the usual. I won't put you to sleep with the details. Here, look, I got us a bottle of Cristal duty-free.' Bella went back into the living room and popped the cork with a 'woo hoo' as it went pinging off the chandelier.

'You never do,' Sera said and she sat cross-legged on the couch waiting for her drink.

'What?' Bella passed over her sister's drink and sat down on the armchair opposite, curling her feet under her bottom.

'You never talk about your flights, or your day, or your life at all.'

'Sure I do, I just don't want to bore you.'

'No, I've been thinking about us a lot lately. All you do is listen to me bang on about my petty worries,' Sera said and sipped her drink, keeping her eyes on Bella's reaction.

'It's my job,' Bella said with a smile. She didn't like where this was going.

'It's not.'

'Sure it is: you whinge, I listen, we drink. Fantastic. Cheers.'

'Isn't there anything *you* want to talk about?' Sera asked.

'Well, there is actually.' Bella's glass clinked as she put it down onto the granite-topped coffee table. 'I'd like to talk about Mum. You really need to go and see her. She misses you, and she misses the kids.'

'Oh, she misses the kids, my arse – she wouldn't even know their names.'

'Sera, don't be like that, she really wants to see you. She can't understand why you're not talking to her.'

'I talk to her. I told you I rang her, when? Last week?'

'Last month. And the time before that was two months.'

'Yeah, well, whatever. It just ends in such an awful, nasty way. I hate it. But I'm not *not* talking to her. It's just that I don't need the past constantly poking its nicotine-stained fingers into my life.'

'Sera, she's your mother. She wishes she could just phone for a chat from time to time.'

'Chat – ha. More like whinge.'

Bella was getting annoyed now. 'Funny, that's what she said about you.' As soon as the words were out she wished she could shove them back in.

'What?' Sera was on her feet now, her arms folded. 'See, that's exactly the kind of stupid, antagonistic thing she would say. Why should I bother with her when she never bothered with me? She did notice me in the pub that night, you know. I saw her watching me dance. But she didn't even care that her fourteen-year-old was out drinking in a hotel. What kind of mother do you call that?'

'I know she noticed, Sera,' said Bella. 'I got into so much trouble the next day, but I never told you because I didn't want you to think it was your fault.'

Sera's mouth dropped open.

'As punishment she burned all my magazines.' Bella's voice was quiet, barely a whisper. 'That's when I left.'

The realisation that Sera herself had inadvertently caused her greatest fear to happen took seconds to sink in. It was her fault. She'd caused her sister to leave for the mainland. To leave her alone in that cesspit. She became even angrier.

'If I don't see Mum anymore, Bella, it's because it's your fault. You shouldn't have left me there. You didn't see how rotten my life became after you went. I had no one. No one.'

'Oh, it's *my* fault you were a teenager and couldn't do the bloody laundry and look after yourself? Fine, blame me. Blame me for everything.' Bella's voice dripped with sarcasm.

'I may as well blame you. I wouldn't have this fucking scar destroying my body if it wasn't for you.'

It was out. The scar. Sera's words floated in the air in front of the two women in their ugly glory. For all of Bella's guilt about Sera's disfigurement in the past, she was now confronted with it like an open-palmed slap. The time had come to make a choice. So she chose. Then and there, after years of self-recrimination, should-haves and if-onlys, Bella decided it hadn't been her fault. Shit happens. Kids have accidents. Life goes on.

'That was not my fault, Sera,' she told her sister quietly. 'You shouldn't have been climbing.' The freedom of finally uttering the words sent chills down Bella's arms.

An explosion of disbelief hurtled from Sera's mouth. She stood and picked up her handbag. She was leaving. This was crap.

But there were things that needed to be said. Bella followed her sister to the door.

'Kids get injured every day from stupid household accidents,' she said. 'I'm sorry it happened to you. So very sorry. But I was working hard looking after the four of you. You might remember what it was like, Sera, but you don't know the physical hard labour of it all. I would go to bed at night exhausted. I had school all day, then home to a pigsty, to get dinner on the table and then clean up. Then you'd be thrashing and crying in your sleep so I'd comfort you, but I didn't get a good sleep. It was neverending. I couldn't wait to get out of there, to be free of the family. To be free of you.'

Sera stared in amazement at her big sister, her lifelong protector, her guardian angel. It was all a sham. 'How fucking dare you?' Sera shouted. 'You self-centred cow!'

With that she flung her Versace handbag across the room. It thudded against the wall before landing in a heap on the marble floor with little regard for its minute Italian stitches and softly buffed cowhide. Sera stood with her hands on her hips. There was no way she was leaving now.

'How dare *I*?' responded Bella, furious now. 'You cheeky little shit! *You* are the self-centred one. *You* are the one the world revolves around; *you* are the one who took my childhood from me, gatecrashed my twenties, and *still* moan about how I don't give you enough attention.'

'But you wanted me, you said you liked to look after me! You said I could hang with you in Sydney.' Even Sera could hear her whiny little-girl tone.

'Don't you understand, Sera? That was out of guilt. I couldn't not look after you. I blamed myself for that scar for years. I took jobs from Mum so that I could be your special guardian. I told her I'd watch you in the school play, so that she didn't have to. I made your lunch even when Mum was making the boys' lunches. Every time I saw your leg, it pushed me further into that role. Mum wasn't as bad as you think, Sera. I stole you from her.'

Sera leaned against the wall. Her knees shook and she allowed her body to slip to the floor. She hunched up, her arms hugging her knees. She was so confused.

'So all this time...?' She looked up at Bella with mascara-rimmed eyes.

'All this time I've been trying to make amends for that hideous scar on your leg.'

The words tumbled over each other as they spilled out in a rush from Sera's lips. 'But it's not your fault, Bella, it's not. I'm so sorry, I shouldn't have said that it was.'

'I know you didn't mean it. And I know now that it's not my fault.' Bella sat down on the floor next to her sister. 'I finally know.'

They stared at the dust-free skirting board opposite them as they tried on the truth and found it fitted them both better than any designer label ever had.

~38~

Sera signed the bill and relieved the waiter of the room service tray. Before she closed the door she watched as the young man turned to leave.

'Hmm, nice bum,' she commented as she brought the tray back to the coffee table.

'Oh, you dirty old woman. You're old enough to be his mother,' Bella laughed.

'Now, what's for dinner? Time to tell me what your big secret order was.'

'Guess,' Sera said with her two hands over the silver food covers.

'I don't know, pâté de foie gras?'

'Nope. I'll give you a clue, it's your favourite.'

'My favourite . . . Hmm, that means what *you* think is my favourite . . . you probably think it's caviar. Is it?'

'Nope.'

'Okay, lobster bisque and a dozen oysters?'

'Nope.'

'Oh, it's not a boring old Caesar salad is it?'

'No. It's your absolute, secret favourite, that no one in the world knows about.'

Bella stared at her little sister, her eyes widened in hope. 'It's not . . . ?'

'It is!'

'It's not really?'

'It really is!'

The girls both screamed in delight as Sera pulled off the silver lids. They screeched in unison, 'Double cheeseburger with hot chips!'

'And bacon!' Sera added in excitement.

'Bacon, gurghalargh!' Bella let her tongue roll out and drool in a very useless, yet most amusing, out-of-character impersonation of Homer Simpson.

'Do I dare ask what's in those little silver dishes?' Bella said.

'Guess.'

Bella was well and truly ahead of the game now, 'Chocolate ice-cream!'

'With . . .' Sera prompted.

'Chocolate chips?!' Bella squealed.

'And . . .' Sera smiled.

'CHOCOLATE TOPPING!'

'YAY!' The two women leapt onto the feast, shoving chips and burger into their mouths as fast as they could.

'Hey, do this,' Bella said, and dipped her chips into the ice-cream.

'That's disgusting, a bit of decorum, please,' Sera said with her nose scrunched in distaste.

''Snot 'sgusting, 'sbewdiful,' Bella said, her mouth full.

'They've forgotten the sauce!' Sera said.

'Oh, what?!' Bella moaned, 'See, that's the problem with a five-star joint like this, too good for dead horse! Any money they've got *aioli*.' She dragged the last word out and fluttered her fingers.

'At least we get to check out the waiter again,' Sera said from the phone as she rang room service.

Bella watched her sister across the room as she dialled. She took in the bare feet, the track pants, the face washed of tears-induced make-up smudges, the simple pony tail.

'You know, Sera, you look absolutely beautiful.'

Sera turned around with a scoff perched on her face ready to launch. Before it could, Bella hurried on. 'You really do. You should do the "less is more" thing more often. It suits you. You have great skin under all that bronzer, and simple pants and a tee really shows off that amazing figure of yours. You should embrace that look more.'

Rather than poo-pooing the sentiment, Sera looked amazed. 'Really?' she asked, actually taking the compliment on board for the first time in her life.

'Really,' Bella said, 'au naturel, you're a knock-out.'

After every last carbohydrate and lipid had been devoured by the girls, and the tray had been dispatched to the hallway for someone else to clean up, they sat back in the lounges with their champagne flutes freshly bubbling.

Sera looked around at the state of what had been only a few hours ago a pristine suite and which now resembled a sorority dorm room.

'This room is a pigsty,' she said.

Bella giggled. 'Care factor? Zero.'

'What's happened there?' They both knew she was delicately asking about her OCD.

'Well, little sis, as you know I've been in and out of therapy for years. And I've decided I'm done.'

'What?! You've always been a real advocate for therapy.'

'Yeah, I still am. I've just done enough for now. I've had a breakthrough.' Bella smiled eagerly and sat forward to face Sera.

'It happened on the day Curtis got married. I went

and day-spa'ed myself silly, came back to my hotel room, dropped my clothes on the floor, cried all night, and in the morning stared at my pile of clothes and didn't have the urge to put them away.'

'You crazy fool,' Sera joked.

'Then I kicked them. And they flew around the room. My scarf flicked across the bed, my stockings landed in the ice-bucket, my knickers draped from the chandelier. Then I emptied my entire suitcase and kicked that all around the room, too.'

'You didn't! How strange . . . for you, I mean.'

'Yes, strange, but very liberating. Then I emptied my toiletries bag all over the bathroom. And even squished toothpaste into the sink. And then I actually pulled the towels off the hook. And you know how much I like a neat towel rail.'

'I do indeed,' Sera said.

'And I laughed the whole time. It wasn't destructive, and I wasn't hysterical or anything; it was just more of an experiment. To see if I could do it and to see if I cared. And I didn't care at all. It so didn't matter. The sky didn't fall in or anything. Of course, I had to leave the maid a good tip, but apart from that, no impact.'

'Good on you! I'm very impressed.'

'Then – you won't believe it – I couldn't be bothered tidying it all up. I just sat on the couch and vegged out, and when it was time to go I shoved everything into my suitcase. Well, semi-folded. But it certainly wasn't outfit-ordered as per usual.'

'Go girl!' Sera chuckled, thinking of Bella with a disordered suitcase. 'Will wonders never cease?'

They sat and stared into space, reflecting on how far their relationship had travelled in such a short time. Finally, Sera spoke.

'You were always too good for him, you know,' she said, quietly.

'Yeah, I know,' Bella replied, and they clinked their glasses in cheers.

~39~

Today the Stitch 'n' Bitch group was going to help Mallory prepare for her home-coming tomorrow after her week in hospital. Jacqueline, Sam and Chantrea were already waiting in the hospital foyer when Sera arrived. They gave her happy hugs, all delighted that Mallory's journey to recovery was taking a big step forward.

Together they walked into Mallory's room, following their usual practice of softening their voices and offering a calm, sympathetic front to their emotionally exhausted friend.

But they were greeted by a pleasantly surprising sight. Mallory was sitting up in her wheelchair. She'd changed into a funky, hot pink zip-up hoodie, her face was made-up and her hair was shiny and brushed.

'Mallory! Look at you! You look absolutely amazing.' Sera got to her first and leant down to embrace the slight body. The others took turns to proffer their gifts and peck her on the cheek while exclaiming over the physical transformation.

Mallory grinned at her friends. 'He's come back to me,' she said proudly, as if she'd won a marathon. 'He wants me!' Their faces dropped as one. 'Don't you understand, guys? He's chosen me over that little scrag!'

'Mallory,' Sera said as gently as she could, 'are you sure this is the right thing for you?' She had sat through night after night of sobbing, watching the hurt and anguish of betrayal wreak its devastation on Mallory's fragile soul. She couldn't believe that in such a short space of time Mallory could make such a massive U-turn and go back to him.

'Yes, of course it is. He says he's really sorry, that Tilly and I are the ones for him and he's not going to leave us, that he's going to break up with her. He's going to pick me up tomorrow and take me home.'

Nobody quite knew what to say.

'Are you insane?!' Chantrea voiced everyone's thoughts.

'But Chantrea . . . guys?' Mallory replied, quite confused they weren't sharing her excitement. 'Don't you get it? I won! He's finished the affair. It's over; we're all going back to normal.'

Sam had to speak up; he couldn't stop himself. Mallory was such a lovely person, and Vince was clearly a creep. 'I don't think you should do this. At least think about it,' he implored.

'Sam, I've sat here hour after hour thinking. What else can I do, for God's sake?' she said, waving her hand at her crushed leg. 'It's not like I can go out dancing or go for a nice walk.' She swallowed the bitterness that was rising in her chest, determined to hold on to her happy mood.

'Look, of course I've thought about it, over and over, and I know you're all worried about me, and want the best for me, but this *is* for the best. I can't be on my own, don't you see? I wouldn't have a clue how to live by myself. I need Vince. And,' she said proudly, 'he needs me.'

Jacqueline, ever the pragmatist, knew from experience there was little anyone could do to convince a woman in love of anything sensible. 'Well,' she said, 'congratulations, darling. I hope you're both very happy.' She leant in to give her friend a hug.

Chantrea couldn't keep it together any longer. She grabbed Jacqueline by the arm and dragged her into the corridor as the others offered Mallory their hollow congratulations.

'What in the hell are you doing? Why are you congratulating her? That's like congratulating someone who's been diagnosed with dengue fever, for chrissakes. How can you do that?' Chantrea was livid.

A few months ago Jacqueline would have bitten back at Chantrea's anger, but now she could see that her attack wasn't personal. 'Chantrea, I know how you feel, it's very frustrating.'

'Fucking oath, it's frustrating.' Chantrea looked around as if to find something to punch.

'Settle down, this isn't going to help anyone. Take some deep breaths.'

Chantrea looked at Jacqueline in surprise. She was expecting – maybe even hoping for – a fight, somewhere to direct her anger. Instead, she followed Jacqueline's advice and felt less volatile as she flooded her lungs with oxygen.

'The only thing we can do is to be here for Mallory when it falls apart again. That's all. We can't stop the inevitable from happening; we'll just stay close to catch her when she falls.'

'But it's so unnecessary, Jacqueline,' Chantrea said. 'She doesn't need to fall, doesn't she see?'

'I think it's fairly obvious that she doesn't see what we can all see so clearly. But we can't tell her what to do, or how to feel, we just have to be here to help pick up the pieces when she comes to her senses.'

'Yeah, I understand,' Chantrea sighed deeply. 'Sorry for going off like that.'

'That's okay. Let's go back to the blushing bride.'

'. . . and guess where he's taking me in a few weeks to celebrate?' they heard Mallory bubbling to the others.

'Where?' asked Sera, trying to dredge up enthusiasm.

'Skiing! He loves skiing.'

Chantrea looked at Mallory's toe-to-hip plaster cast. 'How thoughtful of him,' she replied, darting a quick look at Jacqueline.

~40~

The thumping tones of Destiny's Child blared at full volume from the electric-blue 300ZX convertible. Sharee swerved into the car space and killed the engine, cutting the doof-doof off mid-beat, much to the relief of two older women waiting at the nearby bus-stop.

Legs as spindly as the stilettos which carried them appeared from the driver's side as Sharee swung herself, her hair and her bag out of the car, slammed the door and stormed into the pub. She was in a filthy mood. When Vince had called an hour earlier with the ominous 'We've got to talk', she knew what was going down. She knew the dutiful husband buried deep inside her dirty little meal ticket was threatening to emerge.

Now that wifey was laid up in hospital, she was sure Vince would try and wriggle out of the arrangement. They'd had it all planned. Vince was meant to leave that twitty little Mallory and set Sharee up in a fantastic Darling Harbour apartment, complete with her own masseuse, plasma screen TV and Vanuatu holidays.

Sharee Burns had been successfully upgrading sugar daddies since she'd turned eighteen. The first bloke had just been a general manager of an insurance company, but on a good wage. But by the time she'd broken up his marriage his wife had worked it all out and had put all the family assets in her own name, then sued the stupid bugger for the rest of the dosh, which had left him so strapped with alimony and emotional baggage he was good for absolutely nothing. Sharee had dumped him quick smart.

She plonked herself at the bar and sat sucking noisily on a raspberry vodka while she sized up the patrons. No harm in a bit of window-shopping.

Her second conquest had been more promising: a wealthy younger guy running a huge corporation. It was his family's business, so he had all sorts of delicious playthings: a magnificent property in Port Douglas, a yacht, and a massive inheritance in the pipeline. But when she'd pissed off his Alice-band-wearing fiancée, she'd also managed to piss off his family, and the crusty old matriarch had whipped away his money and toys faster than you could say 'trust fund'. She'd learnt valuable lessons in love along the way though, namely: don't fuck with the family and find out whose name the assets are in.

She reckoned Vince was it, her last-ditch attempt to land a big fish before she got hit with the ugly stick that came with reaching thirty. Vince meant pay dirt and no wife with broken legs was going to screw up her plan.

Of course the writing had been on the wall since Vince realised that Mallory had seen them doing the wild thing in the spa. He'd turned grey when he caught sight of the picnic basket and the stupid bitch's shoes in the carpark. She'd tried to buck him up with a spontaneous hand job, but he'd simply pushed her aside.

Ever since the stupid cow went and got herself smashed up by that truck, whenever they'd got together it had only been a quickie. Sharee knew her days were numbered. Thank God she'd invested in a timely little insurance package several months ago, when she'd stopped using her diaphragm. She'd known she was up the duff for ages but had waited to spill the beans when it would give her maximum benefit. And that time had come. Now she was armed and ready for action. Just let him try and dump her, she thought. She was ready to give him the biggest friggin' shock of his life.

Vince came in gabbing into his Blue Tooth as usual. His wraparound sunnies were in their permanent position on the top of his head, and his purple shirt co-coordinated perfectly with the complementary tie. He was a hot dresser, she had to admit. His hair was gelled into fashionable random peaks.

'G'day, darl,' he said, and pecked her on the cheek. 'Jim Beam and Coke, thanks, mate,' he said to the bartender. 'So how's tricks, kitten?' He addressed Sharee's cleavage.

'Great, darl. You?' she smiled charmingly and was pleased she'd remembered to undo her top two buttons to ensure the new La Perla lacy push-up bra was attracting his attention.

'Busy, love, so busy. I've got a huge client from Hong Kong nibbling at the bait at the moment. A massive deal. He wants the brand new Boadicea. This deal could put me in retirement.'

'A Boadicea? We haven't got one,' she said.

'Of course we haven't! They're fifty mil US! Not to mention seventy feet long. It wouldn't fit on the whole block, let alone in the showroom.'

'Well, how come the punter is talking to you, if you haven't got one?'

'Well, *he* doesn't know that, does he?' Vince replied. 'I have to let him think I have one until I can actually get my hands on one.'

'So why don't you just direct him to a dealer who does have one?' Sharee asked.

'Because that doesn't put a clear three mil in commission in my back pocket, now does it? Jeez Louise, you don't know much about business, do you, babe?' He glanced at her then indicated to the barman that he and the little lady needed a refill.

'Now, babe, we have to talk. Given the situation with Mallory, it's not such a great time –'

Sharee cut him short. 'I'm so glad you wanted to see me today, darling, I've got some wicked news. You're going to be so rapt, I just know it.'

Thrown off guard by her exuberance, Vince allowed himself to be distracted for a minute. 'What is it?'

'I'm pregnant.'

The peanut he'd just tossed in the air fell downwards and landed squarely in his airway. He choked and gagged, taking a gulp of his drink to wash it back into his mouth before croaking, 'What?'

'I'm pregnant! Almost four months'! Isn't it exciting?'

'But you can't be. I've had a vasectomy.' He shook his head in confusion.

Oh, she'd really fucked up now. Sharee's thoughts were in chaos. She plastered a smile on her face as she tried to grab hold of a solution to this unexpected information. Oh shit, oh shit, oh shit.

'Well, my, my,' she said finally. 'Nothing can hold back your feisty little swimmers, can it?' She grinned at him as she kneaded his bicep. She kept going – if there was ever a time to lay it on thick, it was now. 'What an amazing bloke you are. I've heard of this kind of stuff, of course, in fact they reckon it's pretty common in exceptionally masculine men.'

'Really?' he asked incredulously.

'Yeah! For sure! How is a couple of little snips going to stop your kind of strength?' She went on before he could think too much. 'Don't you see? This is meant to be, we're meant to be together, this is a miracle baby. Oh, you master, you hero.' She clasped her hands over her uterus and squealed in joy before uttering her *coup de grace* – the line she knew was going to be the money shot. 'And I just know that it's a boy.'

It worked. He was all over her. They sat at the bar for another hour, planning, talking and giggling; trying to feel the fetus move; talking about prams and schools, obstetricians and water births.

By the time Vince left the mother of his unborn child, his head was spinning in amazement. It was true, it was a miracle. It was time to move on. He owed it to this woman and to his little son. Mallory would be fine. Tilly was nearly grown-up anyway. It was time for a fresh start. He'd break it off with his old family clean and simple. Rip it off like a Band-aid. It would be a shock at first for them, but they'd be fine. After all, what really mattered was to be happy. For *him* to be happy.

~ 41 ~

For the first time Mallory truly appreciated the large open-plan living space of her home for a reason other than the aesthetic. She was still unaccustomed to negotiating the cumbersome wheelchair about and the wide front hallway and fashionably large front door were a blessing.

Vince closed the door behind them and tossed her hospital bag onto a beanbag in the sunken living room.

Thanks to Sera's hard work, the house was immaculate. The floors gleamed and every surface was clear of clutter. Sera had mentioned that she'd popped in to do the dishes, but she'd obviously worked her fingers to the bone. The place hadn't been this clean for years. Mallory hadn't discovered it yet, but the fridge was crammed with home-made casseroles and pasta sauces, and the pantry shelves groaned with baked treats from well-meaning neighbours, friends and the school community.

Vince pushed her over to the large glass-topped kitchen table where he replaced a dining chair for her wheelchair. As she passed the stairs, she caught sight of herself in the floor-to-ceiling mirrored wall. She'd gasped with shock. When she'd groomed herself this morning in the hospital, she'd thought she looked fairly good, considering her ordeal. But out of the realm of the damaged, ill and elderly, back home in her normal environment, she couldn't believe the vision that flicked past her eyes.

She was truly an invalid. Her face was devoid of life, her eyes were like sunken wells and the bruises yellowing beneath the cuts and scars gave her a creepy jaundiced look. Her broken arm was plastered from her fingertips to her shoulders and her broken leg stuck out straight in front of her.

It felt strange to be at home. Mallory was nervous, vulnerable and unsure how she would cope. She had no idea where she would sleep, how she would mother Tilly, do the washing or go to the toilet without the aid of the nurses she'd come to rely on.

She knew her friends would be there for her, of course, and Tilly was a big girl and was going to be a great help. But most importantly, Vince was there for her. He was still hers, he was home and he was going to help her get through this dreadful time.

There he was in the kitchen: what an amazing guy, popping on the kettle and fussing over a cake that had magically appeared from the pantry. She smiled at him but he seemed to drop his gaze just as their eyes met. He retrieved her bag and efficiently unpacked it, tossing the laundry into the washing machine and running the other bits upstairs. She heard him moving about on the floor above as drawers opened and closed. She was going to be safe in this man's hands, she just knew it.

Her mind wandered and began mentally designing her next art-piece, something in driftwood for the kitchen wall, perhaps. Vince reappeared downstairs again and continued making her tea. He brought it over to her and set her up nicely with a magazine, the cup of tea and a slice of nut loaf.

'Where'd the cake come from?' she asked as she nibbled the corner.

'That old bat that lives up the road, next to the florist's,' he said. 'It's been like Darling bloody Harbour on a Sunday here recently. God only knows how everyone found out you were coming home, but the freaking doorbell hasn't stopped ringing with people bringing around food. I feel like putting up a sign to tell them to stick their Meals on Wheels efforts – a man can't put his feet up for five minutes.'

'Oh, they're so sweet and thoughtful. Who were they, so I can thank them?'

'No idea who half of them were. Anyway, forget them, how are you doing? Do you need any pain relief?'

'No, darling, I'm feeling great, thanks. And thanks so much for today, you've been wonderful.'

'Well, I've made your morning tea, unpacked your bag, I guess my duty here is all done. Is there anything at all you need?'

Mallory looked up at her husband with a watery smile. 'Just you,' she said in a small voice.

'Yes, well, about that.' Suddenly Vince looked decidedly uncomfortable and, turning away from Mallory, he leaned on the kitchen sink that overlooked their swimming pool and tennis court. 'I'm afraid I've got some rather bad news.'

Mallory looked at him, her face frozen in disbelief.

'I'm so sorry to do this to you, Mallory, you're a great girl and all but it's just that I have to do the right thing by my son.' He moved out of her line of sight.

Mallory turned to stone. A gurgled questioning sound was all she could manage. Her head tried to follow him but the plaster cast at her shoulder prevented much movement.

'Whoops,' he said as he moved back into her eyeline. 'I haven't said this very well, have I?' He smiled down at her. 'Sharee's pregnant and I have to be with her and be a father to my boy. You know I actually always wanted a son and, considering you weren't able to give me one, it's just wonderful to finally have one.'

'But you had a vasectomy. We could have had a son, I wanted lots of babies!' Mallory was confused: she knew she was focused on the sub-text here, but she couldn't face what he was really saying.

'Yeah, right, what with you from your family of all girls, that's all I needed, a house full of chicks!' He laughed as if he'd just made a light-hearted pun. 'No, apparently one of my swimmers snuck through, it's truly a miracle.'

Mallory's desperate pleas were hushed. Her bruised and battered eyes stared silently up at this stranger.

'Oh, crap, look at the time. I must be off. We have an obstetrics appointment. Sorry, babe.' He leaned forward and stroked her hair apologetically as if she were a puppy left outside on a rainy day. And with that, he left. The slam of the front door resounded throughout the empty hallway and the living room.

Mallory sat statue-still while the silence invaded the corners of her house. There was no pain now. It was all gone. Everything was all gone. A little voice inside her whispered, *I told you so.*

Fifteen minutes later she tremulously reached out to the tepid tea. Her clumsy left-handedness knocked the teacup over. The stream of taupe liquid trickle across the table and onto the floor. She had no way of cleaning it up.

~42~

'What?' Tony had his mobile flattened against one ear and his left hand protected the other one from Cold Chisel's 'Cheap Wine' blaring from the juke box. 'Mum's there to mind the kids,' he shouted into the mouthpiece. 'Come on, we're at the Royal, it's just around the corner.' He listened to the few snatches of excuse that were audible above the pub noise. 'Hang on, Sera, I'll just go outside so I can hear you.'

Tony sidled through the crowd, dodging schooners as they sloshed past. He left the public bar to stand on the skinny patch of sidewalk on Broughton Street.

'Sorry, honey, that's better. So why don't you come down? I'd love to see you. The guys are all here. We're celebrating completion of the Potts Point job. Some of the wives and girlfriends are here too.'

He rolled his eyes as the list of reasons came streaming forth.

'You look fine, Sera,' he tried to reassure her. 'You're beautiful . . . you don't have to blow-wave your hair . . . just chuck on some jeans or something, it's just a pub.'

He knew he was fighting a losing battle. It was impossible to get her out of the house with no notice, especially to the pub. He gave up. 'Well, honey, I'd love to see you. If you can make it down, it would be great. We never go out together anymore. Okay, bye, love you.' He sighed and clicked end call on his phone. A grey Volvo shooshed by in the rain-slicked street, spraying his jeans with mist. He felt so alone. He missed her. He missed having a partner, a girlfriend, someone by his side. They weren't united anymore; they were no longer a team. It was as if they were just two people living under the same roof – like flatmates.

He went inside and up to the bar to wait for service. More and more each day he could feel Sera pulling away. Every time he kissed her or tried to hold her she'd merely endure it. She didn't push him away or anything, it was more subtle than that. It was her lack of enthusiasm when they embraced that was so heart-breaking. He just adored her. She was so clever, she managed her life – hell, all their lives – with such efficiency. And she was so sweet, she was one of those people that everyone who met her gushed afterwards about how *nice* she was, so *charming*, so *delightful*. And she had the cutest little smile when something tickled her fancy. I used to tickle her fancy, he sulked.

Tony was well aware that a woman's libido dropped off considerably after babies. He wasn't expecting to have sex with her every time they touched or anything. But he knew she was worried about that, he could read the signs when he reached over for her in bed at night to hold her and her rigid body lay there frozen, emitting every possible message that it just wanted to be left alone.

But he only wanted a cuddle. Was that too much to ask? It wasn't always about sex. Contrary to popular belief, men did have other needs, he thought, shaking his head and starting to feel quite indignant about his plight. He was just after respect, affection, conversation: the simple delightful elements of every healthy relationship. But, come to think of it, he was actually pretty horny right now.

The Royal was at its frenzied best. The pool tables were packed and the beers were being knocked back in a fashion that suggested the punters feared imminent prohibition. Freddy and George, two of Tony's apprentices, invited him to join them in the men's for a few lines.

He laughed. 'Not for me, boys, I'm a family man, you know, not into that stuff.' He was having an in-depth discussion about flooring with Shane Peterson, his chippy, and was feeling nicely mellow. He guessed he'd drunk more than he should, but it didn't stop him from saying yes when one of the lads slapped a shooter in front of him. The flaming sambucca took his chilled, mellow feeling, put it in a blender and transformed it into a shaken and stupefied sensation.

The men leaned into a circular bar table in the middle of the room and began a deep and meaningful conversation about women, which neither would remember in the morning. Shane suddenly leaped wide-eyed into the air. 'What the . . . ?' he exclaimed and turned. 'Oh, it's you,' he accused a petite platinum blonde who had just accosted him with a butt pinch.

The girl's locks were piled atop her head with stray pieces stringing about her face and neck. Tony could tell she was young. It wasn't just the unlined visage that smiled prettily up at him awaiting an introduction, but also the bizarre get-up that only someone with the confidence of youth would wear. Skinny-leg jeans clutched her calves and a billowing top scooped down to proudly display rock-solid breasts. A tiny useless piece of quilting stopped under the bust-line in a flimsy pretence at being a jacket.

'This is Tony. Tony this is Taylah, she's . . . umm . . . an old friend.'

'An old root, you mean, Shane,' she joked and put out a hand made twice as long by the length of her pearlescent fingernails.

'Nice to meet you,' said Tony.

Taylah smiled and shimmied in response. 'Nice to meet you, Tony. Hey Shane, why are you keeping all the good ones from me? This guy's gorgeous.'

'Aww shucks,' Tony said. He glowed at the compliment and instantly decided that the girl before him was a charming young lady.

Shane muttered something about watering the horses, and scarpered. Tony smiled broadly and fell into an easy conversation with the provocative Taylah. The flirting was like flint on a stone to Tony, who revelled in the seductive sparring. It had been a long time since anyone so attractive had paid him any attention.

The sambucca and the Bailey's that followed numbed his body and he was hardly aware that she'd snaked one arm around his waist, under his jacket. She was very sympathetic about his lower back pain that had gotten worse lately. And said she knew the perfect cure.

'It's all about stress management,' she advised. 'You need to relax. To let the stress out, you need release.'

'Really?' he asked, fascinated by this insight. 'I usually just see a chiropractor.'

'No, there's a better way to get release than that, beautiful Tony.' She gave him a look so lusty that only a dead man would miss the innuendo.

Tony's heart pounded. She was so sexy.

'Nobody needs to know,' she said. 'You deserve a good time.'

He *did* deserve a good time.

'So, Tony,' she whispered loudly in his ear to drown out the pub ruckus, 'there's a quiet room out the back, do you want to come?'

~43~

The tiny nymphette wrapped Tony's great log of an arm around her waist and tugged him into the direction of the rear stairway. Tony stumbled to the ground and staggered back to his feet again.

'Sera!' A shout came from the other side of the bar. 'G'day, Sera, how you doing?'

The guys loved Sera. Often, when they were building locally, she'd bring them lunch or a slab of beer at knock-off time. George and Freddy swept her off her feet in a big bear hug.

'Sera, Sera, Sera!' the chant went up in greeting as each of Tony's team kissed her on the cheek or hugged her hello.

Shane sidled up to Taylah. 'That's Tony's wife,' he whispered. 'You lose.'

'Damn,' she said, and blended into the background to sniff out another target.

'Sera?' Tony said thickly, his addled brain trying to process this latest development. 'Sera!' he called out when the reality of his wife's arrival finally emerged through the fog. He lumbered over to where she was surrounded by his men. The crowd parted to let the boss through. Tony grinned a big goofy smile and threw his arms out, knocking a glass of wine from a rather displeased patron's grip. 'Sera, you came! You came!'

'Hello, drunken one,' Sera said, and endured his crushing embrace with a squeal and a laugh. 'What have you been up to?'

'Just a few drinks with the lads. I'm so glad you're here. Let me get you one. Bar-keep, a glass of your finest chardonnay for my missus! And a round for the boys!' Tony leaned against the bar and beamed at his wife. ''T's so good to see you. Jeez, you look good.'

'Good to see you too, Tony, how was work?'

'Work's great, drinks after work are great, I'm great. Jeez, you look good.'

'I know, Tony,' she said, patting him on the back of the hand. 'You just said.'

'But you do,' he insisted. 'You always do, you're gorgeous. And so lovable, everybody loves you, you know that, dontcha? Everybody.' He turned to the room. 'Who loves Sera?' he yelled into the crowd.

'YEAH!' the crowd yelled back. The rabble was pissed enough to love anybody at that point.

The jukebox finally stopped its homage to INXS and someone with a bit of musical taste took over the DJ-ing. 'Boulevard of Broken Dreams' by Green Day came on.

'Remember this?' Tony grabbed Sera's hands and stared earnestly in her eyes. 'Remember? Dance with me – come on.'

They wrapped their arms around each other, enjoying their bodies moving in time to the song that had meant so much to them nine years ago.

Back in 2000, on the day they had met, Tony had been the last to board the plane, his overgrown black curls flopping in his eyes, and his cheeks flushed with running from the bar at the end of the terminal to his flight from Hobart to Sydney.

'So sorry,' he'd said to the flight attendant as he tried to juggle his laptop, brown suede jacket and fumble in his pocket for his boarding pass. He flashed her a cheeky smile. 'I was deep in conversation with an old Digger at the bar, couldn't get away from him.'

He finally retrieved a slightly soggy boarding pass from the back pocket of his Calvins.'Ah . . . Oops, I seem to have used this as a coaster.' He grinned again.

'Never mind, sir,' Sera said. 'Your seat is easy to find: it's the only empty one.'

'Oh dear, did I keep everyone waiting for long?'

'Never mind,' Sera said again, her professional demeanour firmly in place. 'If you could just take your seat, the captain can get us all on our way.'

Tony found himself staring at her lips, watching them move as she spoke. 'Oh, of course, yes, I'll do that,' he said, snapping out of the moment.

As he apologised his way toward his seat, Tony felt flustered and slightly confused. He put it down to the Guinness. He threw his jacket in the overhead locker as the seatbelt sign dinged, then squeezed past the two other passengers into the window seat, pushing his laptop under the seat in front.

Sera's face was a mask as she delivered the safety routine, her hair tamed by pins and spray, and those lips hidden behind a veneer of red gloss. In his mind Tony saw her face break into a smile, her hair fall soft and golden onto her shoulders and those lips – ah, those lips. Right then, he decided, he had a mission. He would make that beautiful girl smile – not just a regulation Air Australia smile, but a true smile, just for him – by the end of the flight.

*

Sera's heart had banged so noisily in her chest when the guy with the curls came on board that she was sure he would hear it above the clipped professional voice she struggled to maintain. There was something so endearing about his ridiculously messy hair, his cocoa coloured eyes – even his scent gave her tingles of pleasure.

He didn't make any effort at subtlety during the quick pond hop, taking every opportunity to try and make her laugh. 'Nuts?' she'd asked when serving drinks. 'No, perfectly sane,' he'd replied.

His charming attempts at winning her smile were actually working a treat, but only on the inside. She wasn't going to give in that easily. It took all her will power to remain professional and cool. She rushed back to the galley a few times to lay a cool flannel on her burning cheeks and take some deep, calming breaths.

She'd had plenty of passengers try to pick her up in the past. It was one of the downfalls of the job. She'd even accepted a few offers of dinner and one had actually become a relationship for a short time. But she'd never felt anything like this.

After landing, Tony stood and retrieved his things. He'd been pretty sure she had a fun-loving and cheeky personality underneath – he'd seen the sparkle in her eye as she snubbed his gags – but he had failed to crack her professional shell . . . hadn't he?

One last chance; she stood at the door bidding her passengers goodbye like an automaton: 'Good evening, thank you for flying Air Australia. Good evening, thank you for flying Air Australia.'

Surely she'd personalise her farewell for him, he thought, as he reached the door. Hadn't they bonded?

'Good evening, thank you for flying Air Australia,' she said to him.

His shoulders slumped. He hadn't touched her. Despondent, he stepped onto the air bridge to make his way up the tunnel.

'Excuse me, sir?' He turned as he heard her voice. The same mask of polite indifference greeted him. 'You dropped your boarding pass,' she said and handed a crisp piece of board out to him.

'Oh, that's not mine,' he started, but when he looked at the paper he could see a phone number written across the top. He took it and looked back at her.

The open smile that wreathed her face was as genuine, pure and giving as he'd known it would be. Dumbstruck, he could do nothing but stand there, holding the pass and smiling back. 'Thank you for flying Air Australia,' she said once again, but this time it smacked of mirth and warmth.

He'd practically skipped down the concourse. The baggage carousel reminded him of a merry-go-round, the planes were a flock of doves and the taxi queue was a daisy chain.

As soon as he got home, with shaking fingers he dialled the number that was written on the boarding pass.

The Fringe Bar was jumping with its usual crowd of revellers when Sera walked in later that night. She should have suggested something more intimate than Oxford Street's ultimate party venue, but she needed to be sure her mind agreed with her gut before she took this thing any further. After all, this Tony guy was a complete stranger.

The music was thumping, the joint was jumping – and so was her pulse. She'd never been so nervous on a date before. What was it about this guy that made her so edgy?

She was sick of being single but she hadn't actively

looked for a partner in months. It wasn't worth the let-down and the disappointment – she just knew they'd be turned off once they saw her scar. She was sick of walking the lonely road. But maybe this would be different.

Her eyes went instinctively to the table in the corner window just as Green Day's haunting hit started with its opening lyric.

At that moment Sera's eyes met Tony's. She walked over, they both started speaking at once – 'I was just thinking of this song!'

It became their song and Green Day their band.

'Do you remember, Sera? Do you remember?' Tony's eyes were closed as his head hung, supported by her shoulder.

'I remember, baby,' she murmured, at peace in his secure hold.

'God damn it, Sera!' His mood switched in the classic manner of the truly intoxicated. He pulled back and gripped her upper arms. 'What happened to us? It was so perfect, we were so great. What happened?'

'Don't do this, Tony, not now, not here,' Sera begged.

'Then when, Sera, when? In between your bloody manicures? Will you schedule me in?'

Sera nervously glanced around. Interested looks were coming their way; conversations halted.

'Tony,' she said, as calmly as she could, 'let's go home and talk there.'

'No, Sera, this is hopeless, you don't care about me. Taylah does, Taylah thinks I'm hot!'

'Who is Taylah?' Sera's voice was ice.

Taylah, witnessing the spectacle, took a step back and hid behind two security guards who were standing at the ready.

'Doesn't matter, no one! What about this Sam character?

You spend more time with him than you do with me.'

'Tony, you're making no sense.' Sera was getting angry: this was not her idea of a night out. 'I'm going. Are you coming?'

'No, I've had it, I'm sick of just being the service provider in that house. I'm staying with my mates, they care about me.'

Sera looked around at the slack-jawed beer-guzzlers and the bright, speedy eyes of Freddy and George. 'Yeah great, Tony, have fun.'

'I will, Sera, you better have a good hard think about us, because I'm jack of this shit!'

She picked up her coat and headed for the door. She turned back to ask him once more to come home but he was at the bar ordering whiskey.

~ 44 ~

Sera'd imagined the dress she'd wear, the death notice in the paper and even what music she would play at Tony's funeral. 'Oh, for God's sake!' she shouted out loud at her own macabre thoughts as she threw back the sheets and gave up any hope of sleep. Where in the hell was he?

She crept into the laundry to make herself a decaf. And who in the bloody hell was Taylah? What had gotten into Tony tonight? It was the hundredth time she'd asked herself the same questions. She moved into the living room and looked out the front window at the black sky.

She was waiting while the rest of the hemisphere slept. But waiting for what? For the cops to knock on the door and tell her about a terrible accident? For Tony to come back to say he was leaving her? For the sky to fall in? She didn't know what it was, but she was on the edge of her toes, ready to launch, ready to react when 'it' happened.

She'd arrived home from the pub in a filthy mood and after slamming the kitchen door with little regard for sleeping children or Joan she'd poured herself a fishbowl of white wine. Tony was acting like such a dick. How dare he get drunk and throw accusations around like that? And who in the bloody hell was Taylah?

Her fury was quickly replaced with worry, then usurped by self-blame. It was her fault. She flung herself into the family-worn sofa and stared at the purple glowing bars of the old electric heater. She had been so cold towards him lately. No, fuck it! It was his fault: how dare he stay out all night like this and worry her sick? She was going to kill him.

She took a deep breath and tried to meditate. This roller-coaster of emotions would give her an ulcer if she wasn't careful. But she couldn't help it. There was so much going wrong in her life at the moment; everyone around her seemed to be losing the plot. Her mother was useless, she'd just sorted things out with her sister, and now her husband was acting like a complete bastard! What had she done to deserve so much misery?

From above the fireplace a row of family photos smiled down: the kids; she and Tony on their wedding day, grinning like the madly-in-love couple they were; she and Bella at her sister's thirtieth, smiling at each other with affection. For a few minutes, Sera stared at the photos, remembering the moments, the people who made her life so rich. The stillness of the house hung heavy around her and tears began to slide down her cheeks. She was blessed; truly blessed. Her children, her husband, her sister, her friends – and yes, even her parents – loved her and cared about her. She'd been so caught up with her own petty nonsense that she'd lost sight of the important things in her life and now here she was blaming everyone around her for her own discontent. She felt a flush of hot, red embarrassment flood her cheeks. She was acting like a spoilt child in a toy shop.

Poor Bella, she was just trying to break free of the shackles of motherhood that she had wrongly had to carry for so long. But Sera was scared: scared to let go, scared that she would have no one to turn to without Bella being there to tend to her every emotion.

'God, I have to grow up,' Sera whispered to herself, suddenly shocked by the realisation of how she had behaved toward those closest to her. She inhaled deeply, her breath shuddering with taut emotion. It was time to behave like an adult and take some responsibility for her own life. Fear swept over her as she wondered whether it was too late to save her marriage.

Sera leapt up as she heard a car. But it just drove by. She flopped back down and picked up the phone again, but there was no point: it would just go to voice mail like it had all night. She tossed it back on the couch.

A surge of fear swelled up from her gut and she almost burst into panicked tears. But the emotion was forced back down with anger as she remembered how cross she was at him making her so worried. She was so confused.

She thought back to the events of that evening. When Tony had called and insisted she drop everything and come to the pub, she could have killed him. All day she'd been looking forward to an early night, tucked up in bed with her favourite show and a cuppa. And then he'd clicked his fingers and expected her to come running to his side because *he* felt like partying? Typical.

After she'd hung up the phone, suddenly her night under the doona didn't seem so inviting. She'd felt terrible that he was asking her out and she'd rejected him. She considered how lucky she was that her husband was begging her to go out with him. How many husbands did that? Most probably loved the opportunity to be out without the ball and chain, yet there was her darling Tony on the phone pleading with her to come to the pub. She'd been rotten to him lately. She knew it, he knew it; she knew he knew it.

But they were both pretending all was harmonious in their marriage. That was dangerous. That was just asking for relationship cancer. She needed to make more of an effort. She needed to show him she cared about him. The Royal was only around the corner.

Darling, drunk Tony had been so happy to see her. The past month's tension had flown out of the window. It had been a warm and mutual embrace. She'd laughed with him as they stumbled around the dance floor reminiscing about their first date.

And then he'd done the Jekyll and Hyde thing. She knew it was the alcohol talking, but often it worked like truth serum. He was right. The poor man, he was right. Turning up at the pub once wasn't about to right months of negligence.

Sera's face dropped into her palms and this time tears of remorse flowed for the damage she'd caused to their marriage by being so selfish, so self-absorbed. She suddenly realised why she had done this to him. He was too amazing. Too good. She didn't deserve him. She wasn't good enough. He was so perfect and wonderful, supporting the family, backing her on all of her ideas, taking her side in the Joan war. She didn't deserve such a great man, so she'd shut him out.

But seeing him tonight, drunk, aggressive, in all his imperfect glory, made her see that he was a man. Flawed, pissed, aggro and beautiful. He was struggling just like she was. Please let him just have stormed off in a tantrum and not be in some dreadful accident, Sera prayed. Please, please let me see him so I can tell him I love him and that I'm sorry.

She stared again at the blackness outside. A couple of tentative bright birdcalls warned of the impending day. It was coming: the sunrise would be here soon. So she waited.

★

Tony staggered up the front steps, dead on his feet. He was experiencing the blissful few minutes between intoxication and hangover but was achingly aware of how brief this eye of the booze storm would be.

He turned the key as quietly as he could and slipped into the house. Sera was going to freak. He'd never stayed out all night before. Now that the alcohol had cleared somewhat, he realised how crazy his actions had been: walking mindlessly until he'd arrived at Bondi, at the place where he had proposed to Sera so long ago. He wasn't angry anymore, just exhausted and very sad.

He tiptoed into the lounge to crash on the sofa, but jumped as a white figure stepped out from the shadows.

'Sera, you startled me. I'm so sorry, really, I should have called –' His words were cut off by her soft lips as they kissed his. Okay, he was confused now.

'No, *I'm* sorry, my beautiful husband,' she said. 'I can't tell you how much I love you.' She led him to the couch, laid him down and stroked his head for the twenty seconds it took for him to fall asleep.

~45~

Jacqueline sighed deeply with contentment as she flipped through her precious cookbooks, scouring the well-worn pages for inspiration. She couldn't believe how much her life had changed in such a short time.

Working with André and the rest of the team at Laurent Boulangerie had been the best decision she'd ever made. She'd become friends with the other members of staff, she enjoyed being recognised in the street by customers and she particularly enjoyed discovering her obvious talent for working in the service industry.

Her self-esteem had blossomed as she'd flourished as a person. She was more confident and relaxed; quicker to laugh, slower to judge. Her own family were startled at the transformation but had embraced the new and improved Jacqueline. The boys were coming to her for advice rather than treating her like a mere domestic servant, and even Thomas had begun to discuss work issues with her.

But the person she'd surprised the most was herself. She honestly hadn't thought she could be a valuable employee. She'd taken to her chosen occupation as smoothly as butter to hot toast. She served her customers with as much reverence as she served the food. André was thrilled with the care and precision she took with presentation. Her smoked salmon on rye had more finesse than if Neil Perry himself had stacked the capers, and her tomato-peel rosettes almost had her new boss swooning in admiration.

It was such a thrill to be working with a sense of purpose; to have appreciation from the customers and other staff members. Jacqueline really felt that she was a valued team member, making a contribution, working towards a common goal. She got such a thrill when she cleared dishes that had been practically licked clean.

But it had been a tough road getting to that first day. For a while there she believed she was going to have to phone André and quit before she'd even started, given the reaction at home.

To her surprise, the opposition had been strongest from her boys, not from Thomas. She'd called them to the table for dinner two nights after accepting André's job offer and, instead of a casserole, she'd presented them with her new job prospect. The three faces had looked at her blankly, then in bewilderment.

'But you can't,' Joshua had whined. 'You're supposed to be here when we get home from school. Who'll bring us our afternoon tea?'

'You're both old enough to let yourselves into the house and make your own afternoon tea,' she said.

'Yeah, sure, we might be old enough,' spat Damien in a sulky tone. 'Doesn't mean we want to.'

'Yeah, you're supposed to do it. And how are you going to make dinner if you're working all day anyway? And do the other stuff like, I dunno, drop my sports bag off like today when I forgot it?' Joshua was hunched now, his bottom lip stuck out.

'Dad.' Damien turned to his father with a voice-of-reason, man-to-man kind of tone. 'You're surely not on board with this idea. I mean, you can't both work. You bring home enough money, you work long hours. We need Mum here, don't we?'

Thomas had been sitting silently, taking in the family conference. All faces had turned expectantly to him. As the man of the house, everybody knew his word was final. Jacqueline remembered how closed his face had been; how she'd thought her dream of a life of independence was finished before it even began.

'All right,' he said. 'Let's look at this logically, men, let's list the pros and cons of your mother getting a job – from her position.'

'Okay,' Daniel said, holding up his index finger. 'Con: she won't be able to bake for us if she's baking for other people. Con: she won't be able to pick us up from school as often. Con: she won't have time to get the housework done, and I really like my room tidied every day.'

'And she won't be able to do tuck-shop duty and I always get free food when she's on tuck-shop,' Joshua piped in.

'And pros?' their dad inquired with one arched eyebrow.

'I dunno, more money for stuff for us, I guess,' Daniel said.

'Okay, everything you've listed is one hundred per cent based on your own selfish needs. I asked for pros and cons from her position. What do you think she'd get out of it?'

'Well,' Daniel started slowly, unaccustomed as he was to thinking of others. 'I suppose it'd get her out of the house.'

'Good start,' Thomas said.

'And it would broaden her CV, teach her some new skills.'

'She could bring home some good food – for her to eat, of course,' Joshua said.

'What about fun?' Thomas asked. 'Does anybody think

Mum might have some fun and satisfaction in going out and working with people who have similar interests to her?'

The trio had turned their heads to her, sitting in shock at the far end of the table. She'd been utterly gobsmacked by Thomas's support.

'Mum?' Daniel asked. 'Would it be fun for you?'

All she'd been able to do was nod and smile, her eyes pricking with tears. It was the first time her family had ever asked her that question.

Then Thomas had delivered his verdict. 'Jacqueline, I do agree with the boys to a certain extent that the family always has and always will come first.'

She'd nodded her agreement eagerly, sensing a win on the horizon.

'You do a wonderful job maintaining our family, but now that the boys are old enough to start taking on more personal responsibility, and' – he glowered at his sons – 'especially in view of how selfishly they see your part in this household, I think it would be beneficial for you to have a little part-time job.'

'Oh, that's wonderful!' she'd cried. She was just so thrilled to have their support, albeit tenuous. 'I may not be able to drop everything the minute you call, but I'll certainly always be here for you all,' she added.

'It'll do them the world of good, Jacqueline, to learn to be a bit more self-sufficient.' Thomas was reassuring. 'Now, where's that delicious smell coming from?'

Jacqueline neatly jotted down some dessert ideas in a brand new diary and thought back to her first day of work. It had flown by in a flurry of flour, lattes, high tea and white paper bags brimming with delicacies. It had also coincided with payday, and an envelope of cash was waiting in her pigeonhole at the end of her shift. Sixty-seven dollars. Of her own. She'd earned it.

She'd stepped out into the sunshine and patted the envelope. It felt like so much more than sixty-seven dollars. It felt like five thousand dollars. In the past, when handling her husband's money, one hundred dollars was like petty cash. But now her own earnings felt substantial, meaningful.

She'd wandered down the footpath, glancing at, but not seeing, the wares displayed in the Knox Street boutiques. She strolled down Guilfoyle Avenue, happy the boys were off at their own activities that afternoon.

The taupe serenity of Empire Homewares had called her in. She looked at the price of some candles, then stroked a toile quilt in admiration. A white china soap dish in the shape of a pineapple caught her eye. It was so sweet, such a delightful little piece. She'd turned it over to see the price. Sixty-seven dollars. What a coincidence, she'd thought.

Then she'd felt the familiar prickle in her fingertips. Instinctively, she'd glanced back to see that the shopkeeper was deeply involved in re-merchandising the window display, then turned back to the soap dish. She'd really wanted it. It was ideal for the ensuite. Adrenalin started to ooze into her system, and she'd felt the familiar heat invade her cheeks.

She'd earned sixty-seven dollars that day. At work. You could buy this if you wanted to, she'd whispered to herself. But it had taken hard work and time to earn that money. She put the soap dish back on the shelf. She'd think about it. As she walked out of the shop she bid the girl in the window goodbye.

Jacqueline pushed the cookbooks to one side and picked up her shiny new calculator. Her fingers flew over the keys as she slid her plans around in her mind. After only a few weeks working at Laurent Boulangerie she'd become efficient in every aspect of the daily running of the business, and was even managing orders. It was as if something had lain dormant inside her and had been ignited into life. Suddenly she was hungry for bigger challenges.

It had been such a short time, but nevertheless Jacqueline felt it was already time to move on. She'd only needed to get her feet wet in order to feel the urge to dive straight into her new life, she realised. Not that she'd let the Laurent team down – she'd keep her job, of course – but there was a new challenge for Jacqueline Bouvier on the horizon. She was going into business.

She'd already informed Thomas, making it clear that she wasn't asking for his permission. She didn't need funding: she had her inheritance accruing interest nicely in a trust fund. Thomas had blustered for a few minutes about Jacqueline needing to ensure that the household would remain in order, but then admitted that she seemed happier than she had been in a long time, and had pledged his support again, much to her surprise.

She'd scoured the internet, bought books on starting up a home business, spoken to local small business owners and now knew more about OH&S, BAS, GST, and ABNs than Kerry Packer ever had.

Her company name registration had already arrived in the mail and The Cake Lady was in business. She had her eye on three prospective clients; local café owners, who had already tasted Jacqueline's wares at the school fete and had given her pavlova, fruit flan and carrot cake high praise. She could easily see a projected eighteen hundred dollars in turnover per week, she noted with pleasure, as she tapped away at the keys. And she'd found a mentor in André, who had been an enthusiastic adviser as long as she promised not to make any French desserts that competed directly with his business.

That night, when Thomas arrived home with the boys, they were shocked to walk in and not smell the aroma of their evening meal warming in the oven. Although she'd been working hard for weeks, with precise time management she'd still always managed to have a hot meal on the table at the end of the day.

'What's for dinner?' Thomas asked suspiciously as he entered the kitchen and saw his wife sitting at table strewn with paperwork.

'I thought you could pop out and pick up some takeaway please, Thomas. I've been busy with work all day.'

Thomas started to voice his displeasure at the request, but was drowned out by the boys' high-fiving each other in excitement. Takeaway was a rare treat. Suddenly the career-mother life had perks.

'I say, Jacqueline,' said Thomas. 'If this little hobby of yours is going to impact the family like this, I can't say I'm at all pleased.'

Jacqueline looked up and took off her glasses. 'Well, Thomas, considering it's not a "little hobby", but a business, I can assure you it will impact this family occasionally. Maybe you can just make the odd sacrifice for me for a change. Takeaway food once in a blue moon isn't going to kill you, you know.'

'Well, I don't know if that was the plan . . .' he mumbled under his breath as he wandered back off to the car to fetch the family's evening meal.

'Daniel, darling,' Jacqueline said as she went back to scouring the cookbooks. 'Can you please pop the washing into the dryer?'

'Sure, Mum,' her son said, now eager to please his new feisty career mother. 'Muuum!' came his call a minute later. 'Which one's the dryer?'

~46~

By Wednesday afternoon Tony was starting to feel almost normal. As he got closer to forty, his occasional hangovers took much longer to shift than they had in his twenties, when a couple of Beroccas and a cold shower would see him right. As he unloaded the tools from his truck and locked them in the back shed, he wished he still felt that youthful sense of being bullet-proof.

Nowadays a really big night out meant he was dogged with energy-sapping lethargy, short-term memory loss and a short temper right into the next week. And this time was even worse; because he had to drag a great bucketful of guilt through his days as well. God, he felt terrible. Poor Sera, she'd been making such an effort at reviving their relationship by dropping everything to come to the pub and he had to run off at the mouth like that. And then not coming home! He'd felt sick with remorse all week.

He walked into the house through the renovation, picking through the builder's rubble, pleased to note that they'd made some progress. He didn't have to call out to know there was no one home. He could sense the house's emptiness.

His blue mood sank down a notch from flat to downright miserable. He hated coming home to an empty house. The children's squeals, his mother's grumbles and even Sera's constant activity made him feel good, like being in a secure nest. But empty, the nest was merely a pile of sticks.

He sat on his mother's Jason recliner without even chasing away the gloomy twilight by flicking on a light. He should make himself a cuppa, he thought, but he couldn't be bothered. It wasn't worth it if he couldn't make a pot for two.

Sera had been so nice to him since Friday night. She'd been sweet, cuddly and attentive. He couldn't work it out. It had been bliss falling asleep in the wee hours of Saturday morning with her delicate touch stroking his forehead. Then she'd taken Mum and the kids to the museum for the day to give him recovery time. She was a bloody angel sometimes. Why she hadn't put his nuts in a vice for staying out all night was beyond him.

They hadn't had a chance to talk properly since the weekend: life had been its usual merry-go-round of kids' stuff, visitors and work, so they hadn't been able to manage more than a few moments alone – except in bed, and then they'd both been too exhausted to do anything other than cuddle and fall asleep.

He needed to talk to her. She needed to know he didn't mean anything at all by his stupid, stupid words. Where was everyone? He knew it was the delayed hangover making him feel like this, but he was so tired and emotional he almost felt like crying.

Then he noticed the note on the coffee table. His pulse hammered in his throat. Empty house? A note? No! He knew he was in strife, but not a note! He scooped it up and nearly tore the letter in half in his haste to rip it open and read the words.

It was brief, and in Sera's hand. The tears swimming in his eyes blurred the writing and he angrily brushed them aside.

Dear darling husband,

Do you remember how we used to make treasure hunts for each other? Well, surprise! I've made you one. Hope you're up for it and not too tired. Lots of love, Sera.

PS – You have to start right away because I'm waiting at the end of it! See you soon, don't get lost.

Clue No. 1

Roses are red
Violets are blue
There's five, but one
makes me ah-choo!

Tony stared in amazement at the paper. He flipped it over, still half expecting to see a PPS that said, 'By the way, we've left you.' The back was blank.

He turned it back over; his smile so wide his ears hurt. He kissed the note, then kissed it again. She loved him! Her daggy, silly treasure hunt proved it. Tony leaped up and punched the air in jubilation. He took the stairs three at a time as he ran to his room. He flung his work gear in a corner, dragged on jeans, a polo shirt and a navy, woollen jumper and was back in his truck within minutes.

He started the engine, then realised he had no idea where he was going. As he stared at the note, his butterflies distracted him from collecting the logic needed to decipher it.

Okay, violets and roses, flowers, ah-choo, it was obviously referring to Sera's allergy to gypsophila, the white flower spray that florists use to tart up an arrangement. The first time he'd given her flowers he'd caught her tossing the gypsophila in the bin while arranging the remainder of the flora in a vase. She'd told him she was allergic and it wasn't until years later he discovered that it didn't actually make her sneeze, she just thought it was seriously ugly but hadn't want to hurt his feelings.

So it was something about a florist, but what about the reference to five? 'Of course!' he said aloud. The florist at Five Ways. He gunned the engine and arrived at Sera's favourite haunt within minutes.

'Hey Jo!' he called as he entered the shop. 'You seen Sera?'

'Stop fishing!' Jo laughed from behind the counter. 'I'm not allowed to help you.'

'You don't have to, I've worked it out,' he said with a smile and pulled open the door to her fridge. Sure enough, stuck to the bucket of gypsophila was another letter.

This time he experienced flurries of excitement rather than pounding dread.

'You're clever!' Jo said.

'I know her too well,' he answered with pride.

Back in the car, he opened the letter.

Clue No. 2
Nowhere near the finish line
Fast hackers you might be
In tiny little shorts
Can you keep up with me?

What? He read it again. Fast hackers? What in the hell? Okay, 'tiny little shorts' rang a bell. When they were dating, she used to tease him about his running shorts being so small. They used to run together on Sunday mornings down at Rushcutters Bay. Of course, 'fast hackers' – Rushcutters! He laughed as he started the engine.

At Rushcutters Bay Park, he pulled over and stared at the letter. Where would she put the next clue? 'Nowhere near the finish line'. So that would mean the starting line. They used to meet on Waratah Street. He drove around and at the bus stop where they met was another letter taped to the advertisement. He laughed as he saw it was an ad for City Search. She must have enjoyed that coincidence.

Clue No. 3
YY UR
YY UB
ICUR YY 4 Me

This one had him stumped. Some kind of weird code. So he first had to crack the code then work out the clue that was no doubt hidden within.

He sat in the car frowning. It was dark now and the park was empty of the usual end-of-day joggers and dog-walkers.

He stared at the characters. 'Why why your?' No. 'You are?' That was it. 'Why why you are?' That made no sense. The end bit was 'I see you are'. But 'Why why?' Tony looked away from the letter, then back again, staring harder. 'I see you are . . .' what's with the two whys? Hang on, two whys or too wise? At once the message was as clear as day: 'Too wise you are, too wise you be, I see you are too wise for me.'

Excellent. He sat back and smiled and went to turn on the keys in the ignition. Hang on. Where to? What did it mean? 'Too wise' . . . so, the library? That didn't mean anything in particular to them as a couple. Encyclopedia? University? No. No. Wise, wise, wise. A glimmer of something sparkled in the depths of his memory. Wise.

Hang on a minute . . . Wyse! Wyse and Son. Two Wyse. The Italian tile importers. They'd spent a wonderful Saturday afternoon there, just after Maddy was born, scouring through piles of imported pottery pieces. They'd felt like archaeologists. It was the most amazing little shop, with a basement filled with mountains of dusty old crates. There was no doubt in Tony's mind and he chuckled as he sped off in the direction of Woollahra.

Sure enough, as soon as his headlights stroked the peeling façade of the old building, he saw the letter tucked into the locked wrought-iron security door. He leapt out and tore it open with excitement. This was the most fun he and Sera had had together in years. He'd completely forgotten about her crazy little treasure hunts. Even an event as simple as a picnic used to be accompanied by similar notes. She was such a darling to re-kindle a part of their past he'd enjoyed so much.

Clue No. 4
Eighteen thirty-five
Sandman not at the shore
By any other name
This clue is four.

Now she was getting random. He'd never work this out. He looked at the car clock. It was seven already. Should he call her? Tell her he was running late? No, that would wreck the game.

'Eighteen thirty-five', what in the world did that date mean? 'Sandman, not at the shore'? There's shoreline and sand all over Sydney, but the word *not* threw him. What sand's *not* at the shore? 'By any other name'? A rose by any other name still smells as sweet? Sweets? Lollies? Roses. 'This clue is four' – that was weird because it's a waste of a line. He knew this was the fourth clue, so why was she repeating herself?

Four? 1835? Sand not at shore . . . hang on just one minute. He knew, what she meant. Sand *not* at the shore –

a sand bunker! The rose was Rose Bay, this clue was 'fore' not 'four'.

He laughed at his own cleverness. Sera had thrown him a surprise thirty-fifth birthday party at the Royal Sydney Golf Club in Rose Bay. He'd just played eighteen holes with his three best friends and when they came in for a cold one at the end she'd been there with fifty of their mates.

She was really taking him down memory lane with this treasure hunt. The treasures were the memories, re-visiting the past. Forcing him to go back to see the happy moments in the history of their relationship. He couldn't wait to see her, to hold her.

He sailed down Kent Road in Rose Bay and leapt out at the large Sydney Golf Club Sign. He looked behind it and, sure enough, taped to the back was another letter.

'Last Clue – No. 5' was written on the front.

He didn't even have to read it. He knew she would be at Icebergs, the restaurant where he had proposed to her.

Tony's truck flew down Curlewis Street and he took a punt there'd be a car-spot in the impossible-to-park-in Notts Avenue. He was so eager to get his hands on Sera that he didn't want to waste time hiking up from the beach public carpark.

His memories danced around his mind. The night he proposed, she'd been ridiculously beautiful in a long, slinky, pale blue halter dress. He was so nervous; sure she was going to turn him down. He remembered the first renovation on their Paddington house, shopping together, oohing and ahhing over each design discovery. He thought back to the surprise party; jogging together; their babies; the holidays.

They'd had so much fun in the past eight years. It was difficult to keep a marriage going; nearly bloody impossible sometimes. But God, it was so worth fighting for, so worth working on. To have a friend forever, like he had in Sera, was the most precious gift in life.

He got lucky and slid the car into a welcome space. He leapt out and ran into the restaurant, ignoring the maitre d's approach as his eyes scanned the room. In the corner his search was arrested by the vision of the most familiar and welcome sight in the world. His wife.

Sera was sitting facing the entrance, grinning inanely that her clever trick had worked and he'd arrived sooner than she'd expected. Tony strode across the restaurant and threw his arms around her. As he intended, her funny little squeak came out with the squeeze.

'You did it!' she said, when he finally released her. 'Clever thing!'

'That two whys one threw me,' he said.

'I knew you'd remember,' she replied as they sat down opposite each other, holding hands across the table.

'It was like a living photo album – you sent me through real-life snapshots of our time together,' he said. 'You're bloody brilliant, woman!'

'Ah, you got that, then, did you? I thought it might be a bit subtle,' she said.

'I got it.' He gazed at her. 'Sera, I am so sorry about the other night.'

'Oh Tony, please don't, I'm the one who is supposed to be sorry. I drove you to it. I've just been so cold toward you lately.'

'I understand, believe me, if anybody knows the pressure you've been under, it's me.'

'But that doesn't mean I have to treat you like shit just because I'm having a bit of stress,' she protested.

'Sera, I shouldn't put pressure on you like that, I should back off a bit.'

'Tony, I just feel so ugly and plain and boring at the moment. Maybe it's a mid-life crisis coming early or something, but I just can't bear myself and I cringe every time you look at me, fearing what you must see.'

Tony looked at her in amazement. 'I don't believe I'm hearing this, Sera. My darling, you are more beautiful today than the day we met. And believe me, when we met I'd never seen such beauty!'

'Tony, I'm serious. I'm not looking for compliments. I think my scar's actually getting worse with age. I know it sounds shallow, but the sheer hideousness of the thing creeps me out.'

'What scar?'

'Tony! I'm serious.'

'So am I, Sera. For a start, I haven't seen it for years, you keep it so covered up, and secondly I never even noticed it much in the first place. It's just one more part of you.' He looked closely at her. 'There's something else, isn't there? This isn't just about your physical appearance. What is it?'

He was mortified that his innocent question caused fat tears to roll from her eyes and down her cheeks. 'Sera, what's wrong?'

'I'm not good enough for you, Tony, don't you see? I just can't keep up anymore. I'm tired of trying to be perfect. I see what happened to Mallory, to Bella, and to half the mums at the kids' crèche and I am so worried that I'll be left too. I look at you and you take my breath away. You're gorgeous, you're clever, accomplished. Look at your business going from strength to strength, you've got private school education, your mates are in the "right" circles. I'm just a tarty little strumpet of a shop-girl who never deserved you in the first place and I'm terrified I'm going to lose you. I think I've been steeling myself against the inevitable, getting ready for the moment you leave me for someone younger, prettier, smarter. I've been detaching myself from you, from us. I mean, I know you're not that kind of bloke, Tony, don't get me wrong, but beautiful women can be very persuasive and you're an absolute goldmine to any predatory prospectors out there.'

Tony sat and listened in disbelief. 'You can't be serious,' he finally said.

Her downturned mouth told him she was.

'Sera, when I got home tonight and saw the house was empty . . . Where are the kids, by the way?'

'Movie with Nana Joan.'

'Cool. When I came home and saw that note on the coffee table, do you know what I thought?'

'No, what?'

'I thought you'd left me, I thought it was all over red rover, you'd taken the kids and gone.'

'What? As if I'd do that, and just leave you a note.'

'It's what I thought. And you know I nearly chucked with grief. Right there on Mum's Jason recliner.'

Sera laughed at that vision.

'And then, when I saw you were playing your funny little game with me, I could have screamed with joy and laughter. I was so relieved and so happy that I hadn't lost you.'

'So both of us were worried the other was going to leave?'

'Yeah, it looks like it.' They looked at each other sheepishly when they realised how silly they'd been, and how their miscommunication could have actually threatened their relationship.

'So best we talk about things in the future, then, before it's too late?' Tony asked his wife.

'Definitely,' she agreed.

'So you liked the treasure hunt?' she asked him as she picked up her menu.

'Yeah, the clues were hard, though,' he said.

'The last one was pretty easy,' she said.

'You know, I never even read it. When I saw it was the final one, I guessed you'd be here.'

'You're kidding. I'm that obvious?' She laughed.

He reached into his top pocket, took out the scrap of paper and read the last clue she'd left him.

We fell in love
You thawed my heart
You proposed to me here
Over ricotta tart.

~47~

'Oh, all right, Bella, I'll ring her, stop bloody hassling me, will you!' Sera's tense tone was more about being stuck in afternoon traffic in Bondi Junction. But also, she didn't need a lecture right now. Since their big blue in the hotel, her relationship with Bella had settled into a completely different, far more solid place, but it didn't stop Bella continuing to nag Sera about their mother, or make Sera want to talk to her parents more than she ever had.

Bella's tinny voice from the car speaker competed with the roar of the bus that went past Sera's car. 'I'm not hassling you, it's just that she sounds a bit down and needs a friendly ear, that's all.'

In the past Sera would have meekly agreed with Bella while internalising her resentment. At least now she could snap back her frustration.

'Look, sorry I sound snippy; bloody traffic. What's Mum's problem this time?'

'The caravan park is putting up the rent and she's beside herself.'

'So I suppose she wants money?' Sera said.

'Well, she didn't mention it. Just talk to her, will you?'

'I'm really busy, I'll see how I go.' Sera wasn't about to make any promises. They said goodbye and hung up.

Sera sat at the same red light she'd been stopped at for three changes now. She drummed her fingers on the steering wheel and flicked on the radio to distract her thoughts. She stabbed each button to change the inane chatter and commercials of each annoying station, then punched the off button.

Bloody Mum and Dad, she thought. Can't they sort out their own lives for a change? What's the point of them, I mean really? Parents are supposed to be there to help their kids. Not the other way around. Look at me, she thought, that's my job, I run around after my kids constantly and love it. It's my duty, it's what I'm here for. So where's the payback? When do I get to be a little girl, indulge in a whinge and get some support? It's just not my job to be a counsellor for every petty problem the woman has.

She glanced at her watch. She still had an hour before she needed to pick up the kids. Chantrea was in town; she might pop in and have a chat with her. Chantrea's no-nonsense attitude could be brutal at times, but at least you got guidance. She texted her. The reply came back immediately.

Yep, drop in, just grabbing Sally from crèche, back in 5.

Dara Kim opened the door. 'Come in, come in, Chantrea will be back very soon. Look at you. Too thin. You girls all too thin. Why don't you eat? Come here, sit down. I will feed you.'

All the protestations in the world wouldn't stop Dara from unloading the fridge, so Sera sat at the kitchen table to enjoy a moment of being mothered.

She looked around the tiny little kitchen. She loved the craziness of Dara's knick-knack collection. One entire shelf was devoted to animal salt and pepper shakers. Another wall groaned under the weight of photos of Sally and Chantrea. Souvenirs from the family's travels around Australia took pride of place on another bookcase: a gold nugget from

Broken Hill, an opal letter opener, a koala snowglobe, a Santa-in-boardshorts ornament.

'Here, you eat this,' Dara said and shoved a dish of rice and very fragrant chicken in front of her. 'You want tea? Green tea? Black tea?'

'Yes please, a black tea with one sugar would be lovely.'

'You don't want milk in it, do you? Milk in tea, still can't understand that rubbish.'

'Er, just a dash would be great.' Sera felt like apologising for her appalling western taste.

A derisive puff burst from Dara's lips as she slapped the milk carton on the table. 'You do it,' she said, as if it were too disgusting a request for her to participate in.

Having set her guest up with all she could possibly offer, Dara sat down opposite Sera.

'So how are you, Dara?' Sera asked as she lifted her chopsticks. 'Working hard still?'

'As always. I did fifty hours last week, but I don't complain.'

'You're good, but you're allowed to, you know,' Sera said and tucked into the chicken. It was delicious. What was that herb?

'No, how could I complain? Look at this wonderful life I have. Look at this wonderful city I live in and my Sally, what a princess. I'm sure she's royal, you know, the bearing, the grace. Very talented girl. Nothing to complain about. Too much complaining nowadays. People are too greedy, want too much.'

Sera noticed Dara grimace as she stood to pour the boiling water into the teapot.

'Are you in pain, Dara? Does your leg hurt?'

'Oh, it's nothing, just my knee. Doctor says I might need an operation. But it's nothing. I'll survive. It's the lifting. We don't have a boy at the shop at the moment so I have to lift the big boxes. But they'll get a boy soon who can do that, then all will be okay again.'

'You're amazing.' Sera didn't like to let on that she knew about Dara's past from Chantrea, but the woman was something like a hero to her. What she'd endured, how she'd managed to single-handedly set up a new home in a new country for her daughter. 'I wish my mum was like you.'

'She is,' Dara said simply and looked point blank at Sera.

'Oh, no, she's not. You haven't met her. She's nothing like you.'

'She's a woman. She's like me. She's like you. Same.'

'But she's not a real nurturing type of mother, you know? She's always got her own problems, she complains a lot, she doesn't seem to cope with life like you do.'

'She's a person. She has . . . what's that new word? . . . issues too, maybe she doesn't have friends to talk to. Maybe she trusts you and wants to share with you.'

'Well, I hadn't thought of it quite like that before,' Sera said. 'But it's really her job to be there for me, and my job to be there for my kids. You know, the cycle goes on.'

'Oh, pshaw. You should be a grown-up by now. What are you? Twelve?'

Sera looked up at Dara, startled. She could see where Chantrea got her forthright manner from. 'No, it's not like that at all, it's just that she's always whining on the phone to me about stuff. And never listens to me at all.'

'That's what she's like. She is the person she is. What about that Jacqueline woman, she's your friend isn't she?'

'Well, yes, she's my friend.'

'Well, at the brunch at her house, she was going on and on and on about her two boys. Very good to have boys, yes, very proud woman but not very humble. She wouldn't shut up about them.'

'Oh, yes, Dara, I know, but that's fine, that's what she's like. She needs validation. I actually feel sorry for her, she doesn't get any attention from her family, she doesn't have parents anymore, she needs her friends to listen to her. I don't mind at all being her sounding board. And you know, she's getting so much better now that she has her business up and running. And now that she has a group of girlfriends to listen to her, she doesn't seem to shout for attention anymore.'

'Hmmm,' Dara said cryptically and just sat and stared at Sera.

Sera understood that was her cue to think about what she'd just said. 'Oh, you think I should give my mum the same respect. That's different though. She's my mother.'

'Not mother, woman – woman first. If you treat her like you treat your friends, you would get along much better.'

Just at that moment Sally barrelled into the room and threw herself at her grandmother. '*Gaela Yay*!' she said from the depths of Dara's bulk.

'*Gaela* Sally, little one, how was crèche?'

'Very good. I am the best at collage. See?' She thrust a piece of board with all manner of backyard detritus glued all over it at her grandmother.

'This is very good.'

'Yes, I have to agree,' Sally said. 'And now I'm going to stick it on the wall in my room. Hi Sera, bye Sera,' she said and was out the door.

'What a nice surprise!' Chantrea said as she walked in the room carrying bags of shopping. 'Sorry I took so long. I had to stop at the supermarket. Wine?'

'No, I won't darling, thanks anyway. I have to fly, I've got to pick mine up now. We'll catch up soon, promise.'

'But I just got here!' Chantrea said. 'Didn't you say you wanted to talk about something?'

'Nope, changed my mind, sorry. I'll call you. Bye, darling. Bye, Dara, thanks so much for the snack and the chat.' Sera hugged the two women and left.

As she walked down the long drive to where her car was parked in the street, she felt like she was taller, stronger, more independent. Dara had made so much sense just then.

Why hadn't she seen it from this angle before? Marlene was a woman, with her own upbringing, her own story, her own life all coming together and making her the person she was today. Sera needed to readjust her thinking. This person was struggling with her own difficulties, feeling her own joys. They were all in this together. What on earth had Sera been expecting?

As soon as she shut the car door, she pressed speed dial number four on her mobile. After two rings it was answered. 'Hello?' came her mother's voice.

'Hi, Mum, it's me. How are you?'

~ 48 ~

Joan found it was impossible to be in the house with the builders constantly crashing and banging about. There was too much noise for her to watch television in the living room – not to mention the filthy mouths on the lot of them – so she'd had to remain in her bedroom.

She'd read the *Women's Weekly* and *New Idea* from cover to cover and realised with a start it was already 2 pm. She was well overdue for her daily ablutions. Buggered if she was going to use the downstairs bathroom. With the amount of times those bloody great men lumbered down the hall to do God-only-knows-what in her private bathroom, one of them would be sure to burst in on her. If she went upstairs to use the family washroom she'd be guaranteed her privacy.

And today of all days. Her right hip was really playing up. It had stopped her from getting around a lot lately. Not that anyone cared. Sera was forever gallivanting around town and poor Tony was working tirelessly of late. Poor dear.

She'd booked in to see the doctor, but since her regular doctor had retired she'd had to visit some young upstart who looked like he was straight out of primary school and clearly his inexperienced flibbertigibbet of a receptionist knew nothing, otherwise she wouldn't have made a woman in terrible pain wait until Friday for an appointment.

Joan mumbled and grumbled her way up to the stone-tiled haven and took her time drawing a lovely hot bath. She poked in the bathroom cabinet for some Epsom salts to ease the ache in her hip. But nothing so practical existed in this Aladdin's cave of luxuriant lotions and potions, she noted with displeasure. There'd have to be thousands of dollars worth of top-end nonsense here, she thought as she picked up one, wrinkling her nose at the ingredients. We made do with a tub of cold cream in my day, she thought.

She found a sample of Clarins bath gel and poured a liberal dose into the water. 'Probably have me break out in a rash,' she muttered as she sank into the hot water.

After a long soak, Joan emerged from the bath feeling a lot less cantankerous. She finished drying herself and wrapped her body up in her old favourite chenille dressing gown, then wandered into the master bedroom to look out over the construction site. At least the idiot builders were packing up early and heading off.

The roof of the new renovation covered what used to be her beautiful patio. A huge lump of sadness came up into her throat. She knew that Tony and Sera were planning on landscaping a beautiful courtyard at the rear of the property, but that didn't reduce the pain she felt about losing the patio.

They didn't know how much it meant to her. They didn't know what had happened there so many years ago and how that had changed her life forever. But how could they? How could anyone know? Only one other person had been there and even he didn't know the full story.

She pulled herself out of her miserable trance and left her memories in the broken patio.

Halfway down the steep staircase, Joan stepped on one of the kids' toys. Her right foot folded into an instant sprain that threw out her failing hip. She fell forwards and tumbled gently down the stairs to lie in a heap at the bottom. She tried to move, to crawl to the phone, but the searing pain from her dislocated hip prevented even the slightest movement. She was stuck. In agony. And there was nothing she could do. Nothing at all, except wait until someone came home.

Oh my head, Sera thought, climbing the stairs from the carport, loaded down with shopping bags and with two children in grizzly tow. What a day. What an enormous, ridiculous day. She'd had one too many at Icebergs the night before.

Since getting up at six am, she'd completed enough tasks to make a ward-nurse look like a lay-about. The builders had arrived at seven, as always, and having grown quite accustomed to kicking off their work day with early morning caffé lattes, espressos and cappuccinos, were unable to pick up a tool until Sera the barista had done her duty.

Maddy had a last-minute show-and-tell requirement involving a permanent marker and sticky tape. The make-shift laundry kitchen was having ventilation issues so the burnt toast smoke not only filled the house but also triggered the ear-splitting smoke alarm, accompanied by Harry's terrified scream.

Joan moaned and complained about her dicky hip; Tony had to fly, with apologies, to another building site. 'What's wrong with this bloody building site?' Sera had bitterly complained a little too loudly to his retreating back, which had sparked an entirely unnecessary marital spat. They might have just had fantastic make-up sex, but they were still a normal couple.

Then her day seemed to just get worse. Each Freedom Furniture sent her to another more out-flung Freedom to view a couch in a particular colour of Greige that was guaranteed to be on the floor. But at each outlet she found the couch had been mysteriously misplaced by a Stone couch. Not Greige at all. Very different. And the five-centimetre-square fabric swatch the staff kept showing her was hardly sufficient information for a furnishing decision.

She'd only just made it in time for her afternoon shift at DJs. It was pension day, so the department store was full of old ducks clucking over gloves and hats, sampling creams and perfumes and enquiring after each of her product lines in the most minute detail before purchasing a bottle of Vaseline Intensive Care and popping off to Dot's Diner for the Soup and Sandwich Senior's Special ($4.95 on Tuesdays).

Then the builders rang to say they were knocking off early because the materials they needed hadn't been delivered. She'd winced. Her fault: she'd forgotten to order the splashback last month.

She was the last to pick up her kids at crèche, and the children certainly weren't going to let her get away with that. With empty tummies and exhausted bodies, they squabbled relentlessly on the way home. 'Why is red?' Harry asked her repeatedly, growing increasingly enraged by her apparently insufficient answers.

When Sera finally reached the back door, she was emotionally and physically drained. She put the key in the lock. What else could possibly go wrong today?

At the base of the stairs lay Joan's bizarrely twisted body in a crumpled heap. The voice that floated up from the depths of her dressing gown was muffled and weak.

'About time you got home. Where in the hell have you been?'

~49~

The cyclists' bells behind her forced Bella to the side of the Centennial Park running track. She'd left Parklands restaurant two kilometres ago and was feeling quite chuffed that she hadn't stopped for a breather yet.

Since her tentative Palazzo Versace epiphany, Bella had re-discovered so much about herself. And one of her most exhilarating realisations was that she loved to run. She'd stopped her daily jog several years ago when Curtis had cringed at her ruddy-cheeked appearance and sweaty armpits.

But now she was back on track, beating the asphalt with little care that wet strands of hair plastered her face and neck. It was so lovely to be back in Sydney and she couldn't believe she'd been avoiding the city for so long. But while the spectre of her failed marriage had loomed, and as her sister had grasped onto her like a drowning woman, it had been a difficult place to enjoy. But now that both situations had eased, she felt free to revel in Sydney's remarkable views, architecture and entertainment.

Bella was enjoying her sister's company more than ever since the dynamics of their relationship had shifted. They were now more like equals than big sister and little sister, and able to enjoy a healthy friendship.

Bella was also relieved to see that Sera had been able to accept their mother's limitations and manage a warmer relationship with her. She was never going to be an ideal mother – her needy and demanding behaviour would be likely to continue – but with her daughters now ringing her on alternate days she spent her phone conversations talking more and complaining less.

The restaurant was coming back into view and Bella was thrilled at how much faster her time was getting. She didn't run to keep her figure trim, she ran because she loved the power of pounding the pavement. It was her meditation.

A horse clopped past and blew an equine raspberry in her direction. Bella laughed and brushed the droplets of horse spit from her face.

She wasn't rostered on with Air Australia for a whole week and was using her free time to meet up with one of her old friends each day. There were a lot of new baby and house-warming presents to buy. There was so much to catch up on. Her next flight was to Hong Kong on Saturday and for the first time in years she felt disappointed about leaving town.

Bella increased her pace at the final one hundred metre mark and sprinted to complete the circuit. She walked in a circle, hands on hips, until she stopped panting. Wiping the sweat from her forehead with her forearm, she cringed as she noticed the streak of grime left on the back of her hand. She wiped it off with her T-shirt. It was going into the wash anyway.

A bus full of office Christmas party revellers unloaded at Parklands for their end-of-year celebration. Bella's breathing eased off as her heart rate slowed.

A great idea suddenly flashed in Bella's mind. A girls' weekend – just Bella and Sera – in Hong Kong would be perfect. This time, without a massive fight. She could book them both in at The Peninsula, they could go shopping, and it would give Sera a much-needed break. And besides, now that Sera didn't need her so much, Bella was free to give her treats whenever she felt like it.

Bella pulled her iPhone out of her back pocket and rang her little sister with the exciting invitation.

~50~

Sera flew out of the childcare centre and rushed to the car. Right, six glorious hours to do ten hours' worth of jobs. The painters were putting on the final coat today, so she had to duck back home to let them in. She'd have to ring Joan in the hospital and see how the nurses had offended her today. The new furniture was being delivered this morning and Telstra had promised to arrive sometime between nine am today and Christmas to install a new telephone outlet.

Now, if she could will her mobile to not ring, she might have a chance of getting everything done. She glared at it. For such a small piece of technology, it was a godsend and an almighty headache rolled into one.

As if on cue, the little bugger trilled. The caller ID announced that it was Tony. She smiled, he'd been so adorable lately, but he wasn't adorable when she was this busy and she knew he only rang when he wanted her to do something.

'Hi, honey,' she chirped into the phone, determined not to let him sense her angst and stress.

'Hi, honey,' he repeated. 'Listen, I need you to do a favour for me.'

Oh, good God, she thought, how on earth will I fit this in?

'It's quite important. I need Mum's health card, health insurance policy and membership card. I was on hold with the insurance company for twenty minutes, so there's been no joy there and I need to know her level of health insurance.'

Sera knew Tony was reaching boiling point with his mother's hospitalisation. 'The surgeon wants to do her hip replacement tomorrow and the hospital needs this sorted out today.'

Having spent the last two days running about after Joan – ferrying licorice allsorts, slippers and clothing to and from the hospital – Sera had had quite enough. But she smiled instead, hoping it would sweeten the tone of her response.

'Of course. I was on my way back to the house anyway. Where's the paperwork?'

'She says it's in a pink box on the top shelf of her closet in an envelope with my name on it. Can you please bring it to the hospital? You were planning on coming in, weren't you?'

'Yes, yes, of course,' Sera lied, and turned the car in the direction of home.

Back at the building site, she dumped her day's collection of renovation swatches and samples on the hall table and went straight to Joan's room. It was nice to walk into the room and not have it smell like a second-hand shop. The usually dim space was bright and cheerful since she'd pulled the curtains all the way back and left the window ajar.

She opened the closet door and clucked in horror at its tightly packed contents. An array of navy blue, teal and maroon assaulted her stylish eye. Coogi knitwear, parachute-silk leisure suits and bucket-loads of boucle fought for hanger space.

She saw a pink box buried beneath a pile of orthotic footwear on the bottom shelf. That must be it. The box was full of memorabilia; photographs, newspaper cuttings and greeting cards. How bloody disorganised was this woman? Hadn't she heard of a filing cabinet? Or at least a scrap-book?

She flicked through the sepia-toned memories swiftly, searching for the envelope. She smiled at the yellowed snippet cut from the classifieds of March 1968 proudly announcing the birth of her husband. Finally, at the bottom of the box, she found a dog-eared envelope with the name 'Tony' on the front.

Opening the envelope, she found several pages of handwritten paper, worn thin on the folds as if it had been handled many times over the years.

She read the first line: 'My darling Tony, this is the hardest letter I've ever had to write . . .'

Sera hurriedly folded the letter shut. This wasn't for her eyes. This was obviously an intensely private missive. She couldn't read this letter . . . could she?

It was impossible. She was torn. But she couldn't stop herself. Shelving the guilt she was feeling about prying into Joan's personal life, she re-opened the letter. After all, she assured herself, it was addressed to her husband and they happily opened each other's mail.

It only took a few lines to realise that the letter was not directed to her husband at all. As she read on, Sera started to shake her head. 'No,' she said out loud. 'No, it can't be true, it just can't be.' By the time she reached the last line, Sera fell heavily back against the wall as if she'd been shot.

Her family was about to change forever.

Three weeks later Joan was ready to come home. Sera collected her and settled her in, and Tony whipped home from work briefly to greet his mother, kiss her on the cheek and drop off a bunch of flowers. Just enough time to win brownie points but not long enough to endure her tirade of complaints.

As soon as he left the house, Sera locked the front door, took the telephone off the hook and walked into Joan's room.

The patient was sitting up in bed supported by a tower of feather pillows. Magazines were strewn across the bedspread. The pen in her hand flew across the *New Idea* celebrity crossword, proving that her intimate knowledge of the famous was on par with any paparazzi.

She didn't look up as Sera entered. 'Tea please, Sera,' she ordered, her pen didn't pause, quickly answering 'Antonia' to 'sister of Dead Calm redhead'.

Sera ignored her mother-in-law's request and pulled the desk chair up to the side of the bed. Leaning forward, she gently took the magazine from her mother-in-law's grip.

Joan looked up over her bi-focals in shock at such defiance.

'We need to talk,' Sera said.

Joan went white and her hands flew to her lips. She knew.

~51~

Joan's eyes watered as she stared out of the window, the landscape blurring to indistinguishable colours and shapes. She sighed deeply and then looked back at her daughter-in-law.

Sera was shocked. Years had melted from Joan's eyes. They were softer, younger. Her familiar steely stare had disappeared. Sera had never seen her looking so fragile; almost beautiful.

'It was different in my day, love,' Joan started. 'Girls were raised to be dutiful women. Sure, there was a wave of bra-burners out there, but we all thought they were crazy. We were the good girls – the debutantes – and besides, why would you want to run around making speeches, having a career, doing it all when you've still got to put a roast on and get the mending done?

'Career women were frowned upon in my set. I married young, was really forced into it, you know, not in the arranged marriage way, mind, but the women of the family and the rest of our community all decided that because Barry was a CPA – a reliable, hard-working type – he was "a catch". In those days your husband just had to be a good provider. Forget about your best-friend, soulmate, kindred-spirit rubbish. I tried to get a job in the beginning. Just as a nurse, you know, but Barry wouldn't have it. My place was in the home. It was the only real row we ever had in our entire marriage.'

'You never had a blue, during the whole time?' Sera was astonished.

'Just that one. And it was a doozy, let me tell you. He punched a hole in the wall of our beautiful kitchen. I'll show you where later. I quickly learnt how to keep the peace. What's the point of screaming the house down every second night? Young people today have no restraint.'

Joan described her years of cleaning, shopping and cooking and how she tried to fill the empty hours with her needlework. She desperately wanted a baby to fill the lifelessness of the house in Paddington, but the years went by and pregnancy evaded her.

'You have to understand, love,' Joan explained to Sera, 'my marriage was like living in domestic handcuffs. Lust and passion were merely the stuff of romance novels. And what in the hell was an orgasm? I had no idea!'

Sera sat back in her chair and listened to the story from so long ago that had never been told.

Joan was desperate to love. She'd never truly loved anybody, never given herself up completely and thrown herself into a relationship with that urgent need to sacrifice all for another being.

After eight years of failing to get pregnant, she sank into a depression. She'd given up and could barely keep the house running as she lived with the daily pain of her childless state. Barry became increasingly hostile with his wife, blaming her for their barren union. He began avoiding the silent house as much as he could, spending all his time at the office or at the club.

Joan was desperate to feel better. She'd spent two years grieving her apparent infertility, cycling through emotions of denial, shock, anger and finally the dark hopeless place called grief, where every day is bleak and interminable. When she came out of the tunnel, she realised there was nothing in her life. But Joan was a survivor and turned towards her beautiful Paddington terrace house. It became her baby. She threw herself into beautifying the property.

She made curtains, crocheted doilies, put up wallpaper, macraméd hanging basket holders, nurtured her maidenhair ferns, and baked beef Wellington. And bit by bit, what had started as a coping strategy became a way of life. She experienced little joy or passion but she soon became able to get from dawn to dusk without wanting to kill herself.

Then one day her husband decided to embrace the trend for outdoor cooking and bought one of the new-fangled barbecues. The back door of the Paddington terrace house led directly to lawn and clothesline, so he planned to install a patio to house the new equipment. Joan was given the job of project manager, which was a relief because she'd painted, papered and knitted every square inch of the interior of the house and was looking for a new target for her homemaking skills.

The lawn was cleared, the Hills Hoist removed and the ground levelled in readiness for slate crazy-paving. Barry's boss recommended an Italian chap for the job: 'You know what those wops are like at stonework, old man,' he had advised. 'Have you heard of St Mark's Piazza in Venice?'

Antonio turned up at eight am on day one to be briefed by the man of the house. Barry instructed Joan to bring coffee. She carefully mixed a Nescafe and cringed when the new Australian grimaced at his first sip. He smiled in apology and said that he might just have a glass of water instead. It was a challenge, she decided.

By the end of the week, while Antonio laboured in the forty-degree Sydney heat in the north facing backyard, Joan had discovered how to buy coffee beans and grind them to perfection. In a small Italian delicatessen she found a Bialetti aluminium coffee maker that sat on the stovetop. She enjoyed such a frisson of satisfaction when the coffee began to release its rich aroma and Antonio would call out from the construction zone, 'Ahhh, *bella*, the coffee smells *magnifico*!'

She would deliver it to him and watch him savour every sip. She revelled in his clear affection for the cup of black ink. She'd never met anyone who so thoroughly embraced life; whose every waking moment was directed at discovering something new and wonderful. She marvelled at this man of passion.

But she particularly marvelled at how another human being could be so impressed with her doing something as simple as making a coffee. '*Grazie, bella signora*' were the words Joan lived for. She scoured Italian cookbooks at the library and began bringing Antonio little treats with his morning coffee. Biscotti, pasticciotti and, of course, his favourite – cannoli: a fried pastry shell stuffed with a sweet ricotta filling. She made it so feather-light he said it was almost as good as his darling mama's in Positano. He asked her to call him Tony, like his friends did back home.

His kind words became a drug to Joan. She would whip through her household chores by eight o'clock every day so that when he arrived she could start her baking and present him with her offering by morning-tea time. She would then spend the rest of the day sitting near him and listening to his rich voice as he sang Italian operettas, the Beatles, and even some Doris Day.

They talked about everything: the state of the world, the state of the Royal family, even the state of her vegetable garden. He encouraged her to plant zucchini, a vegetable not widely used by the Australian housewife in the 1960s.

Joan didn't know she was falling head over heels in love. How do you know you're flying if you've never done it before?

As the patio came to its inevitable conclusion, Joan suggested to Barry they really needed a retaining wall to stop the backyard from encroaching on their spiffing new courtyard. He readily agreed, because, after all, Smith from the office had just installed a retaining wall.

Day two of the building of the retaining wall arrived and so did Antonio, complete with a bunch of sweet peas and an embrace for his *bella signora* that caused a flush of heat to sweep through her core. The next time she brought Antonio his morning espresso and placed it on the pile of bricks beside his work area she laid a hand on his shoulder. He turned from his crouched position and looked up. He stood slowly and wrapped his arms around her. The wall did not develop much further that day. As the sun dropped behind the west fence of the backyard, it was only the threat of a home-coming husband that tore them apart.

Antonio was desperately in love with Joan. He begged her to leave her husband and be with him. But she refused to even consider it. Even with her recently unleashed passion, Joan's sense of duty was tattooed on her soul. Her parents, her in-laws, her local community, would be so torn apart with disappointment and hurt should she dare follow her heart – she just couldn't do it.

She said no to Antonio and the tears tumbled from her face to mingle with his on the crazy paving at their feet.

Antonio closed up. He completed the retaining wall without another word to his *bella signora* and when it was done he left forever.

Joan sank back into her familiar dark depression. She stayed in bed most days; glorious sleep was her only friend, the only escape from the reality of having lost her love. She maintained the household with bare minimum effort, just so Barry didn't notice anything was amiss.

Antonio tried one more time, a few weeks later, to convince her to leave. He was out the front of her house one afternoon when she dragged herself to the corner shop to buy food for her husband's dinner. He leapt out of his truck and came over to her. She was shocked into silence: she'd thought she was never to see him again. She felt her resolve weakening and put her hand out to stop him. It rested on his hard chest.

'You must listen to me, Joan,' he said.

She looked at him mutely, her eyes filled with pain and tears.

'I am going back to Positano. I cannot stay here in your beautiful country one more day without you. Every ray of sun reminds me of you, I can't even enjoy my espresso anymore because it makes me think of you. I leave tomorrow. You must come. You must come with me.'

'I can't,' she said. Her whisper barely made it to his ears.

He turned and walked back to his truck and drove away.

Three weeks later, Joan realised she was pregnant. That morning it felt like someone had turned a light on. Her joy was practically hallucinogenic. The sun was warmer, the colours more colourful, the outlines on the leaves sharper. And the crazy paving was the craziest, most delectable piece of stonework she'd ever seen.

The only minor downside, of course, was that she had to force herself to have sex with her husband that night.

Naturally Barry was thrilled to become a father. And, when he wasn't at the office, he would occasionally even hold the baby – when Joan wasn't feeding or changing him.

Infant Tony grew into big boy Tony then into a young teen. Joan and her son were inseparable. Tony and his father, however, were always at loggerheads. They didn't agree on anything and Barry's strict parenting techniques set up an impenetrable barrier in the father–son relationship. When Tony, at age sixteen, announced he was quitting school to take up a builder's apprenticeship, the camel's back collapsed.

A screaming match of hideous proportions ended with Tony leaving the family home and moving into share housing to follow his own dream, rather than his father's dream that he should go to university.

Eighteen months later, with not a word between the two men, Barry died of a massive heart attack while yelling at the office boy at work. Tony, with dry eyes, attended the funeral.

Joan had told Sera her story while lying back on the pillows, her eyes closed as if seeing the series of events taking place all over again.

Now she opened her eyes, and looked at Sera. The transformation was complete. A smile played at the corners of her mouth. Her dark green eyes twinkled as the beautiful memories faded slowly. But the secret was out. She was no longer the gatekeeper of the family scandal. Let the repercussions commence.

'But the letter I found?' Sera asked her. 'You never sent it?'

'I was torn, Sera, what was I to do? I loved him so much; he needed to know he had a son. But how could I do that to him? Offer him a son he couldn't have? The scandal, Sera, the dreadful scandal. You must realise how ostracised I would have been by my community.'

'There would have been a way, surely.'

'Sera, you don't think I've thought of that, over and over. The number of times I've regretted my decision. The great shame I've had to live with, it tears me apart every day.'

'Why didn't you tell him after Barry died? Why didn't you go to Antonio then?'

'Because I had kept it a secret for too long. My parents were still alive, so were Barry's: imagine the betrayal! And I thought Antonio would hate me for not telling him nineteen years earlier, when we first conceived Tony.'

Sera leaned over to her mother-in-law and gave her an embrace. 'Well, it's out now. It must be such a relief for you.'

'Yes, Sera, it is a relief, thanks for letting me get all that out and for helping me keep this secret. Now I won't feel so alone.'

Sera frowned. 'Um, Joan, you are going to tell Tony, aren't you?'

Joan's eyes widened in horror. 'Oh God, no! Sera, you mustn't. I couldn't, you can't, it would destroy him to know he's illegitimate.'

'Oh for goodness' sake, Joan, we're not living in the Dark Ages. Illegitimacy is completely a concept of the past. Half the mums at childcare aren't married and no one even notices.'

'But to know he's been raised in a lie, that I've lied about his father. He'll hate me, he'll hate me!' Joan started to sob hysterically, tears running down her powdered cheeks. She clung to Sera as she begged. 'Please don't, Sera, I couldn't bear it if my Tony hated me.'

'Joan, calm down,' Sera handed her a box of tissues from the side-table. 'I won't tell him if you don't want me to. But I think you'd be very surprised. Besides, it would be very important for him to understand his heritage. He's half-Italian, his father's a stone-mason – that's all very exciting news. It explains so much; his passion for life, his precision in his work and love of creating. I really think you need to consider it.' She got up and slipped back into nurse mode. 'But more importantly, right now you need to heal, you need to rest and let that hip of yours mend.' She got up from the bed and fussed around the room; tossing out tissues and picking up empty teacups. She opened the bedroom door to leave.

'It's funny,' Joan suddenly said. 'It will take six weeks for my broken hip to heal but it's been a lifetime and my heart still hasn't.'

~52~

The gravel path seemed fluid as the sunlight fell from the trees and played with the leaves' shadows on the ground.

Their pace was slow, almost a shuffle really. Tony wanted to be sure his mother didn't over-do it on her first day out. 'How's the new hip holding up, Mum?' he asked as they approached a park bench. 'Would you like a rest?'

'Probably a good idea,' Joan admitted and gratefully sank down on the seat. They sat in silence and sheltered from the early summer sun under the gracious boughs of a Moreton Bay Fig. The sparkles bouncing off Sydney Harbour reminded him of the flash photography in the audience at the Olympics; a constant twinkle of pea lights.

As he stared out at the scene that fell before him – the iconic Opera House to his left, the bridge directly ahead, the architectural sentries perched atop the cliffs on the opposite shore – it occurred to him again how lucky he was, they all were, to live in this remarkable city. He'd always had a weird feeling that he'd won the lottery, living in this place; that he'd just barely escaped a very different path.

He had been feeling extremely serene lately. Everything was going so much better. His world was bobbing along in a light zephyr, where sweetness and light abounded. The reno was over and they'd re-structured their crazy living arrangements, stretching into the new space with relief. His relationship with his beautiful wife had reached an entirely new level: the comfortable companionship of long-term now sizzled with fresh flirtation. He was thoroughly enjoying her, but, more importantly, she was enjoying him.

Something had altered in his mother since her accident, but he couldn't quite put his finger on it. She was more relaxed, less prickly, less likely to snap at imagined slights. And she wasn't as critical towards Sera: she was almost friendly.

He nodded with pride. He'd done it, achieved the great Australian dream. All he had left to do was kick back and enjoy the patch of paradise he'd created for himself and his family. He felt a spring inside him slowly uncoil for the first time in decades. He stretched out his legs, put his hands behind his back and enjoyed the feeling of release it gave him. Tony finally let go. It was all good.

'Tony, there's something I need to tell you,' his mother said.

'Hmmmm,' he replied, only half-listening.

'And I don't quite know where to begin.'

Tony could start to sense his internal spring tightening up ever so slightly, resentful it had recently been fooled into the luxury of release.

'Why not from the start, Mum? What is it?' He forced himself to sit up.

His mother looked at him, her eyes filled with tears and he shook his head. Jesus, no, not more drama, damn him for jinxing the situation with all the self-congratulation.

'I really don't know how to tell you this, but I have to because if I don't, Sera will, and it's not her place to tell you, it really is mine. It's something I should have told you years ago but I didn't have the guts, anyway your father was still alive and I could have gone to the grave with it and then you'd be none the wiser, but that's really not fair on you, and it's especially not fair on the children, for that matter . . . you see your children are crucial to this news . . . your children are . . . but here I am starting at the end, I must start at the beginning.'

At the mention of his kids Tony interrupted sharply. 'Mum, stop it, you're raving. Tell me right now, what's this got to do with the kids?'

'Well, it goes back to 1967 –'

'The kids, Mum, tell me about the kids.'

'Well, I have to start at the beginning. You see, we needed a crazy paving patio –'

'Mother, what about the children?'

'Tony, don't fluster me, you men don't understand the art of story-telling.'

'Mother! The children are . . . what?'

'Italian!'

There was silence. Tony wondered if his mother had Alzheimer's. Then he wondered if she had suddenly gone deaf and hadn't heard the question properly. How could his children be Italian? He looked at her. She looked back at him.

'Well, one-quarter Italian, really,' she said, as if reading his mind, 'but still Italian enough to get those lovely chocolate brown eyes of yours.'

One-quarter Italian. That would mean his father was Italian, but his father was descended from the Dutch. He and his ancestors were very blond. It was funny how blond they were, actually, he'd often wondered where his own black hair and brown eyes had come from . . . Hang on. Tony's past flashed before his eyes: the years of feeling like he didn't fit in, the sense that his father didn't understand him, the fights, the unrealistic expectations.

'Mum?'

Joan looked as contrite as a fallen woman of sixty-six could. 'Sorry, Tony, I should have told you years ago.

I am so sorry, but I just couldn't do it to you, I knew how disappointed you would be with me. I didn't want you to hate me. You're mad, I knew you would be.'

He continued staring at her. He had never considered his mother as a person before, just as a mother, carer, nurse, cook, and wife to his father. He saw her fear that she would lose him, her fear that he wouldn't support her.

'Mum, I'm not mad at you.'

'You're not? Oh, darling, that's wonderful. You should be, I know.'

'I wouldn't be here, if it wasn't for you. And now it all makes sense. I always felt so dreadful that Dad and I never got along like other fathers and sons. He never seemed to enjoy my company or my ideas. I felt it was my fault the whole time that I couldn't win him over. It makes perfect sense after all. We weren't even related.'

He stared back at the water, letting this new revelation sink in. His dad wasn't his dad. It was the most bizarre feeling he'd ever had. His every sense of who he was seemed to dissipate into the Sydney sunshine. But rather than feeling lost, he felt free. Released somehow.

'It wasn't just because you weren't genetically related that you didn't connect to Barry, son. He was also a king-sized arsehole, too, you know.' Tony laughed at Joan's flouting her number-one rule of never speaking ill of the dead.

'This is amazing, Mum,' Tony said, and to Joan's obvious delight he squeezed her tightly. 'So one question remains to be answered. Who *is* my dad?'

~53~

The year was fast coming to an end. The group couldn't believe that November's Stitch 'n' Bitch had come around so quickly. That night's session had the air of a teen slumber party. The giggles and squeals floated up to the limed, exposed rafters of Sera's extension like the champagne bubbles that drifted up in the slender flutes.

As Sera passed around the pretty little teeny-weeny strudellini she'd picked up at Gusto in Five Ways late that afternoon, she marvelled at the transformation that each member of the group had been through in just a few months.

Jacqueline accepted an apple strudel and, without a hint of snobbery, declared it delectable. She had softened, unwound; she didn't act in such a superior way anymore, Sera thought. Of course she was run off her feet with her new business, but the work suited the manic redhead. At least now she was working for herself instead of the spoilt and overbearing menfolk in her family.

'Two hundred and twenty units a week!' Jacqueline declared to Joan, who was a new and welcome addition to the group. I've become quite adept at freezing pie crusts and pre-mixing fillings. And I've just put on a driver: the deliveries were getting quite time-consuming, especially the North Shore orders. I need to steer clear of André's turf, he's been wonderful.'

'Well done,' Joan said, squeezing Jacqueline's arm. 'I am

very impressed. You have really done a great job. Let me know anytime you need a hand.'

Sera shook her head and smiled to herself. Talk about unlikely allies.

Joan was a new woman since her big confession. The years had dropped away. The terse and tense manner had dissipated and now that she was relieved of the burden of guilt and shame she'd relaxed into a different woman. The judgments had dried up, the snappiness had disappeared. It was like a total mother-in-law transplant. Joan had expected to be judged herself for her adulterous past and was utterly surprised to find the news was greeted with congratulations and support from the other women. Mavis had sniffed in a superior manner when she'd heard, but Joan hadn't cared a dot. She was too amazed at the acceptance she'd received from Sera's friends.

She was now a valued member of the Stitch 'n' Bitchers and was eager to show the others her advanced knitting and needlework secrets.

It had been such a relief to be able to sit in the bosom of this group of friends and pour out her heart, explain her feelings about Antonio for the first time, whisper the details of the intimacies the young couple had shared and enjoy the gasps and coos of her audience. She felt safe and secure within this group, a feeling she'd never had among friends before. It felt extraordinary to be accepted as Joan the Woman and to be proud of that person, with all the flaws and history that came attached.

'And after that we're off to a little village in the east where her aunty was raised.' Chantrea was regaling the group with the details of her impending holiday to Cambodia. It would be a surprise for Sally.

Chantrea explained that it was tradition in her mother's family that when a child reached school age he or she was taken on an adventure to celebrate the journey from babyhood into childhood and, as Sally was about to enter Prep, her mother and grandmother were indulging her wish to visit Cambodia. 'I really have to brush up on my language skills, though, I won't have a clue what anybody's saying,' Chantrea said and laughed.

'I haven't seen you this excited about going on a trip in years, Chantrea,' Sera said and topped up the champagne. 'I'm so happy for you, you're all going to have a ball.' She was genuinely thrilled for her friend and was so pleased she'd finally come to accept her heritage.

Sera looked around at her newly renovated house. The new kitchen gleamed with granite and glass and gave the house the heart she'd always felt was missing. Joan had finally given the domestic facelift her blessing, especially since Tony had been able to reclaim the original slate crazy paving and had re-built the now famous patio.

Now Joan sat every morning in her special courtyard, sipping her espresso and admiring how her Tony had recreated Antonio's courtyard with such immaculate detail.

And Mallory, darling Mallory. It was typical that only Mallory could make facial scarring look endearing and sweet. It added to her natural vulnerability. She was still in terrible pain over her marriage break-up, of course, and the girls had taken turns spending large chunks of time counselling her and helping her to mend both physically and mentally. But at least this evening she was finally laughing again. It's going to be months before it gets easy, Sera thought, but at least she's still with us, she still has Tilly, and thankfully the prick is letting her keep the house.

Sam looked shattered, Sera thought, as she opened a beer for him and passed it over. He was working too hard and the girls were running him so ragged that his mother had just flown in from Brisbane to help him out for a couple of weeks. And by the sounds of things, his string of disastrous dates was taking its toll.

'A monk!' He declared in response to Chanrea's probing about his love-life. 'That's what I should become. So easy: a cave, some chanting, a bowl of rice every so often, no dramas. Then at least I wouldn't have to endure the hell of the dating scene.'

'Oh, come on, it's not that bad, surely,' Jacqueline said. 'It must be fun getting out there and meeting new people.'

Chantrea and Sam both looked at her with dubious expressions. 'It is awful,' said Chantrea. 'It seems single people are single for a reason – except us, of course,' she hastened, throwing an apologetic glance towards Sam.

'Absolutely,' he agreed. 'We're single because everybody else is completely wacky!'

'That's right,' Chantrea said, 'completely and utterly wacky. I had a date recently and he seemed so very, very normal – entertaining, interesting, charming – then we went back to his house and from crockery to wallpaper it was decorated with Lucy Liu images. He had a freaky Asian thing going on. I couldn't get out of there fast enough.'

A flurry of bad date stories ensued. Even Joan joined in and told a story about a strange doctor she had afternoon tea with during her nursing training who had a fetish for cadavers and spent most of his free time in the hospital morgue. 'It wasn't sexual, mind,' she reassured the group, 'he just really enjoyed talking about them. It was quite creepy.'

Sera noticed Sam lean his head back on the couch. 'You need a break, Sam,' she said, 'just a few days to yourself.'

'Sera, I'd love a break, just to sleep in for a couple of hours, read a newspaper – hell, I'd be happy to simply sit still for a day. It's all go, go, go running a business from home, and those dear little girls – do kids ever stop moving?'

'Listen,' Sera said, striking on the perfect answer. 'Bella's given me a business class ticket to Hong Kong with three nights at the Peninsula. It's for this weekend, and I can't possibly go. We're flat chat, so I was about to call her to cancel.'

'It sounds like heaven, Sera, it really does, but I couldn't,' Sam said.

'You're crazy to pass it up, Hong Kong's fantastic,' Chantrea said. 'Your mum's here with the girls, why not?'

Sam shook his head in the manner of a typical parent, in complete disbelief that it would ever be possible to get any time alone. 'No, it's just not doable. I've got clients, the girls, Mum . . .'

'Big deal: cancel, re-schedule, do it. A weekend at the Peninsula is the closest thing anybody's going to get to paradise on the planet, let me tell you,' Chantrea said. 'You simply have to.'

'I can't just go to Hong Kong for the weekend,' Sam scoffed, as though she was nuts.

'Why not?' the women all asked in unison.

'Well, it's too crazy. I mean, what if something happens while I'm away? What if something goes wrong?' He made excuses then looked from face to face in wonder. Sera watched his thought processes click away, mirrored in his face. Was this possible? Dare he do it? What a concept. A long weekend to himself. 'Won't Bella mind?'

'Course she won't,' Sera said. 'You know Bella, she won't care at all. She'd be thrilled.'

'No, I don't know Bella,' Sam pointed out. 'I haven't met her yet.'

'What? Didn't you meet her a few weeks back?' Chantrea asked. 'She came to the last Stitch 'n' Bitch.'

'I was on a date that night with the purrer.'

'Oh, that's right.' Chantrea laughed at the memory of the story. 'The one who thought she was part feline.'

'That's the one. She even wore a bell around her neck.'

'See, they're all wacky!' Chantrea said.

'You're telling me!' Sam replied. And at the thought of the tentative date he had set up for Saturday night with another potential fruitloop, he made his decision. 'Sera, thank you so much, I'll do it.'

The girls all cheered and raised their glasses to him.

'You'll have a ball,' Sera said.

'Absolutely,' Chantrea agreed, 'and it's only for three days. What could possibly go wrong?'

~54~

The seething masses of humanity lined up barefoot and resigned at security – each bored passenger awaiting his or her turn to remove belts, bangles and other unassuming items that might make the sensitive metal detector sound its suspicious alarm.

Huffs and sighs from one queue burst forth as an elderly woman was caught trying to smuggle nail scissors aboard. Those more experienced travellers, impatiently tapping their feet in the line, shook their heads – they'd all been there before, the old duck might as well try and convince Dannii Minogue to quit plastic surgery for all the good her pleas and tears were going to do.

Bella took the scene in, grateful for her own incident-free queue. She was well-versed in this minefield of inconvenience and had quickly assessed which line had the fewest likely troublemakers. Certainly not the line on the far left with the mother, the stroller and the three children, that's for sure. The infant was asleep in the stroller and the mother was in tears after being told she had to remove the sleeping baby, fold up the pram and put it through the X-ray.

Metal-free and sans pointy implements, Bella entered the far side. She checked her watch for the tenth time since entering the airport. She had to meet Sera's friend at the bar to give him his accommodation voucher for the Peninsula. She was more than a little annoyed that her gift to Sera had been re-gifted to a person she didn't even know. She'd been looking forward to a night out in Hong Kong with her sister but when she'd heard the sad tale of the dead wife she'd swallowed her irritation and forced herself into a more charitable frame of mind. Who was this bloke, anyway? When she'd last caught up with the girls in Sydney they all seemed so taken with him.

She found the bar and flicked her eyes around the room. The dimly-lit space was peopled with solo travellers sucking down their drinks, too desperate to wait for the free grog on their flights. All she had to do was hand over the voucher and then she could head to the flight attendants' lounge. The flight was due to board soon and she needed a little freshening-up time.

At the bar, however, was a man who was obviously not the typical airport barfly. He had a long black fringe that touched his narrow black rectangular glasses. He wore a black polo top with a charcoal suit coat and faded jeans. A canvas computer bag sat at his feet. She looked back at his face and realised he was smiling tentatively at her.

He stood. 'Bella?'

'I guess you're Sam.' Holding her hand out in greeting, she moved over to the bar.

'It's so good to meet you. I can't thank you enough for this. I hope you don't mind that your sister re-gifted your present.'

'Not at all, I haven't thought about it twice.' Bella couldn't help herself and smiled again. He was really quite sweet; it was rare to meet a good-looking man unsaddled with arrogance. 'And here is your accommodation voucher.'

'Thanks so much, it is very good of you. I really appreciate it. Can I get you a drink to say thank you?'

Bella hesitated – she really needed to get moving – but he was so grateful, not to mention charming. 'All right then, a quick bitters, lime and soda, then I should get to the gate. We board in forty-five minutes.'

'So you fly?' He attempted light conversation as the barman served their drinks.

'I do,' she replied.

'Do your arms get tired?' he asked, deadpan.

She looked at him strangely for a second, then laughed.

'Sorry, I make stupid jokes when I'm nervous,' he told her.

'Are you a nervous flyer?' she asked.

'Yes, a little,' Sam admitted.

'Then your arms must get really tired!' She returned the gag and they relaxed into each other's company. They chatted away in the manner of new friends: comparing stories about Sera and her family, international cities, airport dramas, the latest episode of *Border Security* – a secret weakness they shared, they realised. Bella even opened up so much to Sam that she shared the story of her rough upbringing, making him laugh with stories about her wild brothers.

She couldn't put her finger on it. She felt warm in this man's company, safe and relaxed. She'd never experienced that with anyone before. Usually she had a gatekeeper in her mind who monitored her every word to ensure she didn't let loose any private thoughts, but it was obviously on strike today as all sorts of opinions and anecdotes came tumbling forth.

She suddenly realised she hadn't checked her hair or her make-up since she had walked in. Her watch remained unchecked and her posture had relaxed into a languid lean instead of her usual rigid stance.

Just as Bella reluctantly glanced at her watch to see if it was time to go to the gate, the announcement came that the flight to Hong Kong was delayed by two hours.

Amongst the exasperated moans of their fellow travellers, Bella and Sam found it difficult to pretend to be disappointed.

~55~

When Bella and Sam left the bar to board their plane, they joked that the pilot must have finally found the keys to the 747. They said goodbye at the gate and she promised to visit him during the flight.

Now it was back to being Bella the professional, Bella the serious. Her smile quickly switched from the natural beam she'd been shining on Sam to the pleasant, tight-lipped countenance she reserved for her first-class passengers.

Her chignon was neat enough; Bella didn't bother checking.

'Cabin crew, secure doors and cross-check,' the first officer announced over the PA. Asif giggled at her as they crossed paths to double-check the door.

'Oh, put a sock in it, will you,' she said to him over her shoulder. She was well aware he was laughing at her old habit of cross-checking, triple-checking and quadruple-checking the doors were secure. She may have recently begun tackling her OCD but she was still a stickler for safety.

'What?' he said, all wide-eyed and innocent. She poked her tongue out at him and walked up to the head of the aisle, pasting on her most winning flight attendant smile.

She picked up a lifejacket and went through the motions of the safety procedures to the pre-recorded voice. She could do this in her sleep. Bella shuddered to think how many hundreds of times she'd performed this ritual. But she liked it. It soothed her in a strange way, to have this routine performance that was simultaneously crucial yet mind-numbingly mundane.

It fascinated her how many passengers steadfastly ignored the safety demonstration. Perhaps they'd heard it so often they knew it by heart, she wondered as she stood there in front of them as if invisible. Or perhaps they were in denial that there was any chance of an accident. When the demonstration was over, she went up to the exit area to buckle herself into her seat.

Sam stowed his carry-on luggage in the overhead locker and sat down next to an earnest bespectacled fellow. They exchanged brief pleasantries before Sam picked up the in-flight magazine and his fellow passenger went back to madly texting on the in-flight telephone.

After take-off, Sam's seatmate finally put the phone down and breathed out a tremendous sigh. It was so melodramatic Sam turned to him questioningly. 'Oh, sorry,' he explained. 'Steven Blakely's my name. I'm a journo with Reuters and I've just texted a story through to my bureau. It's no mean feat writing an entire article in SMS.'

'Why didn't you do it on the ground?' Sam enquired, intrigued about the man's job.

'It only just broke. My contact in Iraq phoned just as they were closing the doors. There was an explosion in a shopping centre in Baghdad literally minutes ago.'

'Really?' Sam exclaimed. 'Many injured?'

'It's too early to tell yet, but it doesn't look good. It's peak shopping time there and it's a suspected car bomb.'

'Oh, jeez, that's terrible.'

'It would have been terrible if I hadn't received that call. Talk about by a bee's dick. I would have landed in

Hong Kong to find the story submitted by somebody else. It'd be old news by then. But now, it's on the internet as we speak.'

'That's amazing,' Sam said. As they chatted more, he learned that Steven had worked the international circuit as a foreign correspondent for fifteen years. He didn't look the flakjacket, adventurous, devil-may-care type, but Steven explained it was just the front-of-camera telly journos who fitted that stereotype.

The first few hours went by while they each drank a beer and chatted about world politics, carbon emissions and life in the internet age.

Apart from a chatty elderly lady, the first-class passengers were a fairly easy group to handle once the alcoholic in 2A passed out, which was a relief because the Sydney to London via Hong Kong flight could be a tiring one.

Twenty-two hours with belligerent passengers was hell on earth. Although the layovers were generous, it often wasn't worth it. Thank God she was stopping over in Hong Kong this time. She'd arranged to meet up with Sam and pleasant thoughts distracted her for a moment from her task at hand.

A few hours into the trip, Bella couldn't conceal a shy schoolgirl grin as she told Asif about Sam sitting in Business Class. He threatened to go and check him out, but she begged him not to.

'Oh, come on, Bella, just a quick peek,' Asif taunted. 'I have to give my approval, you know. I'm not letting you go out with a fugly.'

'He's not fugly,' she hissed and tried to push him back into the galley, 'and be quiet, he's just on the other side of that curtain, he'll hear you.'

They rolled their eyes at each other as the impatient ding of the call button sounded. They peeked out of the galley and sure enough it was 3A. 'North Shore Princess's fizzy needs topping up,' Asif groaned. 'Here, you do it.' He thrust the bottle at her.

'I'm not doing it. She's your passenger.'

'I'll buy you a Chanel handbag when we get to Honkers if you do it.'

'Big whoop, they're a dime a dozen.'

'No, real one, promise,' Asif said with his hand behind his back. Bella knew he had his fingers crossed but she took the bottle anyway.

'Chicken,' she said, as she turned to leave the galley.

'I prefer spatchcock,' he shot back and turned to restock the refreshments trolley.

The cabin thrummed as the plane continued across the continent. After she topped up her passenger's drink, Bella glanced around and took in her steel tube world in a slow gaze. It seemed calm enough, business as usual. Napping, sipping, TV-viewing passengers; quietly spoken flight attendants. A passenger leaving the toilet. It was like an ecosystem in a bell jar. In stasis. Nothing could change, nothing could happen, they were all just trapped there, under the guidance of the pilots, trusting, waiting for the moment they arrived back in their lives.

Bella returned to the business class galley to catch Asif admiring himself in the stainless steel reflection of the Atlas locker. She was just about to tease him when a deafening crack rocked the cabin. The passengers shrieked as the floor beneath Asif's feet crumpled up in a steel hump. He was flipped to one side, his head smacking hard into the metal bench, leaving him unconscious and bleeding.

~56~

Gale-force winds flushed debris through the cabin. The metal wall of the toilet was smashed and one lethal piece came to rest near Sam as if it had been a throwing star wielded by a ninja. Sam looked at it two feet away and swallowed hard. The roar of wind and yelling was deafening.

'We're being shot at! We're being shot at!' a middle-aged man two rows back screamed hysterically.

The oxygen masks dropped down in front of each passenger. It gave them a job to do, albeit a minor one, which helped distract them momentarily.

Sam fought past the dangle of yellow plastic and made his way back to the hysterical businessman, who was still yelling. The cabin had depressurised. He didn't have much time.

'Hey mate, stop panicking. We're not being shot at. Put your mask on and don't say another word. We'll be fine.' The man looked up at him mid-sentence, then nodded mutely and started fiddling with his mask.

Sam sat back in his own seat and grabbed his own mask. The oxygen was hissing reassuringly and he took three deep breaths before pulling the elastic over his head.

Steven Blakely turned his ashen face up to Sam before he grabbed the plane telephone and started texting again.

'What the hell are you doing?' Sam hissed from the side of his mask.

'Texting the bureau,' Blakely replied, his voice lowered several octaves by the yellow rubber interference. 'This is an airline disaster story, you don't get bigger than that! This is a guaranteed front page by-line.'

'What the fuck?' Sam said, 'We need to do something, we need to help!'

Steven Blakely's thumb was a blur as it flew over the keypad. He didn't look up as he replied, 'No point in helping, what can we do? We're screwed. Must get story out before crash.'

He put the phone back after a few more seconds. 'Well, that's it. The word's out.' Sam looked at him and a chill ran through his bones as the journalist sat back calmly and waited grimly for the inevitable.

Sera stood in her bathroom and smiled at the glass jars in either hand. She shook her head in disbelief that she'd once had so much faith in their contents. This ridiculous white cream wasn't the answer to her issues with the scar. The answer was inside her, and had been the whole time. She didn't care about it anymore. Sure it would be nice to have smooth legs, but it would also be nice to win Lotto and that wasn't about to happen either. She was sick of casting herself in the role of victim. This was the hand life had dealt her, and it was about time she accepted it. The classical music pouring from her bathroom radio soothed and enhanced her new found sense of inner calm.

Sera moved towards the bin to add the jars to the batch that had already been discarded. Suddenly the music ground to an abrupt halt. She looked at the radio in surprise. That's not very ABC, she thought.

An officious female announcer started to speak. 'News just in: A mid-air explosion on Air Australia Flight 96 en route to Hong Kong from Sydney has just occurred. Reuters journalist Steven Blakely is on board the aircraft and has reported that an explosion on the left-hand side of the plane has penetrated the hull. Debris and wind are inside the cabin. One flight attendant is unconscious but there are no other apparent injuries.

'Details are limited at this stage. Air Australia CEO Kevin Janeway is about to make a statement to the press.'

Sera screamed and dropped the jar onto the tiled floor. It exploded into shards.

Tony came running in. 'What is it, Sera, what's wrong?'

She looked at him dumbstruck and simply pointed to the radio. The CEO of the airline was repeating what the news reporter had just said. He also explained the type of aircraft it was and details of the passenger and crew manifest.

'Shit, that's bad,' Tony said. 'Let's clean up this mess, and then we'll go down and turn on the television. It'll be on all the stations.'

He knelt down with the bin and a roll of toilet paper.

'Tony,' Sera said, her voice strained.

'Yeah, what hon?' He said and turned up to face his stricken wife.

'Bella and Sam are on that flight,' she whispered.

Chantrea walked down the wide airport concourse towards her gate. Two small boys were playing chasey from one side to the other and she nearly tripped over them twice.

'Stop it, you little buggers,' she snarled at them when they came close to her a third time. She glanced at the clock on the departure screen overhead. Ten minutes: plenty of time to slap on some face, drag on her kit and play Hostess Barbie for the next cattle car full of Bali-bound punters.

Suddenly her mobile went nuts, ten new messages coming in at once. Then it started ringing with an incoming call. She was about to answer it when her attention was grabbed by the mass of people crowded around a television at one of the gates.

The phone continued its insistent bleating as she looked in disbelief at images of the Air Australia flight and old footage of the Qantas oxygen canister accident of a year ago flickering up on the screen. She moved closer to hear the news. Hijacked? Surely not. What on earth was going on? Which flight was it?

AA-96. Her world tumbled in sickening lurches as her phone kept ringing. That was Bella's flight, and Sam was on it.

The crutches went flying across the room and bashed into the opposite wall as Mallory crashed to the ground in tears. 'I can't do it, I'm telling you, it's too hard!'

'Yes, it's very frustrating,' Francesca, the physiotherapist cooed as she retrieved the crutches, 'but you're making tremendous progress. Look, you took six steps today, and the crutches only really held your weight for the last few.'

'Six steps? That's crap. I used to do Step Reebok. I used to do fun runs. I used to wear high heels.' And with that last, most tragic, announcement she put her head down and wailed. 'I'm . . . never . . . going to wear . . . high heels . . . again,' she sobbed.

Francesca couldn't help but roll her eyes. Mallory was a fairly easy-going patient usually but really, high heels?

The door to the workout room slammed open. 'Hey,' Francesca scolded the receptionist who came flying into the room,'I have a patient.'

The girl rushed to the television and picked up the remote. 'A bomb or something's just exploded on an Air Australia plane,' she explained.

'Oh, shit,' Mallory and Francesca said in unison and stared at the screen. The room was dense with silence as the trio watched in horror.

'Apparently the plane was on its way to Hong Kong,' the receptionist said.

'Oh no,' Mallory said in a little voice, 'I think my friends are on that plane.'

'You're very kind to help me, Joan. You really don't need to,' Jacqueline said.

The two women were up to the rims of their pink soapy washing gloves in dishwater, cleaning up after the day's bakefest. They'd made forty-two chocolate cheese-cakes, a dessert that was fast becoming Jacqueline's signature dish.

'I said I'd help you and I'm a woman of my word,' Joan said. 'Well except for that "to have and to hold, to love and to cherish and forego all others" load of codswallop.'

Jacqueline laughed at the callous disregard of the sanctity of marriage. Joan was a funny old bird. Jacqueline thoroughly enjoyed her company and couldn't have grown her business so quickly without the older woman's help. In fact she'd expanded her range to include a line of tasty little Italian pastries at which Joan seemed to be quite the dab hand.

A repeat of *All Saints* babbled away in the corner of the room as the women washed the last of the baking trays.

Suddenly Chris Bath at the Channel Seven news desk interrupted, all worry lines and shaky voice. 'Breaking news: an explosion has just occurred on board Air Australia flight 96. Reuters journalist Steven Blakely is on the flight and witnessed the blast first-hand. Terrorist activity has not been ruled out at this stage. The award-winning journalist sent a message from on board the plane.'

A close-up of a mobile phone was shown on the screen. A text message was scrolling:

Explosion abrd AA96. Crw mbr dwn. No O2, masks in use.

A male voice-over translated the SMS in a sombre baritone, 'Explosion aboard Air Australia flight ninety-six. Crew member down. No oxygen, masks in use.'

The newsreader continued with ultimate professionalism, her head tilted sightly to one side. 'This text message was received by the Reuters bureau in Sydney at 4.10 pm eastern standard daylight savings time and it has been confirmed by telecommunications experts as having been sent from Flight 96. This is not a hoax. At this stage we cannot confirm if Sydney Control Tower has been able to get in contact with the captain of AA96.

'In July 2008, a Qantas jet experienced what seems to be a similar mid-air explosion . . .'

The women grasped each other's pink, soapy, rubber-lined hands and stared at the screen in horror.

~57~

Sam leapt out of his seat and tore through the curtains to the galley. Bella was crouched over Asif. She had an oxygen tank with her and was fitting a mask over his face. She looked up at Sam. They both knew words were a waste of valuable air. Sam started to feel foggy. His lungs were burning. Asif took a breath and came to. He looked at the others and put up a thumb to indicate he was okay. Bella took a breath from the tank's second regulator and passed it on to Sam, who also took a breath. The rush of oxygen cleared his brain.

'What happened?' he asked. She shrugged as she took the mask back from him and breathed.

'Some kind of explosion. Look up the aisle.' The cause of the constant scream of wind became obvious as Sam saw the hole ripped through the floor.

'We have to cover it before it gets even bigger,' he shouted.

'But how?' she asked.

The captain's voice on the PA was competing with the chaos. 'Everyone, please remain calm. It's essential you do not panic. I have control of the aircraft. I repeat, I have control of the aircraft.' His commanding tone convinced the passengers to accept his order and as the squealing, wailing and crying began to calm somewhat, they realised the plane, although descending, was doing it in a controlled way, not in a nosedive, end-of-the-world kind of way.

Sam scanned the area around him. His eyes rested on a large silver serving platter. The hole was the size of a bowling ball. The platter might just do it. He approached the tear in the floor and slapped the tray down. It immediately buckled in the centre as the suction tried to pull it out.

Sam returned to Bella and gratefully accepted the oxygen mask from her. She in turn took Asif's from his outstretched hand.

'We need more of a barrier, that's not going to be enough,' Sam said. 'It'll be sucked out any minute.'

'The seats?' Bella suggested.

'Do they come off?' Sam asked.

'We can try,' Bella said and Asif nodded, his face as white as the laminate on the cupboard doors of the galley. 'The captain should have us at a safe altitude within minutes,' she added.

Just then a high-pitched scream came from the business class section. 'Shot at shot at shot at!' The wails came louder and louder.

'We've got a situation back there,' Sam told Bella and Asif. 'A guy's completely lost it. You guys work on releasing one of the seats. I'll go and see what I can do with the panicked one.'

As Sam went past his own seat, he glanced over at Steven Blakely, who was texting again. Who could think of work at a time like this?

The businessman was up and standing in the aisle. He saw Sam coming and pushed into him. 'Parachute, I need a parachute, I need to get off this plane. WE'RE GOING DOWN, DO YOU HEAR ME, WE'RE GOING DOWN!'

Sam knew panic was more infectious than any disease and potentially more deadly. The other passengers joined in with the hysterical screaming and clung to each other in desperation.

Sam grabbed the man by the shoulders. 'We're not going down. The captain has the plane under control. We're about to hit breathable altitude, but you need to sit down and get your mask on.' Sam grabbed the man's mask and gulped a lungful with the intention of handing it over and placing it on the passenger's head.

'No!' The man screamed in terror. 'That's mine, that's my oxygen, give it here, give it to me.' His powerful arms thrashed out. Sam ducked but got the bloke's forearm in the ear and side of his head. Stars swam in front of his eyes for a moment before he regained clarity.

'For God's sake, calm down,' Sam said. He put his arms out to steady the guy but again, the man tried to punch him. Sam defended himself by landing a crack on the guy's nose. The man's head ricocheted back, his eyes swum back into his skull and he sank down into his seat into blissful unconsciousness. Sam, after taking one more breath, put the oxygen mask over the man's now relaxed face and rushed back to the first-class section.

Bella and Asif were wrestling with a crew seat. 'It's only two large bolts, here and here, and we can get it off,' Bella said, offering the small spanner to Sam. He quickly unscrewed the first bolt but the second one was jammed.

His thumb caught in between the seat and the bolt as the fastener folded back onto itself, catching Sam's thumb in its grip. He swore as the blood sprang from his hand. An eerie crunch forced Sam and Bella to look at the hole. The heavy stainless steel tray was sucked out like a sheet of tinfoil. Only a curved lip of metal remained visible. 'It's gonna suck through,' Sam shouted.

The trio pulled on the seat until the second bolt snapped. They grabbed the seat and flung it over the silver tray just as it was sucked out into the baggage hold, which presumably had a hole in its side much bigger than the one in the cabin. The vacuum from the hole greedily grabbed the seat and it held fast.

The captain's voice filled the now quieter cabin. 'Ladies and gentlemen, we are flying at fourteen hundred feet. The cabin should be filling with oxygen but I highly recommend you keep your oxygen masks on until we land. We have emergency clearance at Darwin International Airport and we will be landing in approximately six minutes.'

The passengers gave a half-hearted cheer, but weren't prepared to really believe they were safe until they were on solid ground.

The calloused thumb of Steven Blakely spread the word of the hopeful conclusion of the drama to fifty million readers, viewers and listeners within twenty-seven seconds.

~58~

Chris Bath continued to look out at her unseen audience in concern as she repeated the same words she'd been saying for the last fifteen minutes. Sera and Tony stood in the middle of the living room, transfixed by her commentary. They were holding their breath, for the next update, each in their own bubble of worry, alone in their thoughts, not daring to let their imaginations play this drama out to its inevitable conclusion.

A disembodied arm handed the newsreader a piece of paper. 'News just in,' the on-air reporter said to the camera. Sera and Tony grabbed for each other's hands. 'Air Australia Flight 96 has landed safely at Darwin International Airport. Reuters journalist Steven Blakely, on board at the time of the drama, reports that the hole in the airplane is likely to have been caused by an oxygen canister, similar to the incident aboard a Qantas 747 last year. One passenger has been reported as injured and one crew member has also suffered minor injuries. To repeat, the air emergency is over. The Air Australia flight, on which an explosion took place thirteen minutes ago, has landed safely in Darwin.

'If you've just tuned in, late this afternoon on a routine Air Australia flight to Hong Kong . . .'

Sera felt her knees buckle in relief. Sheer nervous tension had been all that had kept her standing for the last thirty minutes. Tony sensed her weakness and leaned in with strong arms to support her weight. His solid presence allowed her the safe place to unleash and the tears flowed. She was so lucky to have him, to have this beautiful supportive man here by her side during such a traumatic moment. She needed him so much right now and, as always, he was here. She felt a sudden rush of horror. What if it had been him on that plane? She sobbed into his arms for what might have been and out of relief for what hadn't.

Maddy and Harry came running down the stairs into the room. 'Mum, what's wrong? Why are you crying?' Maddy demanded. 'Why are you sad?' Harry asked.

'They're not sad tears, darling,' Sera said and she peeped out from her husband's embrace. 'Happy tears.'

The fright was over. They were safe. Joan stripped off her gloves and hurried home to be with her family. Jacqueline turned off the television and leaned against the wall in sheer exhaustion. Everything became so clear. In the last thirty minutes her list of priorities had just been thrown into the air like a deck of cards and had landed in a completely different order.

Suddenly petits fours, puff pastry and BAS statements seemed petty and irrelevant, and re-connecting with her family stood on the top like a beacon.

She walked down the corridor and leaned on the study door to look fondly at her husband. He had been glued to the television like the rest of the country, and was watching the passengers disembark.

She moved across the room and knelt at his feet. He dragged his eyes away from the screen in surprise. 'What?' he asked.

Jacqueline turned away from him and, sitting on the floor with her back against the couch, said, 'I'd love a massage.'

'Oh, sure, dear,' Thomas said and his strong, gentle hands kneaded the drama's stresses from his wife's shoulders while they watched a passenger being wheeled away on an ambulance gurney.

Mallory squealed and cheered with the rest of the patients, nurses and physios who'd come in to watch the drama unfold on the only screen in the clinic. She gabbled explanations to all present about her relationship with those on board. Her audience hungrily gobbled up the story of Sam being a last-minute passenger.

She was so happy, so ridiculously joyous and happy! She couldn't describe it to herself. She'd been so black and dark and miserable and, well, quite frankly, depressed lately, that this wonderful feeling of gaiety was intoxicating by comparison. Forget about walking, she felt like she could fly!

What a waste of energy being bitter about Vince and his pregnant girlfriend. Who gave a shit about them anyway? Live and let live: let them play their happy families, let them live their lives. All Mallory could think about was that Sam and Bella were safe, that the plane full of people were alive and that the terrible crisis had ended.

'Hey, Francesca,' she said, 'check this out,' and she picked up her crutches. She did ten steps across the room before her body needed to support itself on the metal frames.

'Wonderful!' her therapist cried out and the room cheered her on.

Chantrea sank into one of the lounges at Gate 10, away from the hordes still glued to the screen. It was every flight attendant's nightmare. Thank God it was over. She shook her head in shame. She'd been such a selfish cow. What if that had been her on that flight? What if it hadn't turned out well? Her mother would raise Sally and Chantrea had to be one hundred percent convinced that was a good thing. Her mother was a wonderful woman; yes, raised in a different time, in a different place, in a different culture, but both Dara Kim and Chantrea had one very solid thing in common: they loved Sally fiercely and would do anything for her. All Dara Kim wanted was what Chantrea wanted: for the little girl to grow into a well-rounded, happy, confident young woman.

It was time to tell Sally about her surprise birthday adventure. Chantrea leapt up and rushed to a quiet corner so she could use her phone to break the exciting news to her daughter. She wanted to speak to her mother too. She needed to tell her how much she loved and respected her. It was a task that was well overdue.

~59~

It was Sam's idea. The group was shaken by the mid-air ordeal and needed to bond. Funnily enough, Bella and Sam, as the main characters in the drama, were less rattled than the rest of them.

Perhaps it was having been there, having survived it together, that made them less affected than the others. Of course it could have had something to do with the fact they had spent the remainder of the weekend in bed together at the Crowne Plaza Darwin and had thought of little else but each other since.

Whatever the reason, Sam knew that it was up to him to host an emergency extra Stitch 'n' Bitch evening so that everybody could come over, hug each other, re-group and reassure themselves that Sam and Bella were fine. It had been a week since he'd returned and the catch-up was long overdue.

The December evening was warm as they collected for pre-purl drinks in Sam's vegetable garden. The women oohed and ahhed over Sam's garden creation, the summer growth shooting a fine show for the group.

'Here's the fun bit,' Sam explained. 'Your hors d'oeuvres,' and he picked a snow pea from the trellis and popped it in his mouth. 'Cherry tomato, anyone?' he said, gesturing at the garden bed behind them, where the bright red baubles against the lush green growth shone like Christmas decorations.

After the group had feasted on the organic beans, strawberries, tomatoes and peas they moved inside to take up their knitting. They were far more industrious nowadays than they'd been in the beginning. The real reason for their charity work had been pushed to the fore given recent events and they were all determined to supply a range of completed knitted goods to Woollies for Wars in time for the Christmas dispatch.

Joan had given them a real rev-up too, teaching them a range of new skills. Jacqueline was on her tenth beanie, having long ago discarded Thomas's argyle sweater. Sera was making her third children's blanket in a good quality merino, while Chantrea had found woollen bed socks to be her forte.

'So, Sam-the-Man,' Chantrea started with a twinkle in her eye, 'how'd it go with Bella?'

'Nope!' Sam held up a flat palmed hand, 'you can all stop right there. I do not kiss and tell. Or, in this particular case, have the hottest, most delicious sex for twenty-four hours straight . . . and tell.'

The women stopped their knitting as utter silence descended on the group. They looked at him with dropped jaws. Chantrea finally broke the silence, voicing everyone's thoughts: 'I am so effing jealous.'

They laughed out loud, fully agreeing with her sentiment. Even Joan nodded, wide-eyed, with an embarrassed flush creeping up her neck.

'Would you mind? That's my sister you're talking about,' Sera interjected.

'*Not* talking about,' Sam corrected her. 'You can hassle me all you want, but no details will be forthcoming. End of story.' He picked up his scarf. He was casting off a thick wool wrap. 'Ta-dah,' he announced, holding up his finished piece.

The room broke into applause. 'Absolutely tremendous. Now: tassles,' Joan said, and got up to sit by Sam in order to teach him a whole new skill.

'Well, can we at least ask where she is?' Chantrea said.

'Apparently a roster stops for no man or woman in that industry,' Sera explained. 'She had to have a few counselling sessions with the airline then start the LA run again. But she really wished she could have come, and you know what? This time I believed her.'

Just then Sam's phone rang. He grinned like a schoolboy. 'It's her!' he said and answered the phone on speaker. 'Hi Bella, you're on speaker, so no dirty talk.'

'I beg your pardon!' came Bella's voice over the phone. 'Hi everyone!'

'Hi Bella,' they all chorused.

'Hey listen team, Asif and I are at this crazy Versace sale and of course I thought of you all. Anything and everything's here at ridiculous prices. So how about it, little sister, what can I get you?'

Everybody squealed and tossed their knitting aside.

'Gosh, I don't know, Bella,' said Sera. 'By the way, I spoke to Mum, she's feeling a lot better, now her cold's gone.'

'Great news, thanks,' Bella replied.

'Anyway, what is there?' Sera leaned towards Sam's phone, sitting on the coffee table, as the catcalls and screeches from the warehouse district of LA echoed around the Bondi Junction living room.

'Belts? Bags? Tops? Frocks? You name it. What about a tee?' offered Bella.

'Nah, I think I'm over labels at the moment,' said Sera, to her sister's surprise. 'What about Chantrea?'

'Chantrea,' Bella said, 'there's this purple lycra skintight dress that'd you'd love.'

'Thanks for thinking of me, Bel, but I'm budgeting.'

'Mallory? You there?' Bella asked.

'Yeah, I'm here, but I'm fine, Bella, really, I can't really spend up at the moment.'

'What, so none of you want to take advantage of this incredible sale?'

'Er hem,' Jacqueline tried not to call attention to herself as she called attention to herself.

'Oh, Jac might,' Sera said.

'Jacqueline?' Bella asked, unable to hide the surprise from her voice.

'I'm . . . er . . . not usually into Versace, it's a bit flashy. Does anything come in navy?'

Bella laughed across the phone waves. 'Versace comes in two colours, darling: glitz and glitzier.'

'Well, no then . . .' Jacqueline said, tucking her ballet flats firmly under her seat.

'Oh, go on, Jac,' Sera encouraged. 'Don't you have that Bakers' Conference coming up? You could wow them with a bit of glamour.'

'Well yes, I do,' she admitted slowly, 'and I would like to splurge on a little something for the new me, as it were.'

'Jacqueline, hang on,' Bella said, 'I've got a dress here that would be divine on you. It's gold, of course, but no sequins. It's a satin off-the-shoulder full-length number that clings but not tightly. It would be divine with your colouring.'

'Oh my, it sounds heavenly,' Jacqueline said, beaming. 'How much?'

'Two and a half down to, ohmigod, four hundred!'

'Get it, get it!' Jacqueline squealed, the bargain frenzy infecting even her.

'Okay, done, anybody else?'

Sera looked around the room. 'Joan, get something for Joan.'

'Oh, don't be ridiculous, Sera, they'd laugh at size sixteen. You'd have to sew two frocks together and it still wouldn't fit,' the older woman protested.

'Bags, heaps of bags, what colour?' Bella called out.

'NOT BLACK!' Sera, Chantrea and Jacqueline all yelled at once.

Joan looked quite miffed at their response.

'Red?'

'Yes,' Sera said, 'that will be brilliant.'

'Red? But I don't own any red,' Joan protested.

'Joan, you don't carry a red bag with red, you carry a red bag with taupe,' Sera explained.

'Oh,' Joan, said slightly mollified. 'I've got tons of taupe.'

'Sounds great, Bel, good work, thanks for the call.'

Back in Bella's hotel room in LA, the two shoppers sorted through their purchases.

'Look at me, I'm a supermodel,' Asif announced as he came out of the bathroom in his new Versace suit teamed with wasabi shirt and tie combo.

'You are, you're drop-dead gorgeous,' Bella agreed.

'Whatjaget, whatjaget?' he chanted as she opened up her parcels.

'Beautiful dress for Jac, great bag for Joan, I bought Sera a little top for Chrissie, and a couple of belts and shirts for Sam.'

'For your boooyyyfriend,' Asif sang, fluttering around the room in a circle like an executive fairy.

'Shut up, Asif,' she said as she packed everything up.

'What about you, what did you get?'

'Nothing,' Bella said.

'What?' Asif stopped mid-ponce. 'What do you mean, nothing?'

'Nothing. Didn't feel like it.'

'You're not quitting designer, are you?'

'Well, I'm not starting the twelve-step program just yet, don't worry. I just thought I might start saving up for a terrace in Paddington, so I can be close to home.'

~60~

'I can't believe we're standing outside the Elephant Bar,' Chantrea squealed with excitement. 'It's one of the most famous bars in the world, you know!'

'Of course I know,' her mother scolded. 'Your father and I were well-known here when we were in our twenties,' she said with pride. 'Often the manager would pay for our drinks, he held us in such high esteem.'

'Really, Mum?' Chantrea asked. 'That's amazing. You were quite famous, weren't you?'

'I try and tell you this for years and you don't listen,' Dara Kim retorted and the three travellers turned to climb the terracotta stairs to the iconic powder-blue arched French doors.

Chantrea looked down at Sally. 'Are you too tired for one more stop, sweetie? We've had a very busy day.'

The solemn little eyes looked up. 'No, Mummy, I really want to see the elephants.'

Chantrea laughed. 'You know they're not real elephants, don't you?'

'Of course, Mum.' The little girl rolled her eyes in derision. 'They're paintings of elephants.'

Sally's Cambodian adventure had officially started that morning when they'd awoken at their hotel on the Riverfront Promenade. The Tonle Sap river sparkled in front of them and the hydro traffic competed with the road traffic for chaos and drama.

They'd tuk-tuked it to the Royal Palace, one of the few national treasures the Khmer Rouge had spared during its reign of terror, now home to the current royal family.

Chantrea, infected by Sally's excitement for the fairytale princess palace, skipped with her daughter through the elaborate grounds and gasped in delight at the sculptures, small palaces and stupas, commemorating past royal family members.

The Silver Pagoda was the little girl's clear favourite. When Sally first saw the silver floor tiles adorning the pagoda she instantly suggested they replace their floor-boards at home with similar ones. 'What a splendid idea,' Chantrea had agreed immediately.

The emerald Buddha, looking down in solemn beauty from his golden dais, subdued their excitement momentarily and they stared back in awe. However, the moment passed when Sally squealed at the sight of the statue of 'Buddha of the Future' resting in front of the Emerald Buddha. It was solid gold and covered in diamonds. 'Wow, he must be worth kazillions!' she'd exclaimed.

The tour of the Royal Palace had taken the small group most of the day. Chantrea had been determined not to miss a single historical fact or bas relief.

'You know your father and I were honoured guests at a banquet at the Royal Palace once,' Dara Kim boasted. 'I wore a long gown in shell pink. I looked like an orchid.'

'Oh, Granny Yay, you must have been beautiful,' Sally sighed and she gazed in delight at the European dollhouse cuteness of the Napolean III Pavilion.

Their feet ached in thanks when they finally sat down in the Elephant Bar. As they lounged in the wicker chairs awaiting their drinks, Chantrea looked at her travelling companions. 'Mum and Sally, thanks so much for suggesting this trip. I am having a great time. It's a beautiful country, you were right. So rich with culture and architecture and the French food is to die for. I finally understand what you mean: it's magnificent.'

Dara Kim assessed the coloured elephantine motifs on the wall as the waiter deposited their Femme Fatales, for which the bar was legend, and Sally's Sprite.

'Mmmm,' the older woman said with a shoulder shrug, 'yeah, sure, it's a nice place, but it's no Sydney – now there's a city!'

Jacqueline gazed out at the rolling pastureland. A distant moo reverberated around the undulating green hills. The backdrop of the Blue Mountains shimmered in its eucalyptus haze. She had been thrilled when Thomas had suggested a weekend farmhouse getaway.

The boys were on holidays, Thomas's business was expanding into a second surgery and everybody had become very supportive of Jacqueline's burgeoning Cake Lady enterprise. She looked over at her husband sitting in the other white cane chair and smiled.

'Wouldn't mind a Crown Lager, darling,' he murmured from behind his collector's edition of *Teeth, Roots and Gums*.

'You know where the fridge is,' she replied and, closing her eyes, leant her head back onto the floral cushion to enjoy the late afternoon sun.

'Oh, yes, right, of course,' he said and leapt to his feet.

Within seconds the wine glass at her elbow was being topped up.

'Thank you, darling,' she said.

*

Mallory stopped for a moment to recover. The last section of the Coastal Walk was a killer. The steps were so steep she didn't know how people actually jogged them. She stepped onto the grass to let yet another Eastern Suburbs Angel bounce by, all perky buttocks and velour tracksuit with a ponytail in a rainbow of blonde shades.

She arrived at the tip of McKenzie's Point and entered the circular sandstone paved viewing station. As she breathed in deeply to try to catch her breath she looked out over the ocean. Bondi Beach lay behind her and the South Pacific Ocean stretched in front like a giant teal shag carpet, textured and deep.

The waves churning at the sandstone cliffs below were the colour of raw glass – deceiving in their innocuous frothiness. The famous Bondi Coastal Walk was an inspiration at every turn. This morning's shower had caused impromptu waterfalls to skip down the dappled cliffs. The rivulets leapt over cantilevered rock shelves and ducked through ferns, turning the algae cover a bright emerald.

Mallory turned around to take in the elongated new moon that was Bondi Beach. The structures that perched on the far point of the bay and crept into the beach town reminded her of the clifftop dwellings she'd once visited in Skiathos, each seemingly straining against the other to get the better view.

She looked back at the variegations of the cliff's rugged face. The pockmarked bulging beast was humbling when she'd walked under its bulk a few minutes earlier. But from here it looked fragile in its pastel palette of oyster, rust and tan.

Her fingers itched; she wanted to somehow own the beauty, to recreate it, to make it hers. She made a promise to bring her camera next time so at least she could capture it that way.

She'd never noticed the beauty of the area in such detail before. Her tentative walking pace had forced her to slow down, giving her the time to look and really see her surroundings. In the past, she had simply counted the kilometres she'd conquered while measuring her pulse. But this time was different.

The lead in her right hand tugged and she looked down at the white shaggy furball she and Tilly had christened Miffy, who was desperately pulling to get closer to the interesting smell embedded in the flowering gazania lining the path.

Miffy's short shitzu legs were good for nothing more than digging and play, Mallory had quickly discovered, and the puppy preferred to be carried when the two went out on their daily walks. Mallory didn't mind at all: there was something very soothing about having the warm bundle of fluff tucked under her arm as she strolled around the eastern suburbs. But at every rest stop Miffy would scramble to get down and sniff around the immediate area to ensure all was well in her olfactory world.

The Sculpture by the Sea exhibition was on display and woman and puppy stood for a while longer. Mallory took in a piece depicting sailboats laser-cut from red rusty Core Ten, while Miffy admired an impressively sized dog turd.

The sailboat piece, titled 'All at Sea', by famous Melbourne artist Robert Delves, had a rustic, industrial quality that complemented the rugged brush landscape.

Miffy started up her gutsy little yapping and Mallory turned to see what the commotion was about. The puppy was leaping up in the air, endeavouring to give a large friendly labrador what-for. The labrador simply smiled its big-jawed goofy smile and laid a lick on Miffy so powerful it toppled her onto her side. She leapt up, yipping at the indignity. Mallory smiled at the labrador's owner who was as muscular and blond as his pet, though with a much less goofy grin.

'So funny,' he said. 'What kind of dog is it?'

'She's a shitzu,' Mallory replied and scooped up the animation on legs. Miffy's legs drooped on either side of Mallory's forearm and only one black eye peeped out from the silky curtain of fringe.

'She's adorable,' he said and scratched her behind the ear. Miffy's legs waggled in pleasure. 'Do you like the artwork?' he asked, indicating the sculpture.

'Yes, it's beautiful, although I've only just started. I planned to walk to Tamarama and see a few more pieces.'

'There's a stunning one three along, made from some kind of acrylic, it's transparent,' he said. 'A fascinating take on the Emperor's new clothes. The artist uses it as a metaphor for Sydneysiders and their obsession with beauty.'

'Really?' Mallory asked, intrigued to learn more, 'how cool.'

'Yeah, very cool. I know the artist's work and I reckon this is the best I've seen. Although not as sophisticated as this Delves piece, of course. I'm Paul, by the way.'

Mallory extended her small hand formally. 'Mallory,' she replied, smiling widely.

As Mallory and Paul wound their way along the Sculpture Walk together she discovered that he owned a gallery in Darling Point that featured street art and industrial exhibitions. Boris, the labrador, and Miffy were getting along very well, now that Boris had learnt who was boss.

Paul gave Mallory a crash course on sculpture and form as they wandered through the coastal artworks, her head spinning with new ideas and perspectives. The lesson was over too soon, as the couple and their dogs arrived at Tamarama Beach, or Glamourama as the locals called it because it was a favourite among the gorgeous young things that frequented the topless haven. Today an impromptu wet T-shirt competition with a twist was taking place on the water's edge. Buff young men stood in the shallows, their tight shirts clinging to their pecs, while equally beautiful young women in the adoring audience soaked up the sight.

After a quick mango lassi together at the beach cafe, Paul invited Mallory to an exhibition opening that night at his gallery. They said their goodbyes and Mallory walked back to her car, excited about her future for the first time in months.

'. . . and Space Mountain, and Nemo Submarine and Pirates of the Caribbean –'

'And the Mad Hatter's Tea Party,' Alexandra interrupted her sister's wish list of which ride to try first at Disneyland.

'Yes, yes,' Sam laughed in joy at their enthusiasm. 'But we've only just walked in the gate. Any chance Bella and I can get a latte on Main Street first?'

'NO!' The girls yelled and ran off as Pluto and his entourage rounded the corner.

Sam wondered if he was allowed to be this happy. The bright Los Angeles sun bathed the fake dominion and enhanced the feeling of benevolence and wellbeing Disneyland was famous for. Chirpy music filtered through the hidden speakers.

He gazed in wonder at the hordes of tourists who flooded into the theme park. The Japanese were buying every trademarked product from pencil toppers to ice-cream makers. The Europeans were taking photos and reading the history markers and the Americans were eating.

The pristine streets were dust mote free, the walls unmarked by grime, and not one tiny pea light was blown in the strings of eleven thousand that draped the candy-coloured faux facades. It truly was a fantasyland.

He looked at the beautiful woman standing by his side, smiling at his children, and wondered if she too was simply an illusion. Touching her gently on the arm he felt her warmth, her blood pumping. Her soft skin was silky under his fingers. She was very real. She turned to him and wrapped her arms around his waist. Her shoulder slotted perfectly under his arm as he returned the embrace.

'This is brilliant, Bella,' he told her. 'Thanks so much for organising it.'

'Hey, in my game, the world's your playground,' Bella said and watched as the girls jumped up and down, waiting their turn with the famous dog.

'Well, it's good of you, darling, to sacrifice your precious holiday time and spend it at a theme park filled with children – and my children at that.'

'Are you kidding? I love your girls. We had so much fun shopping yesterday.'

'You spoil them rotten, Bella,' he said. 'You mustn't spend so much money on them.'

'Oh, we're on holiday, I promise it will be back to wicked stepmother when we get home.'

'Will you wear the cape and boots and brandish a sceptre?' he asked with a cheeky grin.

'Only if you promise to be the fairest in the land,' she replied.

Bella turned her face up to his and, with the Magic Castle looking down on them in the Happiest Place on Earth™, they kissed.

~61~

The chilling, primal scream ripped through Vince's serenity. He'd been immersed in the sports pages while reclining on the armchair in the hospital room when Sharee's cry made him jump through the roof.

'You right there, Sharee?' he asked, more in irritation than concern.

He'd been rudely dragged from a deep sleep three hours ago when she'd thumped him unceremoniously and yelled, 'It's time! Move it!'

Mallory would never have treated him like that. Sharee was proving to be more trouble than she was worth. Still, he was a man of honour: he'd knocked her up (with his super-swimmers, he reminded himself proudly), and he was going to stand by his new family. He owed them that much. Besides, it would be so brilliant to have a son. They'd go to the footy together; hang out; drink beer; go bush-bashing; sailing – it would be fan-fucking-tastic.

Poor Mallory, though, he sometimes felt a twinge of guilt about dumping her. She was a good kid. They'd had some laughs, some good times. The thing is, he thought as he stared unseeing at his newspaper, I love her, but I'm just not *in* love with her. He deserved his happiness, and having this little guy would be great.

And besides, Sharee was usually a top chick, a tiger in the sack (not that he'd been getting much action lately, but that'd change once the kid was born). Sharee was more like him, they had a real blast together – and wasn't that what life was all about? Having a good time? Still, it had been really hard breaking up with Mal, he'd felt lousy for literally days.

Anyway, Mallory wouldn't take him back now anyway. Just after Christmas he'd gotten a bit sentimental and tried to reconcile with his missus. It was sheer brilliance on his part that he had the plan to dump Sharee *after* getting back with his wife in case it didn't work out with Mal.

So when Mallory rejected him (amidst peals of highly unnecessary and slightly hysterical laughter) there was really no harm done. He'd always been one to keep his options open: 'Don't burn your bridges, son,' his old man used to say.

So here he was, back at plan A. Not a barrel of laughs yet, he had to admit, but that would all change when he took his new family on a surprise boating holiday around the Whitsundays in six months' time.

'Where's the fucking anaethetist?' Sharee demanded of the midwife. 'I need that epidural NOW!'

'You're too far gone, love,' the midwife said in her most soothing manner. It was obvious she was accustomed to abusive, freaked-out, labouring women. 'You've reached ten centimetres, and very quickly too I might add, good job. You're about to have your baby. See if you can push on the next contraction.'

'Where the fuck is my obstetrician?! I don't want some nurse delivering my baby. Especially since he's decided to come a bloody month early!'

Vince sighed and hauled himself out of the chair; he figured it was time to get involved.

'We've called your doctor, he's on his way, but the traffic is shocking out there apparently and who would have guessed you'd progress so quickly,' the midwife replied, smoothly ignoring the insult. 'Okay, the baby's crowning, oh, here it comes, try and push hard with the next contraction, dear, you're doing a great job. Oh, dear,' she said as she caught the first glimpse of the baby's head.

'What is it?' Vince asked, 'is something wrong?'

'Not at all, it's probably best if you don't come down to the business end of things; just stay up there and hold your partner's hand.'

The other midwife bustled about the room preparing the cot, the heat lamp and the baby's first tiny outfit.

The attending midwife glanced up at the monitor. 'Here we go, dear, here comes another contraction, now push as hard as you can, we have to get the head out.'

'You think I don't know there's another one coming, you stupid cow, what am I –' Sharee's volley of abuse was cut short as the contraction tightened across her back and belly as if she were in the jaws of a crocodile. She screamed and crushed Vince's small hand.

'Ow, that hurt,' Vince whinged and pulled his hand out of her grasp. 'You can hold your own hand if that's how you're going to behave.' He tucked his tender appendage under his other arm and stuck out his bottom lip.

With an almighty push, Sharee forced the tiny creature out into the world in one fast swoosh. The midwife caught the new little body before it hit the deck.

'Oh, how beautiful, you've got yourselves a daughter,' she said as she hurriedly wrapped the child in warm blankets.

'What the fuck?!' Vince demanded. 'You told me it was going to be a boy!'

'I thought it was,' Sharee protested. 'I dunno, it looked like one on the ultrasound.'

The midwife rolled her eyes. These two were a right royal treat. 'Be thankful she's healthy,' she said and turned to present the child to the proud parents. 'And she's such a beautiful colour!'

Vince was staring out the window in a sulk when the new mother took hold of her infant for the first time. 'Uh oh,' Sharee said in a little voice.

'What?' Vince demanded and turned to see what his girlfriend was talking about.

He looked down at the tightly wrapped bundle as she turned her tiny head, her mouth pulling at the corners as it instinctively sought the nipple.

The satin newborn skin was the colour of the darkest caramel and her wee head was capped with silky tight black curls.

~62~

The Paddington house hadn't known such a flurry of excited activity since Tony and Sera's wedding day. Suitcases were bumping up and down the staircase, children were running in and out of bedrooms on futile errands designed to keep them busy and out of the way (but often resulting in the inverse effect), phones rang, Sera and Joan were discussing, deciding on and discarding outfits with lighting speed, while Tony checked and re-checked documents, secured the house and made last-minute arrangements with his building team.

They were going to Italy.

After the news of Tony's parentage had sunk in and the family had embraced their new Italian heritage with dinners of linguine amatriciana and stereo speakers bellowing Verdi, Puccini and Bellini, Tony and Sera had pressured Joan into calling Antonio.

Tony had been thrilled to discover his real name, Tony Donizetti, and had threatened, in his excitement, to have his name changed by deed poll immediately, until Sera had calmed him down by reminding him about the kind of administration headache involved in changing a name halfway through life.

After hours on Google and many phone calls, they had finally tracked down the Antonio Donizetti they were after. There were four who lived in the Positano area but only one was a master stone-mason, recently retired. It was late at night in Sydney, mid-afternoon in Italy, when they made the call.

'*Pronto*?' came the voice down the line, and although gravelly with age, Joan knew in an instant she'd reached the right number. Even time couldn't affect the rich baritone she'd dreamed about for the last forty years.

'Antonio?' she whispered, her throat threatening to close over.

'*Joan*?' came the reply.

'Yes,' she said.

The crackle of the international phoneline was the only sound for several seconds as each was overcome with emotion. They were unable to say anything, charged with longing, with remorse for the years that had passed, for the life that hadn't been.

Finally, the man in Positano spoke. 'My *bella signora*,' he said with such need it sent tears flowing down Joan's face. Tony and Sera perched on the edge of the couch on the other side of the room, staring as the moment unfolded.

'Oh, Tony,' Joan replied. They both burst out laughing in joy and relief that they were finally back in contact. Tony grabbed Sera's hand when he heard his father's deep chuckle for the first time, spilling from the mouthpiece of the telephone and into their living room.

The call was the first of many. Over the next few days introductions were made, secrets were shared, passionate recriminations were laid to rest, apologised for and forgiven, reunions and greetings took place, and loving endearments were whispered. A cable, two millimetres in diameter, faultlessly ferried this family theatre from one side of the world to the other.

A family decision was made. Too much time had been wasted. Not another second of this fragile relationship should disappear in the temporal sinkhole. They were going to meet him, this man who had so indelibly tattooed his being onto the little family in Paddington.

Tony got onto the internet and booked tickets to Naples, while the children ran around in a circle squealing and chanting all the Italian words they knew: spaghetti, cappuccino, Roma, Florentine.

Sera mustered up all her courage and cornered Joan in her bedroom. 'Joan, darling,' she said and smiled to soften the blow of what she was about to say. 'It's about time you had a makeover.'

It was like dealing with a giggly debutante, Sera thought, as she had Joan plucked and waxed at Paddington's Benefit Boutique – day spa to the stars. A recent arrival from San Francisco, the chic pink salon sat prettily in Oxford street while Sydney's womenfolk raced though the door desperate to be given the Benefit treatment and, better still, boast about it later.

Joan's conversation had regressed to teenage level. 'Do you think he'll like me? Did I tell you what he said last time we spoke? Do I look fat in these pants?'

'Yes, yes and no, Joan,' Sera said, supervising the metamorphosis from the chair in the corner. She was flipping through the David Jones fashion catalogue, dog-earing the pages advertising clothes suitable for a woman of certain years about to embark on a European tryst.

The hair was next. Joan's Lady Diana brush-back was softened and straightened until it tapered to her ears and against her neck in a more flattering style. The L'Oreal Luscious Red Joan had used for decades was replaced with a honey-brown, highlighted with subtle warm blonde streaks.

Joan's eyes went from the colour of algae to the colour of emeralds in contrast to the new hair colour and they sparkled in excitement as she admired the new do. 'Gracious me, I look ten years younger,' she said, and Joh Bailey's premier colour technician smiled in pride.

It was time for Sera's specialty, and she perched Joan on the stool at the Dior counter. She covered her mature skin in Diorskin Sculpt number 010 which completely hid the sun spots and age spots and minimised time's cruel lines.

She had always known Joan's colouring would far better suit the paler shades in the summer palette instead of her usual maroon and moss, which made her look like death warmed up. Diorblush in Naïve Rose set off her prominent cheekbones and eyeshadow 855 Diorsweet – a duotone of oyster and pink – on her lids with liner and mascara made Joan appear sophisticated yet pretty.

'Never believe the younger labels are just for the kids,' Sera advised as she rifled through a rack of Lisa Ho she'd dragged into the expansive dressing room. 'Every designer has a piece for your shape. You just have to know what you're looking for – aha!' she pounced and retrieved a taupe canvas jacket fringed with a frilled collar and pinched-in waist. 'And you're not a size sixteen, Joan, you've got a slim figure. You should wear items that hug your shape, not hang off you like a bag. You're a fourteen or even a twelve.'

When Joan arrived home that night, after her intense grooming overhaul, Tony stood as a glamorous older woman entered the room, and prepared to meet Sera's new friend. It took him a few seconds to realise the stylish woman with the broad smile was his mum.

~63~

Sera turned this way and that, admiring her new swimsuit. It was a special figure-hugging number she'd bought at a boutique in Rose Bay and it was guaranteed to make her look five kilos lighter.

As she turned to look at her derriere she decided the swimsuit was worth its exorbitant price. The sheer architecture of the piece certainly lifted and flattened where it was supposed to and she felt positively trim.

'Ooh, Mummy, you look beautiful,' Maddy cried, running into the room.

'Thank you, darling,' Sera smiled, her hand instinctively moving to cover her scar.

Maddy stared at the rarely exposed purple stain and puckered skin on her mother's leg and Sera slowly took away her hand and allowed her daughter to see the full damage. Maddy had never mentioned the scar before, It was as if she instinctively knew it was a taboo subject, but now she asked, 'Mummy, how did your leg get hurt?'

'Well,' Sera answered, a twist of anxiety knotting in the base of her stomach, 'I was just a little girl, littler even than you, about as young as Harry, and I had a very bad accident.'

'Oh Mummy, you poor thing.' Maddy looked up, her eyes filled with concern.

'Luckily Bella was there to help me, though,' Sera said, hugging Maddy.

'But what was the accident, Mummy?'

Sera sighed quietly. 'You know how you kids aren't allowed near the kettle, or the stove, or the fireplace?'

'Yeah,' Maddy replied, her eyes still on her mother's leg.

'Well, that's because sometimes accidents can happen, like it did with me. I accidentally tipped a saucepan of boiling water on to my leg.'

'Oh no!' Maddy gasped. 'Does it still hurt?'

'No, not anymore, though it did then. I had to go to the hospital for a very long time.'

'Did you?' Maddy looked up at her mother. 'Were you lonely? Did you miss your mum?'

'Well, yes, a bit,' Sera smiled gently, 'but mostly I missed Bella. Even though she came and visited me every day.'

'Aunty Bella is so nice, Mummy. She used to come and play with us all the time. Why doesn't she do that anymore?' Maddy asked, the scar forgotten.

'I know, I miss her too, but you have to understand, Maddy, Aunty Bella's got her own life. She's very busy. Besides, she does visit often, just not constantly.'

'But she used to help me do cartwheels. And colouring-in. She did great unicorns.'

'But look at your unicorns now, darling, they're brilliant without Aunty Bella. You can do wonderful unicorns and cartwheels without her.'

'Yeah, I guess, you're right.'

'And besides,' Sera smiled, 'I think Aunty Bella's going to be spending heaps more time in Sydney now because she's got a boyfriend.'

'Really, is he nice?'

'Yes, it's Sam – you know, Issy and Alex's dad.'

'Wow, that's fantastic!' Maddy said, clapping her hands. 'They're really nice.' Maddy's brow wrinkled as she thought a bit more. 'So now that I don't need Aunty Bella so much anymore, she's coming back?'

'Yes, that's right,' Sera smiled, shaking her head at the irony of the conversation.

'Isn't that funny?' Maddy said.

'It sure is,' Sera said. 'Now why don't you get out in that spa with Daddy and Harry, and I'll be there in a few minutes?'

'Okay, Mummy, I love you,' Maddy said, skipping out.

Sera turned to the mirror again and took a close look at her ravaged leg. Somehow the scar seemed to have shrunk – not in size, but simply in importance.

For so long, all her life, she had allowed it to define who she was. It was as if the slash down her leg was embedded in her psyche. She ran her hand over the puckered flesh. This was hers, this scar; this damaged stretch of skin, but it was no more than that; no deep emblem or representation of anything other than an awful accident, a moment in time that was seared into her flesh.

Sera didn't want to hide anymore. She wanted to live and laugh and enjoy her husband and children.

The sounds of splashing and squealing floated up to her. She gave the mirror a smile and grabbed a towel from the bathroom before stopping to wipe up the morning's toothpaste parade from the charcoal tiles.

They'd added a spa to their new courtyard. Of course they were hideous-looking things, spas, so very Kath and Kim, but it didn't matter. Sera didn't care anymore. Although she still admired beautiful things, they didn't run her life as they used to. And when it came to something fun, like the new spa, she became completely blind to the aesthetic. The kids were crazy for the new toy and she and Tony had enjoyed many a languid hour floating into the night, sipping bubbly and romancing the togs off each other.

Joan was happy with the spa idea when they phoned her in Italy to suggest it. She didn't know when she'd be back, maybe for Easter, but just to re-new her visa. She and Antonio had travelled from one end of the Amalfi coast to the other and were currently enjoying the beaches and nightlife in Sorrento. They were to return to Positano at the end of the week for another flurry of far-flung family reunions.

Antonio had never married: his heart was taken by another, he'd explained sadly to the many girls he had known. But his patience had been well rewarded, he'd explained to his cousins and second cousins as his arm refused to leave Joan's waist. His *bella signora* had come home, and she even spoke their language beautifully.

Sera hurried through a few last bits of tidying up so she could join Tony and the kids. She popped into the children's room to do a quick straighten up. The room had recently been re-decorated in her much-wished-for hues of tangerine, pumpkin and lime – but with plenty of flexibility for the children's own style.

She plumped up a regency stripe cushion and popped it on the daisy motif tub chair in Maddy's corner. She tsked at Harry's effort at bedmaking and smoothed the Spiderman doona into place and tossed a stray Dora the Explorer cushion onto Maddy's Dora bed.

'There,' she said as she pivoted on bare legs at the door for one more look back into the room. 'Perfect.'

Acknowledgements

Michelle Hamer would like to thank:

Her beautiful children Harley, Ruby, Darcy and Oliver for their love, affection and support through the difficult time that accompanied the writing of this book. Thanks to Harley for the wonderful author photo.

The gorgeous Kelly Cooper and Tracey Caulfield, who constantly offer their unfailing support and belief in me. Where would I be without the girls at the end of the phone? Thank you both for everything, I would be lost without you.

Cate Kendall would not be possible without the dedication and committment of my co-writer Lisa Blundell. I would like to thank both Lisa and her wonderful husband, Ian, for their support. Love your work!

Thanks, too, to John Meriton for his patience and feedback during the editing process, as well as his expertise on all things technical! And a huge thanks to the wonderful team of publishing professionals at Random House who make writing these books such a joy. Thanks to our publisher, Larissa Edwards, senior editor Roberta Ivers, editor Jessica Dettmann and the enthusiastic Random House marketing team.

As always, my agent Selwa Anthony continues to be a pillar of support, inspiration and good advice at the end of the phone. Thanks Selwa!

Lisa Blundell would like to thank:

Selwa Anthony, a patient, skilled and outstandingly diplomatic woman; the lovely Larissa Edwards, our publisher, who seems to have limitless time to hash over issues as they pop up; Roberta Ivers, our talented structural editor; and Jessica Dettman, our proficient copy editor, who made a molehill out of a mountain.

Thanks must also go to the people of the Cambodian community who shared their stories and helped with our translations; the rangers of Waverley Council for their intimate knowledge of the Bondi Coastal Walk; and Gabriel McMahon from Qantas, and flight attendants from Virgin. Thanks, too, for the guidance of Melbourne artist Robby Delves, and Sydney artist Jo Neville, Paper Couture, Darlinghurst. To Lucy, Phil and Sam for listening to me go on ad nauseum about this book during the writing process: I am so grateful for your friendship. Thanks, too, to Steve Weller for my author photo.

And thanks, of course, to my co-writer Michelle.

I would also like to thank australiasbiggestbookgroup.com for choosing Cate Kendall as their author in their valiant attempt to raise much-needed funds for Muscular Dystrophy. Thank you to all who participated in this important fundraiser.

And as always, enormous thanks to Darling Husband, without whom our four children would probably never get fed!

For more information about Cate Kendall's work please go to www.catekendall.com.